Sky Bird

Also Written by Nancy Larsen-Sanders

All Stubborned Up
Earth's Memories Series (Book I): The Mourning Dove's Message
Earth's Memories Series (Book II): Women with Backbone
Earth's Memories Series (Book III): The Marrow of Life
Earth's Memories Series (Book IV): For the Duration

EARTH'S MEMORIES SERIES, BOOK V

Sky Bird

NANCY LARSEN-SANDERS

*1st Place Winner of the Historical/Western Novel Category
in SouthWest Writers 2003 Writing Contest*

iUniverse LLC
Bloomington

Earth's Memories Series, Book V
Sky Bird

Copyright © 2013 by Nancy Larsen-Sanders

All rights reserved. No part of this book may be used or reproduced by any means, graphic, electronic, or mechanical, including photocopying, recording, taping or by any information storage retrieval system without the written permission of the publisher except in the case of brief quotations embodied in critical articles and reviews.

Certain characters in this work are historical figures, and certain events portrayed did take place. However, this is a work of fiction. All of the other characters, names, and events as well as all places, incidents, organizations, and dialogue in this novel are either the products of the author's imagination or are used fictitiously.

iUniverse books may be ordered through booksellers or by contacting:

iUniverse
1663 Liberty Drive
Bloomington, IN 47403
www.iuniverse.com
1-800-Authors (1-800-288-4677)

Because of the dynamic nature of the Internet, any web addresses or links contained in this book may have changed since publication and may no longer be valid. The views expressed in this work are solely those of the author and do not necessarily reflect the views of the publisher, and the publisher hereby disclaims any responsibility for them.

Any people depicted in stock imagery provided by Thinkstock are models, and such images are being used for illustrative purposes only.

Certain stock imagery © Thinkstock

Cover art by J. Shad Sanders

ISBN: 978-1-4759-9247-2 (sc)
ISBN: 978-1-4759-9249-6 (hc)
ISBN: 978-1-4759-9248-9 (e)

Library of Congress Control Number: 2013909444

Printed in the United States of America

iUniverse rev. date: 07/03/2013

For
Katie Jo Sale

Acknowledgments

Fremont, Kansas, the town and county, are located in western Kansas … within my creative mind only, along with the rest of the story, *Sky Bird*. Students and survivors of the 1930s decade will recognize historical events and details of the time.

Love and thanks to my amazing family for their support over the years as these books were being created. You're finally going to know the ending!

Colby Writers, thank you for your steady presence.

Thank you, Jamea Jule Sale, for being my daughter and an early reader.

Thank you, John Shattuck (J. Shad) Sanders, for being my son and for creating the book's artwork.

John, we will win the battle through our love and your editing.

Norm and Judi Linville, you've helped to keep me going through a most difficult time while completing these books. Thank you.

A special thanks to Stacey and Frank Cory. Who else would travel from Georgia during the hottest of summers to give me that final nudge?

Chapter 1

Nature's Attack

Wyoming, in early January, spewed out a storm front toward the tri-state corners of Nebraska, Colorado, and Kansas. As the storm traveled southeast, the wind was what folks called a general wind. It stirred leaves beneath trees, gathered corn shucks against barn foundations, and rattled yucca pods in the pastures. It was a necessary wind, needed to turn windmill wheels and to dry winter underwear on the clothesline.

But with its arrival in western Kansas on a frigid night, the wind seemed to feed on the howling of the coyotes and prairie foxes, taking on their voices. The silenced animals retreated to their tunnels, leaving the pastures, fields, and farmsteads to the growing wind.

Overwhelmed by the gale, the darkness froze. In protest, tree limbs along dry creek beds and near houses sometimes cracked like rifle shots that didn't reverberate. Perhaps the wind mistook the sound for starter pistols. Suddenly, its power was stimulated into further action, and it searched for prey to fuel its energy. It snarled along field edges, ate at dry, powdery soil void of vegetation, and sent grit along the ground in a murky, blizzard-like cloud that filled drill rows and shallow ditches before spiraling up to obliterate the stars and moon sliver. In pastures, it set its greedy teeth on more dry soil that struggled to protect grass roots. Creatures in their homes in tunnels beneath the grassland shuddered at the sounds above their heads of roots being ripped out.

The previous spring, despite the drought, there had been a prolific growth of Russian thistles. Now the weeds, dead and dry, were on the move before the wind, rolling and bouncing, each followed by a trail of dust. The thistles had many stems bristling with pods that ejected their tiny seeds, and, once the pods were open, they took on the shape of miniature shovels. The shovels dug at the soil, flinging dust upward into tornadic shapes.

Out in the choking dust, range cattle and horses circled in groups and thrust their heads against the protective bellies of one another. Pigs crowded together and snuffled from the fallout in the hog house, and chickens tucked their heads beneath their wings.

The first Kansas dust storm of 1937 had begun.

Chapter 2

Anxiety and Dust

The wind knocked at the house. Windowpanes shuddered, and beams creaked in response. Dust crept through the cracks where windows and doors met sills. It coated the oilcloth of the kitchen table, dulled the living room oak floor, and faintly outlined Deborah Nelson's head on her pillow. She slept uneasily, dreaming of a wind that pelted her face with a confusion of crystals that were explosive with light upon contact. She woke, a sharp headache was behind her eyes, and her nasal passages felt swollen and congested. The air in the bedroom was peppery. Granules stung her eyes, nostrils, and chest. Grit scoured at the windowpanes. She groaned with disappointment and pulled blankets over her head, trying unsuccessfully to shut out the wind's noise.

She heard restless stirrings from the baby's crib and knew there were things to be done. While she changed Baby Half Shell's diaper, he responded to her touch and voice, smiling, making nestling dove sounds. The paperwork for his adoption had been completed recently, yet she felt as though Half Shell had been hers since the day he was born. She loved him as deeply as Jonathan and David. Thinking about Half Shell being the great-grandson of her old Indian mentor, Grandfather Blue Sky, Deborah felt a warm thrill go through her chest. She leaned to kiss his cheek and sorrowed that the baby—all of the boys—must endure yet another storm. She wrapped him warmly in his blankets and covered the crib with a sheet to keep out the filtering dust.

In the next bedroom, David and Jonathan sleepily fumbled with their bandana face masks, and she helped place and tie them. They too made their quiet responses when she rearranged blankets and tucked them about their shoulders. "Thanks, Mommy."

Deborah didn't go to the back bedroom to check Sonja, the young woman who lived with them as hired help. Sonja was used to dirt storms and the routine that came with them. She had undoubtedly put on her own mask by now.

She rolled rags and rugs in the living room and kitchen, placing them against window- and doorsills. She took a whisk broom to the stove in each room and brushed off its dust covering. She added kindling to the banked coals.

As she usually did when something disturbed her, Deborah traced her fingertips over the frames of significant photos on the small parlor table: Grandfather Blue Sky in full Indian garb; Christian, Lendel, and her posed in the swings on the Nelson farm in Minnesota; and Christian and her on their wedding day. She found comfort in anchoring herself, visualizing in the darkness. Other photos of her parents, Christian's parents, and the little boys were there. Carrying their images in her mind, she wandered about the rooms, looking out windows and seeing only her reflection and listening to the sweeping sounds on the glass.

She held Blue Sky's photo. "Grandfather," she said, "here we go, once more."

The power of the wind had not lessened and neither had her despair. Deborah sat at the dusty kitchen table and hid her face in her arms. For six years, windstorms had been threatening her farm and other land in the area. She and her closest neighbors, Victor Whitesong and the Goodmans, had fought together with what she could call only middling success, holding the topsoil down with soil-catching trenches, ground cover and shelterbelts, and mulch and terraces. They didn't try to grow a crop to sell—there was no market. With windmill irrigation they had grown enough food for all of them, including John Strate and his five boys, until they had moved to Leavenworth.

Just this week, Deborah had received John's letter containing his worries for her. *"I'm aware of the calendar, little lady. It's that time of year when the winds usually begin to blow in western Kansas. I also know you've had no moisture, so I'm sure you expect the dust to blow.*

"I know, you're going to say you won't go to Minnesota because you don't want to live near your folks. Now, don't misunderstand me (you and I are just darned good friends). Why don't you and the boys come live with us until the drought is over? Of course, I know what your next argument is—you don't want to desert the old folks and Victor. Shoot, load up August and Audrey and Victor and all of you come! My little house and farm are just that, little, but we sure don't have to breathe dirt. The boys and I lived with you. Why don't you folks come live with us?

"Now, why didn't we think of that before? Sell your livestock or bring them here. We'll find room! We can even add on to the house like we did Victor's."

She had written back. *"John, why am I not surprised at your offer? You are a dear man. But you know we need to keep watering the shelterbelts and listing the fields when they blow. Who knows, maybe rain will come, and the winds won't blow this year."*

That was just two days ago.

Was this storm bad enough that she'd have to work the fields as soon as the wind let up and there was enough light to see? Some of her farmland should never have had its protective growth of grass plowed. By plowing the marginal ground, Christian had made it easy for the winds that could easily scour the soil down to infertile hardpan, that concreteness that repelled earthworms and vegetative growth. The poorest ground had the soil that most often blew, and she had learned long ago to be alert.

Deborah complained as she usually did at times like this. "Darn you, Christian." She slammed the table surface with her palm.

Frustrated with her worries, she took her journal from her desk. Sometimes writing made her feel better.

So, here I am, facing the blowing again. With each year of the drought and onslaught of the winds, I'm reminded Christian plowed some grassland without talking to me first. I know he must have thought I was so obsessed with keeping the ground in grassland that I didn't want to debate further.

I had always wanted to live where I could see so far into the distance that my imagination would have to take over where my senses left off. Grandfather Blue Sky put that desire in me. He told me how, years before when he still lived in Hopi land, he had seen both the ocean and prairie. He described them to me when I was a child.

He said, "In those places, just as with the desert, my heart soared. I could see forever. Doing that, I knew that even with death I could still experience 'forever.'"

I didn't want to alter our land, because Grandfather said it shouldn't be scarred. If man owns land, he should be its careful custodian.

Sitting back in her chair, Deborah studied what she had written. Ironically, being custodian of the land involved more than just following Grandfather's teachings. Laws said she had to attempt to control the blowing. She smiled bitterly with the thought. If she didn't work her fields, Sheriff Stoddel, the last man in the world she wanted to see, would enforce the law.

Sounds at the windows caused her to look out. The wind was still strong, the odor of the air suggestive of how suffocating the dust could be during a far worse storm. The cold coming through the windowpane seemed to reach with fingers, the touch stinging her skin, and she pulled the robe closer to her neck.

She thought about Clifford and Bethany Strong who had built this very house. From 1870 until their deaths in 1929, they had kept their land as a ranch. At first, Christian had seemed impressed with what the Strongs had done, and he wondered how many acres of grassland they had handled when they were *big* ranchers, before barbed wire.

"Imagine, Deborah, 1870," he had exclaimed. "The Goodmans say there was still an occasional buffalo eating this grass in 1870. It's so difficult to picture how hard the Strongs worked to develop this place so beautifully."

Yet Christian began to talk about plowing even more acres. He wasn't totally to blame. Before they left Minnesota, they had both talked about raising wheat. But when Deborah saw the farm, she changed her mind, saying the land shouldn't be "broken."

"Christian, I can feel all the memories that are here. Leave them," she said.

Her words caused their only disagreement of any consequence. He had started to plow, and she stopped him. Even now, she thought at times he might have left her and the boys because of the disagreement—that he wasn't dead after all.

Victor, always Christian's loyal friend, had said more than once, "No, he didn't leave you, Deborah Jorgenson Nelson. He wasn't that kind of man, not that kind of daddy to his boys."

Once, when he said it, she had replied, "But maybe he was that kind of husband to his wife."

"Deborah, you are frustrated and even angry at times, not having any evidence of what happened or where he is. But this I know. He didn't desert you and the boys."

How many times had she promised herself to never start the debate, the questioning, all over again? Why was it, with the beginning of each year's winter winds, she experienced the revival of her doubts about Christian? With his disappearance—more than six years ago—her trust in him had begun to falter. Why did it even matter now what became of him, except to satisfy her curiosity? She still loved him, only in a far different way. Now she loved Victor with a depth that made her very soul joyful.

The seventh year of the drought and blowing was beginning—she raised her head and wiped her face with the backs of her hands, taking in deep breaths. Her hopes were destroyed one more time. Going to the window again, she saw that daybreak was coming, and the wind was lessening. She began to feel her usual determination. Yet something else, an anxiety, was still with her, and that worried her. She seemed to sense something to come, disruptive as a feeling. She preferred to think a fluctuating barometric pressure caused her tension, but that seemed unlikely.

She added coal to the kitchen range and mixed biscuits for breakfast. She dressed in warm clothing and braided her hair. Standing at the mirror, she coiled and pinned the braids to her head, an attempt to keep her hair out of the worst of the dust. She noticed the beginning of red smudges on her cheekbones. Already she was feeling the bronchial irritation and fever that Dr. Hocksmith said were her body's reaction to breathing in dust.

"Move back to Minnesota, Deborah," he had advised her. "At least you have that option. Most folks don't."

She had ignored him. She would never leave Victor, the Goodmans, and the land.

"Don't forget pepper on the eggs and cinnamon on the oatmeal," she said to Sonja as they prepared breakfast.

"So we won't notice we're eating dirt." Jonathan adjusted his mask.

"Shh," Deborah gently cautioned, not wanting David to hear. Jonathan was eleven now, and his understanding of the seriousness of the drought had grown.

David, who was nine, wiped dust from the high chair and tried to get Baby Half Shell to sit down. Laughing, the one-year-old buried his hands in David's curls and hung on, something he did every chance he got. "Oatmeal and cinnamon," David sang as he worked at fastening the high chair tray and putting a bib on Baby.

Deborah stood by the stove, waiting for the biscuits to be ready. She felt Sonja watching her.

"Are you all right, Deborah?"

"I'm so full of anxiety," she admitted in an undertone, "that feeling I have when something's wrong—or going to happen."

Sonja's mouth tightened. "What, I wonder?"

Jonathan had heard. "A bad storm? A black blizzard?"

She turned to reassure him. Ever since the first "black" storm, both boys could easily become alarmed at the possibility of another one. "Don't you worry. I don't know what it is. As soon as I eat, I'm going out to do the chores and check the fences. Perhaps my tension has something to do with the livestock. You boys stay in the house. You hear me?"

"Maybe you shouldn't go out," Sonja said.

"Don't worry, I'll be careful, you know that."

Later, Deborah kissed Jonathan and David, whispering, "Remember what I said. No farther than the front steps to shake rugs." Baby kissed her, giggling over the smear of oatmeal he left on her face.

In the mustard-yellow light, she walked west beyond the yard trees, turning about to look at the sky, alert to any black clouds of dust that might silently roll upon themselves and swallow the land, eating at its surface, sucking up the soil. But the skies were just an ugly brown. Now that the worst of the storm was over, only numerous small patches of dust swirled here and there in the open fields.

The farmstead was quiet, except for the bickering of crows in the orchard. A small flock startled her when they lifted from the trees and flew to the south.

The anxiety was still with her.

She cared for the livestock, feeding and watering in the dismal light. She brushed down the hides of the two milk cows and washed their udders but still had to strain dirt from the milk when she did the separating. The small herd of beef cattle, some belonging to August and Victor, had found shelter near the haystacks in the corral and were eating the bundles of dusty sudan grass she had thrown into the bunkers; they would soon move out to graze. That meant they might get through any fences that had wires broken by the weight of weeds and drifted dirt.

"Be strong, granddaughter," she heard Grandfather Blue Sky say in her head. "Be strong in mind, as well as body."

The horses milled about in the corral, wanting her attention. Deborah spread a blanket on Lady, lifted the saddle, and tightened the girth. She positioned her bandana over her nose and mouth. Then she placed a cotton sugar sack on the mare's lower face and nose, fastening it to the bridle straps. Damp masks would have been better if it weren't for the cold air. Neither the sugar sack nor the bandana did enough good; still, the greater danger was going without them. Breathing the dust today would be constant. She also knew to be prepared in the event a bad storm should catch her away from the house.

"Come here, Marco." She had designed a smaller sack to fit over the dog's muzzle and fasten to his collar. He didn't protest or try to shake it off. Resignation was in his eyes.

She was dressed for the bitter temperature, long johns beneath her jeans and flannel shirt, a sweater under her heavy jacket. Over everything she wore coveralls, feeling encumbered by the clothing despite her slenderness. The layers were necessary, for the wind was biting and still managed to work its way inside the edges of her stocking cap.

Victor hadn't come to do chores with her. That meant he was helping August and Audrey sweep out their sod house. When that was finished, he and August would probably ride fences together, for the old man worried about their condition even though the cattle were in Deborah's pasture.

Holding a pitchfork on her saddle much the way she might a rifle, Deborah began her ride, trailing along the fence line, knowing she would ride hours before she finished. She carried a sandwich and canteen of coffee already grown tepid.

The fence that ran parallel with the lane and its big cottonwoods had packed-in thistles, but because the wind was strong up on the flat lands, any weeds she might pull out of the fencing couldn't be set afire. That was a job for a calmer day. She heard the crisp, dry sound of the brittle grass beneath the mare's hooves. Before long, the men would help her rotate the range cows to new grazing ground.

Deborah found the east fencing reasonably clear of weeds and piles of blow dirt. Going north, she crossed the creek, its hard bed shattered with wide drought cracks. She stopped the mare and watched the Goodman house across the road east. Her heartbeat seemed to hasten with anticipation. Sure enough, before long Victor stepped onto the porch, waving and blowing a kiss to her. She smiled beneath the bandana, wishing he could see her face and be close enough to touch the hand she waved.

He called, "If August and I finish riding our fences early, I'll track you down and help with yours."

"That's good. I love you." She rode away from the creek, back up onto the heights where the wind stung her eyes.

Still wondering about her anxiety, Deborah turned in her saddle, looking around at the skies. Her eyes traveled over the hills, down to where trees obstructed her view of the creek. The cattle now grazed toward the creek. She counted them and noted their movements. They seemed normal. In the distance, she saw no sign of dust trails. No one was driving or walking. There were no smudges or columns of smoke. She listened. Sometimes calls or alarm bells carried long distances. There was nothing.

Scanning the fence along the way, she turned and rode to the west fence line. She would need to get down soon and walk, for the windchill was numbing her. In a big canyon, where the creek bed had channeled the wind and its gathering of tumbleweeds, the barbed wire was full and weighted. She pulled out the debris, piling and compressing with her feet and pitchfork. It would be safe to burn here.

The tumbleweeds to be burned brought back the image of Christian when he was eleven, barefoot, standing as though mesmerized in a pile of burning weeds from his dad's fence. She had pulled him out. Lendel had used a saddle blanket to smother the fire in his brother's pant legs … burning his own hands and agitating his ailing heart. Deborah shuddered, remembering her worries about Lendel and the weeks of Christian's suffering, despite Grandfather Blue Sky's careful attention.

Now she studied the air for wind currents and positioned herself on the upwind side of the debris. She set the thistles on fire. The weeds were tinder dry and flared up in a flash, their consuming sound like innumerable whispering voices. Yellow smoke and sparks floated above the blaze. The shallow layer of embers smoldered to ashes, and she stirred them with the fork tines, looking for any sign of life. A draft blew into the ashes, and they merely scattered. They were dead.

As she worked, she remained alert and watched the bend of the creek that shut off her view of the farm of Tony Van Ricker, whose pasture bounded hers. This was the very place where he had cut the barbed wire one day and rode his horse at her with intentions of attacking her, venom in his voice as he called her a squaw, telling her Indians didn't belong here.

Could her anxiety be tied in with Van Ricker? What if he were to come again? She hefted the pitchfork. Just as she had trained him to do, Marco sat on the creek bank, looking about, nose to the wind, ears cocked. His job was to listen and look for a threat. She didn't let herself imagine what the dog might do if the man rode around the creek bend.

Where a big draw spilled out of Van Ricker's pasture into her own, Deborah wrinkled her nose at the foul odor that the wind brought to her. Van Ricker had lost a cow as far back as October, and the word was that the cow's teeth had been ground down to uselessness by dirt in the feed, slowly starving her to death. The stench had been hovering ever since.

August had lamented to Deborah, "Tony should have noticed the cow's condition long before it got so bad. Should've put her out of misery long before." There was a stricken look on the old man's face. He hated to see any animal suffer.

The scree of a hawk turned her eyes upward. The large-winged bird soared in ever-widening circles until it disappeared over the wall of Van Ricker's canyon. The hawk was undoubtedly headed for the dead cow—even death had its attractions.

Moving on, she headed up to the knoll where Marco crouched. She twisted and turned in the saddle, looking for anything out of the ordinary. There was only the dust-ridden sky. That was no longer unusual.

She rode to the south end of the pasture and opened a gate that led into her half-section field that had once been a separate, fenced pasture. Dalton Strong had left the fence standing when he broke out the buffalo grass to grow wheat. The fence was well made, three strands of strong barbed wire fastened to yellow rock posts. It was a fine fence, and she wanted to keep it in good condition in case she planted the field back to grass.

Marco ran ahead of her, swerving about, his nose to the ground. At a distance, a rabbit sprinted away, raising its own little trail of dust, and Marco watched. The uneven ground was hard riding due to its drill rows, but she was grateful for the ridges. They held stubble from last year's sedan grass, a drought-resistant fodder crop. Its roots were successfully holding the soil down, although some dust had blown in last night, apparently from Van Ricker's field to the west; the loose soil had fanned out within the stubble instead of forming drifts. That was good—for her field, not his.

She heard Marco growl; he crouched a short distance from the southeast corner of the fence, his body rigid, hackles raised.

A brown grocery wrapper appeared to be flattened against the corner post and barbed wires, held there by the wind and flapping up and down, its edges stirring the soil drifted against it and creating brief clouds that fogged the air. Packed in and around the post and wires, tumbleweeds and other dried growth provided a base for the drift that was peaked and scalloped like blown snow. Deborah rode her mare closer.

A few yards from the fence, what had looked like grocery paper was not. Her heart thudded as she swung down from the saddle to peer more closely. What she saw caused her to thrust her shoulder under the horse's comforting neck and head, and her hands cupped Lady's nose and mouth.

A person's arm and shirt were caught in the wires, along with the metal clasp and button of an overall strap. Nothing else could be seen because of the blown dirt—except a foot, twisted unnaturally, the dangling laces of its scuffed shoe blowing in the wind, leaving tracings in the drift much the way a bull snake might do.

Gasping from the shock of seeing someone's feet protruding from a drift of blow dirt and an arm hung up in a guy wire, Deborah reluctantly but hurriedly crawled through the fence. It wasn't the wind that sent a bitter chill down her back. Here was the source of her anxiety.

She squatted and dragged dirt away from a body small enough to be a boy. She dug faster at the drift, hoping yet knowing no one could breathe with his nose and mouth covered by so much soil. He was a young boy she recognized, only nine years old, the same age as David. His skin was colorless and frozen. He was sandy haired and blue eyed with long, blond eyelashes.

"Aw, Robby," Deborah wailed softly. She lost the balance of her squatting position, and sat in the dirt, bending her knees to sit cross-legged. "Robby," she cried again.

She removed her gloves, took off her face mask, and pulled her cap closer about her face, beginning a slight rocking motion of her body. Her fingertips gently brushed the dirt from the child's face. There were punctures near his left eye, probably caused by the barbs of the fence. Beads of blood, ruby red and glistening, curved from the eyebrow downward, and the trail of blood had frozen before the dust covered the face.

"Robby," and this time she sang a keening chant. Adding sounds and rhythms taught many years ago by Blue Sky, Deborah mourned over the boy. His name was Robert, but no one, including his parents, Wave and Jenny Vogl, called him Robert. He had always seemed younger than he was, and the diminutive version of his name was used.

She chanted a song of grief, Hopi words she couldn't translate, didn't need to translate, for the rhythms and tones communicated the sadness of the loss of a soul. Tears ran down her face.

The dirt covered a good share of his body, and the sleeve of one arm was entangled in the post's guy wire. His fingers, cold and stiffened, seemed to be reaching out. He wasn't wearing a coat or face mask, and his shirt collar was hung up in the barbs. Another barb had torn his pant leg.

Years ago, Audrey had told Deborah about Robby's birth. "I sat with Jenny while we waited for Dr. Hocksmith. She was doing well, everything happened so normally. Carl delivered her, and as soon as I saw the baby I knew. The cord was around the dear baby's neck, and his color was bad. Carl had to breathe into his mouth to get him going. But he was already hurt … his poor little mind."

With the memory, the old lady had cried, for one of her own babies had died from the same cause a long time before. "Jenny and Wave love Robby desperately. She says he is sweet-natured and willing, and I know she works hard to teach him."

Sitting on the frigid ground in the biting wind eventually brought Deborah to her senses. She stood and looked about her at the sameness of the flat land, its shades of desolate brownness fogged by falling dust. She loved the land. She had heard people say they hated it because of the blowing dust. If anything, she loved it all the more because of the agony it was experiencing with the drought … but at this moment, with the body of the child at her feet, she was finding it hard to relate to the land's pain.

Sounds startled her. A number of black birds perched on the fence line, which stretched west, and Marco growled. Their raucous calls made her realize what she had been seeing but not recognizing in the powdery dust surface—footprints of crows, carrion eaters. Most of the birds were immobile, others crouched with a slight lift to their wings; all watched her intently. She studied the ground where the toe marks led up the side of a drift near where Robby's eyes had been covered, and fresh droppings were in the dirt. She had arrived just in time to prevent a further indignity to the child.

Deborah was stirred to action. Directly to the east of her section line was Wave's farm, two miles down the road, and she knew Jenny and he must be out of their minds with worry. With pliers, she untwisted the top two strands of barbed wire from the rock post, bending them out of the way, and led the horse across. She drove the tines of her pitchfork into the ground, leaving it to stand by the post. Removing the saddle, she hooked it over the post with the saddle horn pointed to the east. Victor would understand.

When she had the body wrapped in the saddle blanket, she placed it across the horse's back. She clicked her tongue and walked beside the mare, steadying the burden. Lady went through the road ditch, and they began the cold trek to the Vogl farm with Marco in the lead.

At the Vogl yard gate, she lifted the bundle down, holding it close to her chest. She heard the house door slam, and Jenny ran to meet Deborah, her voice sounding much like the keening song Deborah had sung in the field.

"He's dead?" she asked. "I thought so." She joined her arms with Deborah's. The woman's face was swollen, and her eyes were red.

Smothering dust blew in their faces. Jenny gasped for breath and caressed the blanket over Robby's face. "The poor baby. What a horrible way to die. Where was he?"

"Jenny, let's go in." Deborah led the way, calling the dog. Inside, she gestured, and Marco crouched near the door.

They placed the boy on the kitchen table. Two girls older than Robby were in the dim living room. Their eyes were big, and Deborah heard sobbing. Jenny hurried to them. She sat on a divan and pulled a girl down on either side of her. They talked and cried together.

Deborah removed some of her outer clothing and the sack from the dog's muzzle. She smelled perking coffee and poured a cup. The taste was thick and bitter, but it was hot and thawing to her senses. After a few sips, she noticed the mirror above the sink. Her forehead was black with dirt, and there were streaks on her cheeks where tears had run through the dust. She poured warm water into a basin and washed; her skin burned from its exposure to the wind.

Jenny joined her. "They're awful worried about their dad right now. I'm not sure they fully realize about Robby—but they will. They loved him so."

"Where is Wave?"

"I don't know." Her eyes darted about the kitchen as though looking for him. "He went searching at dawn."

"What can I do for the girls?" Deborah asked. "Some warm milk maybe?"

Jenny thought for a moment. "You know what? Extra pennies are few and far between in this family, so I hid away the cocoa can and the last of the sugar for some special occasion." Dismay was on her face. "Dear Jesus our Savior, there's nothing special about this occasion ... but Carol and Joyce are awful special."

Deborah went outside to put Lady in the barn. She got milk from the well house.

Jenny measured the sugar and cocoa with shaking hands. Deborah poured the milk and put the mixture on to heat.

"Deborah Nelson, you have to be one of the most caring people I know."

"You have done the same for me. You helped me when Christian disappeared. When I lost the baby, you came out in the bitter, bitter cold and snow."

"Pfft." Jenny waved her hand. They watched the milk begin to heat. "How far did you walk with Robby?" Her voice was strained and husky.

Deborah patted her hand. "Two miles. I found him in the corner of my half section. I thought ... I thought his brown shirt was grocery paper moving in the wind."

"My heart wants to believe he didn't suffer too much in the miles he walked last night, but my mind knows different." Jenny clutched her fists to her chest as though she were in pain.

Deborah reached out to her again. "Jenny?"

"I'm okay. I'd appreciate it if you would take that chocolate to the girls."

After spending some time with Joyce and Carol, Deborah helped her friend remove the saddle blanket. Jenny was pale, and she was biting her lip. They sat on opposite sides of the table. Both of them studied the boy's face.

"He doesn't look like he suffered, but you know he did," Jenny said.

"He isn't suffering now," Deborah said.

"Life wasn't fair to him."

Deborah was startled, wondering where she had heard those words before. Then she remembered saying them in 1918 when Lendel died.

Jenny jerked upright in her chair. "Wave! Oh, dear Lord above, take care of him." She held her clasped hands between her knees and rocked back and forth, her eyes wild. "I've got to tell you about the dear man. He went out looking for Robby within a half hour after the storm started. We didn't know until then the boy wasn't in the house. We don't know when and why Robby went out, maybe to the outhouse. Wave finally came back—it seemed so long. He intended to go out again. I put myself in front of the door there, and I said, 'Over my dead body, Wave Vogl.' He knew

I meant business. We stayed up the rest of the night, trying to figure out how Robby got out of the house without us knowing. We watched the lamp globe get smoked up.

"Deborah, you, of all people, must know what it's like to search an attic over and over … the cellar … the barn and other buildings. You did plenty of it. Poor Wave. So scared. He breathed his share of dirt out in those buildings. Over and over he looked, hollering and hollering, thinking maybe he had just missed seeing Robby, you know, hadn't looked carefully enough." She was agitated, and her hair was beginning to straggle out of a loose knot, hair the same color as Robby's.

"I understand. In many ways I searched for years," Deborah said. "I guess a good share of me has given up by now—after six years."

"That's one blessing with Robby. You found him for us. At least we won't always be wondering where he is, the way you have with Christian."

Jenny looked at the boy. "Oh," she cried, "he didn't have a coat or hat. How did he get so far, with no more than what he had on?"

Deborah went around the table, leaning over to press her head against Jenny and hug her. They rocked back and forth.

Jenny said, "I've lost my mother and dad, my two grandmas and grandpas before that, and Wave's mother. I thought that was terrible."

"I've lost people too but to lose a child …" Deborah didn't want to think about it. She had lost her baby.

"I imagine adopting Baby Half Shell has helped you. He's such a dear boy." Jenny rocked harder. Deborah got a dish towel and helped Jenny blow her nose.

"I just couldn't seem to teach Robby everything he needed to know. Most of all, I couldn't teach him judgment, hard as I tried."

"I understand." Deborah remembered the last community picnic in September. David and she had played ball with Robby, and when the ball escaped the boy, he had run precariously close to the edge of a rocky ledge.

"Jenny, is your telephone working? I'd better call Dr. Hocksmith."

"Oh, yes, do that." Jenny went to the window. "How bad is it out there, really? I made Wave stay inside during the worst of it, but he went out at daybreak. He was going southeast, thinking Robby might have walked before the wind. Do you think I'll lose him too?"

"That husband of yours has a good head on his shoulders. You know that."

Jenny nodded. "I do know." She went to the body. "I'm going to wash him. Get the hateful dirt off him."

"I'll call, and then I'll help you, if you like."

"I would like that."

Deborah washed the boy's hair, and Jenny cleaned his face. She examined the blood, which looked like a chain of jewels. "What caused this, do you suppose?"

Reluctantly, Deborah said, "I believe it was the barbed wire fence."

Jenny cried at the thought and washed away the dried blood. Marco was disturbed by the noises she made and came to his feet. "Stay," Deborah said. He went back to his corner, the sugar sack dragging from his collar.

The boy's mouth had fallen open, and Jenny wiped the dust from his teeth and tongue. "Dear Jesus who suffered on the cross ... this boy suffered too." She tore a strip from a cloth and tied up the jaw to hold it closed.

"He has such delicate features," Deborah said. Tears made her eyes feel less gritty.

"He never seemed to age. His mind didn't grow. His body got bigger, but he always acted younger than his age. I used to pray he would catch up. I learned better ... or I guess I accepted."

Jenny described how Robby had worked hard to learn the simple, routine things. "Toilet training." She smiled through her tears. "What a struggle."

"Toilet training is not routine," Deborah said. "My boys had problems. Their aim wasn't so good."

The women laughed, and there was relief in the sound. They were silent as they dressed the body in clean clothing. Jenny was buttoning a shirt cuff when she said, "Buttons. Oh, they were hard for him."

"Yes, buttons. David still buttons only one overall strap."

Jenny put a small pillow under Robby's head. "I don't know if it matters, the pillow, I mean."

Deborah said, "It matters."

A noise at the door startled them. Wave came in. Jenny went to pieces, her calm features seeming to collapse before Deborah's eyes, her voice painful to hear.

When Wave saw Robby's body on the table, the man had even less control than Jenny. "The poor little guy. I tried, I tried, Jenny." Bending his tallness, he buried his dirt-blackened face against her hair while reaching out to grasp the dead boy's arm. "I wore my horse out, I'm afraid. I left him at the schoolhouse in the shed and walked to Herman's place, and now he's out looking too. I sure don't want Corrine to worry—"

"I'll call Moses," Deborah said. "He'll see to it Herman is found and told about Robby."

Footsteps on the porch took Jenny to the door. "Come in Dr. Hocksmith." Her voice was hoarse, almost gone.

Hocksmith had a white handkerchief over his nose and mouth, and he removed it and his stylish wide-brimmed felt hat. He was wearing soft leather gloves.

Marco was growling, his teeth showing, fur standing on his neck. Sheriff Stoddel was behind Hocksmith. Deborah snapped her fingers, moving Marco over by the stove. She suppressed an angry sigh. She should have known Stoddel would come with Carl. The small man looked at her coldly. He unbuttoned his coat, drawing the lapels back just enough that he could maintain his usual posture, his hand on his hip near the gun. The narrow slits of his eyes matched the grim line of his mouth.

There were more footsteps on the porch and a knock at the door. Wave let Victor in and held out his hand. "I figured you'd be coming, Whitesong. The wind's come up some, hasn't it? Bad enough to make you feel like the north end of a goose going south." Deborah watched Wave pull himself together, making commonplace references to the weather, grasping Victor's hand firmly, helping him remove his outer coat. Both men ignored the tear streaks on Wave's face.

"Visibility is worsening, for sure." Victor removed his hat. He turned to Deborah, relief in his expression, and warmth in his brown eyes. He gave her his slightly lopsided smile. "I tracked you. Those tracks will be gone soon."

"Tracked?" Stoddel snorted. "You ain't Indian like her. Only Indians track." He stared at Deborah, and she ignored him.

Carl was examining the body. "How'd it happen?"

Wave's voice was intense, full of emotion. "After the storm started, we realized Robby wasn't in the house. We don't know what happened. We supposed he went to the outhouse. We looked everywhere we could. I finally had to quit and wait until morning."

Jenny leaned over the body as though to shield it from Stoddel who had stomped across the room to stand close to the table. "The poor child smothered or froze ... or both. It doesn't matter which at this point. A storm like that is a terrible threat to even the most experienced person. I was telling Deborah, one thing Robby lacked was good judgment—"

"Idiot, wasn't he?" Stoddel's question was more a comment than a question.

Deborah could have clawed his eyes. "You don't have to talk that way. It isn't appropriate."

"Sheriff Egbert Stoddel," Hocksmith said, his voice loud and haughty. He stared down at Stoddel. "The only idiot in this room is still breathing."

"Why's he clean if he was out all night?" Stoddel demanded in his unreasonable voice.

"We washed and dressed him," Deborah said.

"Deborah's the one who found him and brought him to us," Jenny said. "He was in her fence, two miles over."

Victor had come to stand beside Deborah. He wasn't touching her, but she could feel his warmth. Just as she expected, and she knew Victor expected the same, Stoddel abruptly turned to stare at them, moving his small eyes from her face to Victor's.

"Why is it," he said, "wherever there's trouble or someone is dead, the two of you are there?"

"Just a minute!" Wave's voice was even louder than Hocksmith's had been, and Jenny jumped at his sound. "What the devil you getting at?"

Deborah struggled for calmness. She had been through this before. "I was riding my fences, looking for broken wires—"

"Two miles over ain't your pasture." Stoddel glared. "It's a field."

"A field that's still fenced. I wanted to see if the fence needed repair or if I needed to list the field to control blowing." She spoke with patience she wasn't feeling. "I found Robby in the southeast corner. He was ... caught in the barbed wire and guy wires."

Stoddel wasn't finished. "But then you washed him up. Took away the evidence. How do we know that's what happened? It's just like Lydia Bogart. The two of you say she drowned herself. You cleaned her up and brought her to the undertaker—"

"And she had drowned herself," Carl said in disgust. "Moses had no reason to lie about his own wife, a sad woman with dementia. Just shut your mouth, Egg. You're being a horse's ass."

"The last thing we womenfolk can do for a dead child, for anyone, is to bathe him the way it was done when he was born." Jenny struggled to control her sobs. "Getting that dratted dirt off his body and face was the only thing we could do for the poor thing." She hid her face against Wave's chest.

Deborah said to Stoddel, "You'll find my saddle at the place where Robby was."

"Why? Why's your saddle there?"

She sensed Victor wanted to put his hand on her arm, for he knew how Stoddel could get her stirred up. She said each word slowly, for hadn't Dr. Hocksmith suggested Stoddel was an idiot? "I left the saddle because I wrapped the boy's body in my saddle blanket and put him across the horse."

Stoddel wasn't quitting. "How many years since your husband up and disappeared?"

Victor answered for her. "Six going on seven. You know that, don't you? Like you know the number of fingers and toes you have."

"And everywhere we turn, the two of you are together—"

"We work together," Victor said. "We work with the Goodmans, trying to see ourselves through the Depression and the drought. We're all friends." He was mad, and Deborah reached for his hand. A mere touch was all it took, and he breathed deeply and slowly.

Wave's face was contorted, his voice choked. "We got a dead boy here, and like the good woman she is, Deborah brought him to us—"

"Your husband disappeared six and a half years ago and the two of you—"

"We know, we know," Carl said. "Stoddel, you've been accusing these two ever since. Trouble is, no one can figure what you're accusing them of doing. Despite all the searching, there wasn't evidence of anything—and certainly no body. I've had enough!"

"But—"

"You aren't welcome in my house, Stoddel. Get out," Wave said.

Hocksmith took a folded paper out of his pocket. "This is the death certificate. No question in my mind, and it's my business as coroner to fill it out."

Stoddel leaned close to Robby's head. "Any marks on him? Any marks on his throat?"

Wave grabbed the sheriff's shoulders from behind and pushed him toward the door. He pushed Stoddel so hard that the man almost fell.

Hocksmith said, "Jenny, Wave, I'm sorry he came with me. He was in the drugstore when Deborah called, and you know how he is. Doing his 'sheriffly duty.'"

The doctor signed with a flourish. "I'll file this paper with the state." He hurried to the door and spoke to Stoddel. "You coming or walking back to town? Doesn't matter to me." He pushed the man through the door and slammed it behind them.

"That son of a—"

"Wave," Jenny said, "the girls are in the other room."

Wave clamped his lips together and sat down. "It must make Stoddel feel awful powerful, adding to the misery of folks like he does."

Chapter 3

A Childhood Disease

Deborah knew she wasn't alone in considering February a deadly month, a time hard on the body and emotions. The weather was cold, with sharp winds that defied layered clothing, carefully caulked houses, and thick bedding in the barns. The nights seemed exceptionally long because the hidden sun made the days bleak and short. February was when spirits were low—it seemed spring would never come—and germs invaded stressed bodies low on immunity.

A measles epidemic was going through the school. Word from Carl Hocksmith went about the neighborhood that measles alone were not a threat to the children, but measles combined with breathing the blowing dust might reduce a child's resistance and possibly bring on pneumonia.

Audrey's face tightened at the news. "We need to keep a close eye on those darling boys. I've seen enough breathing illnesses to last me a lifetime. The first I heard of such a thing, my uncle worked in a coal mine. Something about the coal dust getting in his lungs, and it killed him. I wonder how different coal dust is from field dust."

With each dust storm, Deborah worried about Audrey, and on a few occasions the old lady had taken to her bed. "I've breathed my bushel of dirt," she would say. Hocksmith said breathing the dust put a strain on Audrey's heart.

"It seems to me," August said, "lung disease can be pretty sneaky. None of us thought Baby Half Shell's daddy was sick with lung problems when he visited here. Maybe Fleet Foot knew, but he never let on."

"Back where we came from, I knew of old folks who died of pneumonia." Audrey twisted the skirt of her apron. "I've never taken care of anyone with pneumonia. For sure, I wouldn't know what to do. In my opinion, even doctors don't know much about treating it. It's common to hear of old folks dying of pneumonia in the winter."

Deborah remembered hearing August read to Victor from the newspaper about dust pneumonia. It was what worried her about Audrey. Dust pneumonia could be her downfall.

She wrote in her journal:

> *John, the dear man, encouraged me to get out of the dust bowl until the drought is over. If it were simple to do, I would put those old folks in my car with the boys and do just that—leave, take them away because I believe them to be vulnerable. But I can't leave Victor behind, and then I start naming people I love and worry about ... I can't leave behind Mary and her girls, then there's Moses, Sonja ... her entire family. By staying with me there's one less mouth to feed at her home. She needs me, and I need her. What about Corrine and Herman and the babies—everyone with children should leave the dust bowl ... Jenny and Wave and the two girls. After all, they have suffered the greatest of tragedies because of the dust.*
>
> *And there I am—it's impossible to add and subtract from a list of people I care about. This is my community, my life. The people I love most are right here, breathing the air we share.*
>
> *I love and am loved.*

Baby Half Shell was the first in Deborah's house to come down with measles. David was puzzled. "I thought you fellers said it was school kids who are getting measles. Can't call a baby a school kid."

Sonja laughed. "Sure can't. I'm afraid it's my fault. I took Baby to see my folks one day, and I think it was about the time one of the kids must have been getting sick." Half Shell was fussy. "You can blame me."

"Don't blame yourself, Sonja," Deborah said, holding and rocking the little boy. His dark skin was pale, making his eyes look bigger and blacker. "You know it had to happen sometime. Measles don't just hit school children, David." She brushed the baby's flyaway hair from his damp forehead.

"That's a relief," he said. "I thought maybe the little feller was getting extra smart all of a sudden."

The baby seemed to take the illness in stride after the first day. "You know why, don't you?" Victor asked. "I think after that trip with someone from the reservation, Half Shell can handle just about anything." He looked closely at Deborah. "Hey, I didn't mean to make you cry."

"Oh, you know how I am. Every time I think of how scared he must have been, I get upset. I tell myself it wasn't a long trip, and when he got here, Leonard took care of him. But he still was scared, poor little thing." As with every time they talked about Baby Half Shell's trip, she reached out and hugged the baby close to her, comforting and loving him at the same time.

She had received an indignant letter from Many Stars about Half Shell's recent trip to Kansas. He had paid a visiting Indian woman from Colorado to deliver Baby Half Shell to Deborah's farm, but the baby was left in the train station for the mailman to deliver. With each letter, Many Stars made some reference to his sadness over the fear Half Shell must have felt, voicing Deborah's feelings exactly.

He wrote, "How could a woman, a mother herself, leave a twelve-month-old baby with a station master? Be sure you tell the mail carrier how grateful this family is to him."

One morning, Leonard Heickert brought the mail down the lane instead of leaving it in the mailbox. "Deborah"—he had never called her by her first name before—"look at what the baby's grandfather sent to me." He climbed out of his car and took off his coat in the frigid air. He proudly modeled a sheepskin vest. "Handmade! Real fine work. That man wrote a letter saying his daughters made this to say thank you. Now, they're good people, I'd say."

In a few days, Jonathan came down with measles. He was a good patient, tolerant of being kept in the house as long as he had his books and dictionary. He had discovered Scott and Dickens on Deborah's bookshelves and alternated his reading of the two authors. He used the dictionary for words he didn't know. She sat near him, doing as she had done with Baby Half

Shell, brushing his hair from his forehead, feeling his cheeks, checking his eyes, and thinking how with each year he looked more and more like her. And with their dark hair and skin, Baby and Jonathan resembled one another enough to be real brothers. She studied his features.

"I'm okay, Mom," he said restlessly, conscious of how she was looking at him.

"You're right. I'll check in with you later."

Victor came early one morning, driving his truck instead of riding horseback. They had been saving tires and gas by using their horses as much as possible, so she knew something must be up. She met him at the truck.

"It's Dad," he said. "He's sprained his ankle bad. Mom said he didn't have enough sense to not chase an ornery cow on foot." He grinned as he climbed out of the truck. "She says, in her words, 'the stubborn old fool will get better fast just knowing you're coming for a couple of days. He hates being dependent.'" Laughter gleamed in Victor's brown eyes.

"So that's where you got your stubbornness. Two days? Is that enough?"

"Aw, I think so. I figure by then he'll have the crutches figured out—or broken for kindling." He grinned. "What I thought I'd do is send Stoddel out to help you. Suppose that's a good idea?"

"A real good idea," she said dryly. She tugged his too-large ears and smoothed his hair. "Your mother's going to think I'm neglecting you. You need a haircut. You're always needing a haircut."

"If we were married, we could keep up on the haircutting. I'll tell Mom she should go to town and straighten out Stoddel. Clear out all the old suspicions. Then we can get married." He kissed her. "I hate to leave you with everything to do, especially with Jonathan sick."

"Don't you worry. With Sonja here, we can do the few chores we've got."

"I worry about the old folks and the dust."

"Victor, you'll have your hands full with your dad. Don't worry. I'll see August and Audrey often and get their milk and cream to them."

"I know you will. I want to go tell the little fellers good-bye. Then I'd better get going. A sprained ankle doesn't make a feller sick to where he willingly stays down."

When he came out of the house he gave her a long kiss. He said, "I'll bet anything David's about to get sick. I can see it in his eyes."

"Look at how well you know those boys. Give your folks my love."

He turned to crank his truck. "I love you, dear Deborah. I'll be back in two or three days, and maybe Baby Half Shell will be walking by then."

Deborah watched Victor's truck go down the lane, dust fogging out behind it. Immediately, a feeling hit her, an anxiety that tightened her chest. It had been a while since she and Victor had not seen one another daily. She was going to miss him.

The anxiety stayed with her. Was there something more than missing Victor?

Victor was right. David did become ill next but in a different way. At first, he fought the "stay down" routine, preferring to play with his toys on the floor or chase about the house. Then he grew pale, and a cough and congestion developed. Deborah built a fire in the fireplace, bedding him down on the divan. She sat on the floor, reading a Dickens book to him.

He listened intently, only saying occasionally, "That poor feller, Oliver." He had little appetite, and sometimes he dozed off, despite his coughing and congestion. As soon as he was awake again, he demanded to know more about Oliver Twist.

The next day he grew quiet and sleepy after lunch and went to bed. That was the day Sonja had to go home to help her mother who now had three children sick with measles. Her dad came to get her, and David barely noticed when she told him good-bye.

"Looks like David's hit hard," Sonja said. "I've heard the most rambunctious child is often the sickest. Dad said Joel has been pretty sick, and he's the one who acts so tough."

"Today's dust doesn't help," Deborah said. "When I hung damp sheets over David's bedroom windows, he just slept through all my thumping around."

She watched a truck, the Beckman truck this time, go down the lane in a cloud of dust. The inexplicable anxiety seemed to increase. She hated to see Sonja leave, but her mother, that poor woman with too many children, needed more help than Deborah did.

She put a rocking chair by David's bed and sat there for some time, just watching him sleep.

Baby Half Shell and Jonathan ate supper with good appetites. Deborah debated if she should wake David for food or let him rest. He hadn't eaten at noon, saying, "Chicken broth's for girls and babies."

There was a lull in the storm at sunset. Then the wind rose again, and the dusty odor increased. Deborah carried the half-asleep boy to the divan and covered him. Jonathan went on to bed. She checked the windows and doors and, for what seemed like the thousandth time, rolled towels and rugs against their sills. She alternated between listening to dirt hit the windows and another disturbing sound—David's feverish breathing. He didn't breathe deeply, and she wondered if his chest hurt the way hers had with the flu last year.

For a long time, Deborah watched the boy. She could tell by touch that he was growing hotter, and even though he stirred restlessly and coughed, he seemed to sleep. Sometimes she woke him enough to give him a drink. He was listless and barely responded to her voice. He swallowed weakly, much of the water dribbling out of his mouth. She worried, wondering what it meant. She wished Audrey or Victor were with her. If she couldn't get liquids into the child ... that was serious.

She thought of people who had died in recent years. Many of them, like Mary Cressler's old dad, were probably pushed over the brink by the dust storms. David Nyfeller's aunt had died in South Dakota. The doctor said her lungs were filled with dust. Robby Vogl had either died from the cold or smothered in the dirt storm. Deborah shuddered and wondered if David had dust in his lungs. The thought of pneumonia came to her, and it wouldn't go away. Dust pneumonia, any kind of pneumonia, was a big possibility.

Deborah walked nervously about the divan, and the anxiety, like a pressure against her very soul, was great. The wind increased, and there were sweeping sounds at the windows. She bathed David with cool water, hoping to bring his fever down. The sound of his breathing was more than worrisome.

She changed from her nightgown and robe into a skirt and long socks. She combed and rebraided her hair, wrapping it about her head and wondering why she was doing these things. By then, her anxiety had surfaced like choking scum on a pond lake. Victor ... if he were here, he'd know what to do. Should she send Jonathan on the mare for Audrey? She listened to the dust at the windows and knew her thought had been reckless. He was recovering from the measles, and neither Jonathan nor Audrey should breathe more of the dust.

Chapter 4

Take My Five Dollars

At two o'clock in the morning something warned Deborah that David's condition was desperately serious. She held her cheek against the boy's hot face and listened to his shallow breathing, wondering how such a simple, slight sound could suppress her own chest and squeeze her heart.

She woke Jonathan. "I need your help. I've got to get help for David. Change Baby's diaper and dress him warmly while I start the Ford. There's just enough wind to make it pretty cold out there."

Deborah hurried about, gathering a jug of water, face cloths, and blankets. Her hands trembled as she dressed David in a sweater over his flannel pajamas and put a cap on his head and two pair of wool socks on his feet. Should she drive to town or try to reach the doctor by using the Bogart or Vogl telephone? No, the Vogl phone had been disconnected, and Moses's phone did not always work during a dust-blowing wind. Who could help her the most, Audrey or Carl Hocksmith? Just a few days ago Audrey had talked about having had no experience with pneumonia. She'd better take David to town fast. Carl would know what to do. She took the car key from the bureau and buttoned five dollars in her shirt pocket.

She ran to the shed and struggled to open the doors against the northwest wind. She cranked the car. The engine was cold, causing her to work hard. There was the strong smell of gas, and she feared the car was flooded. Patiently, she tried one more time. The car started. She drove close to the front gate and thought about what must be done. The range and fireplace were burning low, and surely they were safe. She ticked off in her mind the things she had put in the car—water, blankets for Jonathan and Baby.

Jonathan handled Half Shell while Deborah carried David and the lantern. Dust swirled in eddies about them as they hurried to the car. She put David in the front seat, his head by her thigh, and Jonathan got in the back with the baby. Half Shell giggled through his face cloth, his eyes excited. "Good boy, Baby," she whispered, as Jonathan tucked a blanket around him. David's mask had slipped down. She adjusted it, feeling the heat of his face. He seemed unaware.

The drifting dust was alive on the county road. Its streamers crawled along the roadbed, except where they were caught by the edge of a drift. The wind seemed to grab and throw them into the air. What if the wind increased? What if she didn't make it to the doctor? Urgency made her drive faster—six miles—and then there would be six more to go on the gravel highway.

Not long after Deborah turned onto the highway, the wind suddenly hit harder, buffeting the little car.

Jonathan was aware. "Baby's asleep," he said, as though to reassure her.

"Good. Jonathan, I'm going to speed up. If we hit a drift … we need to hurry."

Much of her driving was instinctive. She watched for the ditch, using her side window more than the front. Soon she was crawling along at ten miles per hour. Conscious of David's hot head against her body, her fear grew. A sour taste rose into her mouth. The wind was worsening. She was desperate to get help for the boy. In the dust-filled air, the headlights reflected back, and she drove almost blindly.

Without warning, just when she estimated they were two miles from Fremont, the engine quit, stopped by static electricity. Deborah was horrified. She glanced down at David and then directed Jonathan. "Sit tight. I'm going to crank."

The wind cut at her with sand and bitter cold and tore at her long coat, causing the inevitable twisting about her legs, threatening to trip her. She closed her eyes against the grit, feeling her way to the front of the car. Why had she worn a skirt and the long socks? Her knees were bare, and wind whipped beneath her coat. As she jerked at the crank, she railed at herself.

She should have dressed better. What if she had to walk, carrying David? She should have worn jeans.

She turned the crank, again and again, knowing a car that had shorted out in such a storm wouldn't start until the weather conditions were right. She heard the rumble of thunder, but years ago she had ceased to respond with hope for rain. Static electricity jumped along the lines of barbed wire in the nearby pasture. The thunder boomed, and its sound, along with the wind, seemed to rock the little car.

Perspiring from the heavy coat and exertion, with tears washing the dust from her eyes, Deborah stopped cranking and looked about, knowing with desperation she couldn't carry a sick child and find her way in the stifling blackness. Besides, she couldn't leave Jonathan and Baby. She felt her way to the car door and slid in.

"I'm sorry, Mama," Jonathan said.

"I know." Deborah cried, her grimy fingers touching the sick child's face, feeling his irregular breaths on her hand.

Wind shook the car. Had a little Ford ever been overturned by such a storm? She moved over in the seat and cradled David in her arms. She berated herself for not going to the doctor sooner. What if she had brought the truck? Would it have withstood the dust better than the car?

David's breathing slowed, and fear made vomit rise up into her throat. What could she do? The wind howled about the car, and gravel was flung against metal and glass. She prayed, gently rocking the boy, her cheek lightly pressing his forehead. She crooned toneless, gentle sounds. She wanted to allow her own good health to seep into the boy.

Before dawn, David died.

Deborah knew the moment he took his last breath, and she held her own, willing him to breathe again. There was only silence in her ear, no small breath against her cheek. She clasped his body, her face against the springiness of his curls. "Jonathan," she cried, "he's gone. He's dead." She knew her voice carried the emotions of centuries and centuries of mothers who had said the same thing.

She said, "Hang on to Baby Half Shell. Don't let anything happen to him or you." Jonathan sobbed wildly, and she reached over the seat to grab his hand. She couldn't see his face in the darkness. When Baby became alarmed and moved about, whimpering, Jonathan gained control. She heard him comfort Half Shell, and the baby went to sleep. Deborah gripped the steering wheel.

"We're okay, Mama." Jonathan's voice was thick with tears.

The car rocked, and Deborah smelled dust anew. She covered the dead child's face and cried quietly, not wanting to upset Jonathan further. Shortly after daybreak, the wind dropped as suddenly as it had risen. There was still plenty of dust, but she could see a short distance.

"We'd better start walking, Jonathan. You've got to try to carry Baby, and I'll carry David. Can you do it?"

"Yes." He murmured to Baby Half Shell who stirred.

She held her emotions at bay, fearful of letting down again, and Jonathan seemed to be doing the same. She tightened the blanket about David's body, securing it over his head and under his legs. Outside the car, she helped Jonathan lift the baby onto his back and showed Half Shell how to grip Jonathan's shoulders. Jonathan held the baby's legs, and she tied a small flannel blanket around the two of them. Jonathan smiled weakly. "He's my papoose."

The baby boy grinned at her from the blanket's tent, his silky hair blowing on his forehead, and Deborah forced back her tears. "Good boy, Baby Half Shell."

She lifted the wrapped bundle from the car and carried it against her breasts, much the way she had held Robby's body. The weight pulled on her arms and shoulders. Jonathan, his face drawn and eyes narrowed against the dust-filtered brightness of the sun, breathed heavily with Baby's weight but said nothing. Dust still swirled about them, and the boy stopped long enough to hoist the baby a little higher on his back. Deborah took the opportunity to shift her bundle up and over her left shoulder.

When they heard a noise behind them, Jonathan turned. Deborah looked back at a slowly moving vehicle and stood still, staring down at the road. A rusted-out coupe, crowded with possessions and three small children, stopped beside her. A man drove, and the woman next to him held a baby. Baggage was tied to the top and trunk.

When the man called out to her, Deborah turned to him.

"You got car troubles? That your'n back there? We'll make room."

"Thank you. Would you take the two boys?" The family in the car began to move about. "You go right to the mortuary, Jonathan. Tell them I'll go to Dr. Hocksmith, and they can meet me there." She felt as though her voice floated about her, separate from her body.

"We got room," the man insisted.

"No, thank you. I've got to walk."

"Here now! No woman need walk out here alone. We can put your bundle on top, and you get in here in front. My missus can crowd over." His wife tried to say something, but he wouldn't listen.

"You're kind, but I've got to walk."

"No cause to—"

"I need to do this. It's the least I can do."

The woman punched at the man's arm. He ignored her except to shrug his shoulder with each punch.

"No reason to walk—"

The car door slammed. The woman came to stand beside Deborah.

The man bawled at his wife, "Frieda, what you doing?"

"You go on. Take those little boys to the mortuary. I'm walking with this mother here." Her voice was firm, and she glared at him, gesturing with her head toward town. To Deborah, she said gently, "Let's go." Her eyes were warm in her pretty, tired face.

The car pulled away, the gunning engine splattering sand angrily against the rear wheel flaps. As if the man had thought better of it, he brought the car to a halt, and then he drove slowly away. Blue fumes hung in the dust-ridden air. Deborah looked up long enough to see Baby Half Shell at a window, face and hands pressed to the glass, just the way he had stood in Fleet Foot's truck when he first arrived in her life. For a moment, she was fearful she would lose him too.

"You should have a face cloth," Deborah said.

"I'm all right. We'll be there soon." The woman put her arm around Deborah and with her other arm helped support the body's weight. They walked without talking, their feet stirring the dust on the road. At one point, they came to a deep drift and floundered in it, and Deborah felt the woman doing more lifting. After getting out of the drift, they carried the body over both of their shoulders, side by side.

When they reached town, the two women continued down the street, rather than taking to the sidewalk, their eyes turned to the pavement of bricks, drifted here and there with field dust. People were out and about and stopped to stare. The boards of the drugstore walk were warped, and Deborah stumbled. The woman helped her catch her balance.

Gladys Hocksmith, even more trembling and nervous than normal, held the screened door open, her face drawn. "News travels fast, Deborah. I'm so sorry about David." The two women carried their burden into the store.

At the rear of the drugstore, in the little examining room, they put David's body on the table. Deborah smoothed the blanket and reached to remove her face scarf, rubbing her fingers in the corners of her mouth where she knew mud always gathered.

Hocksmith came to stand by the examining table. "Measles?"

Looking up numbly, Deborah said, "Yes." She hesitated. "Maybe dust. Either one. Put what you want on the death certificate. Fever, cough, congestion."

"Pneumonia," he said, "probably pneumonia. Deborah, when there's more than one issue—and pneumonia's one of them—there's not much to be done."

Gladys stood in the doorway. "Come out to the fountain," she said to Deborah and the woman who had helped her. "I'll pour coffee for the two of you."

The women sat at the little round table, the wire-backed chairs feeling spindly under their weight and cumbersome winter coats. Deborah drank the coffee gratefully, and her eyes met those of the woman opposite her.

Gladys hovered nearby. "The boys are at the cafe with Elizabeth. She's feeding them and wants you to come there for food."

"Thank you for everything, Gladys." Deborah looked at the stranger. "Where are you going?"

"East, I guess. Anywhere we can get out of this dirt."

"I should have gone east," Deborah said. "He'd still be alive."

"We came north from the panhandle. We thought it might be better up this way. Now we're going east … before our money runs out."

Deborah heard men's voices in the back room with Hocksmith. She stood, saying to the woman, "I'll be back. Wait for me."

In the examining room, she signed a paper and spoke briefly to Simpson and his son. She watched as they carried David's body out the rear door.

"I'm sorry, Deborah." Hocksmith stood in a pose unusual for him, his shoulders slumped, and his clenched hands thrust into the pockets of his white jacket. "Damn the dust."

"So maybe it wouldn't have made a difference if I'd been able to get here in time. Maybe it wasn't a bad case of measles. Maybe it's what he's been breathing these past years." Deborah felt her face begin to show something other than numbness, as if her frozen expression were cracking away. She took a breath, holding the feeling back. "It seems like everywhere I turn, there are people dying slow deaths. David's death—was it what folks call dust pneumonia?"

"Maybe so. Breathing dust ... you know how it is. You're taking your own chances with it, Deborah."

She turned to leave and then stopped, her shoulders hunched, much like those of the doctor. "You must see it every day. I don't know how you manage."

Back at the little table, Deborah unbuttoned her shirt pocket, removing the five dollars. She placed it in the woman's hand and closed her fingers over it. "Take this. I want to help you get away."

"No—"

"Don't argue. Get your children away from here."

"What about you?"

"I can send my two boys to their grandparents, but for reasons of my own, I've got to stay here."

"But—"

Deborah shook her head. "Money I've got. You've got all of your children. Keep them."

Chapter 5

Minnesota

At the cafe, the boys were eating oatmeal and eggs. Deborah kissed Jonathan's cheek. She held Baby Half Shell on her lap, feeding him and nuzzling her face against the back of his head. Often Jonathan would look up from his plate and smile at her. She couldn't eat, but the coffee warmed her. Folks came by the table and shook her hand, murmuring to her.

"So sorry, missus. This damned country."

"We all oughta get out of here."

"The fellow who brung your boys in, he has the right notion."

"You've had more'n your share."

"What's to do now?" one man asked. He had his own desperation, which she could tell by his voice. His question was directed at more than her situation.

She reached to put her hand on Jonathan's shoulder. "Well, I know I've got to get these two boys away from here. I'll figure it out."

"Power to you. There'll be plenty leaving at this rate."

"There's Moses Bogart," someone by the window said.

The old man was unshaven and gray-faced, and he moved as though exhausted. When he sat beside her, his arm around her shoulders, he spoke earnestly. "I wish I could have done something. I have wanted so much to protect a child against harm more than once in my lifetime."

She remembered how Moses and Lydia had lost two children in terrible ways. "Moses, I didn't see the signs soon enough. If I had realized, maybe I could have gotten help in time."

He closed his eyes for a moment and then said in a low voice, "You're blaming yourself, and you shouldn't. It takes experience, I suppose a doctor's experience, to see pneumonia. And who knows what it takes to cure it.

"I tell you, Lydia sure loved the boy. When she was able to remember things, she would tell me about his visits. He made an impression on her when no one else could. I suspect she saw him the way she would have our boy if he had lived."

"Moses." She held his hand.

"I called Victor at his folks. He said to tell you something. I figure you know what he said." The cafe was filling with breakfast eaters, and Moses was trying to be private. He knew Victor and she were not ready to announce to the community their intent to marry someday. "I brought Wave Vogl with me. We got your car started, and he's driving it to your place. He said to tell you, call on him for help. He wants to do for you the way you did for him and Jenny."

Moses helped her dress Baby for the out-of-doors, and she told Elizabeth good-bye. Deborah saw Elizabeth was pregnant with her first child. Her heart ached for her friend. She hugged her and said, "Bless you, Elizabeth."

"Chicken pox," someone said. "Chicken pox ain't supposed to hurt kids that much."

"It weren't the pox. Measles is what they said."

"Measles? Do measles kill?"

"Oh, well then, chicken pox! I had a thirty-year-old uncle who died when chicken pox hit him so hard—"

"It's the dust. That's what's killing."

"Let's get you home." Moses carried Baby Half Shell, his arm other supporting her.

In the car, he said, "I took the liberty of going by your house. Wave and I did your chores, and then I got a set of David's school clothes, which I took to Simpson."

"Moses, you think of everything. Thank you."

"I thought I'd call your family soon as I get home."

"Those poor people," was all Deborah could say. She bowed her head over the baby, holding him as close to her as she could without hurting him and began to cry silently.

They didn't talk. After the nightmarish drive through the blowing dirt of the night before, the morning seemed strangely still. Only stirring dust from a truck in front of them reminded her the dirt was there to threaten them. Baby Half Shell fell asleep on her lap, and several times Deborah reached back to pat Jonathan's knee. He would smile in return, tears glistening in his eyes. She motioned and pulled at his hand until he climbed over the seat and sat between them. Moses's hands had been clenched around the steering wheel, his jaw firmly set, but he reached to grasp Jonathan's hand. There was much Deborah wanted to say, but she was afraid if she talked, she'd lose control.

Moses let them out by the yard gate. "I see August and Audrey are here. I'll call your folks right away. Victor should be here before long."

Deborah leaned through his car window and kissed him. "I love you, Moses Bogart. Thank you." She took Jonathan's hand, and they walked to the house.

In the dust-coated kitchen, Audrey held Deborah against her small body, a body that seemed so fragile these days. The old woman was crying brokenly. Baby Half Shell patted her cheek. She cried harder.

August joined them, crooning, "Daughter, daughter." He kissed her and reached out to Jonathan.

The boy held on to the old man tightly. "Grandpa," he said.

Audrey's face sagged with grief. "I've been hearing his voice in my head, calling me 'Grandma Audrey.'"

"And 'you fellers,'" August said. "He was always saying you fellers this, you fellers that. He got that from Victor."

Jonathan took Baby Half Shell. "I figure he needs a dry diaper, Mama." Deborah watched her boys leave the room. Jonathan grasped the old man's hand and led him, as though he didn't want to let him out of his sight.

"Poor Jonathan." Deborah kept her body stiffly upright. "I don't know what we're going to do without David. I should have brought him to you, Audrey. Maybe you would have known what to do."

"Girl, I don't know if I could have helped the dear boy. If it was pneumonia ... it's a terrible thing. I doubt if I could have done a thing."

Deborah clenched her fists at her sides. "Carl said when there's more than one complication—you know, measles, dust, pneumonia—there's very little to be done." She threw herself onto a dusty chair, holding her folded arms to her chest. "I should have done something more. I should have realized after Sonja left, even before, something was not right."

"Deborah, you did all you knew to do. I heard a woman say one time that pneumonia fights a great war to win, that sometimes a person might even look like he's getting better ... when he's really hopelessly worse."

"Did you believe that?" Deborah demanded.

"I did," Audrey said softly. "I had no reason not to. Her little daughter had died, and she said that's how it seemed to her."

"If Victor had been here—"

"Oh, dear girl, don't be saying that." Audrey's jaw was solidly set.

"What?"

"The man's going to be so torn up, knowing he wasn't here to do something. Victor loves those two boys as much as Christian did when he was here. You're going to have to pull yourself together so you can help Victor through this. He wasn't David's daddy, but I know what he feels for the boy. Deborah honey, you're going to have to be strong. That man's not experienced with this kind of pain, and I know you don't want him to feel guilty."

Audrey leaned close, and her features were not their usual softness, as though she were toughening herself for what she was to say. "You've got to remember, you've had to endure plenty in your young years, the kinds of things that have stiffened your backbone, painful times that will see you through this.

"You've told me how you lost your old friend, Blue Sky, and some other folks you cared for very much, like your childhood friend who killed herself, all when you were young." She held a damp cloth. Starting at the far corner, she began wiping the dusty tabletop. "And then there was when your folks seemed to quit loving you and how much that hurt." Deborah moved back in her chair, and the old woman wiped the surface in front of her. "You lost Christian, a man you loved so much, and I saw the agony you felt."

When Audrey turned to go to the sink, Deborah followed her with her eyes.

"Far as I can tell, Victor hasn't gone through near what you've lived with. But he's a feeling man. I saw that when he buried your baby girl."

She watched her old friend wipe dust from the counters. "Now this is not to say your loss, your grief, is going to be any less. Losing David is going to be harder for you than losing the baby, for you've loved him that much longer. But there was Victor's pain when he helped us put her tiny body in that little casket and covered her face. Don't forget how angry he was when the deputy beat you so bad and then got by with it. Losing David's going to be awful hard on him, and you can bet he's tearing himself up that he wasn't able to prevent it from happening."

"Audrey, you're so right. I wasn't thinking." She reached out, and the little woman hugged her with strong arms.

Deborah became conscious of a sound in the living room. "Who's sweeping?"

"It's that old man of mine," Audrey said. "And Jonathan's dusting furniture. Let them do what they can. They've got to keep busy. Let me get some food in you. You can't be wobbly at a time like this."

August was talking to Baby Half Shell. "That's right, you hang on tight to the chair and walk around it. Here, let me dust it off a bit so you don't get so dirty. There. Now, keep working at it. That's what it takes—practice. Whoops! I know you didn't plan to do that, but you're sitting in my dirt pile."

She heard the baby laugh and wanted to go to them, but her body was sapped of all of its energy. She put her head down on her arms until Audrey set food in front of her.

His truck arrived—she recognized its sound and waited for him on the kitchen porch. Victor got out of his truck, wearily, she thought, and walked to the house with his shoulders hunched into his chest, his head bowed.

They met on the porch and held each other for a long time.

"I love you," she said.

"I love you. I should have—"

"No, Victor. Don't say it. I truly believe there was nothing to be done by the time I realized—"

"I know you did your best." He held her shoulders firmly, his eyes direct and warm.

She nodded. "It seems that way, from what Hocksmith and even Audrey have said."

"If only I had been here—"

"He was just beginning to get sick when you left. You couldn't know. Despite our joking about it, your dad needed you."

"Doesn't do any good, does it, looking at what we wish we had done?"

"You're right."

He removed his gloves and placed his hands on her cheeks. "I've seen you come through so much, Deborah Jorgenson Nelson. You'll do it again, and I'll be with you all the way."

Jenny Vogl and Mary Cressler were the first neighbors to come. Deborah thought about how Mary had seen her and others through so many rough times over the years, and Jenny's understanding was recent, fresher with pain. "Deborah, why? Why? We loved them so much."

By early afternoon, other neighbors, including Sonja, had begun to arrive. The wind had come up, stirring the usual choking cloud about the flagstone steps in the front yard. When a car or truck pulled into the drive and stopped, dust would settle and slither down its sides in brown sheets like thin chocolate on a cake.

The neighbors brought food, all carefully wrapped against the dust in tea towels and grocery paper. Outside doors were opened and shut quickly and the rag rugs pushed back against the sills. Most of the same people had come when Christian disappeared, and the women had visited Deborah when she lost the baby. Deborah moved among her friends, serving coffee, sharing her grief with them, and holding the worst of it deep within her. They lamented the storms and speculated as to the cause of David's death. The consensus was dirt.

"We're all breathing our bushel," Wave Vogl said. "An active boy like David, I'll bet he breathed plenty. Even if it's not blowing, we stir it up when we walk."

"You're right. No way to avoid it," Rhoda Wolfe said. "Just leading a normal daily life … even going to school, the kids breathe their share. There are days that I wonder if I should keep the school open."

Sonja was crying. "Well, I say losing Robby to the dirt was bad enough. Children don't deserve this. If I hadn't gone home last night, I would have been here to help you. I could have gone for help."

Deborah touched Sonja's cheek and spoke with a seriousness that made her throat tense. "It's all right. We all did what we did. It's over and done with. I don't want you blaming yourself. None of us knew what was happening. I've always felt it was fortunate the boys weren't sick much—but I guess I haven't had much experience with sickness because of it. Everything happened so suddenly. By the time I recognized how serious the problem was, it was too late. I suspect the dust had a lot to do with it, and, if so, it has been doing its damage for a long while, for seven years."

"I loved David, Deborah."

"And he loved you. You've spent some important years with my boys.

Just think, you weren't even eighteen the first summer Christian and I were here, and, as David would say, he and Jonathan were just little fellers." She smiled at Sonja, willing her friend to smile in return.

The conversation moved about the room, comments coming from people with tired voices and eyes. They sipped their coffee hurriedly, as though needing the stimulant to keep their responses alive. She watched them covertly. She saw tired eyes and hair that drooped dustily about their faces. Their eyes were more than tired. It was as though the wind and dirt had sucked and ground out some of the color, and the remainder of their sight seemed to turn inward. It was common for the farm and ranch men to not shave daily, but some of them had more than several days of gray growth, irregular growth, like attempts had been made but left unfinished.

Levi Brownly slumped in his chair, clasping his hands between his knees. "It's getting tough." He sighed deeply. "The blows lasted into October last year, and I'll bet every one of us hoped and prayed that was the end of it. It was like my heart crept down into my shoes when I heard the first storm come up this year … the one that got your boy Robby." Shaking his head, he looked at Wave sadly.

Wave nodded. "I know what you mean. It can get a man down."

"Much more of this, we're likely to go crazy," Elmer Ratliff said. "That's what I fear." Deborah knew Elmer was known for his fears, but no one tried to reassure the old man this time. It was as though they lacked the energy to make the effort.

Herman Vinther said, "Sometimes I look back at Granny Eloise's death, and I kinda get to thinking it's fortunate she isn't living through these times … much as I miss her."

Moses arrived in time to hear the tail end of the conversation. "I understand that," Moses said. "When Lydia was thinking clearly, the dirt drove her wild. She hated it in her hair."

"I hate dust on paper," Deborah said, breaking her silence, "on the page of a book or a paper you're writing on. I can't imagine life without books and paper, but dust takes away some of the enjoyment."

Moses said, "Deborah, Christian's folks are on their way, or at least will be as soon as they can catch the first train coming this way. We'll know more later. Calvin said they were having trouble getting reliable help for the farm, and your folks insisted they would stay and take care of the chores for them. Your dad wanted you to know they were doing that especially because Meredith didn't get to come when Christian disappeared."

Deborah still held the pain back, allowing only tears to roll down her cheeks, unwilling to release anything more. At this point, she was afraid she would give in to the black misery that threatened to corrode her emotions. Victor and August had gone somewhere, probably to the barn to care for the stock, and had taken Jonathan with them. Baby Half Shell slept. Audrey served coffee and tea, her hands trembling the cups on their saucers.

When most of the people had left because they were afraid of the rising wind, Deborah went to the kitchen porch and stared through the glass at nothing. Who would do David's setting hens this spring and shriek in alarm when a chicken hawk flew over? Who would bake cookies for the old folks? The old folks … many of them were gone too—Ol' Paul, Grandma Eloise, Mary's dad Horace, Lydia. Who would tease Idotha and Mary Ann at school?

Wind blew dust through a space between a storm window and the frame. She watched as the little gathering of dirt grew higher until its weight toppled the pile, cascading it down the wall to the floor. Had dust gathered the same way in David's lungs until its weight had overcome his breathing?

Mary, her dear friend Mary, stepped onto the porch. "You make me think of a raccoon. With your crying you've got smudges of dirt around your eyes."

Deborah smiled weakly.

"Come on, honey." Mary directed her to the door. Sonja and Audrey were carrying buckets of water to the little room by the pantry. "Come on, we've got a bath tub in there and fresh clothes."

In the tub of warm water behind a screen, Deborah's body thawed along with her senses, and she cried. Audrey washed her hair, and the women cried with her. Theirs was a mournful litany.

"Such a sweet, dear boy!"

"I never knew it could hurt so much, losing a child I have loved for nine years …"

"Always running to me, hugging me. 'You got cookies, Grammy Audrey?'"

"I should have listened better when Carl warned the neighborhood—"

"You did your best. How was anyone to know he'd get so sick or a storm would come up?"

"At least he didn't suffer too long—"

"You're right. You're so right."

"Mary Ann wants to know who's going to beat her at checkers now."

They wrapped Deborah's hair in a towel and handed her warm clothes. She sat by the kitchen stove and combed her hair while Mary brewed coffee. The wind dropped, and by late afternoon the dust began to settle. Cold seeped into the house, and the women added fuel to the stoves. Baby Half Shell climbed onto Deborah's lap, and she rocked him by the living room stove, feeling herself begin to withdraw from the others. She pulled her hands up in the sleeves of her cardigan sweater and stretched its front opening over the baby and her.

Victor came in with Jonathan, knelt by her chair, and placed his head against the baby, letting the boy bury his hands in his hair. He said, "Simpson called Moses. He'll bring David's body before dark, if it's all right with you. It was that or leave him in that fancy funeral parlor. I couldn't tolerate the idea—"

"Oh, I agree. I want him here. In the bay window. He loved to play there on a winter day. Maybe the sun will shine tomorrow. He liked to sit there, reading or playing, the sun on his head. When he was smaller, he'd even fall asleep on the floor at nap time."

"The Nelsons will probably be here by afternoon, day after tomorrow. I told Moses I would meet them for you."

She reached to stroke his head. She tugged gently at his ear. "Victor Whitesong, have I ever told you what it means to me that you're always here when I need my best friend?"

"Thank you, Deborah."

She tugged his ear again. "And have I ever told you that hairs grow in your ears?"

He grinned at her. "I haven't checked yours lately. I better do that."

With August trying to help, Victor and Big David carried the little casket into the house. August's shoe caught on the sill, and Herman reached out to steady him. They placed the casket on the parlor table in the bay window. With shaking hands, the old man opened the lid. He sobbed audibly at seeing the dead child. Audrey pulled him to her and rested her head against his shoulder.

Deborah moved forward, her arms reaching out, wanting to hold David. She was unaccustomed to seeing him hold so still. She could almost imagine the child was just asleep and dreaming. His face was relaxed, the corners of his mouth slightly turned up. His hands, one resting over the other, were thin and waxy. When she touched them, there was no illusion of sleep in the cold rigidity of the fingers. She reached for his curls, so soft, yet springy. Despite their darker red color, the curls were so much like Christian's.

Christian, I suspect he's with you now. If so, I know you are taking good care of him. Forgive me. I wish I could have done something more. He's so important to all of us here. I know he's just as important to you. God bless both of you.

"That's just his shell," Audrey was saying to Baby and Jonathan. Her voice always sounded old, but now it was even older. She stood beside Deborah and was trying to help Jonathan hold Baby Half Shell.

"I've got him, Grandma," said Jonathan. "See, Half Shell. That's David. He can't talk or laugh anymore." Deborah moved to put her arm around the boys.

"I wish he could sit up and say something," said Jonathan. "I'd like to hear one of his jokes."

Audrey said, "I guess you'd say his body is like a house, only nobody's home. His spirit isn't there. If it was, he'd be breathing and talking."

Jonathan listened intently. "So nobody's home. His spirit's gone. So where is it?"

"Well, death is a real mystery. The Bible says we go to be with our Father in heaven. I believe that's so. Then there are those, like August and me, who think the spirit of a loved one is with God and us living folk at the same time. That maybe his spirit is right here with us, helping us through this. I believe David's happy where he is and doesn't want us to be sad."

"That's right, Audrey," said Deborah. "Jonathan, I think David is with your daddy. I think they are both in heaven together."

"Wow," said Jonathan. He put the baby in Deborah's arms. He went to a shelf and came back with a book. "David's favorite book. Maybe he'll want it." Deborah helped him place the book under David's hands. She could see that their hardness startled Jonathan, and she watched him touch and hold the hands, experiencing, almost as though trying to warm them.

A shiver went up Deborah's back. Jonathan was a year younger than she had been when Grandfather Blue Sky died. She had studied the body in just the way Jonathan was doing, noticing its coldness, the hardness of his arm. Much the way Jonathan had just placed the book, her photo was put in Grandfather's folded hands. "He loved you so," her mother had said.

"What helped me in the past," Deborah said, "was the knowledge that the person I loved was still with me in my mind and my heart. That helped with the loneliness and sadness."

They heard Marco barking, and a car stopped in front of the house. "Who's here?" Mary asked. "I don't recognize the car."

"Why, it's Arlene Van Ricker." Sonja opened the door. "Arlene, come in."

"Is Mrs. Nelson here?"

"Yes, come in."

"I can't," Arlene said. Deborah gave the baby to Mary and stood beside Sonja. Arlene's eyes slid away from their faces. "I can't stay."

Deborah remembered Victor telling her Arlene looked like a person unloved. He was right. She opened the screened door. "The wind is cold," Deborah said. "Please, come in for a while—"

"Oh, no, I shouldn't be out after dark. I can't stay."

"Please—"

Arlene interrupted, "The truth be known, Tony wouldn't want me here. I don't have to tell you. He's gone for the evening, so I took a chance."

She was blonde with skin so pale and transparent that Deborah could clearly see the blue veins in the woman's forehead, giving her a fragile appearance. Wind whipped at her face, causing her to flinch.

"Arlene, Tony's problems are with me. You and I don't have problems. I have felt badly I haven't gotten to know you." She looked over the woman's shoulder. The car was still running. "Your little ones are in the car. Why don't you bring them in for a while?"

"No, I can't. I just came to say how sorry I am about your little boy. There's nothing worse than seeing a little one hurting—and I can't imagine how terrible it must be, living without him. I don't know how you stand it." Along with the almost uncontrollable shaking of her jaw, Arlene's voice trembled. As she spoke, she sometimes closed her eyes. Even her eyelids trembled.

She pulled the collar of her coat up to her cheeks. "And then these dirt storms—one after the other. They don't help. I've got to go. I just wanted you to know how I feel, and I'm sorry—for lots of things."

"I know you're not to blame."

"Tony and The Committee have hurt you and others. He told me about the day he cut your fence and was going to attack you. My own husband—he bragged how he was going to rape you, 'put her in her place,' he said. I'm sorry he has mistreated you because he thinks you're Indian. Christian told him you aren't. He wouldn't listen. I tried to reason with him. I know he threatened your husband's life, and I worry about what happened to Christian. I've told Janie Procek I'm sorry about Daniel's beating and the burning of the cross and her baby's memorial tree. Mrs. Nelson, I would be grateful if you'd tell the Wolfes and Vossermans how sorry I am."

"We need to talk," Deborah said. "Please come in."

"Yes," Sonja said, "come in. No one's here who would tell anyone." But Arlene was off the porch before Deborah or Sonja could say more.

Deborah called to her. "Thank you for coming, Arlene. I wish things were different so our children could play together and we could get to know one another."

Arlene waved and got in her car. Then she was gone.

"My, my," Audrey worried. "There's trouble there. Can't you just hear it?"

"Something's wrong." Sonja frowned. "He told her what he had meant to do to Deborah—how awful. Do you suppose he hits Arlene? She acted scared. She made it clear Tony wouldn't want her here."

Deborah said, "I'm surprised she said all those things, since we've never talked before."

"Would he hurt the kids?"

August heard them. "A man who hurts animals like he did his riding mare? Sure, it's possible he hurts his family. He had a hand in beating Daniel Procek. A man like that is capable of just about anything."

Deborah said, "I'm afraid—"

Audrey interrupted. "You don't need to be worrying about it, dear. You've got enough on your mind."

Another car came into the yard. Bob Lodge from the telegraph office left two messages, one full of love from Deborah's mother, Lillian, which said when Calvin and Meredith would arrive. The second telegram was from her dad: *"Let us help you save those other boys. Come home."* She placed the messages in her pocket where she could touch them.

Chapter 6

Save My Boys

Victor stayed behind after the others had gone. He sat in a straight-backed chair near the casket. "I'll stay the night." Clearly, he intended to keep watch.

"You've got to sleep," she said. "You'll be worn out tomorrow."

"I'm staying right here. I won't leave him alone in the dark. I want to be with him until he's buried. I want him to know I'm here. That's the least I can do."

"I'll stay up with you."

"No, you didn't sleep last night."

"He's my son."

"I know, Deborah. But you already did your damnedest, and I heard how you walked, carrying him to town. Just let me do this for you, for him."

She knew he was right, so she went to her room. The house was quiet, and in her bed, she could hear her own breathing, taking her thoughts back to the sound of David's labored breaths, which had come far between and quiet in the noise of the windblown car. With each of her own breaths she felt pain in her chest, but she could no longer cry. She pulled Grandfather's blanket close to her face. A turmoil of thoughts rather than sleep came.

She would get her journal and try to sort things out on paper.

> *"Let us help you save those other boys. Come home." My dad is right. I've got to save Jonathan and Half Shell.*

My pride, stubbornness, and self-centeredness took my little family away from Minnesota, away from my parents who hurt and angered me. It's time to weigh things more than I've ever done before. To think—I've brought on the deaths of three people:

1. *Christian? I don't really know he's dead because I've no proof, but I did convince him to come to Kansas to buy a farm.*
2. *The baby? Yes! I was stupid and confused enough that I didn't recognize I was pregnant.*
3. *David? He was sick, and I was so ignorant that I didn't know how seriously ill he was.*

I've got to send the boys to safety until the drought is over. They can be with Christian's folks or mine.
There's more to consider: I can't go with them.

1. *I'm responsible for this land and must continue with what Grandfather Blue Sky taught me: I have to take care of the land, especially now during the drought.*
2. *August and Audrey are growing old (eighty-eight). I love them and they need my help.*
3. *I love Victor very much. For that reason I can't leave him. I can't leave him with all the responsibility of the old folks, the care of the shelterbelts, the listing of the fields if they blow, and Stoddel's suspicions that Victor and I did something to Christian.*
4. *This community is my home, and I love it. The people here need me too. We're all under the gun from the drought and the Depression. The old folks, Victor, and I formed our little cooperative to get through these bad times. I can't walk away.*

Christian, if you're dead like I believe you to be, listen to this—please forgive me for losing our freckle-faced, redheaded boy with curls (you've got him now).
I need to send the boys to Minnesota.

Before dawn, it came, hitting the house hard. The storm instantly brought the odor of oppressive dust, and although the house was never without its smells of dust these days, this was thick and heavy. Deborah closed her journal and put it away. She draped the usual sheets over Half Shell's crib and woke Jonathan enough to help him tie on a bandana. Then she went into the living room where Victor sat in the lowered lamplight, his back ramrod straight in his chair, his hands resting on his knees.

"Another storm," she said anxiously. "What if it's so bad Calvin and Meredith can't get here?"

He looked out the window. "It's bad, but we can't predict how long it will last." He carefully closed the lid on the casket. "Poor little tyke," he said in a low voice, "as if you haven't had enough dust."

She sat in a rocking chair, and Victor returned to his straight-backed chair. "Why don't you take the other rocker?" she said. "Be more comfortable."

"I don't want comfort," he said. "The least I can do is feel a little discomfort."

She got up and sat in the other straight-backed chair that August had used earlier.

"Deborah, you don't need to do that."

"I want to. Seems like that's the least I can do," she said, using his words.

The clock said there was full daylight now, but the room was almost as dark as night. Victor went out to do chores and returned, his face grimy with dirt, his eyes red and tired.

He went to the sink and washed and shaved.

Toward nine o'clock the boys were up, and she dressed and fed them. Then she tied fresh cloths over their noses and mouths. She gave Victor a bandana and put one over her own nose and mouth. Jonathan sat with a book he didn't read, and Baby Half Shell played about the room in a quiet, subdued way. She watched him, and he seemed to spend most of his time hanging on to furniture and walking about. More than once she got up to hug Jonathan or clasp Baby in her arms. Victor pulled his chair closer to hers.

They sat for hours, sometimes talking. She worried over the storm, willing it to go away. The room was hazy, but the oak casket seemed to glow, its luminosity a constant reminder of her grief. Sometimes she gasped, the shortness of breath a combination of the smothering dust and grief.

Restlessly, she moved about the rooms, shoving rugs more tightly against the doors, doing for the boys, stopping to rest her hand on Victor's shoulder. "Of all the times I have ever needed someone, I am grateful you are here now."

He held her hand for a long time; the wind howled dismally, causing the walls and ceiling to creak.

She put food none of them really wanted on the table, washed dishes, and wiped down the kitchen. She ran a cloth over the wood of the coffin, cleaning it free of dust. Then she thought of the coffin being placed in the ground and shovels of dirt thrown on it. She didn't miss the irony of trying to keep it dust free, and she laughed out loud, the sound muffled and lacking humor behind her face mask. Victor looked up.

"Dad is right, you know," she said.

"About going home?"

"To Minnesota. This is my home." She walked around the coffin, running her fingers over the smooth wood, memorizing its size and contours in the near darkness. "He's right. And I know what I need to do. I've got to send the boys to Minnesota until this is all over."

He jerked his head up. "Send the boys to your folks?" There was fresh pain in his voice.

"Yes. I'm right, you know. You know I'm right. I can't risk their lives. Seems like there are so many people dying." Jonathan was listening.

"Most of them are old folks," Victor said.

"David wasn't old. Robby wasn't old. It takes only one child's death. Now there are two." She looked at him, and his head was bowed, his hands clasped between his knees, his back no longer straight.

"You're right." Victor sobbed, and Jonathan went behind him, pressing his cheek to the man's head.

"You need to go to Minnesota, Jonathan," Deborah said. "You and Baby. I will barely be able to stand it without you, but I've got to send you where it's safe."

"She's right," Victor said.

"I know." They barely heard Jonathan, his voice muffled in Victor's hair.

"Grandma Meredith's not real well, and neither is Grandma Lillian." She was thinking out loud. "Maybe you could split your time between them. They'd both be thrilled to have you. I've been selfish. I should have shared you boys with them long before now." She moved to the parlor table, her fingers still caressing the wood of the casket.

"The letters I've gotten from your grandmothers—I wrote Meredith about your artistic abilities. Remember, she wrote back, saying she wished she could teach you some things, maybe learn some things from you."

"I remember. That would be good."

"And when I wrote Grandma Lillian about all our garden work, she was so interested. I learned gardening from her, and much of what she knew, she learned from Grandfather Blue Sky." She was thoughtful. "My dad could tell you things about Grandfather Blue Sky that I have forgotten or never knew."

She spoke to Victor now. "I have fought my dad for so long ... because he hurt me. It's with me he feels anger, not my boys. I don't know why, I just know it has to do with me. He'll be good to them."

"Will you go with us?" Jonathan asked.

"I can't. I've got to stay here—finish what I've started. We've got so much time and work invested here. I've got to stay with the new windbreaks and work to keep our fields from blowing." She moved about restlessly. When she turned to face Jonathan, she asked, "Do you know how much I love Victor?"

Jonathan smiled at Victor and nodded.

"I love him in a different way than I do you and Half Shell. I love him, and I can't desert him. You know how we've agreed we're in this for the duration. I can't leave him with all the work of our farm and his ranch—and doing for Audrey and August too. We see them getting older, day after day, and somebody has to look after them. With what has happened to David—well, I just remember what John said when he left here. He wished I would get you boys out of the blowing dirt because it was the safe thing to do."

A gust of wind made the house creak, and the boy asked, "Will you guys be safe?"

Victor reassured him. "I don't think the dust alone would have made David so ill. Doctor Carl says it was measles leading into pneumonia—and the dust sure didn't help. We won't get sick. We'll take care of each other."

"You won't get measles?"

"We won't get measles. We had them when we were young, along with chicken pox and whatever else kids get."

They said nothing more about the boys going to Minnesota, and the storm continued. Deborah could feel dust in her hair, down the neck of her clothing, and under her fingers. The clock said it was after dark now, but they noticed no change in the light of the house. Victor thought the storm had worsened as the day went by. The air in the house was stifling.

Jonathan had now pulled a chair close to the closed coffin and sat without speaking. Baby Half Shell was on the couch, sucking his thumb beneath his face mask. Deborah knew she needed to do something about the boys but couldn't seem to act. Even Victor seemed unaware.

She thought of the Nelsons. "I hope Meredith and Calvin are safe. I wonder if Meredith is all right."

"Try not to worry," was all Victor could say. She knew he must feel as helpless about everything as she.

Baby Half Shell fell asleep on the divan, and when Deborah saw Jonathan cover him with a blanket, she knew she should dress the boy for bed and put him down in his crib. Before midnight the wind increased, and the one remaining kerosene light was dimmer.

The rising wind seemed to galvanize Victor into action. "Deborah, you gather Baby's bed clothes. Let's dress him for bed but let him sleep right there. I think we'd better dampen our face masks. Jonathan, will you do it?"

The boy took their masks, and Deborah and Victor roused Half Shell long enough to change his clothes. He protested when the damp cloth was put over his nose and mouth again, but Victor convinced him to leave it on.

Jonathan fell asleep, teetering back and forth in his chair, and Victor lifted him to the divan and covered him. Then he worked at refueling the stove. Deborah looked in the coffin briefly, as though to reassure herself that David's body was still there. Her eyes were irritated and hurting, and the increased dusty atmosphere of the room made the boy's face difficult to see. She whimpered. Victor came to her side and slowly loosened her grip on the coffin lid. He closed it gently and seated her in a rocker. This time he sat in a rocker himself, pulling it close to hers.

"Do you know, we didn't eat supper? All those boys had was what they got at breakfast and the little lunch."

"I know. It's like I can't think straight. I didn't even think about it."

"Neither did I. We can't let that kind of thing happen again."

He stirred up the kitchen fire and pumped water into the teakettle. When he came back to sit by her, he held her hand. "This hand has shown that little boy lots of love—all of the boys, including John's."

"If only I had done more—"

"Don't say that. You did your best. All a caring person like you can do is the best."

She held both of his hands between hers. They sat facing one another, their heads bowed close together. The noise of the storm frightened her, but Victor's eyes above his mask were reassuring. She could see dust collecting in the corners of his eyes and knew hers had the same.

The night was long and dismal. She prowled about the house, stirring the fire and seeing to it the boys were covered. They drank tea and nibbled at sandwiches someone had left. When she looked out a window, she could see nothing and only heard the wind noises, a wind that she irrationally feared would swallow them up. She felt like there wasn't much left to swallow—a part of her had disappeared with Christian, another with the baby's death, and now with David.

She turned away from the window, putting her back to the cold and noise, and saw Jonathan and Baby on the divan and Victor with his face buried in his hands. Going to him, she placed her hand on his bowed head, smoothing his hair.

He looked up, his eyes blurred with tears. "I was just thinking," he said, "we've got to be tough for the boys and for each other."

She nodded. "Maybe we'd better start with some rest."

He stood. "Let me hold you. I need you to hold me."

Their embrace was long and comforting. Then she brought each of them a blanket—hers was Grandfather Blue Sky's—and they slept fitfully in the rocking chairs.

When Deborah woke about eight, Victor was standing by the casket, his hands resting on it. She stirred, and he turned to her, saying, "I can tell there's a slight letup in the wind."

She placed her hands on the wood near his. "I couldn't have done this—and getting through the storm—without you."

"Yes, you would have. You would have done it because the boys needed you to do it."

By noon, it appeared travel was possible, and they began to think of Calvin and Meredith. Victor would need to go to town.

Then Moses came. He had heard from the Nelsons. "They spent the night, what was left after the train got in, with the Hocksmiths and should be on their way here. Carl is bringing them."

Deborah was concerned. "Meredith? Is she all right?"

"I talked to Calvin. He said they were fine, and Meredith did get some rest. Word is going around. I figure folks will be here within an hour or so, bringing a meal."

August and Audrey were the next to arrive, and Deborah was concerned about the old folks. August seemed to move slowly, cautiously, as though tentatively putting one foot before the other. Audrey's face was an unhealthy gray.

"You ran out of milk, didn't you?" Victor asked. He and Deborah had August's cow at her place and milked for the Goodmans.

Audrey shrugged. "Oh, it was nothing. You know as well as I do how well supplied we are with everything. What's doing without milk for a meal or two?"

The old folks were seated at the table with the boys, and their eyes were tired as though they had spent a sleepless night. Deborah said, "I've got to tell you what we're thinking, Victor and me." Victor moved to her side.

"We're thinking of sending the boys home with Calvin and Meredith." She leaned close, touching the old couple. "Until the drought is over."

Audrey's jaw quivered, but without hesitation she said, "I think it's a good idea, painful as the thought is to us." August nodded and wiped tears from his face.

Victor said, "This boy here knows what we're thinking. He understands."

Deborah went about setting the table with bowls and milk. The oatmeal and coffee were ready. She handed August the can of cinnamon for his cereal, and he grinned.

Audrey said, "Let me feed this baby. He looks hungry."

The Cresslers came, and the girls carried Mary's coffeepots. Audrey gave a little laugh. "I was just thinking you'd be coming any minute with your big pots."

"We'll get them brewing," Mary said, "and the girls can help me sweep."

"I'd better do the milking and throw a few bundles to the cattle," Victor said.

"I'm here to help," and Norris Cressler went out with him.

After his breakfast, Deborah took the baby to her room to dress him for going to the cemetery. Audrey helped. Deborah moved about with a sluggish body, her mind dull with tiredness and a headache. She wore her black wool suit, the one she seemed to only wear now to funerals. It was out of style, but what did it matter?

Baby Half Shell talked and laughed, and Deborah responded. "He's better for me than any happiness pill."

"I guess I was thinking about the same thing." Audrey bent to tie the baby's shoes and give him a kiss. "Life is worth living when we've got children depending on us."

Deborah said, "You're so right. I'm trying to concentrate on that."

Chapter 7

Tragedy

When Deborah saw the Nelsons get out of the doctor's car, she rushed out of the house, forgetting she needed a coat in the cold wind. Meredith, dressed in a gray coat and close-fitting hat, her neck wrapped in a thick muffler, was looking about her. Deborah came to a sudden halt on the porch, holding Jonathan close to her side, and saw what Meredith was seeing.

Dust was still stirring in the air, its effect like a cataract's film over the eye. The sky was a mustard gray, for some reason causing Deborah to think of an old decrepit dog that once belonged to John Strate, the ugliest of dogs, its mustard fur mottled with an under cast of gray.

Gray—there was so much everywhere—the gray rock wall around the yard and the rock house, her beautiful house, surrounded by a gray, dusty pall over every growing thing. Small, scalloped drifts of dirt covered the walkway up to the porch. All of it ceased to matter when she hugged her old friends at the gate.

"Deborah dear," Calvin said, just as she had known he would.

"My sweet girl." Meredith cried.

Calvin still looked so much like Christian, and Meredith's eyes were those of both Christian and Lendel. Deborah's throat ached to see them. Then they were kissing Jonathan and exclaiming over his size. Victor was there, and the two men spoke warmly.

Meredith remained standing outside the stone wall. A gust of wind flung dust in their faces, and the woman watched with shock as Deborah,

Victor, and Jonathan pulled their bandanas from around their necks to cover their mouths and noses.

Deborah tugged at Meredith's arm. "Hurry to the house. You don't have a mask."

Audrey sat near the bay window, and Baby Half Shell stood by her chair, teetering, grinning. Meredith saw him. "Baby Half Shell, look at how you've grown." She had seen the baby months before when Fleet Foot visited Frank and Lillian. "Are you walking?"

"He's close," Audrey said, holding out her hands.

Meredith leaned to kiss the old woman's cheek. "You have to be Audrey. You're the one who's been taking care of our girl. Isn't it something—how I can love someone I've never met until now?" She kissed Audrey again and picked up Half Shell, snuggling her face against his. Calvin took the baby from her, lifting him high in the air, and Baby Half Shell giggled.

Deborah joined them by the coffin, and Calvin held Meredith tightly as they grieved.

Calvin asked, "Doesn't he look like Christian?"

"Oh, yes." Meredith's face was colorless. "His hair is a darker red but the same curls."

Deborah noticed how they continued to talk of David in the present tense, as though he were still living.

"There's Lendel in his face too," Calvin said.

"I've thought that," Deborah said. "Oh, you've lost too many boys."

She turned the Nelsons to face her. She struggled to talk through a throat that was tight and hurried to say what she had to say. "When we get back from the cemetery, we've got to talk. I feel I've got to send Jonathan and Half Shell home with you for a while—until the dirt storms are over—if you're willing."

Meredith was speechless but nodded through tears.

"Oh, Deborah," Calvin said. "Of course we're willing."

"We'll talk first chance we get," Deborah said.

"Look, Mom," Jonathan said. "John and all the boys!"

The Strates were coming in the door. John's tallness—his long legs and arms—and the big grin filled the room along with his five boys. He completely lifted Deborah off the floor with his hug.

"Oh, I didn't expect you," she cried.

Big tears rolled down his cheeks. "It's so terrible to lose a child. I'm so sorry, Deborah. I used to think some of the things I went through during the Great War were the worst I would ever have to endure. Then little

Melonie died. I have never hurt so much in my life, and now I have some idea of what you and Victor are going through."

He had pulled off his hat, and his hair stuck out in tufts. She reached to smooth them. "And now I understand even more what *you* went through, John. It helps, you being here."

"Me and the boys decided we had to come. It took some doing, with the weather, but we have to say good-bye to David."

She hugged Lester Strate. He was crying, but he managed to give her the silly grin she loved. She tried to kiss away his tears while she said to John, "You told me I should get away from the dust. I should have listened to you."

She heard the laugh of the youngest and turned to pick up Jimmy. Big as he was, he wrapped his legs about her waist and snuggled his face against her neck. "Deb'r," he whispered. His odor of dust and small-boy scent reminded her of David.

"Hi, Pretend Mom." Harlan and Lawrence hugged her, warm against her thighs. All of the boys, including a much taller Paul, crowded close to Jonathan and Deborah.

"Oh, it's so good to see you … so good. It takes away some of the emptiness, having all of you boys around me again. John, thank you."

"That's all right, little lady. I sure remember what you meant to me when Melonie died."

She reached to put her hands on his cheeks. "You look good," she said. "Eastern Kansas has been good to you."

John grinned, his usual big grin, except with a difference. "The WPA has a good dentist," he whispered. False teeth filled the gaps.

"Is eastern Kansas still free from blowing dust? Are you safe, John?"

"We're safe. We get moisture. Don't you be worrying about us, little lady." He kissed her cheek.

Deborah introduced John and the boys to the Nelsons. "You dear boys." Meredith teased them, "The things I know about each one of you. Deborah writes wonderful letters."

The house was full of neighbors and friends. Victor's parents had come, as well as both sisters, the married one very pregnant, and it appeared all of the children from the school were there.

Rhoda Wolfe actually hugged Deborah, something she didn't do easily. "In recent years I have selfishly thought one of the worst tragedies was for a woman to never have a child. Today I know a far greater tragedy is to have a child and then lose him." Rhoda's father-in-law Raleigh looked at Deborah with eyes blurred with tears and wondered who was going to bring him cookies and sit in his big old cottonwood and sing like a bird.

"I'll come, Raleigh. I'll come when I'm not in school and bring you cookies," Jonathan said. Deborah noticed he had forgotten he was going away. A lump filled her throat, and she felt sad for the old man as well as Jonathan.

Raleigh dropped his cane and hugged the boy to him.

Deborah walked about, sometimes eating a bit when Mary thrust a plate in her hands but preferring the talk and closeness of her friends. When the meal was finished and the food was covered against the still-moving dust, everybody filed past the coffin and out to the cars.

She drew Victor beside her to the coffin. "Thank you for being with him all these years," she whispered. She hid her face against his shoulder. Her voice was hoarse by now. "David's life has been so rich because of you. He didn't really remember Christian, and you became his daddy."

They studied David's face.

Victor said, "Well, look at that." The boy's hands rested on his favorite book, just the way Jonathan had placed them, but something else had been added.

"Raleigh's pocket watch," Deborah said. "Why, that dear old man." The chain and watchcase shone in the light from the window. "David asked to see it every time we visited."

"The boy touched a lot of lives in his short time."

She patted Victor's cheek and fought to control her voice. "We'd better get ready to go. I don't want folks out in this dust any longer than necessary."

The cemetery was desolate from past dirt storms, the cloudy day even darker with blowing dust. The cemetery was buried in blow dirt, from several inches to drifts, and people sometimes choked and coughed from the dirty air. A cedar tree, dull green and rusty in its winter colors, stood by the oldest headstone, and wind soughed in the branches. Deborah had always wondered if the tree had been planted there because someone thought its mournful sound in the wind was appropriate for the burial ground. She held Baby Half Shell, and Jonathan crowded close to her. The warmth of Victor's body shielded her from the cold northwest wind.

The open grave was next to where the baby girl was buried. There was a stone for the baby, as Victor had promised, but Deborah still had not thought of a name for him to carve on the marker.

She watched the casket being lowered with ropes. The sight of the newly dug grave, its frozen clods piled high to the side, came as an added pain to her. Some of the clods fell with finality onto the wooden coffin, and she whimpered, keeping a firm hold on the boys. Victor put his arm about her waist.

The neighborhood children shared remembrances of David. They gathered about the grave opening, the wind flinging the grave dirt in their faces. Deborah hurt to see them rub their eyes against the grit and to hear them talk through their bandanas.

"He could sure beat the socks off me at checkers," Mary Ann Cressler said. "I was the one who taught him, but it wasn't long before he began to outsmart me. David could always see things I never could." She was crying.

Deborah worried the open grave might be frightening the children when she saw Mary Ann and others staring down at it.

A boy spoke. "David liked books. He liked them so much, he got me to liking them better. Maybe I won't anymore, now that he's gone." Deborah wasn't even sure who the child was.

A young Kolter boy talked, his words lisping because of missing teeth. "I'm a first grader, and David looked out for me. One time he told Junior he'd sock him in the nose if he pestered me one more time!"

"David was just like having another brother, only better," Idotha Brownly said. "I could go home if we had a fight." Deborah couldn't see her face but heard the smile in the girl's voice. "He was one of the persons in my life who helped me see things most people don't notice. Things you need to see if you're going to be an artist or a writer. Have you noticed cows lie down when a storm's coming? He figured it was because of the lightning."

All of the Strate boys, from Paul to Jimmy, had memories. Lawrence was especially upset. "Me and him have been writing letters back and forth. When I lived here, he taught me how to set hens on their eggs. He showed me how you have to stroke their heads and get them all settled down so they don't break eggs. I plan to set some biddies in a few months. I'm going to do it just the way he taught me, but I wish David was here to tell me what to do. He was good at teaching you how to do something."

Jimmy said, "Hard as I tried, I couldn't holler as loud as David. He could holler the loudest of all of us. Jonathan always said David was too loud to be an Indian, so he had to be a cowboy."

"I've never saw a guy who could eat so much homemade ice cream, even when he knew it would make him run to the outhouse." That was Lester.

Harlan said, "More than once my dad was taking a nap on Deborah's porch, and David tickled his ear with a feather. My dad almost knocked his own ear off and mumbled about flies. He never knew it was David." John made a noise, which was a mixture of a laugh and a sob.

Rhoda grouped the children together. "All the children want to sing 'Jesus Loves Me' for David." She was trying to control her tears. "I don't know what we're going to do without that boy at school. I never saw anyone so eager to learn. I've been thinking, maybe he knew he was going to be taken early. Maybe that's why he seemed to leap feet first into everything I set in front of him." She laughed. "Sometimes his red hair got him into trouble before anyone else. I could pick him out faster than anyone. I'll tell you, he kept me on my toes."

The masks of the children muffled the simple song. When they finished, Deborah wanted to sink down into the dirt by the grave, wishing for the pain of the frozen clods on her knees. But she didn't dare. The children were watching.

Moses prayed, thanking God for the loan of a young boy so good at inspiring others and sharing his love of life and freshly baked cookies. "I saw him talk to my Lydia, and often she would talk in return when we all feared she'd never communicate again. Eloise used to talk about what his visits meant to her too even though, as she put it, he scared a year's growth out of her by pulling a garter snake out of his pocket." Deborah thought Moses exhibited a control he didn't usually have when talking about ones who were gone.

"I understand, Lord, this redhead occasionally incited riots among the other children but always in the name of joy and fun. I suppose things must have been a little boring in heaven, Lord, or you wouldn't have taken him so soon. Thank you for letting him leave his mark on each and every one of us. We won't forget him easily.

"Help these children go away from here today with smiles, not fears, and with a desire to follow David's example in his love of life and people. Help us realize a boy like David wouldn't want us to cry in sadness. He'd want us to look at one another and smile and maybe even crack a joke.

Amen." Moses added one more thought. "If he could, I suspect he'd say what he always said to Lydia and me. 'See you fellers later.'"

Holding Baby Half Shell, concentrating on him, Deborah was turning to leave the grave site when she saw people stir and look toward the entrance to the cemetery.

"It's Daniel. What's he running for?" Victor asked her.

"Well, he's late—"

"No, something's wrong. Look at him."

Daniel Procek was pale, his breathing uneven. "It's Arlene," he said. "It's Arlene Van Ricker and those three children." The man was openly sobbing, and John Strate, standing next to him, reached out to hold his arm. Daniel collapsed on his knees in the dirt beside the open grave.

"What is it, man?" John crouched beside him. He held both of Daniel's arms.

"She killed herself." Daniel still sobbed. "And she killed those dear children ... more dead children."

Deborah felt shock, much like a physical blow to the center of her being. She thought of David, and she imagined three small coffins in the lonely graveyard. A sudden gust of wind lifted the loose dirt, flinging it into their faces, and part of her pain was in trying to get the next breath of air and clear her eyes. She was worried about all the children around the grave.

Daniel was out of control now. "You know what I mean, John. You lost your little girl—in such a terrible way—then there was Robby ... David ... seems like they're dying all around us."

John was so wobbly, Deborah was afraid he would collapse. More dust swirled up, and Daniel, who wasn't wearing a mask, didn't even duck his head. He slipped on the slope of dirt. John grabbed him. "Here, now!" John pulled him up and away from the grave opening.

"Daniel." Janie Procek held his arm. Their children crowded near them.

His face wet with tears, John asked Daniel. "What happened?"

Daniel swallowed and lifted his shoulders. "Near as Janie and I could tell, Arlene must've gone out during the storm—it was an hour or two before the storm let up—the first thing we knew, we saw something burning, a building on the Van Ricker place. Bad as the storm was, we could see the fire. It looked like a big one, and we thought it was the house." He was choking from dust.

Deborah had a spare bandana in her coat pocket. She handed Baby to Victor and hurried around the grave to Daniel. John tied the bandana on the man.

"We found our way across the road," Janie said. "Their house is just across and down a way from us. It wasn't the house. It was the shed where they keep the car and truck. There were explosions, and we ran to the house. Tony was in bed. He didn't know where Arlene and the kids were. He said he'd been sleeping—"

Daniel said, "When the fire let up some so we could get close enough, we could see ... we were far too late." He sat in the grave dirt.

Janie seemed to have more strength than Daniel. "She was inside the burning car with the babies. There were gas cans all around. On the phone, Hocksmith said they died fast."

Deborah heard people gasp, and Daniel sobbed. She remembered how he had cried years before when a kitten was run over in his yard—the day of his baby's funeral.

"Lord in Heaven, have mercy on them," Moses said.

"What did she do? She did what?" Deborah heard one of Mary's girls ask in disbelief.

A child replied, "She burned them."

Daniel's voice was stronger now, and he looked about at the people beside the grave. "She didn't have God to turn to. And she didn't have us. We should have helped her. I don't know what caused her to do it."

"I know at least one thing." There was no expression in August's voice. "Victor and me went to see her sometime back. I know the dirt storms ate away at her. She told me and Victor. She said something about the dirt and the children ... I don't remember exactly. I just knew something was wrong—and I didn't do a thing. She must have felt terrible and all alone."

More people cried now, and women especially wailed much the way Daniel had been doing. It seemed to Deborah that all around her were people who had lost children—from Moses many years ago to herself now. Children sobbed, and the emotions seemed to spread like wildfire from child to child. John's boys were openly upset, and Paul looked at her pleadingly.

"Please," Deborah said, "please, listen. We've got to help each other with this. Let's go back to my house where we can be out of the dust. We need to talk."

"Daniel," Janie said. "We've got to think of the kids who are here." At first, he didn't seem to hear her.

John said sharply, "Procek, people are getting upset, especially the kids. You hear me?"

Daniel nodded. John moved him along. "I'll go with you. We're going to Deborah's to talk. You hear?" He directed Paul to gather the boys.

"I'll help, John." Deborah took Jimmy's hand, and Lawrence held so tightly to the length of her coat that she had difficulty walking. She looked across the grave, and Calvin said, "Meredith and I will take care of Jonathan and Baby. We'll be with Victor."

She crowded into John's truck, holding Jimmy on her lap. Harlan was sobbing loudly. "Shh," she said, murmuring calming sounds. Paul was driving. She saw him grip the wheel so hard his nails dug into his palms.

Harlan needed reassurance. "They're with David and Melonie, aren't they?"

"Yes, oh, yes. They're all together. Here, put your head on my shoulder. It's a good thing Lester is holding you, Lawrence. You've all grown so big, my arms have troubles holding you."

Chapter 8

What Neighbors Do

Clasping her arm, Calvin helped Meredith, who was unsteady as they walked to the house. Deborah carried Jimmy, his long legs wrapped about her waist, his face buried against her neck. "She burned them, Deb'r," he whispered.

"I know, I know, Jimmy."

"Burns hurt. I burned my hand on the stove, and Paul put it in cold water. It kept burning. It kept hurting."

"I know, I know." She sat on the braided rug with him, removing his coat, and Harlan and Lawrence crowded close. Jonathan joined them. "Now, listen," she said, "when there's a big fire, it burns up the oxygen—the air we breathe—fast. When a person can't breathe, he's unconscious, you know, like he's asleep. The children didn't feel the fire. They were unconscious." Deborah wondered if she sounded at all convincing in light of so many questions.

Mary came to take their coats. "I'm fixing hot tea for the Nelsons." She crouched down to look in Deborah's face. "Honey, are you all right?"

"I'm all right. Right now, I don't have time to think about everything. It looks like some others aren't doing so well. Could you and Corrine make cocoa for the children—and coffee for everyone? Let's be sure we put all the sandwiches and cakes and pies on the table." She could hear crying all around her.

"I think Meredith is better now," Mary said. "She has her mind on Baby Half Shell."

In the crowded living room, August was moving about, comforting a child here and there. Deborah saw Paul and John doing the same. The room became quiet, almost too quiet now, and Deborah worried that thoughts might seem loud in their minds.

Audrey spoke, her voice soft but intense. "Arlene's children are with Jesus now. He's got them gathered all around him. I'll bet the littlest girl is sitting on his knee."

"Like the picture you see in churches," Nila Meyers said. "The one where the children are with Jesus." She was clutching her little boy, and Reub loosened her hold. He took the child and removed his wraps.

Audrey smiled. Deborah thought the old woman was remembering Nila's stubborn assertion years ago that Jesus had to have been white, just as portrayed in those church paintings. "Yes, Nila, that's right. Most of us have seen the picture, I'll bet."

Jonathan said, "I've got a copy of it, in my picture Bible. I'll get it." He went to his room, and the book was soon being handed from child to child.

"I need to see it too," Rhoda said. Janice Cressler took the book to her.

"Jesus took away their pain as soon as he touched them," Audrey said. She had her arms around Harlan. "Their pain is gone, and they're happy to be with him."

"But why did she do it?" Lawrence asked.

Deborah was expecting the question. "It's probably like your mother, Lawrence. We couldn't figure it out for sure. All we know, she was terribly upset about something, so upset she couldn't think straight when she hurt Melonie. That's probably the way it was with Arlene."

Mary and Corrine took some of the younger children to the kitchen for cocoa. Others went with Jonathan to his room. Idotha touched Deborah as she went by and gently said, "Hey."

"Arlene wasn't a church-going person," Daniel said. "If you don't have God to turn to in time of trouble, what do you do? Maybe turn to your loved ones or your friends. Very few of us were there for her. I suppose Tony wasn't there … looks like."

Janie Procek said, "It might help to know, when we got Tony back to the house, we found a note on the kitchen table. It was from Arlene. All it said was, 'I can't take anymore. The dust'—the note ended there. She didn't finish the sentence. She didn't sign it, but Tony said it was her handwriting."

"That's what I heard from her," August said. "She seemed upset about the dirt. I'm sure she worried for her children in all the dirt."

"She came here the other night," Deborah said. "She expressed her sorrow about David. She probably was thinking about how he died—measles and the dust. She also was feeling badly about Tony's part in The Committee. We just don't know what all made her hurt herself and the children. If she was depressed, something like I felt when I got so sick, depression's like your mind breaks into pieces, and you can't think straight anymore. Maybe that's what happened to Arlene. It's terrible, what she did to the little ones … maybe her mind was just broken into pieces." Victor sat down near her and held her hand.

"I've told some of you how I've visited with Arlene at various times," Janie said. "I'd wait until I saw Tony leave, and then I'd go across the road." She smiled at her children who sat near her on the floor. "My kids are used to getting in the little wagon for a quick ride."

Rhoda asked, "Weren't you afraid Tony would find out?"

Janie ducked her head. "Oh, the children, hers and mine, knew to not say anything. And when I'd leave, Arlene would go out with the broom and erase some of the wagon tracks in the dirt."

"What a terrible way for a young woman to live, so isolated," Audrey said.

"I learned something from Arlene just recently." Janie hesitated and everyone looked at her. "Well, we wonder if it might be a part of what happened. She said Tony was going to take the boy out of school … because the teacher … because Rhoda is Catholic, like Daniel and me, of course."

"Take him out of school? Then what?" Rhoda pressed her fist against her mouth.

Watching Janie, Deborah sensed there was something more. She got up and went to the woman. "Janie? What else?"

"Tony was going to send him to live with his dad. Arlene was upset. She didn't want Tony's dad to have a hand in raising the boy. He's head of The Committee, you know. She didn't want little Harold away from home, learning those ways."

"I agree," Audrey said. "The boy would know nothing but the klan."

August was both angry and sorrowful. "That young woman was driven to the wall. I know how that man raised Tony. Like Audrey said, you can just imagine the little boy was to be raised the same way."

"I wish I had done something." Janie began to cry.

"What could you have done?" Rhoda sat beside her on the floor. "You did a lot—considerably more than the rest of us. You took chances too, doing what you did. It sounds like you gave Arlene the only friendship she had. Bless you." Rhoda hugged Janie.

Daniel paced in a small space. "I sure wonder about Tony. I saw how he acted after we saw what the fire did."

Janie reached up from where she was sitting to tug at his hand. "Maybe he was in shock, maybe—"

"Maybe. He sure didn't act the way I would expect. Not the way I would act for sure. 'Course you know how I am. I don't like to see anything hurting, especially a child." He was flushed. "I've been living across the road from him for quite a few years now. I've seen a lot of hate in him."

"Well, I think we've got other matters to consider," Victor said. "I think we've got to look at the needs of Arlene's family. Janie tells me she and Daniel went to the Hollowells and made phone calls. Hollowell is a cousin, and he went right over to Tony. Stoddel, Hocksmith, and Simpson were due to arrive at the farm and some other relatives were on the way. Now, Daniel and Janie, of all people, you were there in Tony's time of greatest need. I'd like to know how that went."

"I really do think Tony was in shock," Janie said. "He could have told us to leave, the way he feels about us. He didn't. Who knows what the mind is like in a time like that. I pray I never, never experience anything like it again."

"Daniel," Victor said, "after what you've been through because of the beating The Committee gave you, how in the world were you able to do what you did for Tony?"

"God's grace. I haven't forgotten anything, but I figure God's love is for Tony as well as for me. I don't suppose I'll ever forget, and I'm trying to forgive. I admit, I don't know if I would've done what I did if I hadn't seen Janie go flying out the door. Janie's like an angel to people, you know. I figure God sent Victor and Deborah to help me when those klan men were whipping me, and I'm alive and well to tell it. God sent Janie and me in Tony's time of great need." Daniel sounded exhausted, his voice hoarse.

"What would we normally do, folks, if a tragedy has happened to any of the rest of us?" Victor asked.

"We'd go right to the house," Maude Ratliff said. "Even before we've got food prepared for the family, we'd see to their other needs."

"I've been a neighbor to Tony and Arlene for sometime," Levi Brownly said. "I don't count him among my friends, but he's a human being. His pain must be terrible. I would think his soul is just shriveling up."

"Tony may be a person who can't express his grief," Rhoda said. "Not all people can."

Wave Vogl said, "When you folks heard about Robby, you came as soon as possible. We've got to do the same for these folks. Maybe the children better stay here, though. I think the kids have heard enough to last them a lifetime."

"But what if Tony drove Arlene to do what she did?" Herman was bitter. "The business of sending her boy to his dad—I don't know if I can shake his hand and say I'm sorry for his pain."

"But it isn't just Tony," Jenny said. "Relatives are there. Arlene has parents. Just think what they're going through."

Herman lowered his head. "Corrine and I were raised in the same neighborhood as Arlene. Those folks are good, caring people. You're right."

Mary said, "Some of us will stay. A few of the kids are eating, and others need to be fed." She straightened her apron, as though preparing for the next shift in the kitchen.

"Calvin and I will stay," Meredith said. "You mothers and dads go on."

Hands on her hips, Rhoda looked about her. "Denzil, you go. I think my place is right here with these kids. We may have to do some more talking."

Victor looked at Deborah, and they nodded to one another.

Corrine said, "I'll go."

"Are you sure?" Herman asked. Corrine was pregnant and due soon.

"I knew Arlene when we were girls. I feel real bad for the Barlows."

Mary put her arm around Deborah. "Do you think you can handle one more thing today?"

"I need to do this. Arlene came here. I'll be all right."

Cars and trucks filled the Van Ricker yard, and Victor had to park on the roadside. "I can walk," Audrey said.

Her words reminded Deborah of how she had felt when she carried David's body to town. "And I'll walk with you." She held Audrey's arm on one side and August's on the other. Raleigh had ridden with them, and

Victor steadied him on the rough road. The smell of smoke was in the air, and they avoided looking toward the burned building.

The Van Ricker house was quickly filled. Deborah moved among the relatives. She was introduced to Arlene's mother. "Oh," the woman said, "you're the one who just lost your child too." Her body was rigid, yet her face seemed to crumple before Deborah's eyes.

"Yes," was all Deborah could say. She hugged Mrs. Barlow, and the woman clung to her, her breath warm and damp against Deborah's cheek. John was standing behind Deborah. "This is John Strate. He lost a child under tragic circumstances." She passed the woman on to John, unable to say or do more in the face of raw emotions that seemed so bare of any protective covering.

"Oh, you dear man," the woman said. "I heard about your family. Where did you get your strength?"

"Mrs. Barlow, I believe we get strength from God and people around us. I couldn't have done it without the help of folks. You keep reaching out like you're doing."

Deborah left John and Mrs. Barlow. A man reached for her, shaking hands before she even had a chance to reach out. His jaw trembled as a person might who was shivering, and he put his hand to his mouth. "I don't know you," he said, "but we're sure grateful all you folks came. It means a lot to us. I'm Tony's dad." The man gripped her hand hard. He didn't let go, and she felt strong bones and callouses. His shaking chin was unshaven, the gray whiskers seeming to have drawn all the color out of his face.

"I am so sorry about what has happened." She couldn't think of more to say, but he didn't seem to notice. She studied his face, trying to see him as one of the masked men who had had a role in the whipping of Daniel Procek. He was also the man who raised Tony and probably would have had a big influence on Arlene's young boy, Harold Van Ricker.

He said, "I would like for you to meet my wife." Still holding Deborah's hand, Van Ricker turned to a woman sitting near the wall behind him. "Cora, this is one of the neighborhood ladies."

The distraught woman took Deborah's hand. "Thank you for coming. It's so good of you folks. I understand you all just came from another dear child's funeral. What a terrible, terrible day. I just—just don't understand what's happening." She turned to a man sitting beside her. "This is our son, Walter—one of Tony's brothers."

The man scrutinized Deborah, and frown lines narrowed his eyes, pulling his heavy eyebrows together above his nose. He recognized her. He didn't reach out his hand, and Deborah knew he was remembering when The Committee was lined up at her farm and made to remove their hoods while a list of names was made. She had been there in the torchlight. "I'm so sorry about your tragedy," she said, and slipped away when Maude and Elmer appeared next to her.

While visiting with other people, Deborah saw Victor and the Goodmans work their way across the room to where Tony was standing. The man's face was expressionless and pale, and he talked to people without looking at their faces. Victor turned and caught her eye; a signal went between them. She stayed in the living room, relieved she had when she saw Tony stare at her. Only his mouth changed. His lips tightened into a thin, white line. He turned away.

※

Back at the farm Calvin had the fireplace going. Deborah sat near its warmth. More than her body needed thawing. Victor brought her some food. "Here," Mary said. "Here's your favorite tea. Victor tells me Tony saw you from across the room."

Deborah thought a moment, a shiver traveling down her back. "And I met Tony's dad and mother and Walter Van Ricker, Tony's brother. The parents didn't know who I was … but Walter had it figured out. He saw me that night The Committee came here. The Van Rickers didn't ask for my name. Goes to show, names aren't important at a time like this."

"That's not all that wasn't important," Mary said. "Some folks seem to think skin color is so important. You had the same face as always, yet those folks shook your hand."

"They did, didn't they—rather Tony's parents shook my hand. Walter didn't." Deborah gave a little humorless laugh. "I forget I'm supposed to be Indian, and I didn't even think about it when I met them. I guess the grief of the parents filtered out my looks … and maybe I don't really stand out so much among other farm folk in this area who are burned by the sun and wind."

Chapter 9

Life Can Be Short

"Deborah, Victor, we need a few minutes alone with the two of you," Sonja said. David Nyfeller was with her.

Sonja had been crying and was distraught. Deborah almost hesitated, wondering if she could handle any more demands upon her time and emotions. Yet with no more thought, she gripped Sonja's hand and said, "Let's go into my bedroom." After shutting the door, the women perched on the bed, and the men took chairs.

"We made up our minds—just a while ago—to get married right away." Color rose into David's face, and Victor reached out to shake his hand.

Sonja managed a small smile when Deborah hugged her. The young woman's breathing was shallow and quick. "With little David's death, and then Arlene and the children, we're more convinced than ever that we need to get married—now. Because of all that's happened, we see how unpredictable and short life can be."

Nyfeller was his usual serious self. "We also realize the only way we can do this is leave here, at least until the drought is over. There's no way for us to make a living in the dust bowl."

"Wait," Victor cautioned. "There's no way for anyone to make a living anywhere."

"You're right," David said. "My job gives out Saturday because the Staffords just can't afford to keep me on. That's another reason we're thinking of moving on."

Sonja said, "David and I have always been thinking we don't have the money to have a home. But we saw how in a matter of hours little David was gone. We think we need to do everything possible to be together and quit waiting." She struggled and then said, "I'm afraid."

"I'm afraid for you—for anyone who stays in this dangerous dust. But where are you going?" Deborah asked. "Where can you be sure of a job? I do agree you should be getting away from here. That's the important thing. *Go where the dust isn't blowing.*" She emphasized each word, knowing for the first time how strongly she felt. She could not encourage anyone to stay in the dust bowl.

"I understand," Sonja said.

"So where is that? Where is a place that doesn't have blowing dust but has jobs?"

"We have no idea. We thought we'd buy tickets we can afford, get on the train, and just go somewhere, away from the dust," Sonja said. "We figure we'll just go on faith."

Victor shook his head. "I think of what John saw the summer of 1931 when he went to Washington, DC. He said there were men riding the rails from one side of the country to the other, just trying to find work. I hear it's much worse now. I'm wondering, how are you going to know where to go, when to get off the train—and if you'll find work there? Times are a lot worse now."

David dropped his head. "We sound foolish, don't we?"

"We just thought," Sonja said, "it's time we find a way."

Deborah felt her friend was ready to cry.

"I sure don't want to put a damper on things. I mean, I'm all for you getting married, God knows that," Victor said, glancing at Deborah. "But I'd sure like to see you have some job security and a roof over your heads."

Deborah thought of the little outback house behind her parents' home. Most folks would say it wasn't much, but it hadn't mattered to Christian and her. They had each other and, as Victor had just said, a roof over their heads. She no longer listened to the others, for her mind whirled with thoughts.

Was there some way she and Victor could help them? Sonja and Big David could live with her or Victor and work with them the way John had. But they needed to get away from the blowing. She wasn't going to encourage anyone to stay in the dust bowl, not now, not after losing David. She wasn't imagining the fear in Sonja's eyes.

Levi Brownly had once needed a woman to help him, but then he had hired Marion Scott, and now they were married. Moses had desperately needed help, and Frances had taken care of Lydia. After Lydia's death, Frances stayed on, keeping house for Moses. Was there no more work like that for a young couple? But—again—it wasn't just a matter of going somewhere to find work. They had to get away from the blowing dirt. No one should continue breathing the dirt if they had other options.

"Deborah?" Victor said, "Penny for your thoughts."

She was distracted. She got off the bed and stood looking at the floor.

"You've got something on your mind." Victor smiled patiently.

"Well ... just a minute." She left the room, shutting the door behind her, knowing she had left some curious friends.

Meredith and Calvin sat at the dining room table with the Goodmans. She pulled a chair to the corner of the table, sitting between them, and Calvin reached out to pat her shoulder. "Deborah."

She got right to the point. "Calvin, do you and my dad have a need for a hired man, a couple, actually, who could live in the little outback house and earn enough wages to see them through the Depression?" He was startled, and she added, "Maybe someone who could even help you with Jonathan and Baby if they go home with you?" She didn't give Calvin time to answer. "I was thinking how Mother and Dad couldn't come because you all had trouble finding someone to do chores."

He replied slowly. "I suppose we could have found any number of hands, but not men we knew or if we knew them, we weren't sure they were trustworthy. A hired couple, huh?" He smiled at her. "You wouldn't be thinking of Sonja and Big David, would you?"

"I am."

Meredith chimed in. "What a good idea. They could help both your folks and us." She patted her hair. "Does this gray hair tell you something? I for one would welcome a little extra help with the garden and so would your mother. I think it's been hard on your mother, not having Hannah anymore."

Deborah watched Calvin's face. She could see he was deliberating, and then he began thinking out loud. "They could live in the outback house ... Frank and I could share their help and the wages. Having someone would free us up some." He looked intently at Deborah. "You've written a lot about both of them. I can tell they're good people and good workers."

Meredith asked, "Is there going to be a wedding?"

"Right away. They don't want to delay any longer and are thinking of just going somewhere, anywhere, to see if they can get work. David's job peters out Saturday, and Sonja, well, you know about Sonja."

"You would miss her, I'd think," Meredith said.

"Yes, but they've waited so long to get married … and they need to get away from the dust. I'd welcome them here, but I don't want to be responsible for anyone continuing to live in this dust, especially since I can tell Sonja's afraid."

"They haven't waited any longer than you and Victor." Deborah's old friend had thrown caution to the winds in front of the Nelsons, and Audrey's words took them aback.

August said, "Well, Audrey, maybe now's not the time or place to bring it up."

"Why not?" Meredith asked. "Victor's a good man. Deborah, I could tell it right off when I met him. I knew from your letters and from what Calvin told me."

Calvin still had his arm around Deborah's shoulders. "Just because you were married to our son doesn't mean we'd be opposed to you marrying again. I can tell those boys think the world of him."

"He's a good man," Deborah agreed. "But the time is not right. We haven't decided—" She changed the subject. "What do you think about Sonja and Big David?"

Meredith and Calvin looked at one another. "Well, now," he said, "this is sudden, but where are they? Maybe we could talk."

"Yes," Deborah said, "in my room." She led them to the bedroom. "Victor, you come out now. The Nelsons need to do some visiting with these folks."

Later, a dazed and happy Sonja talked to Deborah. "I can't thank you enough."

"I hope it's the right thing for the two of you, working with my folks. Calvin says my dad is different now, from how I knew him. But I just want you to know, if you're not happy there, the two of you can come back here and live with me. Are you hearing me?"

"Of course. But I really think everything will be okay if the Nelsons are any indication."

"Now," Deborah said, "to other matters. If you're going to Minnesota when the Nelsons go with the boys, we've got to have a wedding right away—like the next day or two."

"Oh, yes." Sonja blushed painfully. "I mean, David and I would like that."

"Then, what are you going to wear for the ceremony? Does your mama have a wedding dress you can wear?"

"She just used her best dress, and she said she wore it out long ago. I'll wear my Sunday dress."

Deborah went to the big armoire, pulling a chair after her. She opened the ornate doors and climbed up, stretching to reach the top shelf. She brought down a folded clothes bag. "I wore my grandmother's wedding dress. It will fit you, if you want to borrow it."

"Deborah!" Between them they laid the garment bag on the bed and unzipped it. "Oh, are you sure?"

Deborah smiled. "I'm sure. It would mean a lot to me to have my good friend wear this on her happiest day. Try it on."

Seeing Sonja in the dress, Deborah began to cry.

"Oh, I don't want to make you unhappy," Sonja said.

"You haven't," Deborah insisted, trying to control herself. "I was just remembering how happy Christian and I were on our wedding day." The dress had opened a flood of emotions, many of them sad, but she wouldn't let Sonja know that.

There was a knock at the door. "Deborah?" It was Audrey.

"Come in. Look, look at Sonja in my dress."

"Oh my, my. Oh," Audrey said, "aren't you the most beautiful thing." She reached out to touch the silk. "No, I'd better not touch it. My hands are so rough from all the dirt. Deborah, you must have been a beautiful bride."

Deborah smiled through her tears. "I suppose. But look at you, Sonja. You are beautiful, no doubt about it."

Sonja asked if she and David could be married in front of Deborah's fireplace. "I've always admired it so, especially with your Indian things."

"I would like that. I would like it very much. Sonja? Excuse me for being nosy, but what is Big David going to wear?"

Sonja's eyes widened. "Why, I don't know. All—all he has is work clothes. Oh, dear."

Deborah went to the wardrobe again and brought out another clothes bag. "Take this to David. I hope he won't mind. Tell him I'd be happy for him to wear it on such an important day."

"What is it?"

"It's a suit Christian wore on Sundays. You and your mama will have to shorten the trousers." She went to her closet. This time she brought out Christian's Sunday shoes. Deborah giggled. "Tell him Christian swore about these every time he put them on. His feet were in bad shape from burns when he was a child, and he hated to break in new shoes. If they're too awful in size, I think Big David's work shoes will be fine. Oh, let me get the white shirt and tie."

Deborah brought the things from the closet and opened a dresser drawer. This time she brought some underwear and socks and added a pile of shirts and overalls.

"Oh, Deborah. Thank you."

"Don't thank me. These things have been sitting here for six years and more. I guess I just never had time to think about them. Sonja? Please don't bring them back. I don't have a need for them anymore. Wait, one more thing." From another drawer she removed a pair of Christian's pajamas. She enjoyed the even deeper blush, which appeared on Sonja's cheeks.

Audrey said, "Why, Deborah Nelson, you wicked girl."

Reaching as though to take the pajamas away, Deborah said, "Of course, David may not even wear anything to bed." The comment was almost more than Sonja could take, but Audrey's laughter was good to hear.

Deborah insisted the Goodmans stay with Victor and her when they were ready to talk with Calvin and Meredith. She invited John to be there also, but he gave her a hug and said, "The boys and me are going to Victor's place and warm up his stove. You know how I feel, little lady. I wish all you folks could breathe better air like we are in eastern Kansas." He left with the boys, promising to come for breakfast.

They gathered in the living room near the fireplace. Deborah sat on the rug, feeling the heat ease some of the ache out of her tired body. Nothing could remove the misery in her heart. She motioned to Jonathan, and he dropped down beside her.

Meredith said, "I had no idea the storms were this bad. I don't know how you folks have endured this, day after day."

Victor said, "Our salvation is that not all days are so bad. We do what

August has always advised. He says don't look beyond the end of your nose when you're doing cleanup. We take one day at a time."

"Except now," Deborah said, "I realize I've got to look ahead, past this day, past tomorrow. I've been stupid for not sending the boys to you sooner. Victor and I have already talked to Jonathan. He's willing to go home with you."

Audrey was trying to not cry. "I know I'll rest easier if you'll take these boys out of this dust. You know how at one point we had seven boys here. Now, we're talking about having no boys at all. I don't know what I'll do without them, but I want them safe too."

"I've told Jonathan maybe he and Half Shell will spend part of the time with Mother and Dad. What do you think?"

"I think it would be good," Meredith said. "Selfishly, I would want them all the time, but I think it would be good for the boys and good for your folks."

"Your dad has mellowed," Calvin said. "Frank's still not his old self, but he's getting there."

Deborah turned to Jonathan. "What we're talking about are the problems I had with Grandpa and Grandma Jorgenson. Like I've told you, sometimes he acted as though he didn't like me, and sometimes she acted like I wasn't there. I've never understood why."

"I'm sorry, Deborah." Meredith's voice was full of sorrow. At this moment, the lines of her face, so familiar to Deborah, no longer were a part of a dimpled smile that could draw warm response. Her face was now drawn and tired. "I'm so sorry you experienced that."

While Meredith didn't hold out her arms or move from her chair, Deborah felt warmth as though they held and comforted one another. In the firelight, the woman's eyes shone with tears.

"I remember the little horse Grandpa Frank bought for me and David." Jonathan sat with his chin in his hand. "He taught us to ride. He was friendly. He never said much, but he was friendly."

Deborah looked up at Calvin who was sitting on the divan. "You're sure he'll be good for the children?"

"If he isn't, the boys will be with us full time." He turned to Jonathan. "Are you a horseman, Jonathan? Your grandpa Jorgenson can teach you plenty about horses. I guess you already know."

The boy said, "I love horses. Horses have personalities—I think all animals do."

Deborah grabbed Baby Half Shell as he crawled around her. "I'll warn you, Meredith, when this baby learns to walk, you'll have your hands full. Be sure you use Sonja's help. I've seen her run her legs off, taking care of the little guys."

Audrey added a warning. "You've got to put all your pretties up high."

"Jonathan? You want to do this?" Deborah asked.

"Sure."

"Why?"

"So you won't worry about us so much."

"Don't tell me what you think I want. What do you want?"

"I want to go. I like school here, but I'd like to see what a town school is like. I figure I can learn a lot about drawing and painting from Grammy Nelson. I'd like to get to know them—and Grammy and Grampy Jorgenson." With no warning, big tears overflowed the boy's eyes.

Deborah grabbed him, and Baby, who was sitting on her lap, slid to the floor. "Jonathan! Oh—what's wrong?"

"Well," he sobbed, "it's the baby there. He lost his mom and then his dad—he visited us with his dad, and he had to say good-bye to you. He had to travel with strangers, but I figure when he saw you, he thought, 'Oh, boy, this is it. I'm home to stay.' And now look. We're just going to take you and Victor away from him. He's going to get to know the two grammies and two grampies, and the dirt will stop blowing and we'll take him away from them. It's the baby there I feel bad about."

Jonathan bowed his head down to his knees. "I feel bad about David too. I think it must be the same way. He lost our daddy, even though he didn't really remember him all that well. But he felt good about Mom here, and he thought someday Victor would be our dad. He lost all that. He must feel terrible too. So I feel sorry for him like I do the baby there."

Victor moved to sit on the rug beside Jonathan. Deborah's throat hurt. She said, "And it's about you too, Jonathan, isn't it? You do remember your daddy, and you lost him. Now you're going to be separated from me and Victor—and Grandma and Grandpa Goodman." She held him close. "I'm so sorry."

He hugged her. "Mom, do you blame yourself for David?"

"Yes."

"Why?"

"Because I exposed all of you boys to an unnecessary danger, the dirt. I let my pride get in the way when I should have sent you to safety like

John said I should. He gave me quite a talking-to after his first trip to Leavenworth. I ignored him."

"Then it's important you send me and Baby to Minnesota."

"You sure?"

"Sure." He tugged at Baby and pulled him onto his lap. "You still got me, feller. I'll still be the same." Baby giggled and grabbed a handful of hair.

Chapter 10

Life on Hold

That night, Deborah slept the hard sleep of someone exhausted from having experienced the full gamut of emotions for hours on end. Before falling asleep, she thought of David and of Arlene and her children, and her very soul was in pain. At dawn, she woke with the leaden and achy feeling of not having moved during the night, the remnants of a dream hovering about her like summer gnats, the kind of gnat that attempts to invade nostrils, eyes, and mouth, even one's very being. This had been a dream about David, much like the one she had after Christian disappeared, the dream in which she felt he had died and was telling her good-bye. Lendel was in this dream, just as in the first one.

As always, the dream took place in the sheep pen where Christian, Lendel, and she had last played together before Lendel died. There were a number of children in the dream, for even Lendel and Christian were young, perhaps nine or ten like David. Melonie was there, carrying on her hip the baby that had been Deborah's. Teddy R was even in the dream. He was the boy who worked and lived on Deborah's farm the summer of 1933—before an accident put a severe strain on his weak heart. A younger Teddy R helped the other boys round up the lambs in the pen, and David petted the lambs' heads, soothing them into calmness, much the way he had his biddies.

While the kitchen was being cleaned after breakfast, Deborah shared her dream. "They were all there with David. Melonie played with my baby." John dried dishes, and she turned to him. "John, Melonie was happy."

He remained quiet, unable to trust his emotions.

"Even Teddy R, a young Teddy R, was there. For some reason all of them were young and played with the lambs. David …" Her voice broke. "David calmed the lambs just the way he did his setting hens. He stroked their heads."

The Nelsons were curious, and Deborah told them more about her dream. "Why," Calvin said, "that sounds like the other dream you had when Christian disappeared."

"Christian was with Lendel in the first one, and they were with Teddy R in a second one. But this time, Lendel and Christian were boys, about David's age."

Meredith asked, "They were happy?"

"They were. I've got to remember that. Christian was happy, they all were. I wish I could keep remembering and move on—although so many things seem to have put my life on hold."

"What do you mean, Deborah?" Calvin leaned forward in his chair.

"Oh, it's not just *my* life. We're all in a similar situation here. The drought, for one. It seems all of our concentration is needed to keep one step ahead of the drought."

"Taking care of all the boys, including mine," John added.

Victor said, "The economy. Trying to make a living when there's no living to be made."

"Taking care of us," August said. "We're getting on, me and Audrey. And these young folks been caring for us the way they would their own family."

"Because you are family," Victor said.

"Sure seems that way," Calvin said. "I'd say you've all been blessed, having one another. I know I've rested easier, knowing Deborah has had you folks." He turned from Deborah to Victor. "What I want to know is why the two of you have put marriage on hold. It's clear you love each other."

"That's right," Victor said.

"Well?"

Victor and Deborah looked at one another and then at the Nelsons. Deborah said, "I haven't told you about the sheriff."

John snorted angrily, and August stomped his feet.

"The sheriff?" Calvin asked.

Deborah said, "The sheriff thinks that Victor and I did something to Christian."

"No," Meredith said.

"Idiot," John muttered.

They told the Nelsons how Stoddel tried to drive Deborah and the boys out of Fremont the first day they arrived and what had been happening ever since. "He's convinced I'm Indian," Deborah said. "He's an irrational man who believes anyone the least bit different should be run out of the county."

August said, "I had a real go-around with the jackass one day. Didn't do any good, near as I can tell."

"Well, I'll be," Calvin muttered.

"I didn't want you worrying about it. We're going on to seven years. Christian will be legally dead at seven years. Victor and I thought if we waited until at least then, maybe Stoddel would let up."

"I wonder if it would've made a difference if I had talked to the man back when I visited you," Calvin said.

"Oh, Calvin, like August said, he talked, and it did no good. Other folks have looked out for me, and the man hasn't let up."

August was worked up. "With his attitude, if he isn't a member of the KKK, it'd be a surprise."

Calvin asked, "What do you mean? You've got the klan around here?"

August turned to Deborah. "You didn't tell them?"

"No, I didn't want to worry them."

"Sorry," the old man said. "I spoke out of turn."

"Deborah?" Calvin leaned toward her. "What's been going on?"

They told Meredith and Calvin about The Committee activities in the neighborhood—frightening Deborah and others, setting a cross on fire, beating Daniel Procek. "Don't forget the night they came when Half Shell's daddy was here," August said.

"Well, I tell you," Victor said, "those were some young men in the area—maybe not members of The Committee—and Fleet Foot and I had a run-in with them in town. Wouldn't be surprised if maybe a few of them have The Committee leanings, though."

Deborah turned to John. "Since you left, they burned all of Vosserman's haystacks."

"You don't say. The Vossermans are good people. Why?"

"You'll be surprised to know they are Jewish. Someone overheard Hilda telling Audrey and me about her sister being put in a concentration camp. It was passed on."

John said, "This kluxer business is why there was some discussion yesterday about whether the neighbors should go to console Tony Van Ricker. I tell you, with that visit, folks treated Tony a lot better than he's treated Daniel and some other folks, including Deborah."

Calvin asked, "Are you safe here, Deborah?"

"You asked me when you were here last time. I'm safe as long as I use good judgment. I have Victor and August close by. Also, the community has organized, and we keep an eye on one another."

"Since yesterday's happenings, I'd say this Van Ricker is more of an unknown now," Calvin said. "It may be hard to tell how he's going to act now that his family is dead. What a sad situation. Take caution, Deborah."

"That's right," John said. "He may be none too happy you went to his house yesterday."

Although there was no wind the next day, the usual dust stirred as they walked, settling into shoe cracks and pants cuffs. The sun shone warmly for February. Deborah helped Meredith dress in coveralls, and Meredith rode Lady, going with the men to see the land. Deborah didn't go, for she had a phone call to make. Jonathan and the Strate boys scattered about the farm. She could hear some of them in the tree house.

"You and I," Deborah said to Baby Half Shell, "have things to do this morning. We're going to visit Moses so we can make a telephone call to Grampy and Grammy Jorgenson." He banged a pan with a spoon.

Frank Jorgenson answered her call, and the instant she heard his voice, Deborah stiffened. When he realized who was calling, his voice broke. "Deborah, girl. How are you?"

Sensing his emotion, hearing his few words, she had to grasp the doorjamb near Moses's phone and fight back the tears. "Oh, Dad, I'm better, just hearing your voice."

"You're going through the hardest thing a mother can go through, in my estimation." Frank's voice was reserved, but he sounded more like the man she had known many years ago. He went on. "From what I've always heard, losing a child must be far worse than what you experienced losing Christian. Well, I guess you knew already, losing the baby."

"Yes, Dad." Her tears came now, and she didn't try to stop them. She rubbed at her cheeks with her fingers, and Frances slipped a handkerchief into her hand.

"I'm sending the boys to Minnesota, Dad, just like you advised in your telegram. Meredith and Calvin plan to leave day after tomorrow, and the boys will be with them. We thought maybe you folks could share in taking care of them. What do you think? It will be until I think it's safe for them to breathe the air here."

He didn't chastise her for not having done it sooner. He didn't use an I-told-you-so tone. He simply said, "We'll do our best."

She told him about Sonja and Big David and the decision they had made with Meredith and Calvin. "I hope you're agreeable to it, Dad. They're two among some of my best friends and such good people. Can they live in the outback house and be of help to you? Especially with the children?"

Frank liked the idea. "From what you've written, I suspect Sonja could be an answer to some of your mother's needs. It will ease my worries. You tell them they are welcome here."

Driving home with Baby, Deborah talked to the boy and sang songs that reflected the relief in her heart.

Victor and John took the Nelsons over Deborah's entire farm and portions of the pastureland and the shelterbelts at the two ranches. Everyone gathered again for the noon meal and talked, especially about the measures Deborah and the others had taken against the drought.

Calvin had examined the pastures. "Your grassland looks far better than some I saw. For one thing, a few of your neighbors are carrying too many cows for the conditions. The way you're rotating your little herd among your pastures is good."

He was impressed with the newly built field terraces, and Meredith had particularly noted the trees. "We take trees for granted in Minnesota. Look at what you folks have done and what Mr. Strong and August did years ago."

"Do other folks around here have shelterbelts?" Calvin asked.

"Not many," August lamented. "I've heard the same arguments from folks about shelterbelts as I've heard about terraces. 'They take up farming space,' is what they say."

John said, "Sometimes it's hard to see beyond our own noses. I sure been guilty of that."

Calvin said, "Some folks aren't going to do a thing that smells of government minding their business."

"Just having the trees planted by men in a government project was cause enough for lots of people to back off," Victor said.

Calvin moved his fingertip around a square in the oilcloth. "We may see the day when the government oversees everything we farmers and ranchers do."

"That may be what it'll take to straighten out things," Victor said. "Something has to change. Many of us have cut back on production by not planting."

"Doesn't do any good to plant, dry as it is," August said.

Victor continued. "I fear another war effort, as the government called it last time. Folks will be encouraged to plow and plant—"

"Got to have rain first, son." August's voice was gentle.

"You're right, old friend."

"What are the answers?" August asked.

They spent a good share of the afternoon trying to find the answers, and then the men did the chores.

Deborah told Meredith how her dad had sounded on the telephone. "He surprised me. You can imagine how I felt. I've told Sonja if she finds things impossible with my dad, she and Big David don't have to endure it. I told her they can come home and live here." Her voice hardened a bit as she added, "I also don't want these boys of mine in an impossible situation with Dad. Promise, Meredith?"

"Of course. I understand what you're saying. But Deborah, I do believe your dad is a happier man. I don't know how anyone can show anger toward an innocent child—"

"Like my dad did with me? Maybe I wasn't innocent. Maybe I did something wrong, maybe I caused Dad to be angry—"

"Oh no, I don't believe you did a thing. Trust me. I don't believe you did anything to warrant the treatment you got."

"Well then! Meredith, hear what you just said to me! You said you 'don't know how anyone can show anger toward an innocent child.' Hear what I said—'like my dad did with me?' What makes sense?" Deborah heard the shrillness in her voice. She hid her face in her hands. "Forgive me, Meredith. I love you! I'm going to my room for a quick cool down and maybe a nap."

"Deborah, honey, I love you!"

That night Deborah's sleep was uneasy, and when she did sleep, the soldier dream came again. In the frightening nightmare, one she had been experiencing for years, birds and people attacked a Great War soldier. He whimpered, and his battered head bled. Deborah wanted to help him, but her arms were being held. She struggled harder when the crowd screamed and surged forward.

Jonathan came to wake her. "It's okay, Mom. It was the old dream." To comfort her, he covered her with Grandfather's blanket and handed her the wood carving the old Indian had made. She ran her fingers over the bird's wings until she finally grew sleepy—but not before wondering how it would be with no one in the house when the recurring nightmare came again.

At daybreak, Deborah was outside. Near the corral, she heard horses nicker, and they came trotting up to the fence. Climbing through the rails, she ran her hands over each horse in turn. She leaned across the pony's back and cried, for Dumper was the one that David had ridden.

Her mare came close to Dumper and nuzzled Deborah's neck. Before long, all of the horses, Christian's gelding and the four big work horses, crowded around her. She laughed through her tears. "You're all comforting me! Thank you. How sweet of you. Now, what is making me suspect it is time to put out grain for you?"

Victor arrived with the Strates. "Another still day," John said. "I pray it doesn't blow until your family's on their way."

"Oh," Deborah said, "I hadn't even thought about that. We'll have to watch the weather and hope we don't have trouble getting them to the depot."

John was worried about his job, the boys being absent from school, and his livestock left in someone else's hands, so he prepared to leave after breakfast. "Little lady," he said to Deborah, "if I hadn't already seen you look trouble in the face so many times, I'd be worried about leaving you with no boys, especially no David. You can do it. I'm one to tell you, as time goes by, I don't hurt so much about Melonie. You know that from your miscarriage. It'll get better, the sadness. And don't forget, this drought's going to end. Then you're going to have a family again."

"I wish we didn't have to say good-bye, John."

"Then don't. I told you before. We aren't saying good-bye. We'll see you later."

Chapter 11

The Arrowhead

The weather was strikingly beautiful. "This day is just for you, Meredith. I didn't want you to think Kansas is all bad." Deborah was standing at a kitchen window. "Jonathan, here comes Levi with Idotha and Byron. Let's go meet them."

The young girl climbed out of her dad's truck and went to Jonathan, taking his hand. "Deborah," Levi said, "there's talk your boys are going home with your in-laws. Have you decided?"

"Yes." The one word was hard for Deborah to say. "Tomorrow, Levi. This is Jonathan's last day."

"Well, then." He hesitated. "Set me straight if I'm not right in asking. But if it's Jonathan's last day home, could Idotha miss school and spend it with the boy?"

She had seen the dismay on the girl's face when she heard Jonathan was leaving. "I think it's a great idea, Levi." Idotha's smile was weak. Deborah pulled the girl to her side. "You come on in. We're getting ready for Sonja's wedding, and you can help Jonathan run errands for us."

Preparations were being made for Sonja's wedding supper. Deborah was baking a devils food cake for David and angel food for Sonja, separating egg whites from yolks. Baby Half Shell walked around and around the table, holding onto chairs and table legs. She worked at the table, and when he came to her each time, he grabbed her legs, pushing his head against her haunches as he moved on. She would reach down to stroke his soft baby cheeks and hair. He talked to her, his grin so delightful that emotion welled up in her. She couldn't imagine what it would be like to not have him with her.

Meredith and Calvin watched the slow progression of the little boy. "Will you look at that," Calvin said.

Meredith said, "He just never stops."

"He and I have been talking about it," said Deborah, "and I've asked him if his little legs are worn out. He chatters away at me and keeps on going."

Baby Half Shell finally grew tired and went to Victor to be held. "You wash him," Deborah said. "He needs a nap. I'll fix some food, and Meredith can help you feed him." Tears threatened to spill over, and she stepped into the living room to ask Jonathan and Idotha to bring milk from the well house.

"Mom? You all right?"

"I'll be okay, Jonathan. I'm just missing you boys before you're even gone." She saw Idotha nod and realized the girl understood all too well.

By five o'clock, friends were arriving for the wedding ceremony and supper, and Deborah helped Sonja dress. "David looks so handsome in the suit, Deborah. I've never seen him in anything but work clothes. He wants to wear it tomorrow on the train."

"Victor will tell him he cleans up real good."

"Did you know Victor is letting us stay at his house tonight so we can be alone?" Sonja giggled in embarrassment.

"Now, there's a thoughtful man. I hadn't really thought about why he asked if he could bunk with Jonathan."

"You don't have to put in all this extra work on my hair."

"Yes, I do. You're going to be done up right. Then we'll attach the veil. It's so delicate—so perfect with your blonde hair. You're going to look more Swedish than I ever did."

The ceremony was meaningful but quick. David had hired the Methodist minister from Fremont and the man's brother-in-law who was a part-time photographer. He said they had agreed to come at a more than fair price if they could stay for supper. Deborah helped them fill their plates from the buffet table, and then she knew why David had gotten such a good deal. They were hungry eaters.

The two cakes were cut, and Big David remembered how little David once asked him why chocolate cake was called devils food. "The boy was always full of questions. That's how he learned so much."

Sky Bird

The house seemed quiet by nine o'clock when the guests were gone. Meredith helped Deborah ready Baby Half Shell for bed, and they discussed things the older woman needed to know about the boys. While they visited, Deborah lay on the bed with the baby, holding him close. He contentedly sucked his thumb and fingered her hair.

Meredith said, "Jonathan was right when he expressed his concerns about Baby being uprooted once again."

"But I also know you'll work to make him feel secure. You did that for me more than once when I was little. Remember the summer I stayed with you while Mother and Dad went to Mayo Clinic?"

"How could I forget? What a grand time we had. For the first time, I had a daughter along with my boys."

"We played like we were Indians, and you made headbands. Baby Half Shell won't have to *play* like he's Indian. You had a little ceremony, and we danced. And you gave us Indian names. I remember mine was Sky Bird. I think of it every time I look at Grandfather's carving." She reached out to run her fingers over the bird.

Baby Half Shell was asleep now, and Meredith tucked him in beside Deborah with a small blanket. Deborah smiled, remembering. "This blanket makes me think of when Fleet Foot showed me how to tie a blanket so I could carry Baby on my back. David liked the notion. He said he wished I had carried him on my back that way when he was a baby. I asked him how did he know I didn't. He said, 'I know.'"

Meredith said, "He sounds like a child old for his years."

"Parts of him, Meredith. Only parts of him. There were the other parts. Sometimes he was a handful, as Rhoda Wolfe said. Does he sound like some other red-haired boys you used to know?"

"Deborah?" Meredith's face clouded. "I think your dream is right. I think Christian is dead."

"You do?"

"I believe that because I don't think that boy of mine would've ever left you. I raised him better than that. He loved you and those children so desperately, he'd never walk off and leave you."

"Why isn't there something to tell us what happened?"

"I doubt if we'll ever know."

"Meredith, I do have one concern about the boys going to Minnesota.

Jonathan will attend the same school I went to. He may run into some of the same problems I had."

"Problems?"

"Things like ... being spit on—"

"Spit on! Who did that? Why?"

"There were those who thought I should be going to the Indian school because I looked Indian to them. Jonathan looks a lot like me, Meredith. He may not be spit on, but it seems like there's always a faction that's fairly free with the racial slurs ... or worse."

"Oh, Deborah, I remember you telling me the Jenson boy thought you were Indian. What do you mean, worse?"

"Carl Jenson mocked me when Christian was gone to college and I no longer had his protection. He attacked me one time, my last year of high school. He bruised me badly—but I got a few licks in too."

"Deborah. You're serious."

"I bit him and put my thumb in his eye. The janitor, Mr. Schwarz, stepped in about then and bloodied Carl's nose."

"I'm proud of you. Good for Mr. Schwarz. I'm so sorry you experienced that. Were you all right?"

"He didn't do me lasting harm. It's Jonathan who concerns me now. Some time ago August told me I need to prepare him in the event there are those who mistreat him, but I'm afraid I've put it off. He's been so accepted here."

"We'll be alert. I'll talk to Calvin, and we'll do what's necessary. You're educating me, Deborah. I'm going to learn how to be a mother again in my old age."

"Then there's this little Indian boy." Deborah stroked the sleeping child's cheek. "Grandfather Blue Sky's great-grandson! I still find it amazing. I can actually touch a part of the old man I loved so much, after so many years."

"You wrote me that Fleet Foot worried about the baby being a half-breed. In the mouths of some people that sounds so derogatory. To me, the little fellow is half white, half Indian. I say he looks more Fleet Foot than he does April." Meredith smiled.

"I keep forgetting you and my parents met this baby's real mama. Tell me about her."

"I liked her because she was feisty and didn't let life control her. I gather she'd had a tough upbringing, an unhappy childhood that would make some people feel sorry for themselves. Not April. 'Gonna move on.

Get rid of that old trash.' I heard her say it more than once. 'Gonna move on.'"

"Was she happy about this baby here?"

"Oh, very. It was so evident. She was almost childlike when she would hold him and sing and dance. But she was also what I would call a 'fierce' mother, like you, Deborah."

"Me?"

"One who would fight to protect her young."

Deborah sighed. "I should have been more fierce in David's behalf. But go on with April. What about when she got sick?"

"She was taken so fast. I was convinced she had been hiding her illness. She knew how seriously ill she was and seemed more accepting of it than Fleet Foot. He barely had time to think … then she was gone."

Deborah felt tears burning her eyes and skin. "And then *he* died of a lung problem. Do you suppose the two of them were exposed to something, breathed something that caused their illness? On the reservation? Lung something … both of them in a matter of months. Maybe it was cancer."

"We'll never know. I believe your dad loved Fleet Foot, for the same reason you mentioned about Baby. The man was a part of Blue Sky. I also thought he loved Fleet Foot because he was Fleet Foot."

"I loved him." Deborah continued to cry, and Meredith didn't try to stop her. "The first moment I set eyes on him, I felt such an attachment. It's hard to explain. And then there was this little fellow." She smoothed the baby's electrified hair. "I loved him when I first saw him, and I hated to let him go to Arizona. I had no idea he would soon become mine. Jonathan's right, this little baby is suffering more than all of us rolled together."

Meredith touched the tips of her fingers to the child's cheek. "His blessing is he's young. We'll give him all the love possible, and when he comes back to you, maybe he won't suffer too much."

Calvin and Victor came to the doorway and looked in. "I feared you'd be cold in here, away from the stove," Calvin said. "Deborah, Meredith's got you and Baby tucked in like two peas in a pod. I should've known she'd have you all cozy."

"Come in here and sit down," Meredith said.

Calvin took a chair, and Deborah felt her heart quicken when Victor sat on the bed beside her. She reached to touch his cheek, and he smiled.

Deborah said, "I couldn't do this if I didn't know the two of you will love the boys and take good care of them with every fiber of your being."

She smiled at Calvin and held Meredith's hands. "These hands did so much for me when I was young. You helped me through some rough times."

Meredith's eyes glistened. "It hurt to see what you had to face. When you took care of your mother after her surgery, you were too young."

"Audrey thinks the things I experienced have made me stronger ... for facing David's death."

"Maybe so. But I wish you hadn't gone through any of it. I wish I could have helped you more."

Watching Meredith's face closely, Deborah said, "You know what was going on between my folks, don't you. You know why they turned on me. Both of you know."

Her friend moved uneasily on the bed, and Calvin gazed at the ceiling. Neither answered. Deborah focused on Meredith.

"You were an adult, a perceptive, smart woman. You surely understood far more than a twelve-year-old kid."

Meredith didn't answer. She stared at her nails, sometimes pushing at a cuticle.

"Meredith?"

"Deborah honey, I wasn't at liberty to say anything then ... nor am I now." Deborah thought she spoke as though reminding or cautioning herself. "Please don't ask me."

"I love you so much. I know you love me. It would help me to understand. I'm thirty-two years old, Meredith. For six years, I've wondered where Christian is, and frankly that's enough. But for almost twenty years I've also tried to understand why Mother and Dad no longer love me, why they literally changed overnight toward me. The pain has not grown less with time."

Tears rolled down Meredith's face, and Deborah sat up to hug her. "I'm sorry. You've always been such a friend, and I shouldn't press you. Mother and Dad don't want you to tell me. Am I right?"

Meredith nodded. "They need to tell you themselves."

"Do you think they ever will?"

"They will."

Deborah knew Victor was watching her. So close, she thought, so close, and she still didn't know.

The next morning the Goodmans came early because Audrey wanted to spend time with the boys and help with packing. Victor crated up artwork and books Jonathan wanted to take with him. Deborah went to the attic and found the book satchel Christian had carried through his years in college. Jonathan put his writing pad and the precious book of writings and drawings he had been doing throughout the drought in the satchel.

Meredith and Calvin had pored over the book. "Deborah," Calvin said, "the boy has talents with drawing and writing."

Meredith nodded. "Very perceptive."

"Yes, I think so. Don't forget singing," Deborah said. "We think he has musical ability too. Maybe he'll want to take some music classes. One time he told me there are so many things he wants to do, he figures he'll have to live to at least a hundred."

Audrey and Deborah reluctantly closed the suitcases. The old woman patted Deborah's arm, and her hand shook badly. "We can do this, I know we can."

Deborah held Audrey's hands, finding them calloused, the fingers crooked and knobby. "We'll do it together. I won't be able to stand the loneliness without your help."

"Mom." Jonathan stood in the doorway. "I've got Snicker and Lady saddled. Could we take Baby and ride out to the arrowhead before I have to leave?"

"What a good idea." She turned to Audrey. "Jonathan's going to move these suitcases. You lie down on my bed. Take a quick rest until we have to go to town."

"Oh, I'm all right. I thought I'd help with the dishes."

"Meredith probably has them done by now. The men were helping her."

"Grandma Audrey," Jonathan said, "let me cover you with Blue Sky's blanket." She didn't protest and willingly pulled the blanket up to her shoulders. He kissed her cheek.

Audrey took her hands from beneath the blanket, patted his cheeks, and smiled through her tears. "Jonathan, I'll think of you every day you're gone."

Deborah rode Snicker with Half Shell in front of her. "This is your first ride, Baby." He answered her by excitedly thumping his legs against the saddle, and chattering to Jonathan.

"That's right. And you're going to see the arrowhead for the first time." Jonathan rode ahead of her, leading the way. She studied his slender, straight back, windblown hair, and gentle hand that patted Lady as he rode, and she stowed the details away in her mind's eye for when he was gone.

The day continued to be still, and the sun brilliant. The hooves of the horses raised dust, but even though some reached the faces of Deborah and the boys, Baby Half Shell was delighted with the ride. He saw Jonathan pat Lady's neck and tried to do the same to Snicker.

"If you look at things through his eyes," Jonathan said, "it's pretty amazing, don't you think?"

"Yes. Very."

"And he's going to want to ride again and again. I'll take him. It'll be something we can do together. I'll be careful with him. Grandpa Frank can help me teach him."

"I know you'll take care of him." She added, "You were so good with David."

"I about dropped the storm-cellar door on his head."

"But it didn't happen. Angels were watching."

"Mom, if angels watched, how come they didn't save David this time?"

The sound of Snicker's hooves pounded in her head. "I don't know, Jonathan. I didn't recognize how sick he was … and I didn't have the experience to see how serious matters were. I've heard Audrey say more than once that we just do the best we know how at the time."

They came to the arrowhead and carefully removed it from its mat of growth, the grass not as thick as it was a few years back. Jonathan held the stone and then helped Baby run his chubby fingers over the surface. "This is important, Baby. This is important." Jonathan's voice was so serious Deborah had to smile. "It's part of what Grandfather Blue Sky taught us. You're going to learn these things too. This is your first lesson."

They sat in the grass with the arrowhead in Jonathan's lean hand, Baby Half Shell's fingers touching the chipped surfaces. Baby chattered, and Deborah said, "That's right, Baby. That's right. Like Jonathan said, this is important." She smiled through tears. "When you boys get back, we'll come see it again. It'll be here. Something like this reminds us that life goes on and on. This arrowhead hasn't been here forever, yet it's a part of Earth's memories. It was left here by people long before us."

Jonathan said, "It's a feeling." He held the small object in both of his hands and startled Deborah by lifting it toward the sun the way Grandfather Blue Sky would have done. "David," he whispered.

When they rode into the corral, Victor was waiting to help them unsaddle the horses. "Just about time to go," he said. He took the baby from Deborah's arms and held him close. He smiled when Half Shell grabbed him tightly around his neck. The little boy looked wistful as he watched Jonathan lead the horses away.

At the depot, Deborah told the Nelsons and Nyfellers good-bye. She hugged and kissed Jonathan and covered Baby Half Shell's face with kisses. Then the little boy squirmed to get down.

Victor held his hands and helped him walk. "You about got it, feller." He grinned as he turned him over to Jonathan. "If he practices walking on the train, I'll bet he'll be able to do it by the time you get to Minnesota." Victor's eyes filled with tears as he kissed and hugged Jonathan. He bent to kiss the top of the baby's head.

They could see the boys through the train window where Jonathan lifted Baby Half Shell up to the glass. When the train began to leave, what she saw last were Baby's little face and moist hands pressed to the train window. Seeing him that way was so much like the very first time he had come to her, his face and hands pressed to Fleet Foot's truck window.

As they watched the train pull away, Victor whispered, "I love you, Deborah."

"I love you, Victor."

They held the arms of the old folks as they walked over the uneven ground to the car. "All the boys," August said, "all of them slipping through our fingers. First Teddy R ... he won't never be back. John's boys ... we'll see them now and then. David ... won't never be back. Baby and Jonathan—"

"Those two will be back before you know it," Victor said.

"Yessir, they sure will!" August seemed to shake himself and moved with stronger legs.

Chapter 12

A Quiet House

That night Victor did the chores with Deborah as usual. They worked at their tasks, each carrying a lantern, its light circling out to include feed pans, a bucket and milk stool, eggs in nests. Then the lights converged in the well house where Deborah and Victor worked together at straining milk and cranking the separator. When they finished the separating, jars of milk and cream went into the water storage tank. They covered the tank with a clean tarp.

"Think we'll ever feel secure enough we won't need to cover the water against blowing dirt?" he asked.

She smiled and lightly kissed his cheek. "The old folks say have faith, the drought cycle will end."

"My faith's a little thin these days."

"Mine too."

Victor built a fire in the fireplace while she laid out some supper. "Come eat in front of the fire," he said.

After they had eaten, she sat on the rug, her back against the divan. Victor brought Grandfather's blanket, wrapped it around her shoulders, and hugged her. "You always know what to do," she said.

"I just figured it would help. We've got to look for ways to help one another. This isn't going to be easy, going from a busy, noisy house to this sudden stillness." He listened and so did she. The fire cracked and popped. That was all.

"Even the wind is quiet."

"That's something," he said. "Almost miss it."

They talked, trying to fill the room with the sound of their voices, reviewing the past few days. "I wonder how Tony is handling the quiet in his house," Victor said. "Do you suppose he talks to folks about his children the way we are about David? It's hard for me to imagine him doing it, but I may be misjudging him."

"I've been grateful many times over that people are talking about David," Deborah said. "That's the way it should be. It's not as though he's never been here."

"If only I could touch him, see him."

"See him in your mind, Deborah."

"Today, when we went to see the arrowhead, I had an image of him standing with Grandfather Blue Sky. I was startled … and comforted."

He held her tighter. "It is a comforting thought."

She said, "Sonja and Big David looked happy. It was good of you to give them your house for the night."

He laughed. "Can you imagine a wedding night in the little Beckman house?"

"Heavens, no." They grinned at each other.

Victor said, "I'd like to stay tonight, if you don't mind. I'll bunk in Jonathan's room."

"I don't mind."

She finally went to bed, removing only her shoes, and wrapped herself in the old blanket. She fell asleep quickly but woke later, thinking the stillness was what had made her sit up in bed. There was moonlight in the room. Her habit, when waking in the night, had been to smooth the blankets over the baby and go into the bedroom where Jonathan and David slept. Often it had been necessary to straighten David in his bed, for he always slept precariously close to the edge. She would tug blankets and smooth the hair of both boys. When John's boys were with her, she had checked them too. And she had always looked in on Teddy R, holding her breath, for she feared—just as Meredith must have feared with Lendel—that his weak heart had given out.

The moonlight reached into the crib, its light sending shadows of the bed's rails onto the quilt-covered mattress.

Now no baby and no boys were in the other rooms to wonder about.

Deborah left her bed and, carrying her shoes, walked silently down the hall. She spent some time touching the photos on the pedestal table, barely able to see their forms in the moonlight. She went outside. The air bit at her face and hands, and she pulled the blanket onto her head. She climbed through the corral fence, going toward the pasture, teetering on occasional frozen hummocks. In the pasture, the mare came to her, and she rode bareback and with no bridle deep into the grassland. She turned Lady loose.

Deborah went directly to the highest spot, the craggy cliff that overlooked the creek bed below with its line of trees. Lady followed, her hooves striking stones. Sitting on a cold slab of rock, a place even higher than the one where she and Victor had sat last summer, she tugged the blanket closer and held its edges, turning her hands inside to her body. She watched ragged lines of clouds move across the blue-white of the half-moon.

When she was a child, Grandfather Blue Sky often sang to express a mood—happiness or sadness—it seemed so right to do as he would have done. She didn't remember many words—she had never really known them—but could feel the rhythm and tonations of the chants. Now she sang the chant, a song of sorrow. Grief for her losses made her rock back and forth. At times she was silent, thinking of David and the desolation of being without Baby Half Shell and Jonathan. She also thought of Arlene and the children.

More often, the chant of her song mixed with deep, painful cries that came from the very center of her being. She was silent again, and she heard coyotes that seemed to pick up her keening call, their wavering chorus repeating the emotion of what she had just sung. As usual, farther to the west where the thick berry thickets grew close to ravine walls, there were the yipping foxes. A breeze stirred swirling dust out of the dry grassland behind her. She pulled the blanket closer over her head, much like a tent now, and continued her incantations, dirgelike and Indian in rhythm and tone. Sometime later she heard the approach of another horse, and Lady nickered.

She recognized the sounds as being those of the gelding's bridle and knew Victor was there. He was riding bareback, for she didn't hear the creak of leather. The horse stopped near her, putting his head down to rest on her shoulder. She stood and moved to where Victor could reach down his hand and pull her up behind him. Holding the edges of the blanket, she wrapped her arms and the blanket around him, resting her cheek against his back. They rode slowly to the farmstead, and Lady followed.

Feeling the warmth of Victor's back, Deborah thought about how it would be to stay in his arms the rest of the night. Against his body, within the grip of his arms, she could find comfort and push away some of the loss. Yet never would her losses be recouped. Never would she do anything to antagonize Stoddel and encourage him to find a case, however circumstantial, against Victor.

They agreed he shouldn't sleep at her house again. Often after that, she stood on the steps or in the yard, watching him ride away, thinking how tired he was and how much more sensible it would be if he didn't have to ride the few miles to his bed. During the quiet of the night, when the only sounds were the creak of the house, the dry rustle of the trees, or the crowing sound of a rooster confused by the moonlight, she turned restlessly back and forth, imagining Victor's warm body beside hers. Those were the long nights.

She had a fear of the long nights for more reasons than her desire to have Victor wrapped about her. The bedroom next to hers was empty, its blinds drawn against shadows, the beds and other furniture covered with muslin dust covers. There was no movement, warmth, or sound in the room. The close air reminded her of the back bedroom in the Bogart house, the room where she had found a baby's crib—with its shattered corner railings and, if she had looked closely, perhaps even spatters of blood from a baby crushed during a tornado, decades before.

Deborah ceased to look in the boys' room, for David was gone forever and Jonathan indefinitely. She stripped Baby Half Shell's crib of its bedding and mattress and had Victor help her take the frame apart, removing its nuts and bolts, moving it from beside her bed to the attic. She swept the floor and placed a chair in the empty space.

On the stand by her bed was a photograph taken before David died. What had motivated her, other than Baby Half Shell's arrival before Christmas, to hire a photographer to come from town and take the picture? They had posed near the barn, Victor on Princess—the horse Tony Van Ricker had abused—Deborah on Snicker, Christian's gelding, holding Baby in front of her on the saddle. Jonathan sat astride Lady, and sitting on Dumper was David, his curls as tight and springy as the horse's winter hide was shaggy and long. She remembered Jonathan's comment as they had all sat at the table one day, "We look like a family." They were a family with a baby … but David was gone.

She stroked the faces in the picture, touching Baby's flyaway hair, Jonathan's longer than he usually wore it, and David's she knew to be a deep red even though the black-and-white photo didn't show it. She outlined his face with her fingertip, remembering the light sprinkle of freckles across his nose and cheeks … so much the way Christian had looked when he was a boy. She could imagine August and Audrey touching their copy of the photo much the way she was doing … and of course Victor, who loved all of them so dearly.

Each day, Deborah worked hard for hours on end, tiring her body physically until she was ill from exhaustion, and then, by lamp light, reading, writing, and studying from books that were remnants of her college days, wearing down her mind until it was as tired as her body. She slept and with the ring of the early alarm, jumped out of bed without allowing a second thought as to the comfort of the warmth beneath the blankets. She used cold pump water, not even tepid from the kettle on the warming stove, to splash her face and smooth her straggly hair back from her face.

She rattled the grate, noisily removing clinkers, and shoveled in coal, putting noise—which seemed to echo—into the house, cold and hard sound. Outside she welcomed the crowing of a rooster, squeals of hogs, and the lowing of a cow ready to be grained and milked.

Deborah and Victor settled into a routine, and the continued calm of February made it easy. She was hopeful. "Maybe it was a mistake to disrupt the lives of my boys, sending them back east. Maybe 1937 is the big year. Maybe the blows have ended."

"May be," Victor said, stretching the word into two, his voice full of doubt.

August did the same. "May be." She knew the two words represented doubt, and she fought against dwelling on their sound, yet hearing them repeatedly in her mind.

"Look," she argued. "We haven't had any moisture, but what winds we've had since David died have been normal enough and even the temperatures have been normal for February."

"Daughter," August looked at her sadly, "remember the time you said you didn't know what normal is anymore? I, for one, am glad those boys are safe. We've got to know the winds are gone, and the moisture's come." He was cautious. "I say we don't change a one of our practices, especially when it comes time for the two of you to be working and planting the gardens. Don't leave something uncovered. Keep at the mulch. Here I am telling you what to do, but it sure looks like Audrey and me aren't going to be much good to you."

"August," Deborah admonished, "you've both worked so hard all your lives. Sit back and let us take care of things."

Victor and Deborah did much of the noon meal preparation at the Goodmans now. After morning chores, they would take milk to them and work in the house. Audrey had begun to fail quickly after the boys left for Minnesota. Deborah feared she was losing her will to live with no children around.

"I think it's true," Victor said, "but I also think her health is simply going with old age."

The milk cows were still at Deborah's farm, and each morning Victor came to help chore and to eat breakfast. At night, they chored and had supper together. Usually, he stayed awhile in the evening, and it had become their habit to sit together and write letters to Minnesota. Victor wrote what he called an on-going letter to Jonathan and mailed it every Monday.

Early each morning, they carried milk and cream to the old folks. Audrey would sit in her rocking chair and visit with them for a while. Then she would go to sleep. Victor and Deborah would work about the kitchen, washing up from breakfast and starting the noon meal. By the middle of the morning, August was usually asleep in his chair by the stove.

When the meal was over and the cleaning done, they would leave food for the old folks for their supper and go out to work. More often than not, they worked about August's place, because he no longer tried to keep up the buildings and fences. They spent much of their time repairing his big barn.

"This is a beauty of a barn," Victor said. "It's well worth the time and work."

They made repairs on the siding and roof and even did some shingling on mild days. Deborah loved being on the roof, looking down on August's trees and buildings and out over the grassland. One day, she stopped her hammering and stared down at the sod house. "It's not looking good," she said.

"I know," Victor said. "I've been around it, and you don't see obvious places where it needs saw and hammer. Not like in these wood buildings. No," he shook his head in dismay, "it just has the sags of old age, and I sure don't know how you repair a sod house that has been here this long."

"I just hope it outlasts them."

"Oh, it probably will. In fact, I fear it will because those old folks aren't doing real good."

"I know."

She didn't go back to work immediately, staring instead at an image in front of the old house. She saw David, as she had seen him so many times, latching the old yard gate behind him and running to Audrey who was on the porch. "Got cookies, Grandma Audrey? If you don't, I brought you some." The two figures met, her arms going about him, his face reaching up to kiss hers. In her mind's eye, Deborah attempted to hold the picture motionless, not wanting the figures to move on, not wanting them to leave. With the memory, Deborah made a sound and then a movement on the steep rooftop.

"Sweetheart?" Victor reached out to her, and his hand was warm and firm on her shoulder. "Are you okay?"

"I'm okay. I guess I just kind of forgot what I was doing."

Chapter 13

She Isn't Lonely

March came, warm and calm. Deborah didn't say it to anyone, but she wished she hadn't been so hasty in sending the boys away. There was no rain yet, but just having the blessed calmness was a miracle in itself. The second week of March there was a heavy, wet snow, a "real moisture producer" was what August called it, and 1937 truly seemed to be the year of the drought's end. The snow went as quickly as it came, for the hot sun melted most of it out of sight in a matter of two days.

Victor and Deborah did some walking in the fodder fields, not a lot of walking because of the sucking, surface mud, and looked at the terraces with satisfaction. The terraces held little ponds of snow melt, the surfaces glistening in the bright sunlight. The unusual sight of standing water gave Deborah even more hope that the drought and winds might be ending.

They planned their gardens and fieldwork carefully, laying out only what two people could do while keeping the growing shelterbelts going. There would be the planting of the African crops, as they still called them, fodders that handled drought, and then the usual vegetables. The basic changes they made were to plant only potatoes on Victor's place and a few things August could manage in his garden.

"He's got to have something to putter around with. He'll like his lettuce and tomatoes." But Victor was concerned. "What you want to bet, he'll plan to harness up his team and cut your alfalfa?"

"We'll cross that bridge when we come to it, Victor."

After the snow melted, they spent much of their time replenishing the mulch in the shelterbelts. It was common to see August walking among his trees, and he often gave progress reports as the different kinds slowly began to develop their spring buds. "Those Chinese elms," he said, "I've never seen the like for growing fast. I thought locust was good, and even cottonwood. But look at those elms."

They used Deborah's team to pull a wagon of mulch or the tank of water and just as often hitched up August's team to give them exercise. Always working side by side, they talked, as Victor said, about everything under the sun. Deborah had thought she had known Christian as well as herself, but now she knew Victor far better, and her love for him continued to grow.

"Victor," she said, "we have to be a rarity."

"How so?"

"How many couples have the opportunity we've had? Look at how well we're getting to know each other before we marry."

"When we get married, do you think we'll have anything left to learn about each other?"

She grinned. "Oh, surely there'll be something."

On a day toward the end of March, they went to the Goodmans soon after breakfast. Deborah was carrying a covered pot of vegetable-beef stew. "Here's your dinner—stew and cornbread. I think it tastes good, if I must say so myself. We're going to work in my north shelterbelt, so we'll just eat dinner at my house and come see you after evening chores." She lifted the lid, and Audrey sniffed appreciatively.

August was at the stove, stirring a kettle of something. "What you got there, old friend?" Victor looked in the kettle. "Oh, cottage cheese. You making cottage cheese? I don't know how to do that."

"You need a good teacher like I've had all these years," said August.

Audrey was in her rocking chair, snuggled under a small comforter. "The best teacher," she said. "I've been making it for close to ninety years. Now it's his turn."

Deborah thought Audrey's voice sounded weaker than usual, but the old woman was closely monitoring August's work. He stuck his finger in the milk to test the temperature, and Audrey smiled. "Don't worry, I made him wash his hands before he started."

They visited for a while, listening to the couple banter back and forth about August's cheese making. When the curds drained in a cloth bag, Victor said, "Well, it looks like you know what you're doing. I guess we'd better get to work."

Deborah hugged Audrey before she left. "Save some of the cottage cheese for me, August."

That evening, shortly before supper time, Deborah and Victor did the milking while arguing amiably about the unconstitutionality of the Agricultural Adjustment Act. In the middle of what he was saying, Victor stopped and listened. "Wonder what's going on in the orchard with the crows? They're kicking up quite a ruckus. I suppose they're fighting over a dead rabbit or something." Deborah turned her head to listen, but he went on with what he had been saying.

She was just finishing her cow, stripping out the last bit of milk, when a clap of wind hit the northwest side of the barn. The pungent, peppery smell of dust came inside.

"Oh, no," Victor groaned, and with the wind and his words, Deborah's spirits dropped. As the light began to dim, she sat with her forehead against the side of the cow and fought to hold back her tears.

"Victor." Deborah's voice was choked, but she tried to sound like she was making a joke. "The cow pie that Patience put down by your feet? My hopes for getting the boys home just fell in there." She continued to sit, lacking the will to move.

She heard him quickly finish the stripping of his cow, and then he came to pull her up from her milking stool. "We'd better get this milk to the well house," he said grimly. "We'll also need to check on the old folks, especially since we didn't eat dinner with them today."

Deborah began the separating, and Victor hurried to take care of the hogs and chickens. When he came back to the well house, he saw the look on her face. "What's wrong?" he asked. She was frantically running hot water through the separator.

"I think we've got to get to August and Audrey. I've been worried about her anyhow, but now I have such a feeling, a feeling something's wrong."

"Let's do it," he said. He capped the jars of freshly separated milk and cream and put them in the water to cool. He took August's milk jar out of the tank and hurried to the garage. After cranking the truck to life, the drive to the Goodmans seemed agonizingly slow, and, at times, Deborah found herself holding her breath. What if the engine were to quit as it did the night of David's death? Victor must have sensed her thoughts. He patted her knee and said, "We're going to get there."

The light was virtually gone now. Thistles thumped the truck, and Victor had to watch the line of trees in Deborah's lane. He navigated the corner onto the road, and she knew matters were worse now with no trees to guide him. Peering out her window, she saw the entrance to August's place. "There. There it is."

"I see it, I think." Victor turned the corner cautiously and then drove fast toward the house. "There's the yard fence."

At the house, August was holding the door for them. Deborah could barely see him in the blackness. "Would you believe, I heard the old bell on the gate?" The old man's voice was shaky.

She removed her coat. "How is she, August? How is Audrey?" There was a flash of lightning and thunder rolled overhead.

August shook his head. "Well, I tell you, I'm remembering over and over what Hocksmith said last week." They all knew what Carl had said, but August repeated it as though trying to believe it. "He says her poor old heart's just wore out, and the dust is messing up her lungs. He reminded me she's eighty-nine years old."

Deborah hurried to the bedroom. The windows were hung with damp sheets, and a partial tent was draped over the head of the bed. "Audrey." Deborah bent over the old woman and kissed her.

"Deborah, my Deborah." Audrey's voice was a whisper, and her eyes caught the light of the lamp August held close.

"I blame myself," August said. "All these years I kept her in this old sod house. It doesn't shut out dust storms. I should've knowed better."

"August," Victor said, "there isn't a house around here that can keep out this dust, and yours is doing better than most."

Audrey roused herself enough to reach for August's free hand. "You stop it now." She coughed weakly. "I'm just an old woman. Let me die in peace, old man."

"You aren't going to die," he said. Deborah took the lamp from him, and August sat on the side of the bed.

"Well, you and God know something I don't?" Audrey pulled his hands to her lips. She kissed the knobby fingers. "We're all going to die sometime."

"I mean right now," August said. "You aren't going to die now."

"I hope not." She smiled. "I got to clean this house when this storm quits."

Deborah laughed, and Audrey turned her head to look at her. Deborah could see a whiter place on the pillow where the woman's head had kept the dust away. Dust was collecting in the moisture at the corners of her mouth.

"Now, let's get down to serious business. I want you to know you're all making me a happy woman," Audrey said. "I got this old man here, holding my hands. And Deborah. And Victor's in those shadows. All the people I love the most. Except for all the boys."

"And we all love you," August said.

"Yes, we love you. You've been my best friend," Deborah said, "my best friend. Don't leave me now."

"Now, you all listen to me." Audrey's voice startled Deborah, for she sounded much like the strong, healthy woman they used to know. "Don't you go wasting your time crying over my dead body. You need to remember, I've had a happy life, and now my old heart's just tired. You hear me?"

Audrey looked at Deborah and Victor, and they nodded. August sat with his head bowed.

"You hear me, August?"

"I hear," he said softly.

"I figure I've done what I planned to do when I came to this old planet earth. Maybe I haven't done things as good as I should have. I've been thinking that at the time I had to do what I did, I reckon I was doing the best I could, but that's between me and God. And I sure did learn one big lesson. If something hurt me, if something wounded me, I couldn't just give up. It was up to me to turn the wound into something right and good." She breathed deeply.

"Like I said, don't cry over me. Like your dear little boy said, 'Don't cry over spilt milk.' He was right. It's a senseless thing to do. You'll be crying because I'm not here with you when all the time I'm right by your side. Just listen to your thoughts, and you'll hear me talking to you." She seemed to rest, and they waited. She spoke again. "You won't be able to touch me, but you can still touch one another, can't you? That's ... called love, and I'll be wherever there's love. You can't see me, but you can still see me in your mind, can't you? You can still see the sun shining and ... hear the birds singing and the old white ... rooster crowing, can't you? I'll be there. You can see things grow and rains come and feel snow chilling your bones. Well, that'll be me too."

She spoke almost feverishly fast. "I'm just saying that I'm not going to be far away from you. None of us who have gone before are far from you. We'll help you out where we can. We'll make things possible, and then it's up to you to decide what to do with them. You understand?

"You two young folk have kept me going longer than I dreamed possible—you and the boys. You know that? You've been doing so much for others, including me, and I do thank you. I know how much you love each other. I know the reasons you haven't married, but I sure hope you can do something about it real soon.

"This drought isn't going to last forever. You just keep on doing what you've been doing, and I know things are going to get better. You keep remembering one thing. Jesus expects us to wash the feet of others. That's all you've got to remember." She closed her eyes. "I guess I'm tired now."

Emotions of love and sadness seemed to be crushing Deborah's heart, a heart already full of despair over one more choking, black storm keeping her boys from her. Now it was going to take Audrey.

Victor and Deborah sat in chairs, August on the edge of the bed. He talked constantly, telling stories of the old days, especially the first years of the couple's marriage. "Remember the dress you wore the day we got married? You wore it every anniversary after that—unless you were in the family way—and then I guess it just wore out."

"Baby dresses," Audrey whispered. "It made good baby dresses."

Audrey smiled occasionally, and held August's hands. Deborah watched as closely as she could in the dim light and was sure the old woman's breathing was growing slower. Her hair was unbraided and fell in thin waves down to her shoulders. In the poor light, her face seemed dark in contrast to her hair.

Whenever he could, August included the others in his talking. He described the first time he had seen Victor and Deborah and Christian. He told the story about Christian setting the smokehouse on fire. "He said, he said, 'Well, we got smoke, don't we?'"

During this story, Audrey appeared to be asleep. Then her weak voice said, "He's … here."

"Who, sweetheart?" August asked.

She mumbled, and Deborah strained to hear Audrey's voice. She thought she heard something like Teddy R, and she was certain she heard David's name. Then Audrey said nothing more.

The three looked at one another, and a shiver went up Deborah's back. "I believe they're all with her," August said. "She isn't alone."

Audrey no longer talked, but August's voice continued. The rafters creaked, and lightning flashed into the room, even through the draped windows. Thunder rumbled, and Deborah prayed for rain or snow, moisture to stop the dirt and ease Audrey's pain.

At three in the morning, Audrey died. Deborah was watching her when the rise and fall of the nightgown over the old woman's chest stopped. August was describing a memory, his face animated, and if he were aware of what had happened, he didn't let on. Deborah bent to put her arm around his shoulders. "She looks so peaceful," she said.

"Don't she now," he said. He folded Audrey's hands together and caressed their wrinkles. "I never was so happy in my life as when I was with her. Times was hard. We had our grief, especially when the babies and the boy died, but nothing ever made me happy like she did."

On Audrey's thin hand was a gold band, worn thin. August worked at it until he was able to slip it over the arthritic knuckle. He turned to Victor. "She'd be proud if you'd take this for your future wife."

Victor held it tightly, tears rolling down his cheeks. "*I'd* be proud," he said.

August turned back to gaze at the still face. "She told me, she told me, I shouldn't forget to shake the tablecloth … and maybe change it once in a while. She said, she said use up the peach jelly first, it's the oldest down cellar." He looked about him, his face bewildered. "We haven't growed no peaches for, I expect, six or more years. My, she could do things with those peaches! The best pie."

They continued to stay with Audrey's body until daybreak, or what they figured was daybreak by the clock. Then August stood, his body cramped from sitting so long. "I'd better cover her face against the dust. We better shut the door and keep it cool in here. No sign of the storm letting up." He gently tugged at the sheet, pulling it over Audrey's face. Then he led the way out of the room.

Deborah stood in the middle of the kitchen, fighting off a tiredness that made her want to sit at the table and put her head down. In the dim light, working more from sense of touch than sight, she made biscuits and served breakfast. They ate.

"Peach jelly," August said, holding his biscuit as though saluting. "Good stuff."

After breakfast, Victor said to Deborah, "I'm going to your place and do the milking."

"No, the cows can wait."

"You know they can't. We don't know how long this one will last."

"But you can't see."

"I'll find myself across the road to your fence and follow it from there. You know I can do it, Deborah."

He wouldn't listen to more argument. She helped him put on his coat and hat. Buttoning his coat the way she might have done for one of the boys, she smoothed the lapels and patted the bandana on his face. He carried a sugar sack that he planned to put over his head.

They held one another. "Be careful," she whispered.

"You know I will. Don't worry. Expect me when you see me." When he opened the door, the wind howled through the chicken netting Audrey had used to train vines up to the porch roof.

"Well, now," August said, sitting by the stove, rocking back and forth, cocking his ear toward the crack of electricity. "The boy will be okay."

Deborah cleaned the kitchen, stored the washed and dried dishes, and swept the floor, barely able to see her work in the gloom. Once she went to the bedroom, opened the door, and looked toward the bed. She couldn't see in the darkness but took some comfort from remembering the image of Audrey's last smile.

She cleaned the sitting room, dusting the tall clock sitting in the corner. It struck the time regularly, every quarter hour, causing August to begin remembering again.

"That clock—Audrey's mama stowed it away in a featherbed in the wagon. All these years of dust from all the storms, it's never given out on us. Its works are shut up in the tight compartment, doesn't let any dust in. They don't make them like that no more. Her mama wrote that her daddy was so derned mad we had his best clock for a wedding present. But when her mama died before he did, he wrote us a letter, saying he was glad we had it. Knew we'd take care of it. That's all we ever heard from him, all those years after we run off and got married. Can see the writing to this day. 'Your ma died last week, the 11th. I'm glad you got the clock. I know you'll take care of it.' Isn't it something? Just a few words can say so much. I folded the little piece of paper, and it's in the compartment of the clockworks. Figured it belonged there."

Deborah built up the kitchen fire, and August talked on for a while. His head fell against the back of the rocking chair, and he slept a deep sleep, his feet propped on a footstool, his intertwined fingers over his chest. She noticed he had pulled over himself the small comforter Audrey had always used in her rocker.

Victor was gone a long time, and Deborah's lips were raw with biting them. She opened a jar of canned beef and made noodles. The food was ready at three o'clock when he came, waking August. "Everything's all right," he said, when he could catch his breath. His mask was muddy where he had breathed.

"Everything's okay, and I milked the cows. I let the horses and cows out of the barn to get water. Those hogs are healthy and strong, just rooting away in their shed. Hens sat on the roost. Probably will sit there in the dark until their bellies tell them to get down." He was exhausted and went to sleep as soon as he had eaten. The storm did not let up.

With nightfall, again by the clock, Deborah made the bed in the spare room, and August slept, seemingly unaware of the continuing storm. She wrapped herself in a blanket on the parlor settee, and Victor was on the braided rug before the stove.

The next morning, he put his hand on the old man's shoulder. "It isn't letting up, August. We have to do something. You've got lumber. I'll bring it and tools into the kitchen, and you can direct me in building the casket. While we do that, Deborah can dress Audrey's body, and then I'll do the milking again."

August answered in a broken voice. "I know. We got to do something. We'll have to nail it shut tight before the neighbors can get here, I suspect."

Deborah carried a pan of water and a cloth into the bedroom. The dust was so bad, she wondered what good was the washing—but it was the last thing she could do for Audrey. She knew how her friend hated dust in her hair and on her skin. In the closet was a pretty cotton dress, one Audrey would wear while she worked about the house, and a starched, white apron. Deborah did the old lady's hair, parting it in the middle and coiling it up the way Audrey would have done, allowing soft waves to sweep the sides.

The men finished the casket and set it on the seats of two chairs near the bed. She lined it with a folded blanket covered with a sheet. Deborah and Victor lifted the small body into the box, and they all sat about the casket, studying her face.

"I swear, through the toughest times and in death, well, there she is, always smiling," August said.

"Many times her smile and those loving arms helped me," Deborah said.

Victor nodded. "Me too." He looked at Deborah. "I told Jonathan in a recent letter … I told him he probably wouldn't get to see her one last time, so to remember her as she was. I told him to remember a time when Audrey took the lid off the cookie jar to offer him one."

August laughed. "Yessir, many a time … Jonathan, David, and even darling Half Shell at the cookie jar." After a brief silence, he added, "And all of John's boys."

Victor got up to look out the window. When he turned to face the old man, August said, "I know, I know. We've got to nail this box tight. The storm isn't letting up." August and Deborah helped by holding the lid snug. Victor nailed the coffin, and then they left the room, closing the door behind them.

The dust storm stopped after three days and another night. Victor left to drive about the community, letting people know about Audrey and to inform Carl Hocksmith. He arranged for some men to help him dig the grave in the little graveyard in the grove of trees behind the sod house.

Deborah brought a ham from the smokehouse and set it to baking with squash. With Mary's help, she cleaned the house, sweeping and dusting, gathering the dirt into a wheat shovel. By hand, she washed the bedding on Audrey's bed and hung it out. For now—in the middle of the afternoon—the wind was still and the sky a cold blue. The sheets froze as soon as she had them hung, and her hands turned red and sore. Out by the clothesline, she could hear men in the grove talking as they dug the grave. The shovels and pickaxes grated on the soil, and the sounds rang out in the frigid air.

As she had done so many times, Deborah worked as though separate from her body, moving from task to task, trying not to think. Each time the clock chimed, she listened for Audrey's voice. "Deborah, my girl, sweet girl, look what you did for me and August." But the voice never came. Mary helped her scoop and sweep the front porch. Neighbors arrived, their trucks and cars stirring up more dust.

August looked about the front yard, his face as dismal as the sight. "I got to uncover the flowerbeds someday. Can't let Audrey's flowers smother." One earflap up, one down on his hat and his wool muffler blowing about, he stood unaware in the frosty breeze. His face was gray with whisker growth and dust. Deborah encouraged him into the kitchen, where she poured hot water in the washbasin and handed him his soap brush and cup.

Victor saw the old man's hands trembling, so he set him down in a chair. "Let me shave you, old friend. If Audrey were here, she'd shave you because she'd notice you're awful tired."

August's tears made runnels through the soap on his cheeks.

Deborah became aware of her own griminess and hurried to put away the broom and wash her face and hands. Death was never expected, and because of its unexpected nature, life around them had to continue. Victor brought milk from the well house, and Mary sliced bread, while Moses carried wood and coal for the stove. Everyone kept moving, doing the routine tasks.

Others came, crowding their food onto the kitchen table, standing about with cups of coffee to warm themselves. She watched August shaking the hands of his neighbors. They comforted him while all along he was comforting them.

I thought she would live as long as I needed her ... until the day I died, I suppose. It came as a shock to me that she died before August. I guess I always thought they would go together. That way one wouldn't be left behind, the way Lendel and Christian left me behind in my dream. One wouldn't be left to cry, always looking, listening.

She isn't lonely. All the children are with her.

Chapter 14

Hitler

With the arrival of spring and then summer, Deborah and Victor set up a routine, which included August in their every move. Victor walked the short distance to August's ranch early each morning and always found him at work with his team, standing on a box to curry the big horses and talk to them in gentle undertones. Together, they would hitch the horses to August's wagon and drive to Deborah's place to do chores and have breakfast.

He seemed feebler since Audrey's death, and he walked with a stiff-legged gait, lifting his feet high as though afraid of stumbling over something. Sometimes in the middle of a conversation, he stopped what he was saying and would cock his head. Deborah wondered if he listened for Audrey. Victor and Deborah checked on him often. They viewed him at almost ninety years of age much the way they would a child. It was important to keep him safe and well.

August decided one of his jobs was to take care of the chickens, and often they could hear his voice coming from the henhouse. He even took on David's old job of setting the biddies and watching over the little hatched ones. "Now, I know why the boy loved the chore so much. I guess I never took the time before to see what it's like to do for something so small and weak as a baby chick."

He seemed happy despite his loneliness for Audrey. He reminded them, "She's with us. Remember how she said if she was in our thoughts, it meant she was with us. Well, she's with us all the time, because I sure think of her all the time."

The old man also took on the churning of butter and produced perfect bricks imprinted with a leaf design. Like Victor, he could mix and bake bread and sometimes surprised them with a cake. On a Sunday in June, Deborah turned the tables on August and baked a cake for his ninetieth birthday. Neighbors came to spend the afternoon, and Victor brought a block of ice from town for ice cream. August was the happiest they had seen him since Audrey's death.

Deborah and Victor went about their heavy, hard work, and August didn't seem to notice they left only the lighter tasks for him. They kept him busy, and he was doing what he was able. He had decided to not plant anything in his own garden and sometimes worked with Deborah's vegetables. When he wasn't doing that, he used his beloved team of horses to pull a full tank of water to a shelterbelt that Victor and Deborah watered.

He kept them supplied with both water and information. Each day, he read the newspaper and reported what was happening with the nation's Depression. "John's in a crowd when it comes to working for the WPA. They're building buildings, roads, and everything. Did you know the government's even paying artists and writers to paint and write? Isn't that something?"

Often there wasn't time to respond before August chattered on. "I envy young folks today who are going to see the good of Social Security in their old age. That was a smart move on the part of the government. I just think they've got to see to it farmers get to be a part of it."

"We've got to start earning a living first," grumbled Victor.

"It'll happen, son. It'll happen."

There were some significant rains in June, a good three inches over a two-week period, and with the mulches, their garden and corn thrived. August thought the sudan and kaffir crops looked the best he'd ever seen. "Those terraces! That was the smartest thing you ever did, daughter."

They discovered the old man, though slow with slightly trembling hands, was an expert at dressing and canning chickens. "It's all my experience at butchering hogs. I wish I had a dollar for every hog I done butchered."

Deborah grinned. "But how come you never let us know about your chicken-butchering talent before? How come the rest of us did the butchering and, as you would say, never saw hide nor hair of you?"

He grinned sheepishly. "I reckon I was busy doing important things."

Sometimes August saddled his horse and rode about the nearby countryside. "Got to check out my neighbors and see what's doing with them," he said. One day in September, he came back, a worried look on his face. "That there Reub, he's planting wheat."

"He must have gotten the inch of rain we got last week," Victor said.

"He did. He sure enough did. But what's worrying me, where's the next rain going to come from? What if it doesn't come? We've only had enough to wet the surface—nothing for the subsoil. We've had the usual drying wind since then and hot sun, and a wheat field don't use mulch like you use.

"Then Reub, daggone that feller. He said he borrowed every cent the seed cost him, and I'm not going tell you the interest he's paying. If he doesn't make a crop, he's ruined, is my thinking." He shook his head in dismay.

"He must be desperate," Deborah said, "to put himself in such a fix."

"He must be desperate," August echoed.

In October, the area received a half inch of rain, and August said Reub was confident. But there was no more moisture the rest of 1937. Reub's wheat never sprouted.

Deborah often thought of Nila and Reub Meyers after that. She remembered Nila's anger when Reub plowed more of their pastureland not long after their new baby was born. She had gone to see Nila.

"He didn't ask my opinion," Nila had come close to shouting to Deborah. "Just more land to blow when the wind comes up! It didn't blow when it was in grass!" Nila was almost hysterical.

Deborah had risked moving close to Nila, wanting to hug her.

Nila had shoved her back. "Don't! Don't touch me. I don't need that! Never did!" Fiery red spots had appeared on her face. She had been holding her baby and put him down on the divan hard, too hard, making him cry. Then she shut herself in her bedroom. Deborah had picked up the baby and comforted him, walking the floor until he fell asleep. She had taken the baby to Nila and placed him beside the sleeping woman.

On New Year's Eve, Deborah and Victor had his cousin's little bottle of chokecherry wine with Minnesota cheese and crackers. Victor had built a fire, and, as usual, they sat on the divan listening to dance music on the radio. Before long, they were in a heated discussion as they debated the government's position on neutrality.

"How can our country sit back and watch Hitler do what he's doing? Victor, how can we?" The platter of cheese was on the divan between them, and she worked at cutting small slices.

He argued back. "How can we get involved like we did in the Great War and have so many American men killed or injured for life? Just look at the bad memories someone like John Strate has."

"Victor, it's horrible what Hitler is doing. And Japan has bombed an oil tanker over by China and killed three Americans. We can't just take their apology and think it won't happen again. Be reasonable."

He sighed deeply. "I am being reasonable. I hate war." He spoke with such conviction that Deborah looked up, startled. She put down the cheese knife and listened.

"I've always hated bullies and fighting." He emphasized what he was saying by thumping his fist in his open hand. "Bullies are people who prey on the weaker in order to make themselves feel bigger and better. They don't take on someone bigger than themselves, and they don't try to protect those in need of protection."

"But, Victor, in this case the bully is Hitler, not the United States."

He was silent for a long while. "I guess you've got me there. I guess all I can say is I hate violence. I hate killing."

"Which is what Hitler is doing in Germany. Which is what Japan is doing in China."

Again, he was silent for some time. Then he said, "I hate war so much I forget the many reasons a war can be fought."

She touched his hand. "I agree fighting isn't the answer. There must be alternatives."

His face was dismal. "You and I were just kids during the Great War. I'm not a kid this time if there's another war."

She suddenly comprehended what he had said. "Oh, Victor, Christian said practically the same thing to me—nine, ten years ago." She clutched his fingers. "No. Don't say anything more about war."

"Well," he said with forced cheerfulness. "This is New Year's Eve. Right. Let's talk about something else. Let's look ahead to 1938."

They made small talk and played their usual game of Chinese checkers. Victor brought out the little container of fudge, setting aside a piece for his horse. They laughed and she said, "We're such creatures of habit."

Deborah felt his eyes on her, and she saw the small movement of the muscles in his jaws, indicating he was working up to say something. She beat him to it. "I know what you're going to say."

"Seven years," he said. "Actually, three months ago it was seven years."

"Yes." Sudden tears came to her eyes.

"Deborah?" He was concerned.

"I have never been so mixed up in my life. I'm so scared of Stoddel. If I could just get the boys home." She walked restlessly about the room. "Years ago, looking ahead I figured the drought would be over by now. I thought farm prices would be straightened out. But look at us. Everything has just gotten worse. We lost David and Audrey. I don't dare bring the boys home. There's no sign of letup in the drought or the Depression. Look at the world situation. I'm scared to death of what may be developing. And there's Stoddel."

"We could marry now," he said. "Being together, we could face things together."

She pictured Stoddel with his fingers tapping his gun handle. "We're already together."

"You know what I mean, Deborah. I want a home with a family. I want someone to show me love in ways we don't dare show one another right now. Dear girl, I want to be able to touch you without being afraid I'll do something wrong. I want to forget Stoddel and how he's controlling us." Victor moved restlessly, and his shoulders sagged.

"I'm sorry," she whispered. She knew he was remembering their shock as they had returned from August's ranch the day before. They had taken a team and wagon to haul some coal to the old man's coal bin and get some canned produce from his storm cellar, leaving August behind to nap near the warmth of her stove.

They had just finished loading when Victor said, "Well, damnation."

Stoddel's car was just leaving Deborah's lane and heading south toward town. Alarmed, she asked, "What was he doing at my place?"

"I don't know, but we'd better check on August."

They hurried back to her farm, and when they parked near the homestead tree, August was standing in the yard. The earflaps on his hat loosely flopped, and he hadn't buttoned his coat. His heavy breaths steamed into the frigid air. "The jackass." The old man's face was red, and he stomped back and forth in the yard.

"What happened? What did he want?" Deborah asked. She stopped his pacing long enough to button his coat and fasten his hat.

"I was sleeping and heard the dogs barking. Stoddel had driven in and was sitting in his car, just watching the dogs. When I came out of the house, Marco and Jake settled down, and he got out. I asked him what he wanted. He didn't answer. He barely said a word the whole time he was here." August jabbed his clenched fist in the air. "You know what he did? He started searching places."

"What for?" Victor asked.

"Who knows. He never said a word. He went through the machine shop, the barn, one of the grain bins. Just one. Don't ask me why. He wouldn't talk. He wouldn't answer my questions. Then he found the swimming tank. Just a stock tank where all those darling boys paddled around to cool off and give themselves a little pleasure time from the hard work. That really got him going."

"What about it?" Deborah saw the old man's gloves in his coat pocket and helped him put them on.

"You know how we've got a tarp over it for the winter and of course the fence around it with the padlocked gate. 'What's in there?' he asked. I told him it was a swimming tank for the little boys. He looked at the padlock. I told him we padlocked it for safety reasons. He told me to unlock it. I told him the truth. I didn't know where the key was. You know what he did? He went to his car and got his lug wrench. He just ripped the locked clasp right off the post."

August was getting mad all over again, and Deborah hugged him and patted his back. "The whole time he was doing it, I told him over and over what was under the tarp and why the gate was locked. He went ahead and did what he wanted."

The old man led them to the fenced area behind the well house. The clasp and padlock dangled from the gate that swung in the wind. The tarp had been pulled back from the tank.

Deborah looked about, and her heart felt as chilled as her face in the cold air. "What did he expect to find?"

"Near as I could tell, he must've been looking for Christian, for his body. I don't really know. He doesn't make sense. What's he up to?" Tears rolled down his face.

"It's okay, old friend." Victor put his arm around August's shoulders. "Deborah's going to cover the tank, and I'll get a hammer and nails. We'll fix things up."

"This is something I'm never going to forget." August swung his head back and forth. "For the life of me, I don't understand the man. Wouldn't you think, if he was really serious about looking for something, he'd search other places too? Places that make more sense? Why one bin? Why not all of them? That sort of thing. Besides, after all these years, does he expect to find a body settin' out in plain sight? Settin' in a swimmin' tank? I don't understand. His mind is worse than sick, I do believe. I don't understand."

"Neither do we, old friend," Victor straightened the bent clasp with his pliers.

They fixed the gate, unharnesssed the horses, and took August to the warm house. It was some time before the old man calmed down. He kept asking, "What does he want from you folks?" They couldn't answer his question, and here they were, mulling it over on New Year's Eve.

"Why does Stoddel have to upset an old man?" Victor tiredly lifted himself from the divan. "I'm sorry, Deborah. I've ruined our New Year's Eve. I'd better go." He slowly picked up the tin with its one piece of fudge. "My pony's waiting for her treat."

She stood in the bay window, still thinking about Stoddel, looking out and feeling the cold of the night seeping through the glass. She heard Victor go into the kitchen and put on his coat. He didn't come back to kiss her as he had other New Year's Eves, and she didn't allow herself to turn to him. She heard him call softly, "See you in the morning, Deborah. I love you."

Chapter 15

Fighting Depression

When she knew Victor was gone, Deborah went to her bedroom long enough to get Grandfather Blue Sky's blanket. Back on the divan, she curled up before the faintly glowing embers of the fireplace. She felt the danger in what she was doing because it reminded her of the time she was so ill with depression. When the kerosene lamp finally burned the last of its fuel, the oil fumes lingered in the darkness. She didn't sleep.

A confusion of images rushed into Deborah's mind as loneliness came, memories painful and guaranteed, as Audrey would have said, to put salt in old wounds. Once the flow of pictures began, she found it impossible to stop them. At first, she remembered David's body in his casket and then how the stillborn baby had looked as Victor placed her in the little box. The pictures were juxtaposed with a delightful photograph from Minnesota of Jonathan and Baby Half Shell, happy and healthy. But then unreal—yet so realistic—images of Jonathan and Baby in caskets jumped out of the shadows of her mind, and she sat up on the divan, shaking herself to get rid of them. Following these images was Victor's face, relaxed and warm, as he had appeared earlier in the evening, contrasted with the sad longing in his eyes as he prepared to leave. He had not kissed her, and she knew that had been her fault. She wished she had turned to him.

This would be the first New Year's Day with no boys, no toys and games, no fireworks or homemade ice cream. It was August's first New Year's Day without Audrey. The day also represented the ending of one more year she and Victor had not been married. The thoughts made her tired, yet she was unable to sleep. She began to see the tiredness was lethargy, and it frightened her.

Deborah, knowing she had to get up, struggled to remove Grandfather's blanket. She needed activity to drive the shadows out of her mind. She tried to fold the blanket and succeeded in only bunching it up. Feeling the necessity to do it right, she tried again. Precisely matching corners, smoothing creases, she folded the blanket neatly in half, a quarter, and an eighth. Feeling her way to her bed, she placed it carefully at its foot. Something seemed to have control of her body, dragging her down until she found it difficult to move. She willed herself to carry out the plan she had.

Lighting a kerosene lamp, she saw its globe was smoky and in need of washing and polishing, so she gathered all of the lamps and began scrubbing the fragile globes in hot, soapy water, polishing them dry. She trimmed the wicks evenly, neatly. Some of the lamps needed refilling with kerosene, and she poured fuel into the glass basins. She did not spill a drop of fuel, yet she used a warm, soapy rag to wipe the bases of all the lamps. Her meticulous work was deliberate, something she felt she must do to gain control of her mind and action.

Taking the oiled mop from the pantry, Deborah began polishing the oak floor of the living room, beginning where David's casket had been in the bay window and working her way to the small parlor table, her fingertips tracing over the edges of frames holding images of people dearest to her. She moved the large Hopi pottery pieces, which sat on the floor, and mopped beneath them. When she carried the smaller Indian rugs outside to shake them, Marco met her at the kitchen steps, and she stopped to stroke his head and look at the clear sky with its cold, hard glint of stars and slice of moon. The first hours of the new year were frigid, and she hurried back inside to stoke the kitchen range and begin mixing yeast dough for rolls.

After she had shoveled the gray, barely warm fireplace ashes into the coal scuttle, she laid a fire but didn't light it. She pulled the dining room table closer to the fireplace and could smell the yeastiness of the cinnamon rolls she had set to raise on the kitchen range. The polished floor in the room glinted where the lamplight reached. When the fireplace was lit, the room would be warm.

Deborah was distracting her thoughts and preparing a special breakfast for New Years Day. She couldn't bring her boys home today or solve the problem of harassment from Stoddel, but she could make the day happier for August and Victor. She remembered how August had said he missed Audrey's cinnamon rolls. "She made them for special times, sad times, happy times. I recall how we had rolls when we got word of our boy. Another time we celebrated a good sale of cattle. She was even baking rolls when she realized she was having one of our babies too soon. She saw to it I took them out of the oven at the right time."

He had smiled sadly. "We always had hot cinnamon rolls for breakfast the day of our wedding anniversary."

Today August would have his cinnamon rolls along with the memories they might bring—sad or happy—with slices of sugar ham from Minnesota and warm, baked custard. She filled a cut-glass bowl with golden half globes of peaches from their last jar of the fruit and set them in the middle of the table. That too was something Audrey would have done. She was also preparing another fruit dish, Swedish fruit soup made with dried apples, apricots, plums, and pears swimming among plump pearls of tapioca, something Meredith and Lillian would do. At the last, she added a bit of lemon, for Calvin had sent a crate of citrus fruits for Christmas.

The beginning sunlight was cold and gray when the men arrived to do the chores. Deborah didn't go outside to help them. She removed the custard and rolls from the oven and prepared to put in the turkey. Calvin had sent the sugar ham and Frank the homegrown turkey. Yesterday, she had thawed the large bird and fixed a bread stuffing.

In her bedroom, she brushed her hair, leaving it loose the way Victor liked, and put on clean jeans and the blouse he always complimented. She did something she hadn't done for years. In her drawer was a tiny bottle of perfume, and she touched a minute amount behind her ear. It was the beginning of 1938, and she was going to make the best of it.

When Deborah had spread the boiled icing with its touch of lemon on the rolls, she lit the fireplace. The men came in, bringing with them frosty air and the odors of the barn and warm milk.

"Daughter, I've never known it to smell so good in here of an early morning." August quickly washed and came to kiss her cheek. "Happy 1938!"

Victor grinned at her from behind a towel. "It does smell good. I'll be darned if I can figure it all out." She pushed the towel aside, placed his arms around her, and gave him the kiss she should have given him the night before. "Well," he said softly.

August hadn't even noticed, for he was bent over the table by the fireplace. "Cinnamon rolls," he said. "I see them on this here table, and I can tell from the melted frosting they're warm just the way I like them."

"Then you hurry and sit down," Victor said. "It looks like everything is ready."

They took their time eating the meal, and Deborah made a second pot of coffee. "It's downhill, folks," August was saying. "The year 1938 is going to be downhill. We're over the worst of it, this drought. I can just feel it. The blowing will be stopping soon."

"I sure hope so," Victor said. "I sure hope so." Deborah could tell he was struggling to sound positive.

August had heard Reub Meyer was barely holding on by dickering and bickering with the bank where he had borrowed.

"Poor sucker," Victor said.

August said, "Reub's a good man. I hate to see him go this way. It isn't dignified. If he could have grown a crop, wheat's eighty cents a bushel right now."

"His oldest boy, he quit school," Victor said. "He's gone to work for the WPA or something like that. Maybe they'll make it yet."

After breakfast, August dozed in front of the warm fireplace, and Victor helped Deborah with the dishes. They talked easily and just as easily were silent at times as they worked together. Hours later, they ate a turkey dinner, and August proclaimed the mincemeat pie to be just as good as Audrey's. The old man slept again.

When Deborah reached for the bucket of garbage, Victor said, "Here, let me take it out for you."

"I'll go with you," she said, and they dressed for the out-of-doors. She tucked her hair up under her cap.

Victor said, "Your hair is beautiful, long like that."

She grinned. "So is yours. I need to give you a haircut."

They fed Marco and the hogs and took brushes and currycombs into the corral where the horses crowded around, patiently waiting for their share of attention. Dumper dozed in the weak sunlight, a knee bent, resting his leg by tilting the tip of one hoof on the ground.

"When I see a horse do that," Deborah said, "I always think of a ballerina about to dance."

Victor stood back to look at the pony. "A ballerina about to outgrow her little skirt maybe."

Deborah felt a little silly when she too moved back to look. Dumper stood with drooping head, his long nose grizzled with a winter's growth of gray hair, and blew steam into the air. "A ballerina with hairy legs maybe."

Victor laughed. "A ballerina asleep on her feet maybe."

They looked at each other over the pony's back. Victor reached out to grasp Deborah's shoulders and pulled her closer. He leaned across Dumper to hug her. "I love you so much, Deborah Jorgenson Nelson."

She tilted her head back to look at his face. "I love you, Victor Whitesong. We've got to get the boys home. We need to have the boys here."

"That damned Stoddel," he said.

She felt the usual chill at mention of the sheriff's name. "Yes."

"I want the boys back too," he said. He kissed her long and softly, yet in a demanding way, causing her to grasp him behind his head where she smoothed the too-long hair that curled on his neck. When Dumper moved restlessly between them, they released one another.

"Did you like that, Dumper?" Victor asked. "I sure did."

They finished brushing the horses and walked to the house, their arms around one another's waists. Deborah liked the feel of Victor's hip against hers and wished the walk were longer.

"Do you think August is right?" Victor was asking. "Do you suppose his feeling is a real one—that the drought is over?"

I don't dare to hope. We keep busy, doing winter work on all three farmsteads. Victor and I have even been doing some reading together. And of course we write lots of letters to the boys and the folks. Even August writes to Jonathan. Jonathan says the letters are good, showing the old man is alert and very aware of what's going on around him. Very aware? That means he's keeping an eye on Victor and me!

Chapter 16

The Sod House

The 1938 winds started early. The first one hit the second week of January, loosening the soil, tearing out by the roots what little wheat there was on other farms. When the first blow began, Deborah knew Victor sensed the pain she was feeling. She put her arms around him, holding him desperately tight.

"How many years, Victor? How many years is this going to continue?"

The boys seemed farther away than ever. Deborah worked hard to control her loneliness for Baby and Jonathan. "You could go visit them," Victor said one day. A sudden light came into his eyes. "Why didn't we think of it sooner?"

"And leave you with all the work. No."

"But now's the time. Before spring work begins. You could be back before the soil warms up."

"No. I can't leave you and August alone in this blowing dust." She knew he wouldn't argue with that. "I can't leave you, dear man."

On a day in early March, Deborah woke with an uneasy feeling in the pit of her stomach. Suspecting a windstorm, she listened for its usual noise. It was quiet, almost too quiet, and she dressed quickly, looking about the house, not expecting to find anything wrong, but she worried anyhow. Victor had left the day before to visit his parents for their anniversary celebration and was due back by this evening. She had stayed behind with August, planning to join the old man for noontime dinner and an afternoon of cleaning his house.

She went out to do the chores and made certain the livestock were all right. Even the sky was clear, and there was only a gentle breeze making the air moderately cold. There was very little ice to chop in the water tank, and she barely worked up a sweat in her heavy coat. Marco, seemingly undisturbed, followed her about naturally, so her anxiety must be due to not having Victor with her.

After feeding the hogs, Deborah walked beyond the corral, looking toward August's place. Was everything good with him? Other than his frail appearance, August had seemed energetic enough yesterday. There was activity at his ranch this morning. She knew because she had seen him go about his work. But just to be certain, she decided to check on him after breakfast instead of waiting until noon.

She had to put her plan aside. The hogs were a problem after breakfast. Somehow they had pushed a plank loose, and all three now rambled around the grain bins, their rooting noses having little effect on the frozen ground. With Marco's help she got them back in, but fixing the fence took considerably more time. The source of the trouble was the bottom plank, which had split away from the nails. It would probably let the hogs out again if she didn't replace it. Leaving Marco by the pen to watch, she went in search of a board. Walking about the old woodpile, she hesitated here and there, looking. Seeing a board she thought might be the answer, she moved closer. There was wood rot on both ends of the old plank.

As Deborah went toward the shop, she looked again toward August's place. This time she saw him on his riding horse, and she could tell he was following the fence line between her shelterbelt and his pasture.

There was no lumber of the right size in the shop loft. Deborah cut two-by-fours and spliced the broken board. She worked quickly, sometimes glancing about her, again wondering why she felt the way she did—a shaky, unsteady feeling in her stomach and tenseness about her chest. One of the hogs, a big, high-backed gilt, watched her work with what she thought was a look of renewed determination. She'd better fix the plank well and maybe check the other rails.

The hog seemed confident. "Don't even think about it," she warned. Marco wagged his tail at the sound of her voice.

By the time Deborah had finished, noontime was close. She hurried to the house. That morning she had heated sour milk and left the curds draining in a cheesecloth bag. She hastily mixed the cottage cheese with sour cream and added a bit of yellow-green tops from an onion that had sprouted in the root cellar. She knew it would taste a little like spring to August. "Just like Mama made," August would undoubtedly say. Whether Mama was his mother or Audrey, she was never certain, but she did know it was his greatest compliment.

She had just covered the cheese bowl with a tea towel and was putting on her coat when wind struck the house. So that was what had been making her feel the way she did. If she had noticed the barometer, she might have known. Deborah set the bowl down and looked out the window. The visibility wasn't poor yet, but from the sounds, the blow was going to be a bad one. She put on a hooded sweatshirt and her coat over that. When she stepped outside, the wind was worse than she had realized. It blew from the northwest, cold and hard. Carrying the bowl of cheese, she ran to the shed to start the truck.

At the end of the lane, she wondered if she had been foolish for leaving home. But she kept going. If she were stormed in with August, that would be all right. Her livestock were okay, unless this was a seriously long storm. She drove faster, suddenly feeling an even greater pressure to get there. It was the wind—always the incessant wind—driving her before it like just one more particle of dust.

And then, just before turning into the Goodman lane, Deborah saw the big, rolling cloud of dust to the west, looking so much like the very first black blizzard in 1935 that had frightened everybody. It was towering, moving fast, and would soon shut out the late noon sun. Her heart seemed to skip beats, and she prayed August had already seen the cloud and was in the house or at least close to it. She increased her speed, the truck's wheels spinning in the gravel and dirt of the lane, and drove into his yard, parking close to the front gate. Already the light was being shut down, and the oppressive increase in dust was choking her.

She looked toward the house, expecting to see the old man at the door or on the porch. But what she saw sent a jolt of fear through her, and she struggled against the wind, which held her truck door shut. She got it open and literally flung herself out. The wind closed the door for her, jerking her shoulder and bruising her arm. The northwest corner of the sod house, where the kitchen was located, was partly caved in. About halfway up the wall, the sod had buckled inward, taking the roof with it. Even a window was ruined, its frame broken and the panes shattered.

"August!" She screamed as she ran through the yard and up to the door. "August!" The screened door wouldn't open due to the warped pressure of the door frame above. She threw her body at the door, and it released, causing her to lose her balance. The screen ripped away from its braces. She had to kick and throw herself against the second door, and when she got it open, cracked plaster and chunks of sod crumbled down on her head. She choked from powdered plaster. Inside, she could barely see. Dirt was blowing through the caved area.

She called, "August." There was no answer. He might not even be in the house. He still could be on his horse, trapped in the storm. Then she remembered she had seen the gelding in August's corral when she finished repairing the hog pen.

Fumbling about, Deborah ran her hands over the kitchen table, expecting to find a kerosene lamp. The shelf—Audrey, and probably August as well had washed lamps every morning, putting them on a shelf above the stove until they were needed again. The match holder would be on the wall near the stove.

She was relieved when one of her hands touched the matches and the other a lantern. She turned her back to the wind and crouched down between the stove and a cabinet, struggling to light the lantern, afraid of what she might see. But the lantern barely helped, the room was so full of dust. The wind howled through the broken walls and window, and she crept about, leaning her weight against the force of the wind, calling for August. The dust stung her eyes.

He was on the floor, next to the caved corner, and she had probably come close to stepping on him when she went to the stove. He was face down, and nearby were some two-by-fours, a hammer, and a saw. It appeared he had been trying to brace the wall. She put the lantern on the floor. Apparently nothing had fallen on him. She turned him over—oh, he was frail, not heavy at all—and put her ear to his chest. His breathing was uneven. His eyes were closed, and he didn't answer.

Deborah sat August up and, bending her knees, grasped him under his arms. Her shoulder that had just been jerked in the truck door pained her, but she was able to pull him toward his bedroom. August was small for a man, but she was still surprised at his light weight as she lifted him to where she could put him in his bed. After finding her way back to get the almost useless lantern, she undressed the old man to his long underwear and then covered him. His breathing was not good, and she put a second pillow under his head, thinking it might help. Was it his heart?

"August? August, can you hear me?" He didn't respond.

She needed Hocksmith, but there was no way she could go or even take

August, for she could barely see in front of her face, let alone out on a road. Victor—if only he were here—Victor would know what to do.

She went to the kitchen to get water and was almost afraid to enter the room. She could see more of the wall had caved, and the wind came close to bowling her over. The curtains on the north and east windows flailed and snapped in the air, and the back door banged, its latch broken. If she didn't get to the pump now, she might not be able to reach the water later. Glass crunched under her feet as she made her way to the sink. As she pumped, the wind blew water everywhere. She managed to fill a washbasin and grabbed a tea towel, rushing back to the bedroom, the slopping basin in one hand and the lantern in the other.

Deborah washed August's face and tied his bandana over his nose and mouth. After rinsing out her own eyes, she replaced her bandana, for even with the bedroom door closed and a rug shoved against the crack, the room was full of dust. She peered closely at his lips but couldn't see in the darkness.

Sitting on the side of the bed, Deborah held August's hands and talked to him, hoping if he heard anything, it was her voice, not the destructive wind. "I must look like a raccoon with the rings around my eyes." She talked about Audrey, how she missed her. She held his hands and touched them to her cheeks.

Hours went by. The wind blew as hard as ever, and she was too much of a coward to check the fallen wall and roof. Every creak in the house and roar of the wind frightened her, and she had visions of the ceiling falling on the bed. She sat with her upper body hovering near August, hoping to protect him if anything did fall.

She continued talking, recalling how she had first met August and Audrey. "That was 1929, going on nine years ago. You both stood at my yard gate. Audrey was holding a pot of Boston baked beans, and you had a box of cleaning cloths and homemade soap. I thought the two of you had the sweetest smiles I had ever seen. I should have said this to you long before now. I have always felt like you and Audrey were mother and dad to me. Do you hear me, August? I want you to know that."

The sick man did not answer.

The wind seemed to howl louder than ever, and she got up to look out the window. There was nothing to see except darkness, and, by the window, there was an even stronger smell of dust.

She sat with August again, and his flesh was tightly drawn over the bones of his face, his eyes more deeply sunk. Uncertain as to how much time had gone by, she continued watching him and talking. Despite all the noise outside, the room seemed to become still, and the quiet was a background to the raspy breathing of the old man. And then, even the breaths seemed to grow quieter, each rattling sound further and further apart.

"August, don't leave us. I'm selfish, I know, but I want you to stay." She bent to rest her head on his chest.

A banging from the other room sent her body rigid, and she clutched the old man's shoulders, her face hidden against his shirt. "Dear God, don't let him suffer more than he has already. Don't let the house fall."

"Deborah?"

Someone struggled with the windblown door of the bedroom. "Victor!" Her eyes wide, she stared at him as he came close to the bed. "I thought the noise was more of the house falling."

"I had trouble opening the front door. August! Did the wall fall on him?"

"No. It looked like he had been trying to brace it. I suppose it's his heart." For the first time since she had arrived, Deborah began to cry, and she felt her courage leaving. "He's dying, Victor."

He knelt beside the bed, touching August's arm. "We're here, old friend. You go if you have to go." Tears were in his voice.

"I wish there was something we could do," she said. "How on earth did you get here?"

"I left my folks this morning. Got as far as Cressler's when it hit. Kept going. Drove right into my yard, and the engine quit. What luck. Had to find my way to the house and get a flour sack. I put it over my head and struck out across August's windbreak. Didn't have much trouble until I ran smack into the hood of your truck. Sure confused me for a minute. You would've laughed, August. I wondered where I was, and when I got on the porch and felt around, I thought the house had been hit by a bomb. You should've told me you were going to redecorate, old friend."

Then Victor cried out, "Damn the wind! Damn the dirt!"

Deborah held his hand tightly and reached to stroke August's forehead, smoothing his hair back. "All morning I felt something was wrong or about to happen. I could see him moving about before the wind came. I got here just as the storm turned black." She kissed the old man's cheek through the handkerchief.

He died soon after.

Victor shouted again, "Damn the wind! Why did it have to hurt

August? It just isn't right. No one can die with dignity anymore. Look at how many have died because of the wind and the dust."

Deborah removed the bandana from the old man's face and pulled the bedsheet over his head. She straightened the blanket and a colorful quilt. "See this quilt?" She choked. "Audrey made this. She said someday I would have her pretties, as she called them. This quilt is one of them. I'd much rather have August and Audrey."

From his sitting position on the floor, Victor clasped her legs and pressed his face against her knees. "They were so good to me, to everyone," he said, his voice muffled.

"Such good people," she whispered, pressing her cheek against the top of his head. "I couldn't have made it all these years without them."

They stayed that way, locked in the awkward but comforting embrace. Then noise from the kitchen area jerked them upright. "Oh my God," Victor said, "the whole house could cave in on us. We've got to do something."

The bedroom door rattled on its hinges, and Deborah's eyes widened. "What can we do? We can't go anywhere."

"We could go to the barn, but it lets in an awful lot of dust. No telling how long this will last." He snapped his fingers. "I've got it. Let's get in your truck. That's about as dust tight as any place."

"I won't leave him. Everything could fall on him. Like you say, he should be allowed some dignity."

"Then we'll take him to the truck too. Let's wrap his body in these blankets and put him in the back of the truck."

"Victor, not out in the open like that."

"There's no room in the cab with us. How can you say he'd be out in the open, wrapped up good in a blanket? Nothing will fall on him there, and in here the whole house could go any minute."

She jumped into action. "I won't let it happen to him. Help me wrap him."

They blew out the useless lantern, and Victor carried the body. Deborah held his arm, trying to guide them. As they went through the front door, they heard more falling noises in the kitchen. On the porch, she could hear creaking, swaying sounds from the porch roof. She led them down the steps. The wind jerked at the handkerchief tied over her nose and mouth, and dust stung her closed eyes. They fumbled their way out the front gate to the rear end of the truck. Victor grunted as he lifted and pushed the body into the truck bed.

She tugged at his arm. "Do we have to leave him there like that? It doesn't seem right."

"Deborah," and the wind tried to whip his words away, "can't you see? August would be the first to tell us to use our sense and get in out of this." He was choking from the dust.

Her shoulders slumped in recognition of his reasoning, and she felt her way to the cab side that was sheltered away from the wind. The cab filled with dust as they got in, and when she pushed herself across the bench seat to make room for Victor, her fingers drew away from the dust-on-metal of the dashboard. She settled in the seat and felt the truck shudder in the buffeting wind.

"Victor?" Deborah's voice quavered. "I was scared in the house, but this scares me too."

"I don't think we need worry. I believe your truck can handle a wind like this. Have you got a water jug? We'd better dampen our face cloths. What—what the devil is this?" He fumbled at something on the seat.

"It's a bowl of cottage cheese. I was bringing it for August."

He laughed. "We're probably giving the old man plenty to laugh about."

She could barely see in the darkness but could tell he was removing the dishtowel. "What are you doing?"

"Well, August would say don't let it go to waste, and I'm hungry." He dipped his fingers into the cheese. "It's good."

"Your hands are dirty."

"Gotta eat my bushel—"

"—of dirt," she finished. "Let me have some. I'm starving too."

Both of them felt desperately tired, and it was cold in the truck. "How stupid of me," Deborah said. "I should have thought to bring blankets from the house."

The wind made a constant sound through the hood. "You can be sure if it's whistling through the vents, it's also letting in dust," Victor said.

They tried resting their heads on the back of the truck seat, but the position was uncomfortable. "Deborah, this is ridiculous, the two of us sitting up in this truck. Let's stretch out on the seat, get some sleep, and keep one another warm. I'm bone tired."

They lay spoon fashion with their knees bent. His arm over her side was comforting, his body warm against her. His breath warmed the back of her neck. The buffeting of the truck was like the motion of a rocking cradle. They slept.

When Deborah woke at the first hint of light, the storm was still howling about them, and Victor was sitting up. "Did you sleep?" she asked.

"I sure did." Victor dampened their face cloths again, and she felt feverish. When they talked, they both gasped for clean air.

Two hours later, the wind began to let up and the blackness slowly eased. "If the wind had gotten no worse than it is now, the wall probably wouldn't have blown in," Deborah said bitterly. "August would still be alive. How many years, sixty? That sod house has stood sixty years, and then a stupid windstorm blows it in. Built double thick."

"It may have fallen even before the wind hit, Deborah. From what you say, he had time to get the boards and tools. August always said there was only one chance in a million it stood this long. He did his share of repairs on it."

"I know. Thank God Audrey didn't live to see it happen."

"She knows."

"Yes, I suppose she does. At least they're together now. August missed her terribly."

When the storm had let up enough that they felt safe to drive, Victor asked, "Can I use your car to take August to town? I'd rather put his body in a car than the bed of the truck."

"Oh, yes. Let's get him out of the truck bed."

Victor managed to start the truck. The trip home was dismal and discouraging. Where piles of dirt had been, there were bare spots, while drifts had formed in new places, and as usual the ditches had caught a great share of it. Because the wind still blew, eddies of dust filled the air.

"It's not a pretty sight," Victor commented as he drove up the lane.

"I left the barn and the hog shed open, and I'm sure plenty blew in. I'm worried about how the stock fared." Deborah sighed wearily. "It seems like far more than twenty-four hours since I chored because so much has happened."

He cranked the car, and she backed it out of the shed. They transferred August's body to the backseat. The yard was swirling with dust as air currents came around the buildings. "Don't look beyond the end of your nose," Victor said, repeating what August had always advised.

She called to him from the well house. "Sure a good thing we've kept a tarp over this water tank." While he attached a hose to the stock tank for draining its muddy water, she began cleaning the well house so she could wash the separator.

When the milking and separating were done, they went to the house for breakfast. The amount of dust was overwhelming. The kitchen was cold in the dim light, and there was a heavy coating of dirt. Both of them had slumped shoulders as they looked about.

"This is close to the worst I've ever seen," Deborah said. "We weren't here to shove rugs up to the doors."

Victor was looking at the range. "I'll start a fire if you'll round up your whisk broom so we can sweep off the stove. We could do with some heat and a pot of coffee." He worked at getting a fire started, and she swept the stovetop. They created a fog of dust impossible to prevent.

He sniffed, his forehead wrinkling above his mask. "Nothing like the smell of scorching dust."

She rinsed the coffeepot under the pump and filled it. Feeling like she was just moving the dirt around, Deborah wiped down two chairs and the table and laid out butter and slices of bread.

"I've never seen bread and butter that looked so good," Victor said cheerfully. "And that perking coffee smells good." She smiled weakly.

She had difficulty swallowing the food and suspected he was experiencing the same problem. His face was tired. She thought she was going to cry and turned her head away.

He grasped her hand. "Deborah." Tears were in his voice. "Are you going to be okay while I go to town? You could go with me."

She shook her head. "His body is just a shell, and his spirit is with us," she said, realizing her words and tired voice lacked conviction when she really did mean them. "I'm going to see to August's horses and chickens after I take care of the stock here. I figure he'll be with me, watching that I do things right."

"I'll meet you there or here as soon as I get back from town." Victor poured coffee after rinsing the dust out of the cups. "I've got to tell Moses. I'll stop on the way to town."

When Victor was ready to leave, he hugged Deborah, raising her chin. "Times like this, we need to pretend we're the same pioneer stock as August and Audrey. Sometimes I think of what those old folks endured, and I wonder why I complain."

Deborah nodded. "You're right."

They walked to the car with Victor holding her to his side. "Take care," he said. "Don't wear yourself down. I'll be back to help you shovel out the dirt."

She smiled. "If you'll let me return the favor at your house."

"It's a deal."

Just as he was about to drive out of the yard, she waved him down. "The quilt, Victor, the quilt around August? Would you be sure to bring it back? I'd hate to see it get lost. Audrey made it."

"You bet," he said. "I won't forget."

Taking one quick look about the farmstead, Deborah decided she had to do what August had always advised. If she dealt with just the task at hand, such as feeding hogs or gathering eggs, she couldn't look at the drifts of dirt piled against foundations and the bases of trees and posts. After the chores, she banked the fire in the house and left without looking at the cleaning to be done.

Chapter 17

The Grandfather Clock

When Deborah parked in the Goodman yard, she kept her eyes away from the house. She walked toward the corral. The team and August's riding horse waited at the gate, and she could hear a rooster crowing in the henhouse. The wind was down, and the sun was warming the air. The blue sky almost began to lift her spirits.

She had brought a can of milk, which she poured in the cat pans and the chicken trough. While she did the chores, she cried again. Her tears were not just for August. The old man's three cats and Jake the dog hovered, even after she had fed them. Jake went off, nose to the ground, sniffing about the buildings. He paused in front of the house, his tail wagging and his body tense as if in anticipation of seeing August. It was a dejected animal that finally rejoined Deborah, and she knelt to hug and pet him. She also noticed the three horses and recognized the same signs as they looked toward the house, their ears cocked forward.

"How do we explain to animals and children?" she murmured as she rubbed the dog's ears and stroked the cats. She spent some time talking to them because that was what August would have done.

As Deborah started back to her truck, she stopped to stare at the house. More of the wall and roof had fallen than she remembered. She walked around the sod house. The worst damage was on the northwest, but big cracks and walls out of plumb told her the stress was growing. Extending back from the fallen corner, sections of the roof dipped down.

The front door had been ajar since they had left last night. She could see into the kitchen, and she noticed Audrey's china cupboard with its glass doors. If the roof fell, the cupboard would be ruined, along with the glassware inside, pieces the woman had treasured because they represented some of the beauty in her life. Deborah thought of the cut glass bowl she had used New Year's Day for peaches. She had been imitating Audrey, for the old woman had especially liked to use hers for her canned peaches. She remembered her saying the bowl made the fruit look like plump, golden jewels. There were the little salt and pepper cellars, a cream pitcher, and of course her bone china set.

"Oh, Audrey," she groaned. "How sad—your fine things with the roof about to fall in." Audrey had worked hard to get what she had, and a few things had been wedding gifts or family treasures.

Deborah stepped closer to the open door. Between the two rocking chairs was a parlor table. On it was the Goodman family Bible and a photograph album. Another blowing wind, a falling roof, both could dirty and mar the photos, tearing them from the pages. The album would be the only remnant in years to come as proof Audrey and August had existed. August's death should be recorded in the Bible and sent to his family back east. He had spoken of grandnephews, two of them, with the Goodman name. The Bible had come from August's father. It should be returned to the only Goodman relatives. There was the grandfather clock. She remembered every word August had said about the clock when Audrey died. She had to save it.

With no further thought, Deborah stepped into the house, crouched down, as though afraid of banging her head on some low-hanging object. She looked around her and straightened her back. Then she was afraid as she heard the creak of board on board, somewhere overhead. The noise worried her.

Deborah studied the clock, wondering how in the world to move it. She grasped it with both arms and rocked it. The clock wasn't nearly as heavy as she had supposed. Inside the glass door, the pendulum still swung back and forth, and she reached in to unhook it, dropping it into her coat pocket. She spread one of Audrey's braided rugs near the clock and tugged at the cabinet, gently placing it on its side on the rug. She pulled on the rug, slowly moving the clock across the floor, over the doorsill, and out onto the porch. Not sure how to navigate it further, she left it near the steps.

She had to save the pair of matching rocking chairs with their ornate, hand-carved arms, for one had been August's and the other Audrey's.

The parlor table held the Bible and album. She carried them out. Victor returned and caught her tugging a large, carved sea chest to the door.

"Deborah, stop!" The tone of his voice jarred her, and she stopped in midstride. "Every jerk on that heavy thing shakes the house. I can see it in the ceiling!"

"Then you take one end, and I'll take the other."

"No! You get out of there now. I don't like the look of things."

"It's full of Audrey's things. I'm not leaving it."

Victor put his hands on his hips. "She's dead. You don't need to join her."

She answered by pulling on the chest. Victor exclaimed in anger and hurried to help her. Between them they carried the chest off the front porch.

"Now!" She ran back to the porch. "The grandfather clock! It's the most important." Victor didn't hesitate to help her. She knew he was anxious to get her away from the porch.

"Do you remember Maude and Elmer Ratliff, rolling around on this porch the day Ed came looking for a wife?" she asked.

"Don't change the subject."

Deborah felt embarrassed. Before he could say anything further, there was a cracking sound, and the porch roof suddenly pulled away from the wall and roof of the house. It moved about a foot and hung there, creaking and groaning in the breeze.

"Deborah Jorgenson Nelson, I could shake you."

She thought of Audrey's handmade things that might be in the trunk. She smiled through tears.

"You are wicked." He pressed her head against his shoulder.

A noise on the road drew them apart, and they watched Moses drive up the lane. "Oh," was all the old man could say as he looked at the house. Deborah put her arm through his. "What is all this?" he asked, looking about him.

"Deborah took a notion to save some of the Goodman things. Did a good job from the looks of it, but I'd say she must have a guardian angel." Victor appeared proud and upset at the same time.

Moses stared at the house. "What a tragedy. I never dreamed this old house would go this way." He looked about sadly. "The last of my oldest friends."

Deborah still held his arm. "I'm so sorry, Moses."

He seemed to look at her for the first time. "Well, you have to be worn out. You both look it. Deborah, if your house is like mine was this morning, you've got a mess of cleaning to do. Frances has put in cleaning and cooking time, and I'd like to see the two of you come home with me for a hot meal and some talk."

Moses was right about their tiredness, and Deborah wasn't ready to face her dirty house. They loaded the rescued items and covered them with the truck tarp. Moses shook his head in dismay. "You took an awful chance, young woman!" A broken board dropped from the mangled porch, adding emphasis to his words.

"Now," she said, "the two of you stop. It's done, and I'm glad I did it."

Moses nodded. "You did bring out things that meant a lot to them." But he wasn't ready to give up yet. "I just don't think Audrey and August would've wanted you to risk your neck for their things."

She said nothing more and neither did Victor as they rode in her car, following Moses to his farm.

After a meal and hot coffee, Deborah began to feel better. "Thank you, Frances. I was so discouraged, but I think this food has really helped me. I might even be able to face sweeping out my house so I can cook again."

When the table was cleared, Moses brought folded papers and sat down with another cup of coffee. Frances cut pieces of apple pie. Moses said, "I've got Audrey's and August's will here, and I need to tell you what's in it and where the two of you figure in."

Victor and Deborah looked at each other in surprise.

"Now, just like I said to Eloise Williams's offspring, this is a will to be trusted. The three of us went to a lawyer over at Richly, and this will is on file with him." He opened the papers and smoothed them. "If it's all right with you, Frances and Harold can just sit here with us and have their pie and coffee. I trust them. Isn't that right, Harold?"

"You bet," Harold said seriously.

"Of course," Victor said, and Deborah nodded.

"First off," Moses said, "any money you're owing to the estate, Victor, is forgiven. You're not to worry about repaying."

"But—" Victor began.

"Now hold on. That's because practically everything has been left to you anyhow. The Goodmans left the homestead and all it contains and their land, cash, and livestock to you, Victor, with the exception of a few specific items for Deborah here."

"You don't say!"

"Yes. They thought very highly of you, both of you. They explained they had no living relatives—at least none they even knew, and they considered you to be like a son to them. Deborah, there's a list of things here Audrey wanted you to have—the quilts, some dishes, and such. I believe she had already told you about some of them."

Deborah nodded sadly. "She told me. They'll mean a lot to me."

"And the big clock you risked your neck for—August said it's for you too. He did say, but it's not here in this legal paper, he hoped and figured the two of you would marry, and maybe you'd be kind enough to share it with Victor."

They all laughed, and tears started in Victor's eyes. He said, "Doesn't it sound just like the old man? Shoot, I miss them."

Deborah said, "The house. I can hardly stand to see it the way it is. And even if it were in good shape, it will never be the same without the two of them."

"I was thinking the same, and I've got a suggestion. I think we ought to get a work crew together a day or so after the funeral," Moses said. "It's, as August would say, a goner. We can take it on down and maybe remove a few more of their possessions before they're damaged. There'd be some lumber to salvage too."

Victor agreed numbly. "I don't want to continue seeing it the way it is."

On the drive home, Victor was unusually quiet, and Deborah knew he must be thinking about what the Goodmans had done. He said, "It's hard to believe. I don't deserve it."

"You don't trust their judgment?"

"Well, sure, but—"

"No more buts." She smiled at him. "They loved you and recognized you were deserving. Enough said."

Neighbors and friends came to Deborah's house before the funeral, and the gathering was not all that different from the day of August's ninetieth birthday celebration. Moses said, "When you talk about August Goodman and remember the kind of man he was, you can't sit here crying. You can't help but laugh, for he was a man to be enjoyed, a good man."

"A good man," someone echoed.

"Just like Audrey was a good woman." Everyone nodded.

"Wonder what'll become of the place?" someone asked. "With no kids to leave it to."

Moses said, "It's in good hands. They left it to a good man." He said nothing more and neither did anyone else. Deborah knew it would be figured out soon who the good man was.

As everyone prepared to leave later, she heard someone say, "So many changes, so many changes. It's hard to take."

That evening Deborah and Victor sat at her kitchen table, writing letters to Minnesota, letting Jonathan know a grandfather was gone. Victor wrote: "'Remember the dear old man sitting upon the rake in the alfalfa field, guiding those big, powerful horses like they were ponies. Remember that sweet-faced lady hoeing weeds in her garden by the windmill, wearing her pink sunbonnet, faded some from the hot sun on her head and back.'"

"That's poetry, Victor."

"In a way. Maybe it will ease some of the hurt in Jonathan's mind. So what poetry did you write?"

"I used the word *remember*. 'Remember Grandfather August standing on his box to brush his big team and how each horse would reach back with its nose and nudge his rear.'"

Victor said, "And Grandpa August would say, 'Well, hello to you too.'"

"'Remember his stories about the old days and the one about the nest of rattlesnakes, how he danced as he described how many he saw. How both of them always met us at the yard gate when we rode in—Grandmother Audrey would reach out with her arms, and August would take the reins to lead our horses to the corral. And there was her smile and his laugh—we always had to smile and laugh in return.'"

Victor wrote about what they would do to the old sod house the next day and why it needed to be done. "'I guess it's only right that those blocks of sod go back to the soil, kind of the way fallen leaves turn brown and sweet as they molder.'"

She lifted his hand to kiss it.

Both of them jumped when the grandfather clock chimed in the living room. Victor smiled. "It works, Deborah! None the worse for wear, the way you got it out of the house." He smiled. "I reckon this is the only way I can share it for now."

"I reckon," she imitated.

Victor has gone home and I thought maybe writing in my journal would be a good idea. I don't think it's going to help. What I have to say can be summarized in two descriptive words: sad *and* depressed. *That means I have to get sleep and then anticipate Victor will see to it I get out of bed in the morning.*

No, that isn't fair to him. My illness years ago was thrust on him too much as it was. Tomorrow we meet with neighborhood folks to salvage the Goodman possessions and tear down the sod house. I have to be there. I have to help. I have to get through the day, and the day will get me through the next day.

Chapter 18

What Does the Future Hold?

Deborah joined with Victor and the neighborhood, tearing down the sod house. She worked hard, trying to focus on the physical rather than the emotional aspects of what was being done. It helped that their neighbors were working, and she had to work too, keeping up with them. That way she had no time to look at the growing destruction, which began with the bracing of walls and the roof so household goods and furniture could be safely brought out. Even Audrey's muslin kitchen curtains were taken down, and the lace curtains, always carefully starched and ironed, were removed from the parlor.

The windows came out, but not before she saw Audrey's face at the kitchen window, smiling, her uplifted hand waving. Deborah had no time to think when the bracing was removed. As the roof and walls began to sway and collapse, memories of times in the kitchen, the parlor, even the bedroom where the two old folks had died, were hidden away in the shadows of her mind to be taken out at a later time. Only the kitchen pump was left standing.

They loaded salvaged household items into a truck that someone drove to Victor's house and unloaded. Others helped Deborah crate what food remained in August's root cellar and transferred it to Victor's cellar. Some of the women gathered bedding, curtains, and rugs, and Deborah took them to her well house to wash another day.

At noon, everyone met at August's place, and in the yard the usual sawhorses and planks appeared for tables. The women set out food. Mary asked Harold to build a fire like he always did for lard rendering, and then she brewed pots of coffee. She poured cup after cup while the food was passed around.

O. B. scrutinized Victor and Deborah who sat side-by-side. "You two going to get married?"

Deborah flushed hotly.

"I'm working on it," Victor said.

"He's legally dead now," O. B. said to Deborah. "It's 1938. I been keeping track and it's over seven years."

Gracie punched her husband's arm. "Now, Overland Byron Dickerson, you shut your mouth! It's not your business."

"You didn't have to go saying my name," O. B. whined. "I never told anybody my name before. Nobody but you."

"Well, now they know," she said triumphantly. "I been aching to tell them for fifty-three years."

"Well, thanks," he whined again.

"You're welcome. You deserved it," Gracie said.

"It's a good name," Deborah said. "Has a ring of authority to it."

O. B., looking disgruntled, ignored her and tackled his dried apple pie. Through a full mouth he asked, "Well?" Everyone looked at him. "You getting married?"

Victor grinned. "Like I said, I'm working on it."

"Huh!" O. B. said. "That's no answer."

"We need a wedding," Herman said. "Something besides funerals. Dance and the works. You two are about our only hope."

O. B. wasn't finished. "Stoddel says if the two of you get married, it'll just be proof you done something to Christian."

Deborah dropped her fork and stared hard at her plate. She held herself very still, fearing she was going to be sick.

Gracie pinched the man's arm. "Shut your mouth. You could've gone all day without saying that."

"What do you think, O. B.?" Victor asked.

"Aw, we ain't dumb like Stoddel. We all know better. Everybody knows you didn't do nothing—and there just ain't no answers as to what happened."

After the meal, Deborah went back to the unpleasant work of demolishing the old home, and it seemed her pain had grown after hearing what O. B. said about Stoddel. Sometimes she felt like her boys and marriage were getting further and further away.

Once she slipped away from the neighbors, going into the grove of trees behind the yard. The raw soil on August's grave was mounded up, free of any clods. Audrey's grave showed the beginning growth of buffalo grass and perennial flowers August had planted the year before. She knelt, smoothing an area of the old man's grave that didn't need smoothing. Patting the soil, she held back her tears. "We miss the both of you so much."

"Hey," said a soft voice. Victor leaned down and kissed the top of her head.

"I'm so glad I still have you." Deborah said to him and gave one last pat to the mound of dirt.

"Always, sweetheart. Our problem—it's too quiet in your house. We'll get those boys home and have all kinds of noise again. Maybe a hollering baby."

"Victor, they know now, both of them—August and Audrey—they know what happened to Christian."

"I suppose they do."

"I wish we could know."

"So do I, dear girl."

The work was finished close to chore time. Salvaged lumber was stacked in a neat pile in the barn, along with cabinets, windows, and doors. The men had loaded into a truck the sod that had remnants of plaster attached, and the load was going to be hauled to low spots in the township road. The remaining sod was leveled.

It was as though the sod house had never existed. The windmill, trees, and barn remained.

Someone poured water onto the embers of Harold's fire. The crate of August's few chickens was lifted into Deborah's truck, and the three horses were tied to the tailgate. Victor slowly drove to Deborah's place, the horses clopping along behind. She had the three cats on the truck seat, and in the back Jake reared up with his paws over the sideboard near the cab. She remembered seeing August drive his truck down the road, the dog standing that way with ears streaming behind him and tongue lolling happily.

Deborah carried the cats to the barn. She introduced them to the haymow and took them down to the alleyway where Victor filled a pan with milk. They squatted down, petting the cats and Jake, worrying about the adjustments the animals would have to make.

"At least Jake and Marco have chased rabbits together," Victor said.

She nodded. "And the horses sort of know one another."

The sun was setting when they turned the horses in with hers. Their backs and Victor's seemed inlaid with gold from the lowering light as he poured grain for them. Deborah's breath caught, and she wished Jonathan, with his eye for light and color, were beside her to see it.

Only the two of them worked about the farm and ranches now, turning more and more to each other in their talk. They cleaned the yards at the old ranch, planting flowers where the sod house had stood. They tended the graves in the little grove of trees.

On Sunday, they prepared a simple dinner and sat on the south porch, enjoying the warmth of the sun. Victor reached across the little table, taking Deborah's hand. "Remember when even two or three of these tables wouldn't have seated everyone? I figured it up. There were twelve of us then. I guess it's easier for all of the boys—with yours in Minnesota and John's in eastern Kansas. If they were here, they'd sure miss those old folks."

"Everyone's going to talk, now that we don't have August as a chaperone." Deborah had barely tasted her food.

Victor lifted an eyebrow. "You figure they thought he was much of a chaperone with all the naps he had?"

In April, small rains totaled an inch and a half. Deborah and Victor planted a garden, beans, and corn. They rode the tractor together in the African field, working the ground and then planting. May turned hot and dry, and they worked in earnest at mulching and irrigating the garden and the four shelterbelts.

One evening, she laid the newspaper on the kitchen table and said, "Wheat's sixty cents."

His face fell. "The last I remember, August said eighty."

She gave more information from the newspaper. "It's definite now. Hitler has Austria and Czechoslovakia."

"It's coming," was all he said. She knew he meant war.

The next day, Victor said, "I've been thinking—we need to keep all of our young heifers this year. I have a feeling, that's all I can say. It's time to begin building the herd, slow but sure."

Slow but sure. Those were August's words. She remembered them from years ago as though they were imprinted on her mind. "But we don't know the drought is ending."

"No, we don't, especially since August predicted we were coming to the end in 1937 … and then this year's storms started."

They were quiet for a while, thinking about the storm that had ruined the sod house and contributed to August's death.

"I think he wanted so much to be right, Victor." Deborah's voice was thick with tears. "And I wanted so much for him to see an end to the destruction. I wanted Audrey to see an end. God, how I wanted it for them."

He turned up her palms and kissed them. "They'll see the end when we see it. Have faith."

"How many times I saw those dear old folks, together and separately, looking about them, so hopeful."

Victor said again, "Slow but sure."

"He said that. August said that."

"Our grasslands are decent because we didn't overwork them. August's grass looks the best." Victor referred to what had been August's land as though the old man still lived.

Victor had more to say. "I don't even want to talk about this, sweetheart … but you know I think war is coming, and if the drought should end soon, we need to be ready for the market to come back. It will—if there's war." He shook his head, and she could hear his anger growing. "What a hell of a reason."

"We've got to be able to feed the cows," Deborah said.

"Sudan, kaffir, alfalfa," he recited. "Maybe even prairie hay. We'll see."

"We need to be doing more thinking and talking about what Elizabeth said."

The cafe owner had sent them a letter, inviting them for food and talk. They met in the back of the cafe during what Elizabeth called the light time of her workday. "My office," she said, leading them into a small room holding a desk and a table covered with red-and-white oilcloth. It was set for three.

"The best privacy I can come up with, folks." She served thick pork chops, potatoes, and gravy and passed a bowl of green beans. Victor tasted his meat. "Good, Elizabeth, good. So moist."

Deborah laughed. "He's used to how I cook them dry."

"The key is thickness, first of all." Elizabeth shook her head, her short, tight curls bouncing. "Most folks cut them too thin. That's rosemary you taste."

She paused to look at Deborah. "How long have I known you? Isn't it almost ten years?"

Deborah thought for a moment. "Yes, going on ten years. Where has time gone?"

"It's gone into worrying about Christian and wishing you could marry Victor here."

"Oh." Deborah didn't know what else to say.

"Here." Elizabeth passed a bowl of pickled beets to Victor. "Taste these."

He did as she said.

"Taste them, Deborah. They came out of a jar that's shipped from back east, just like what you probably make, but they're not as good. I used to have Cora Brown make pickled beets for me. That was a good ten years ago. With this drought, she hasn't grown enough garden to feed a jackrabbit. But you have." She turned her eyes from Deborah to Victor and stirred her mashed potatoes.

"I know how good your canned chickens and beef are. I've heard plenty of talk from folks, especially Marshall Draper, about your gardens. He and Leonard have become good friends. Leonard says Marshall's smart for a guy with a college degree."

They laughed and agreed.

"No one has grown good produce during this drought like you folks have, at least not consistently." Elizabeth waited.

"Well, I suppose," Victor said, somewhat doubtfully. "Well, sure. With a lot of hard work."

"I have a proposition. I want you to grow and provide fresh produce to my cafe during season. In off-season, you can provide canned vegetables, pickles, sauerkraut, anything you have. I can continue to use your canned meats and smoked pork. Of course, I can use eggs, milk, and cream. What do you think?"

They looked at one another. Elizabeth ate hastily, not seeing her food, her eyes on them. She dropped her fork. "Sorry. I'm so used to eating on the run. Listen you two, we've already been doing some of this off and on. What if we do it regularly? I have a use for everything you grow and preserve. If times ever get better, I'd like to look into getting a big refrigeration unit. I saw one once. It was so big, you could walk right in."

Elizabeth looked at Deborah earnestly. "Why should I buy canned goods that aren't as good as yours and have them shipped in when I can get them from you? I'll say this, I've kept a reasonable business going during this Depression—along with a few headaches and worries. If I can't create enough business for you, there are some other cafes in nearby towns I'll bet you can sell to. And I think times are going to get better. They've got to get better before too long. God willing. The drought's going to quit and the Depression will end."

Deborah saw the look on Victor's face. She knew he was thinking the Depression would end if a war started.

Elizabeth had the same thought. "I know you, Victor Whitesong. You're worrying that it looks like war will end the Depression, I'll bet. If that's what you're thinking, I agree with you. It's a sad thought."

They left Elizabeth that day, interested in her offer and worried that yet another person was concerned about war.

Now they sat at their little table on the porch, their thoughts spinning as to what the future might bring. Deborah wished she had Ol' Paul to talk to about possible war. Ol' Paul had known about history, and Moses said he read the signs well enough to predict the Great War.

"If we work with Elizabeth, we wouldn't have to pay shipping costs, other than our own gas for delivering," Victor said. "One thing bothers me, though. I read in the paper about possible government regulations being developed that would put controls on something like we're talking about. Eventually, we may have a lot of hoops to jump."

For some odd reason I'm remembering how I told Maude Ratliff I couldn't marry her nephew Ed because I had too many commitments. We understood one another. Christian hadn't been gone very many months: I had to know what had become of him; I had the boys to raise; and there was the farm to operate, with all the ramifications of the times, namely a drought and the Depression.

My commitments haven't changed. Now may be the time to think of rebuilding for our future, even though we know nothing about ending drought and beginning war. Money has been going out of our pockets for years. We're still faced with the same concerns—a poor economy and planting and growing while taking care of the land. We need to eat, and Elizabeth's customers need to eat. Is this the right action to take?

I am sure of one thing—no matter what became of Christian, my commitment is to Victor and our boys. Then there is the hovering cloud of Stoddel—am I strong enough to continue to face up to his insanity?

Chapter 19

Sheriff's Sale

The summer winds rose, only breezes in the early morning, rising by eleven o'clock, twenty to even thirty miles per hour by afternoon. If turned on, the windmills churned, and with full turns of the blades, in union with the thrust of the shaft, water gushed into the tanks, cold and clear, soon to warm in the heat. By then, the blue of the sky had turned harsh blue-white, hard on the eyes, hard on the body, hard on plants. The wind and heat combined energies, competing with any moisture, sucking it up and out.

Deborah and Victor worked hard to keep the garden going. The new windbreaks were well established and didn't require daily watering. Victor didn't even flinch when they decided the two cuttings of the small crop of alfalfa had to be used to mulch the garden and corn.

"Are you worried about having enough fodder?" she asked.

"Have you looked at the African field lately? It looks good. And there's haying to be done. We'll make it."

There was an occasional rain, and because of the mulch and terraces, the moisture was conserved in the garden and fields. Often weeks went by with no moisture, but they kept the garden going with windmill water. Victor began to worry about the pastures, and each time they rode to check the cattle, he looked about with eyes that reflected his tension. "I'm wondering if I showed poor judgment when advising us to keep the heifers."

She tried to reassure him. "It's still an awfully small herd. Wait and see. Those few heifers will become very valuable to us when it's time to rebuild the herd."

In October, the temperature averages had lessened a few degrees, and the white glare of the skies, picking up the morning's accumulation of blown dust, was murky bronze near the horizon. Victor was reading the Fremont newspaper after their noon meal and muttered, "Damn."

"What?"

"Sheriff's sale. Reub Meyers's place."

"Oh no. I was hoping they could hang on."

Victor put down the paper, stirred and stirred his coffee when there was nothing in it to stir, and then left the house. As Deborah washed the dishes, she could see him in the corral, currying August's team, something he did if he were upset or needed to do some thinking. He didn't have to stand on boxes the way the old man had done. She watched the big horses, as they had done with August, swing their heads back to nudge Victor's rear, sometimes slathering alfalfa slobbers onto his jeans.

He came into the kitchen. "This banker of Reub's has foreclosed right and left when he could've let folks hang on a little longer. I can't respect that. I've got a plan, maybe a way to help Reub. If I can use your car, I'll go talk to folks and see what we can get rolling. You want to go?"

"No, you go. Whatever you're thinking, you'll handle it."

He returned long after chore time was over, and she had his plate in the warming oven. "Well," she said when he came in. "The bad penny returns."

"Good penny this time, Deborah." He bent to kiss the back of her neck, something she knew he hadn't allowed himself to do for a long time.

The kiss made her shiver, and she turned to get his food. "What have you been up to?"

"I can't tell you." She could see he was in a teasing mood. "The sale is Tuesday. You go with me and just see."

"Tell me," she said.

He grinned. "Naw, you just wait and see. It'll be worth it."

The sale was at two o'clock on Tuesday, and they arrived at the Meyers's farm at one fifteen. Deborah counted at least fifty men already there, and she could see dust trails on the roads headed to Reub's place. She noticed the men seemed to have the same self-satisfied grins on their faces as Victor.

"You're not going to do something dangerous, are you?" She had particularly watched to see if he carried a gun to the truck. He didn't.

"What we're going to do is all in the name of the law."

Deborah looked about before she got out of the truck. "I'm the only woman here."

"I don't think it's a problem."

"I'll talk to Nila until time. I should have been here long before now. She's probably in real need of talk."

"Good idea. You do that."

Deborah knocked on the outside porch door and called to Nila, but no one answered. The Meyers children, including the little one Deborah had delivered, sat under a shade tree, and she waved at them. They didn't wave back, merely looked at her with big-eyed stares and motionless bodies. She went onto the porch and knocked at the kitchen door. "Nila?" There was still no answer, so she opened the door.

The woman sat at the kitchen table, holding a cup of coffee, and she glared at Deborah, her receded chin set with clenched teeth. "I didn't say to come in."

"I know. May I sit with you?" Nila didn't answer, and Deborah pulled out a chair. "I'm sorry about your troubles."

"Really? You could have gone a long time not bothering to say that."

"I'm afraid I already have. I should have come to see you sooner."

Nila clamped her jaws, and Deborah couldn't think of what to say. The woman began to drum her fingers on the table. Deborah was about to comment on the weather but contained herself. It was an inane topic at a time like this. She glanced at the kitchen clock.

Nila noticed. "What?"

"Oh, I was checking the time," Deborah said, feeling foolish. A comment like that was about as bad as mentioning the weather.

"Yes. Well, it'll soon be over. Then nobody will have to worry about Reub and Nila Meyers." Her face flushed an unpleasant red. "You know, when Reub told me he was going in debt for seed wheat, I said no. He wouldn't listen." Her voice was angry now. "Menfolk don't listen to womenfolk—unless they're Deborah Nelson's menfolk."

She watched Nila out of the corner of her eye, wondering what the woman was capable of doing in her anger. With a suddenness that startled Deborah, Nila pushed her chair back, scraping the linoleum. She glared and whirled about, disappearing into the next room.

Deborah pressed her hands on the table, as though to get up, but wasn't sure what to do next. Then a noise began, a tinny, discordant sound—a piano badly in need of tuning. She listened and recognized the song, a hymn, 'A Mighty Fortress Is Our God.' Stepping to the doorway, she saw Nila playing a battered upright piano, her head bouncing in rhythm to her pounding hands, her hair straggling over her red face. She lifted her hands from keys missing many of their ivories, and placed them almost demurely in her lap. She bowed her head in the way a concert pianist might do.

"My inheritance," she said, her voice thick with tears, and gestured at the piano. "From my mother." She pointed at the ceiling. "My inheritance … from the drought and winds." Above Nila, the ceiling had broken away, and although cleaning had apparently been done, Deborah could see little siftings of dust floating down from the heavy darkness above. "There was some kind of a vent in the attic. We didn't know until the weight of dirt collapsed the ceiling. My home." She stood abruptly. "Now someone else will inherit it."

Deborah said, "Nila, let's step out on the porch."

"Why? So people can stare at me?"

Time was pressing. "The men have something cooked up, something that's supposed to help you and Reub. I want to see what they're doing."

"What are they doing?"

She had Nila's attention now. "I don't know. Victor wouldn't tell me."

"Something dangerous?" Nila jumped up from the piano stool, alarm in her voice. "They have guns? They after Stoddel?"

Deborah grinned. "No, but maybe it wouldn't be a bad idea—going after Stoddel, I mean."

Nila almost smiled. "I guess from your perspective it would be good to run him out of the county." She worried again. "No guns?"

"No guns—at least that's the plan. Let's stand on the porch. Come on." She tugged Nila's arm.

The east porch was in shadow, and no one turned their way as the two women watched the auctioneer climb into a wagon. He was followed by Stoddel who stood on one side and Deputy Welty on the other. The sheriff wore a holstered gun, and Welty held a rifle.

"Guns," Nila said.

Deborah felt her breathing quicken. Victor had said there would be no guns. She surveyed the gathering, counting close to a hundred and fifty men. She saw no sign of other guns. Even horses tied under the trees didn't seem to have rifles on the saddles.

Another man, probably the bank official, climbed into the wagon and made a few comments about the holdings of Reub Meyers. He ended with, "The whole kit and caboodle, with the exception of the contents of the house, will go to the highest bidder."

The auctioneer opened the bidding. He didn't have a helper to take bids, so his eyes constantly scanned the crowd. There were no takers. Deborah began to realize this auction was unlike any she had ever attended. To a man, the crowd remained stock-still, silent. Deborah had never seen a group of ranchers and farmers so immobile. Victor was toward the front with Reub, and he didn't move either. The bank official looked nervous. Stoddel surveyed the crowd, and his hand, which had stayed at his side, seemed to nudge a bit toward the holster. Remembering, Deborah grew tense.

Suddenly, an arm shot up in the middle of the crowd, and a voice shouted, "Five dollars."

The auctioneer was stunned. He stuttered, "I hear five dollars. Do I hear ..." He shuffled his feet, and Stoddel's hand was on his holster. Welty hadn't moved.

The bank official said, "Hold on just a damned minute—"

The auctioneer's mouth twitched. "Do I hear ten? Do I hear fifteen? Do I hear eight?" The auctioneer finally said, "Do I hear five and two bits?"

There was silence.

The auctioneer inhaled deeply. "Going once, going twice, going three. Sold—" and he thumped the long stick he was holding on to the floor of the wagon.

"Now see here—" The official jumped up.

The bidder pushed forward, waving a five dollar bill. The official sat down with a thump, jerking the wagon. Stoddel and Welty swayed and then caught their balance, and the auctioneer jumped out of the wagon.

☀

Sometime later, Deborah told Nila good-bye. The crying woman stood in the yard, her face splotchy and puffy like unevenly raised bread dough. She tugged at Reub's shirtfront as though she wanted to shake him. She whispered hoarsely to Deborah, "I guess you aren't rid of me yet. We're still neighbors."

On the way home, Deborah sat against the truck door, turned so she could watch Victor, enjoying the look on his face. "You look awfully smug," she said. "Have you seen a cat after it has got into the cream?"

"Is it anything like the time little Jimmy got into the butter churn?"

☀

Lord, I thank thee. Like the spoiled child I was and am, I've thought I had a rough lot in life—family problems, prejudice, losing those I love. Then I look at someone like Nila, a woman the same age as me. Nila has her fallen ceiling and a piano with no ivories. How did she endure today? In a matter of an hour or two she went from having the wolf at the door (Christian used that image) to having her home and livelihood back. Most folks would say she still doesn't have much, but it appears what she has is on her own terms at least . . . in reality, Reuben's terms.

Chapter 20

Snow without Wind

On New Year's Eve, Victor showed up later than usual, fairly close to midnight. "I just don't think I ought to stay too long," he said. There was snow on his coat, and he wiped at his face, adding, "The weather …"

"The weather?"

"Well, it could get real deep out there—already is." He bounced up and down on the balls of his feet, much the way August might have done. "What a grand snow."

"What snow? I know it was spitting some after you left at six o'clock—"

"Deborah, I'm serious! Have you looked out?"

"I went out at eight. But like I said, it was just spitting. What are you talking about?"

"Come on!" He grabbed her hand and pulled her to the porch door.

"It's cold—"

"I'll keep you warm." He was laughing and dancing boyishly. "Look!"

He opened the door. Snow was piled on the steps at least six inches deep. She gasped. "Victor!"

He grabbed her hat, coat, and boots and helped her put them on. In the yard she listened. "There's absolutely no wind, not even a breeze." Holding out her bare hands, she watched the thickly falling flakes land on her skin.

"I know. No wind." He grinned, and she thought his face was more relaxed than she had seen in ages. "It's wet, full of moisture. No wind. And it's still coming."

They left the yard, pushing against the depth piled next to the east yard gate. She gazed at the whipped cream layer on the stone wall and reached out to touch it. She didn't, not wanting to topple its white softness. In the driveway, she became aware of the light about her, caused by the expanse of whiteness. "The blow dirt. I can't see it." The snow covered everything, including the big drought cracks in the driveway.

He put his arms around her, and she thrust her hands in his coat pockets where she could feel the traditional tins of sweets and small bottle of wine. They looked down the lane, and the snow was growing deeper before their eyes. She couldn't contain herself and turned her face to his; they kissed. The only sounds in the eerie stillness were wavering coyote howls. Marco answered from inside the barn. Deborah looked up at Victor, trying to show him with her expression how much she loved him.

"Sweet girl—" He kissed her one more time. "We'd better walk."

"Look," she said. "Ghost cows." Coming toward the corral were the range cows, their backs piled thick with snow, steam coming from their mouths.

"What a sight," Victor said. "I've never seen such a sight."

"Neither have I," she said. "Snow without wind seems so rare." They watched the cattle move toward the feed bunkers. "Do you suppose they're hungry? We could pitch some feed to them."

"I doubt it. They'd be bellowing if they were hungry. They probably fed well before the snow began."

They walked until they began to grow cold. Deborah said, "I have cheese and crackers. You have eastern Kansas wine?"

"Grape. Wild grape." He removed the small bottle from his coat pocket, along with Sadie Whitesong's tins of fudge and marshmallows.

They pulled the dining room table close to the fireplace. Dance music was playing, but they only listened and played their traditional game of Chinese checkers.

They had been concentrating on the game when Deborah broke the silence. "If the drought should be ended soon ... the boys will come home."

He grinned. "You don't say."

"Enough said."

"Eight years, Deborah."

At the door in his coat and hat, holding the tin that rattled from its one remaining piece of fudge, Victor said in a determined voice, "I will kiss you. I will leave right after the kiss." He was reminding himself.

She moved into his arms quickly, and he held her tighter than he had ever done before. Deborah forced herself to break away.

"There's more, Deborah—when you're ready."

She nodded.

"I love you," he said and left.

"I love you," she called to him.

Victor arrived New Year's morning near the usual chore time, plowing his way on foot through the deep snow. Deborah could barely see his eyes, for he had his head wrapped in a wool muffler. She hurried to meet him and led him into the warm well house where the kerosene stove had been heating bucket after bucket of water. Soft cascades of snow from the roof swirled about them as she opened the door.

"I walked because I thought it was too deep for my pony," he said, his lips so cold his speech was distorted.

"I'm sorry." She helped him unwrap his head.

"I'm not! How long we've prayed for snow like this. Lots of moisture in it, no wind, and it's cold."

They hugged and thumped one another on the back. "It's still snowing," she said.

"How did you guess?"

She removed her gloves and held her bare hands to his face. "Oh, Victor, you must be frozen. Let's get you to the house."

"I don't mind it. Got to do the chores first."

"I'm almost finished. Breakfast isn't started, but I'm through with the chores, except for separating."

He was preventing her from taking her hands away from his cheeks. "Victor, we'll never get done if we stand here like this."

He laughed and wiped at the snow melting down his face.

Sometime after he had left last night, Deborah had opened the front door to look at the progress of the snow. When she saw how many inches had already fallen and how rapidly it continued to come down, she knew he shouldn't have gone home, no matter what the neighbors thought. She had paced the floor, worried about him, but reminded herself there were no blizzard conditions. Victor would have to struggle through the snow, but he could see where he was.

"It's a good fifteen inches," he said now, "with no wind. I can't believe it."

When they reached the house, she added more coal to the stove and made him sit in front of the open oven while she made coffee. "Oh, what a way to start 1939." Victor twisted to remove his coveralls.

"That grin is going to split your face."

"And why shouldn't I smile?" He grabbed her and pulled her down on his lap.

"Victor," she warned.

He let her go. "I'm sorry. I'm just so thrilled about this moisture." He jumped up to look at the calendar where they recorded moisture amounts. "Two inches of rain in September. An inch and eighty points in October. Another inch in November, an inch and forty-five points in December, all of them slow and easy, nothing like the flood we had when poor Lydia died. Look at it, Deborah. It might mean the drought has broken … and no wind of consequence. If we can get through the next three to four months with no wind …"

She went to her room and brought him a pair of wool socks. "I don't want to have big expectations. I've been disappointed before."

"I understand. We've never really talked about what has to be done for the land to be healed."

"We've got to have subsoil moisture, Victor. I wonder how many inches we're behind—"

"A bunch. You just wait, Bowers will have a headline story about it."

"I've got to plant the marginal land back to grass—"

"*We've* got to do the planting. I'm going to help. Deborah, I like the way you talk about healing the land. Think about what you done already. I think we should invite Marshall Draper for a visit just to review with us."

She laughed. "The times he's made us work so hard. I don't think that county agent has ever taken time to give himself credit for what's been done—the terraces, shelterbelts, the condition of my soil and pastures, summer fallowing—"

"We'd better have him for a visit before that car of his runs off its wheels. He's worked it hard."

"Coffee," Deborah said. "We'll invite him for coffee and chocolate cake."

Victor raised his head. The clock was chiming. "August and Audrey, I am so grateful! I will be totally happy when the boys are back, and I get to share the grandfather clock all the time."

Their day was a happy one. They fixed simple meals and relaxed in front of the fireplace. A number of books had come from the Jorgensons and Nelsons for Christmas. "New books," Deborah said, running her hand over a fresh page. "A book that hasn't been through a dirt storm. How wonderful."

When they went out to struggle in the snow while doing the chores, they could tell Victor had no business trying to walk home that night. "You have to stay," she said.

"I'll behave myself," he promised.

More snow fell in January 1939, sometimes with wind that made drifts but not bad enough to blow the soil that was becoming saturated with moisture. The temperatures stayed cold, and a deep, heavy blanket of snow continued to cover the fields. Their hopes for an end to the drought and blowing dust continued to grow as the temperatures stayed down during February, and more snow and freezing rain fell. There were no winds of consequence.

"I want to believe it's ended," Victor said, "yet I feel like I'm holding my breath."

"So do I, and a song keeps running through my head—'our boys are coming home, our boys are coming home.'"

"Yes, yes!" He raised his arms in victory.

March came with slowly rising temperatures. There were two more light snows, and the melting began in earnest. By the end of the month, close to all signs of snow were gone and the soil was slowly warming. Deborah began an almost daily ritual of going out into the field to the west or south to observe the progress of the snow melt among the terraces. The blue skies and March white clouds reflected in the ponds of water, and she stood in the sunlight, soaking in its warmth and the beauty around her. Sometimes she found herself entranced with the sight and sound of geese flying overhead and turned her face to them, her arms partly raised the way a bird might lift its wings. Many times she had seen Grandfather Blue Sky do something similar.

Victor would say, "You take pleasure in little things."

She would reply, "Geese are not small."

One day, wearing tall rubber boots, she worked her way far out into the south field and found each terrace holding water its entire length. On top of one of them, she turned slowly in a circle, feeling delight in everything she saw, heard, and felt. She unbuttoned her jacket, and the breezes were cool touches on the skin of her neck.

A movement on the north-south road caught her eye. It was Heickert, and even at this distance she could hear the grind of his gears as his car struggled with the mud. Mail deliveries had been few and far between for weeks, and she was surprised to see Heickert battling the deep mud of the road. He stopped at her mailbox, and she heard the beeping of his car horn. Standing by his car, he waved at Victor who was in the barnyard. When Victor began sloshing his way down the lane, Deborah decided she had better head back to the farmstead. Something appeared to be wrong.

As she hiked through the sucking mud, the two men met. She heard the grind of the car as it plowed away through the mud. When Heickert turned onto the road east to Cresslers, his progress was faster, for that road was in better condition.

She arrived at the house soon after Victor did and saw him sitting on the porch steps, sorting a big stack of daily newspapers and envelopes. "Deborah," he said gently.

"What is it? Something's wrong." She was struggling to remove the mud-laden boots, her eyes on his face.

"Let's sit in the porch swing."

"Victor—"

"Come." He sat and gestured to her.

"All right. Now, what? What have you got there?"

He fingered some of the mail. "Lots of newspapers and letters—and this telegram."

Her breath caught, her eyes shying away to watch the soft white clouds float to the east. "Bad news?" she asked.

"Yes. Heickert apologizes. They've had it in town a few days. He tried more than once to get here. It's from your dad."

Her heart seemed to leap in her chest. "No! The boys?" She wailed, "What?"

She felt him grab her arms. "Not the boys. It's your mother." She collapsed against Victor's chest. He spoke softly. "I'm sorry. I didn't mean to scare you about the boys. Heickert said it's your mother. It's not good news."

Mail slid to the porch floor, and Deborah sat up.

"Read it, Victor."

"*Deborah dear. Have buried your mother. She wanted you to remember her as she was when you went to Kansas. That was her request. She gave me many things to share with you. Will do it as soon as I can, not by letter. Boys with me. I am grateful. They are a joy. She was happy to have them nearby. She went awful fast. Dad.*"

"She didn't want me there." Deborah ducked her head, drawing her shoulders inward.

"It sounds like there wasn't time. And she wanted you to remember her as she was."

"As she was … the Lillian who was so ill and depressed after her breast surgery? The mama I knew when I was little, the one who made me feel so loved? Or the mother who was so distant? One time she stared out her upstairs window, looking into the trees, and I was afraid she was lost among the leaves. I was right there beside her, Victor, only I wasn't."

Victor put his arms around her.

She said, "I hope she didn't suffer too much."

"So do I," he said.

"I wonder … well, does no good to wonder. I hope I hear from Dad soon."

"You will."

She cried, and he held her as they slowly swung back and forth. Deborah didn't want to allow herself to think about why her mother hadn't let Frank contact her so she could have gotten to Minnesota in time. Maybe it had been as Lillian said, wanting Deborah to remember her as she had been. Or maybe there still had been the barrier between them, the one that had caused her mother to look beyond her.

"This will be hard on both Jonathan and Half Shell. Jonathan's letters have made it sound like he and Baby were having a happy time with your folks," said Victor.

She raised her head. "I would be feeling much worse if she hadn't had the chance to get to know them. I'm thankful I sent them."

The little kisses on her face were soft and warm.

She looked again at the telegram. "He says he has things to tell me—but not by letter. Then how?"

"Maybe he'll come," Victor said. "Maybe—I'm almost afraid to say it—maybe the drought and blowing have stopped, and Jonathan and Baby can come home. Maybe your dad will bring them."

She smiled through her tears. "Maybe," she said.

"Tell me about your mother."

"A sad woman. Not always. All three of us were so happy ... then she suffered. She had her surgery, and everything was so different after that. It was like there was a big gap, you know, like a huge canyon, between Mother and Dad, and I was somewhere out there, away from them. It was like I didn't exist."

Deborah cried again, and the pain this time was more for that young girl than her mother. "I just never understood. Now I suppose I never will."

Victor held her, and she knew he was sad too. "I'm sorry, Deborah."

"I should be sorry for just the little girl. I'm a grown woman now and have no business feeling sorry for myself."

He kissed her forehead. "Grown or not, something we don't understand still hurts."

Meredith wrote and, just as Frank had said in his telegram, Jonathan and Half Shell were a joy to Deborah's dad. Meredith said, "You just tell me if it's none of my business, but I think it would be good if you'd leave the boys with Frank through the summer, maybe close to time when school will start. He misses your mother, and they are doing him so much good."

Deborah put the letter down with shaking hands. "But we're so certain the drought and the dust are over now."

"Sweetheart, we're not certain. From what Meredith says, you can ease a lot of his loneliness."

She jumped up from the table, almost upsetting her chair. "I don't owe him anything." Her voice was out of control.

He went to her. "Deborah dear—"

She heard his words, realizing he had picked up the way Calvin—the way Uncle Oscar—had used her name. Deborah dear. She shivered. Her dad's telegram had begun that way. She threw herself into Victor's arms, her face no longer pale but flushed and hot with tears. "Of course he can have them for the summer. Jonathan will understand. Hold me, Victor." He hugged her and she said, "I've got to sort this out. I just don't understand everything that goes on in my mind."

Slowly, they drew apart. "He said he has things to tell me, things from Mother. He doesn't want to do it by letter. Maybe this is what Meredith meant when she said my folks will explain to me. I like your earlier suggestion, that he bring the boys home." She pressed her hot cheek against his cooler one. "Thank you, Victor, for enduring one more temper tantrum from me."

I remember saying or thinking something like this before: I don't deserve Victor because he is so good, loyal, and loving. He doesn't deserve me because he is so good, loyal, and loving.

Chapter 21

Welty Again

They planned their gardens and fields in anticipation of having the boys back home, for more food would be needed next winter. Their pastures were greening up, an intense green Deborah found almost unbelievable, her mind's eye remembering previous years with grass the color of dust-laden skies. They gathered up their small herd of cattle and moved them to one of August's pastures, keeping a pregnant heifer back with their milk cow. When the boys were home, more milk, cheese, and eggs would be needed.

Deborah prepared the biddy houses, and again the memories came, causing her to sit in the hay on the floor of the barn's alleyway until Victor found her. He sat on the floor also and reached for her hand that held the frazzled hen in her lap.

"Softly, sweet girl. Do this, like David did." He softly stroked the hen with a finger, beginning with her beak and smoothing upward over her head.

"Yes," said Deborah. She repeated the soothing action over and over. The hen settled down and shuttered her eyes.

Victor placed the hen on the nest of eggs. "Deborah, for the rest of your life there will be things that will stir up a memory of David. Just when you get to feeling strong, something like this old biddy comes along—or someone like your mother dies—and all the old griefs are renewed again."

She surprised him as well as herself by giggling. "You're smoothing my ruffled feathers just the way you did the hen."

☀

Victor had written Sonja and David, telling them about August's ranch, and he and David wrote letter after letter back and forth, discussing the possibility of David working for him in ranching—if the market should improve. Deborah knew they also discussed the possibility of war, as painful as it was for Victor to think about, and what it might mean for the world markets. If Sonja and David were to come back … they decided to plant a bigger garden and raise more chickens just in case, and there was Elizabeth's proposal to think about.

One day, Deborah exclaimed as she read a letter from Jonathan. "Listen! He's reminding us he's due to go to high school in September. Victor, it's unbelievable. He was just a little boy five years old when Christian disappeared. Fourteen! High school."

"So that means one more thing we've got to plan for. With Idotha already in high school this year, the Brownlys can tell us how to go about finding a room in Fremont for Jonathan. Those two will be happy to be together in school again."

"They'll just be happy being together again."

Victor smiled. "You think so? Well, sure, that's been obvious, hasn't it? They dote on one another. Like some other people I know."

She grinned. "Maybe not the same way, but, yes, they dote on one another."

☀

The first Sunday after Heickert brought all of the old mail, they brewed coffee and sat on the divan to read. A sudden intake of Victor's breath caused Deborah to drop her newspaper. "What is it?"

"An American, a Yale student, tells this story. He traveled through Germany. Back in November, Nazis rampaged through Jewish areas in Germany. Sounds like they destroyed synagogues, homes, and businesses. Apparently, the ones who weren't killed were beaten, and twenty-six thousand were thrown into concentration camps." He lowered the newspaper. "I wonder what it's like, being in a concentration camp. I wonder how they're treated."

"I don't know for sure, but I think Hilda Vosserman has some idea," she said. "She hasn't heard from her sister and doesn't expect to."

He took in her words. "Good God." He shook the newspaper so hard it snapped. "It's being called Crystal Night because of so much broken glass. It sounds like most of their property was destroyed or taken away."

"Ol' Paul," she said.

"What? What about him?"

"He predicted things like this. We talked about the Jews, but I had no idea. What has the United States done about it?"

"It looks like nothing. Here's an article that says there have been refugees accepted by Great Britain. But even though we have four hundred thousand emigrant openings, we haven't allowed very many in. The excuse is our economy. The emigrants might take away what jobs we have."

"Our economy is bad, but to turn our backs on people whose lives are threatened? History isn't going to look at this kindly."

"History doesn't look at a lot of our actions kindly," he said. "The Negroes, the Indians, the Chinese—it goes on and on."

She groaned. "This is just the beginning of war troubles."

Victor rubbed his head as though he had a headache. "I'm afraid so."

The August heat was intense, and one morning they began work early, weeding and irrigating the corn and bean field. By eleven o'clock the heat was bearing down on them. Victor stopped to drink from his canteen. "We're going to have to find a cooler job."

Deborah nodded. The sawing of locusts increased in volume and a pair of mourning doves echoed back and forth between the trees of the barn and the orchard. Grandfather Blue Sky's doves ... she had come to think of them as Grandfather's, for they always reminded her of him.

A truck turned into the lane, and Victor straightened his back to see who it was. "Reub Meyers."

"Maybe he's just here to look things over," she said. They often saw Reub park in their yard and walk out to see the African field, the shelterbelts, or even the mulched field they now worked in.

Victor watched the truck. "Nope, he's waving at me. I'll go see."

The visit between the men was brief, and when Victor came back, his face was flushed from the heat. They went into the well house for fresh water. It was cooler there, and he sat on a bench. She filled a basin and washed up.

"Man, this is good drinking water." He carried her basin to the door where he poured the water on the vines by the well house wall. "I wonder if you'd want to go with me to Procek's this afternoon? That's what Reub's visit was about. That government man's coming to burn the wheat stack."

"You're kidding! They're actually going that far?"

Daniel had mistakenly planted more than his wheat allotment would allow, which would have been no problem if he had cut it for his cattle while it was green. But wet ground had kept him out of his fields, and when Daniel did get the excess wheat cut and stacked, it was ripe.

She said, "Don't tell me they won't let him give it away after all. All he wants to do is thresh it and give it to people who are hungry. How can you fault a man for that?"

"The last I knew he wanted to give the grain to people he knows in his church so they can make bread. What is it going to hurt?" Victor was frustrated. "What kind of a government do we have when milk is dumped and little pigs are killed while people are starving or standing in soup lines? I don't get it. There's a lot about our government I'm not real proud of."

He filled the basin with water and began to wash. "Don't let me get started—I guess I'm wearing August's shoes. Anyhow, folks are gathering to protest and stand behind Daniel. Probably won't accomplish a damned thing, but how will we know if we don't try?"

"Guns?" she asked. "Are people taking guns?"

"Oh no. That was made clear. This is a peaceful protest, a chance to try to reason with the allotment man or at least put on record our thinking. I sure didn't know the government could step in when someone wants to make a charitable contribution to those with less."

"I'll go."

"We've got to be there by three thirty."

"I'll hurry and fix our dinner. Then I'll need to change."

Deborah debated what to wear. If this turned out like usual, she'd be the only woman there except maybe Janie Procek. Should she wear a dress? She decided on jeans but went so far as to tie her hair back with a red ribbon.

When Victor saw her, he touched the ribbon. "Pretty," he said. "Your hair is even blacker with that bit of red."

She felt shy with his attention. "We'd better hurry."

They drove past Van Ricker's place, and Deborah was shocked to see that the site of the fire was unchanged from the day Arlene and the children died, over two years before. Charred boards still leaned here and there against the hulks of the car and truck. She wondered why the location hadn't been cleaned up. Perhaps Tony was unable to do it. Surely others, especially his relatives, had offered to help him. She turned her face away, trying not to think of the dead children and the day David was buried.

Victor read her thoughts. "Nobody knows, Deborah, why he doesn't clear it out. People have wanted to do it for him. I don't think it's healthy. He told Hollowell it was his own mess, and he'd clean it up when he was ready."

"Victor, in poetry there's more than one level of meaning to the words."

"What? Oh, well I'm sure you're not saying this is poetry. I think I understand what you mean."

The stack of wheat was between Procek's house and barn, in the very spot, if Deborah's memory served her right, where the small tree and cross had been burned by The Committee. She didn't think that was coincidental. A combine was parked next to the stack. Deborah and Victor joined the group of neighbors, and the sun beat down, a heady aroma of ripe grain and straw filling the air. She couldn't suppress a longing to reach out to the stack for a filled head. Everyone stood in a semi-circle; except for the fact they didn't bare their heads to the hot sun, it could have looked like a prayer circle. Most of the men were doing as she was, shelling out heads and exclaiming over the plump kernels.

"Lot of work in the pile."

"Lot of grain. Look at those heavy heads."

"He had a good crop for once. Like everyone else, he needs it."

"Warner got a crop too, and even Haskell got some."

"Reckon our turn will ever come?"

Deborah imitated the others, putting the grains in her mouth to soften until she could chew them.

"It isn't right, burning this." Henry Collins slapped his leather gloves against his thigh.

"Isn't this something? Procek himself isn't well off. Those allotment checks barely kept the wolf from the door, far as I could see. But he says he's rich, in comparison to some. He says he's got his milk cows, meat, and eggs. Says they haven't been hungry."

"Well, he's what I call a Christian man, working so hard stacking this and willing to give it away."

They heard a screened door slam, and, when Daniel joined them from the house, he was shaking his head. "Janie's all upset. Says she's got a feeling something bad's going to happen. Says we've got no business bucking a government man." When Procek grinned, the others smiled back. "What you think? She says if we burn it before the feller gets here, that'll be sign enough to him we aren't about to be dictated to, that at least we didn't give him the satisfaction of burning it." He was fingering some matches.

"Hell, no! I still say don't give in," someone said earnestly. "You're trying to follow the rules of the allotment. You aren't wanting it for yourself. You just want to feed those who have less than what you've got."

Collins spoke again. "I think we'd solve this fast if we all had guns. Let them know we won't be pushed around."

"The sheriff will have his," someone added.

"No guns," Daniel said. "Nobody's going to get hurt over this. All I want to do is help folks by putting bread in their mouths. And if we don't succeed, at least we're letting other folks know what we think."

"Well, the government's got the law behind them. If you're going to get your check, you've got to follow the law."

"Yeah," Collins said, "but even the law can be wrong."

"My priest was going to help me," Daniel said sadly. "He knows folks who are in need and had a fellow lined up to do the grinding."

"But," a stubborn voice said, "there's something to think about. Give bread to folks, there's no money in our pockets. They get their bread free, and the price of wheat goes down more and more."

"But I'm talking about poor folks who don't have money to buy with. These are hungry folks who don't have work neither—there aren't any jobs."

They were silent for a while, listening to the constant drone of the locusts. A light wind shook the leaves of a nearby thorny locust. Daniel Procek also had his mourning doves. For some reason Deborah shivered, but she wasn't chilly. She moved a bit closer to Victor. She had draped her light denim jacket over her shoulder and thought about putting it on.

"There's Stoddel." A car was coming, leaving behind a trail of dust that hung in the still air. "He's got the government man and Welty with him. Haven't seen Welty much. Last time was at Reub's." The men looked furtively at Deborah.

She smiled. "Well, I haven't seen him much either, and that's fine with me." The men chuckled.

"You mean you don't count Welty as one of your friends?" Henry asked. "All he did was beat you up."

"Not funny," someone said.

"You're right," Henry said. "You're right. Sorry."

As soon as she saw Welty, Deborah felt a sudden nervousness in her stomach. She was startled, for she had seen the man numerous times since his attack and attempted rape and had been relieved that the sight of him no longer bothered her. She moved closer to Victor, lifting to him what she knew was a worried face.

Sensing her uneasiness, he whispered, "What?"

"I'm not sure. Something …"

The protesters ranged themselves in front of the stack. Daniel stepped forward. "Hello, Sheriff." Stoddel was expressionless and didn't respond. Daniel turned to look at the government official, saying nothing. The man was the same one who had given Deborah her first allotment check. He was as heavy jowled as ever, corn fed, one of the men in her allotment group had said. When Welty stepped up to stand beside the sheriff, there was an audible intake of breath from the crowd. He was carrying a shotgun. The men looked at one another, moving restlessly. Stoddel put his hands on his hips, and Deborah saw the pistol that continued to frighten her every time she saw the man.

"I come to carry out the letter of the law," the allotment man said. He took matches out of his pocket and flicked one with his thumbnail. He dropped the small flame, and it landed on a loose straw. For a moment it flared up before faltering and going out.

"We're asking you to reconsider," Daniel said. "I've got a fellow who'll make this wheat into flour, and my priest has lined up four or five needy families."

"Can't do it." The man's jowls jiggled as he swung his head back and forth. "Not if you expect to get your check."

"I need my check," Procek said. "I've got a growing family—"

"The same priest is at fault for telling you to have all those kids. Let him buy the flour for the needy."

"But it's a sacrilege to burn food. You shouldn't do it." Procek picked up a wheat head and rubbed the grains into his palm. "Look here! It's so derned beautiful—" He looked at the group behind him. "These kernels hold the power to give life to those who are starving. I can't begin to count how many times the Bible talks about wheat and bread."

"Well, I always say," and the official had a sneering smile, "you can't save the world, especially in the name of popery."

"Now, see here—" Another man Deborah knew to be a Catholic shoved up to stand beside Daniel.

Welty made a show of cocking his gun.

"Bad judgment," Victor whispered beside her.

"There's no call to have a gun at this gathering," Daniel said.

A cowbell clanked on the yard gate behind Welty, and the deputy turned, startled, raising his gun higher. One of Daniel's boys, about ten years old, had come through the gate. Seeing the gun, the boy was scared, and he looked at his father.

"Hey, like I said, there's no call—"

Henry Collins rushed forward, approaching Welty from the side. "You heard the man. Put the gun down."

Welty swung on Collins, a surprised look on his face.

Collins reached for the shotgun. "Put it down."

"Why? I ain't doing anything. Get back there."

Collins grabbed at the gunstock, and Welty started to pull back.

The gun went off.

Following the blast, they all heard a rush of birds in the trees above them, and Deborah wondered how many had been hit by the buckshot.

A noise from the ground brought her attention back to the scene in front of her. Daniel Procek, who had been moving toward Collins and Welty, lay on the ground, bits of wheat straw clinging to his hatless head, a crimson mass where the shotgun blast had riddled his chest. Her mind zoomed to another time, another place, the frightened birds battering about in the trees above her, sounding like the birds of her nightmare, Daniel's body on the ground much like that of a beaten soldier at a bus stop.

Deborah forgot the dream as her senses were bombarded with what was happening, for near the yard fence, Procek's three-year-old son—shrieking at the top of his lungs—was clutched by the older boy. As though in slow motion, she turned back to Procek ... and the bloody area had grown in size; the bleeding man was kicking with both legs, much the way a chicken did that had just had its head chopped off. Thinking to hide the blood from the children's eyes, she whipped the denim jacket from her shoulder to put over the man's chest. Before she could reach him, the wailing child threw himself onto the man, thrusting his face into Daniel's neck.

"Daddy, Daddy!" The scream was shrill, piercing to ears sensitive to the pain and shock of a child. The little boy pushed against the man's neck, his movement similar to the muscular jerks of the man's legs that gouged boot heels into the ground.

Someone was there, pulling the boy away, while Deborah flung the jacket over the bloody chest.

Then Janie fell to the ground by Daniel. She tugged at his shoulders, shouting senselessly, "Get up! Get up!"

Part of the crowd stood in shocked paralysis, while others were in action. A truck pulled up, and men rushed Procek's body into the back. Someone lifted Janie into the truck bed also, wheels spun, and the truck was gone down the road. Others held Welty, and he was rushed into a car, the sheriff's car, which sped away. The government man had moved closer to the wheat stack, as though seeking shelter, and squatted there, his face drained of all color.

The wail of the child reached Deborah's ears, and she turned to see him running in aimless circles about the driveway, the cry almost indecipherable. "Daddy, Daddy." She reached Christopher just as the ten-year-old did and held him to her, pressing his bloody shirtfront against her own. Martin held on also, both of them murmuring soothing sounds to the child. But then the little boy jerked, arched his back, and pushed with his legs. Deborah fell on her side, her upper hipbone crashing onto a pile of rocks some playing child had left there, the weight of both children on her. She scrambled up, still holding the child, and headed for the house.

She turned, looking for Victor, remembered it was his truck that had taken Procek away, and saw instead the government man bent and retching at the side of the stack.

The little boy was limp in her arms now, and in the dimmer light of the kitchen, the older boy helped her remove the child's bloody clothing and wash him down. Deborah cried, and Martin and Missy cried with her. She held them to her on the divan, saying, "That's good. You have to cry. You have to get it out."

But the little one was quiet, not even whimpering, his eyes almost unblinking and wide. Pulling him to her, she willed him to respond, but he was limp and silent, and she remembered being told of her similar actions when Grandfather Blue Sky died.

The child appeared to sleep, and she placed him in his bed, praying he would find some release from the shock. The other children slept too. She paced the hallway between the two bedrooms, watching them and thinking of Arlene's three children. The pain within her grew to bursting.

A combine roared, and she heard the unmistakable sound of threshing, the odor of wheat dust in the air. When the machine went silent, she looked out to see a tarp covering the spot where Procek had died ... died? Of course he had died, and even Victor had to have known when he drove away with the body being rocked in Janie's arms.

Sitting on the big tarp were burlap sacks, filled to bulging with wheat, and she watched while a man pulled the edges of the tarp protectively over the sacks. Then milk cows were brought from the pasture, hogs called to the trough, and hens shooed into their shelter. A bucket of eggs appeared on the doorstep, and from the vicinity of the well house, she heard the whine of the cream separator. There was nothing for her to do. The children slept a merciful sleep, the house was clean and tidy, and she had nothing to do but sit on a kitchen chair, her mind blank.

At dusk, Victor came, entering the kitchen door without knocking, finding her in the deep twilight of the room. He lit a lamp and pulled a chair close to hers. "Janie's sister and brother-in-law are coming to stay the night. Janie's with her folks over at that little place called Deer Run." He turned her to face him. "Do you think we can get the blood off your blouse before Dianne gets here? I think it'll be hard for her to take."

She looked down, seeing for the first time where the child had smeared her blouse front. "Oh. I hadn't noticed." She went to the sink and pumped cold water into a basin. She removed the blouse and soaked it, scrubbing out the blood. "I'm worried about Christopher. Maybe sleep will do him good. I think it's sleep. I tried to imagine Jonathan or David seeing something like that at Christopher's age ... when we adults can't even handle it."

After the blouse was well wrung, she put it on, its wet coldness bringing some of her senses to life. She cleaned the basin, and when she bent to put it away beneath the sink, she groaned lightly, unexpectedly.

Victor moved to her side. "What is it?"

"Why, I'm not sure. I remember falling with Christopher in my arms and Martin on top of me. My hip ... I hit a rock." She released the waist of her jeans and pushed them down to reveal the side of her upper hip.

"Deborah!" Victor touched her skin, lightly tracing the hugeness of the bruise. "Is it just bruised? Nothing broken?"

"Oh, I'm sure it's just a nasty bruise." She felt the softness of his touch, a touch both soothing and burning. He moved away, and she buttoned her jeans, sudden hot tears rolling down her face.

"The two older children cried, but the youngest might have been in a trance. We'll have to tell Dianne … I fear for Christopher. I'm afraid of the shock—what he saw. Why?" She whimpered, and he held her, his lips to her cheek, until they both heard a car pull up.

During the drive home, she asked about Welty. Victor said, "Stoddel locked him in a cell."

"For his safety?"

"Charges will be filed—"

"Charges! Doesn't that surprise you? Stoddel let Welty get by with beating his wife and me. He even took care of Welty after someone beat him up."

"Maybe that's it," Victor said. "Maybe he got fed up with taking care of Welty, although I guess Stoddel will be toting meals to him again."

"The man isn't guilty. Sure, he was carrying a gun, but I'll bet Stoddel, or even the government inspector, told him to. Then Henry Collins interfered. First, Welty was startled from behind by the boy, and then Henry came from the side. When Henry jerked the gun, Welty's finger was on the trigger."

"He shouldn't have had the safety off. Why'd he have his finger on the trigger?"

"Where do most people put their trigger finger when holding a gun? If not on the trigger, at least near it."

"If he hadn't—"

"That's looking back, Victor. All the ifs in the world won't change matters now. If he had just had the gun higher—but if he hadn't hit Daniel, he might have hit someone standing behind him. Even you or me. If he had been sick today and hadn't come with Stoddel—"

"Are you prepared to speak in his behalf? I don't think many others would."

"You know what I say is true. Everyone saw it. It was a horrible accident. In my estimation, Henry was equally involved."

"It's not just a matter of talking to Stoddel about Welty. It's bringing ourselves to Stoddel's attention again. Do we want to do that?"

Deborah said, "Have we *never* been noticed by him ever since Christian disappeared? I'm sick and tired of the man. What can he do to us?"

"That's just it. We don't know what he can do to us. Folks tell me he got all stirred up when he found out I started what happened at Reub's sale. If we speak for Welty, it just might be fuel for the fire."

Deborah pictured again Stoddel's hand at the butt of his gun when he confronted her years before. "He's been controlling our lives," she said bitterly. "Since the day he scared me after the incident with Tony by the cut fence, I've been afraid of him." She tried to smile and swallowed a sob. "Having Stoddel after us is kind of like living next door to the klan."

"Well, you do live next door to a klan member. Did you forget it?"

"I guess I did. But we're also neighbors to Daniel. For a moment I even forgot him. I'm sure Janie and the kids haven't forgotten what happened. What should I do, Victor?"

"Nobody feels any love for Welty. They liked Daniel."

"I don't feel any love for Welty."

"But you'd speak in his behalf?"

"I want to because it was a horrible accident, and it wasn't all his fault."

At Deborah's farm, Victor turned off the engine, and they sat in the dark. He said, "He's dead. A good man's dead ... and think of those little kids with no daddy." Victor lowered his face to his hands that gripped the steering wheel. "What in God's name is going on? First, Arlene and the children—and then right across the road, Daniel!"

She pressed against his side, gripping him about his waist. "I know. Were we all wrong, going there, and standing in front of that senseless stack of wheat?"

"If we hadn't gone, Daniel would've stood there himself ... alone."

Victor walked her to the house and lit a lamp. "You fix us a bite of food while I go milk those cows and shut up the chickens." He started to the door. "It's been a hard day, a horrible day."

Facing the door, he hesitated, his shoulders hunched, and he said, "I'm not sure I've got the strength."

"For what?" she asked.

With his back to her, he said, "I tell you what. I'll milk those cows and do the separating. Then I'm going home." He stopped, his hand on the door. When he turned to face her, his eyes glistened in the lamplight. "When I think how quickly Arlene and the children died and Janie lost Daniel ... I can't sit across the table from you tonight. Your eyes are so striking, and if I see you again, I'm not going to want to leave, I need you so." His voice broke. "Deborah, I love you so much. Please stay in the house." He left.

She was motionless, his words repeating in her ears. His voice had registered so much emotion—and something that hurt and saddened her. He had sounded lonely. She moved about the living room, touching with trembling fingers, seeking familiar items, especially the recent studio photo of Baby Half Shell and Jonathan. She sat in the rocking chair that had been Bethany's and began to examine her thoughts and feelings one by one.

One thought, a memory, was Lydia's voice, so strong in her mind that she looked about, almost expecting to see her old friend: "He loves you, you know." And next, just as strong, came Victor's voice: "When I think how quickly Janie lost Daniel ..." and then, the final thought, this one equally strong—the kind of love Victor felt for her and the love she felt for him—it was time to ignore Stoddel's venom, the poison he was putting in her veins. It was time to marry Victor.

Deborah blew out the lamp's light and got into bed. She could see the silhouette of the trees against the moonlit sky. The pain in her hip reminded her again of the afternoon's tragedy, and she turned to lie on her unbruised side, her fingers tracing the outline of the soreness. Not only could she still feel Victor's touch but also the solace of standing in Janie's kitchen with his comforting arms around her, her hands touching the back of his head. It was time to marry. She fell asleep.

She woke in the night to the sounds of thunder and lightning and held her breath, barely able to believe. Waves of moist air came through the open windows. The rain began, settling down to a steady, slow pace, and she went back to sleep with its sounds and two thoughts lulling her—the boys were coming, and she and Victor were going to get married.

Chapter 22

The Old Woodpile

Victor arrived earlier than usual the next morning, his mare's hooves thudding softly on the wet road. Before she could even speak, he said, "I saw what you saw. Much as I despise Welty for what he did to you, I saw what you saw. I think a man like Daniel would insist we tell the truth. If we do the kind of thing Procek believed in, doing what's right, it'll give more power to his memory. If you want, let's go see Stoddel when we're through with the chores and breakfast. I think the roads will be firm enough by then."

"Are you sure you want to? I'm not making you—"

"I want to, Deborah."

They were in the yard, and he had already turned to open the corral gate. "Victor." The name was not a question or a demand but a cry full of emotion. He heard the feeling in her voice, for when he turned, the expectation on his face caused an abrupt intake of her breath. She said, "We need to tell Dad to bring the boys home—now." Then, without hesitation, she asked, "Victor, will you marry me the instant the boys get here?"

When he smiled, she realized a long time had passed since he had smiled the way he was at that moment. "Well, Deborah Jorgenson Nelson, I would be honored."

Welty sat in a cell, his shoulders hunched, his hands clasped together between his knees. He stared at the cracked concrete floor and didn't look up at Victor and Deborah. Stoddel was wearing the stick, not the gun, at his side, but he still stood with his hands on his hips, his fingertips twitching on the top of the stick.

"What do you want now?"

"We don't think Welty is guilty of anything other than bad judgment," Deborah said.

Victor said, "He shouldn't have been carrying a gun, he shouldn't have taken off the safety. He should learn to hold a gun without having his finger on the trigger."

"He was startled by the child and Henry Collins," Deborah said. "Henry should have known better than to put his hand on a gun someone else was holding. It wasn't Welty's intent to shoot." She glanced at Welty. He was at the cell door now, hanging on to the bars. Deborah saw the man's jaw had dropped, and his expression was contrary to his usual hard, set-jaw look.

They waited for a response from the sheriff. Stoddel studied their faces for a time, and Welty moved restlessly at the cell door. Then the sheriff gave a snort of laughter. "I don't give a damn what the two of you think about Welty."

They were taken aback by his words. Victor spoke, "Well, now, Sheriff—"

Stoddel snorted again. "I was there. I don't need statements from the two of you. You're about the least reliable witnesses I can think of."

Deborah wasn't surprised at his words. "I'm going—"

Stoddel said, "I still haven't figured out what you did to Nelson, but I'll find out someday."

The most intense anger she had ever felt flooded Deborah's head with heat. She must have moved toward the sheriff, for Victor stepped in between Stoddel and her, turning her about, opening the door. Looking back at the sheriff, he said, "You know, Stoddel," his voice very calm, "all these years I've let you control me, a man who loves this woman and wants to marry her. I realized just now how stupid it was of me. You're a nothing, Stoddel, an absolute nothing. You're not going to control me anymore, you son of a bitch."

Victor's voice was so quiet Deborah wondered if Stoddel had heard him. But then the sheriff's shoulders seemed to slump, and he went around his desk and sat down heavily, the springs in his chair complaining.

They drove down the brick street, and Deborah waved to people who called to them. Victor raised his finger from the wheel, the expected salute from a person living in a rural community. At the railroad tracks, he stopped the truck, even though no train was coming, and let the engine idle.

He gripped the steering wheel, looking through the bug-spattered windshield. "Did you hear what I said to him? Did you hear, Deborah?" His laughter filled the truck cab. "Both of us took all the wind out of his sails. I really think we did." He reached to hold her hand, tugging her toward him. "We're going to get married. He isn't going to stop us any longer. Do you realize that?"

She moved beside him and planted little kisses all over his face. "The boys are coming any day now, and we're getting married."

He held her, giving her a long kiss. They heard the honking of a horn and the hoots of someone who saw them. Dust from the passing truck fogged the window. Victor released her and shifted into gear. "I do like giving folks something to talk about, don't you?"

Back at the farm, they sat in the swing on the porch, and he kept his arm around her. "I can hug you without going crazy, knowing there's hope for us, there's light at the end of the tunnel."

She rested her head on his chest, hearing the beat of his heart. "No doubt about it, your heart is beating. In case you don't know, you're alive."

Raising her face so he could kiss her, he said, "If your dad brings our boys home, he can be here when we get married. How does that sound?"

"It's okay with me—although I don't know what he'll think about it." They kissed again, and Deborah giggled. "As old as we are, you'd think we'd have more self-control."

"Work," Victor said, standing up. "That's the answer, work. Waiting to marry you is going to work me to death." He pulled back his shoulders. "How about removing blow dirt from the corral fence and the base of the barn?"

"Well, okay, but I'll be so glad when we can do what we really want."

The nighttime rain had left the temperature five degrees cooler than the day before. The soil they dug and scooped was heavy with moisture. "This is almost mud." Deborah strained as she threw the dirt into the wagon. "I'm not complaining, mind you. You can sure tell what nice rains we've had for the moisture to have soaked into this stuff."

At noon, they rested their tired backs against the manure scraper—turned bottom up—and ate from the basket of lunch she had fixed. Their thoughts were never far from yesterday's tragedy. They found it painful to talk about Daniel but couldn't seem to stop themselves. She said, "If I hadn't seen it happen, I don't think I would believe it. Right across the road from Arlene and the children … poor Janie."

"Remember how he cried when they burned the tree." Victor shook his head sadly. "I sure wonder what The Committee is thinking now, knowing he's dead."

"If they're honest, they know he died because of his convictions."

He took her hand and ran his fingertips over her palm. He kissed her palm.

"You've got to stop, Victor. I can hardly stand it."

"I know," he said and kissed her again.

Deborah thought both of them worked extra hard that afternoon, as though sweat and aching muscles controlled the electricity between them and made the painful memories easier in their minds. Victor scraped and hauled with August's team. She hitched her team to the wagon for loading what they dug out.

After they finished the corral, Deborah opened the north gate to the pasture, and they worked along the fence line to the back of the barn. By then, it was six o'clock, and storm clouds appeared in the west. Mourning doves seemed to be riding the wind above her, answering one another, and she imagined she could detect anxiety in their calls. From the shadows of the big barn, she listened to the doves, wondering, but then Victor called to her.

"What do you say to burning the old woodpile? It would be easier to clear up the ashes and blow dirt rather than trying to dig out around the pile. There's a lot of wood rot there." Victor studied the area, lifting his hat and wiping his head with a bandana.

Deborah was too tired to do one more thing, yet she agreed with him. "It should have been done long ago. It's a danger with the nails in those old boards. Every time I've thought of burning it, I've been too busy with other jobs." She leaned against the barn wall, trying to cover her exhaustion.

Victor looked at the gathering clouds. "If we'd burn it right now, maybe the storm that's brewing will dump rain on the coals. We wouldn't have to haul water to put them out. Tomorrow, when the ashes are cold, we'll sift them through a screen to get the nails gathered up."

"It's a good idea." He was going on about his work, and she called to him. "The mourning doves—I think they sense the storm. It bothers me, how they're sounding."

"Are you worried, Deborah? Are you anxious? Those look like thunderheads to me, not a dirt storm. But isn't it great, another rain? A year ago, I wouldn't have believed we'd ever have rain two days in a row."

She looked at the clouds. He was right. Even at such a distance, she could see the lightning, and the doves no longer flew the air currents above her. She went back to work, suppressing her uneasiness.

They finished scraping away from the rear of the barn and worked along the fence that ran from the corner of the barn to the east. Some drifts reached the level of the bottom wire, packed in with thistles. Removing the damp soil, and baring the bottom wire and posts, both Victor and Deborah struggled with their tiredness.

"We've got to stop," he said. "Tomorrow's another day."

She straightened and pressed her hand against her back. "I am so sick of this kind of work, yet at the same time, I keep remembering the fence line between Moses and Ol' Paul."

"Deborah, don't look ahead at all the posts and fencing in that pasture. Do what August said."

Victor helped her unharness the two teams and rub them down with clean sacking. At the edge of the pasture, they watched the four big horses roll on the ground and scratch the day's work out of their hides. "That sure beats having to curry them, Victor. I don't know when I've been so tired."

"When? Probably last night ... and all the nights before that."

"You're a slave driver." She gave him a quick kiss.

He smiled. "You know what's driving me? It's something like that kiss."

He was carrying a can of fuel for the woodpile. "Sweetheart, stand clear while I set this fire."

Starting on the back side of the pile, Victor splashed the fuel high onto the old boards. The kerosene fumes filled the air, covering the odors of the fresh green grass and what was left of hay in the nearby stack. She straightened, stretching her back again. The shoveling had been hard work. She watched him, and the sunlight made rainbows in the arcs of fuel.

And then, as though in slow motion, she saw his feet go out from under him, and with a gasp of surprise, he went down, his arm throwing the kerosene container behind him. The next thing she knew, he disappeared from sight as the ground caved near the edge of the wood, taking away a six foot area.

"Victor!" Her scream was long and wailing, and its sound echoed, rebounding against the back of the barn and the hills of the pasture, which rose to the north. She heard her scream echo again and again and was shocked at its frightened sounds. Marco barked in alarm, his head swinging back and forth in confusion. She dropped her shovel and started toward the caved area.

"Deborah! Stay back!" The shout came from below the woodpile, its order so sharp she stopped dead in her tracks and lost her balance, crashing down to her hands and knees. Marco was suddenly beside her, pushing his body against her.

"Stay back! It might cave in some more. I'm in a hole, an old well, is my guess, probably about twenty-five, thirty feet."

"Are you hurt?"

"No. Not hurt a bit. I slid down with the dirt." It was strange to hear his voice from below the pile of wood. "Listen to me!" He was asking her to focus on his words in a way she had never heard before.

"Yes!"

"Saddle Princess. My lariat is on the saddle. Use the best knot Christian ever taught you. Loop an end over the saddle horn and throw the rest down here. Don't bring the horse any closer than maybe twenty feet. Hear me?"

"I hear you. I'm going." She turned to leave—and then whirled back. "Victor?"

"It's okay. It's okay."

She ran, Marco and Jake close to her legs. In the corral, she grabbed the bridle off the fence post where Victor had left it that morning. Praying the mare wouldn't spook, Deborah approached her, talking all the while.

The roan didn't move. She saddled the horse and rode around the barn, near the old well. She firmly tied Victor's lariat on the saddle horn.

"Victor, I'm throwing the rope to you!" She was surprised to see the loops land in a neat pile at the edge of the cave-in and just as neatly slither on and down into the well.

"Good girl! Perfect!"

The rope tightened, and she visualized him pulling up the side of the well. Hearing clods of dirt fall, she watched with horror as more of the side caved off where the rope cut at the edge.

"Victor!"

"It's okay. I'm all right. Stand back with the horse."

Victor clambered out of the hole, his head just grazing the edge of the board. His clothes were muddy. He came to her.

Deborah held him, clasping her hands at his back. "I was so afraid it would cave. I thought I was going to lose you too, along with David and everybody else." She gasped for breath.

An object was in his shirt pocket, pressing against her. Victor pulled back, reaching into his pocket. He placed something in her hand, cupping their fingers together to hold it. A shiver, like a bolt of lightning, cold and jagged, traveled down her back. She was holding a pair of glasses, one lens missing, the other lens cracked.

"Christian's glasses." Victor's voice broke.

A weakness rolled over her body, seeped through her bones, turned them to elastic, and she sat on the ground. Victor crouched in front of her, holding her arms. She stared at the glasses, moving her lips but unable to speak.

He worked to relax her fingers that clutched the glasses so hard. "He's there. While I waited for you to get the horse, I found him." He drew an overall strap buckle from his pocket. "Here's more."

She still could not speak, instead remembering August saying, as he thumped his forehead, "I'll be darned if I can remember where Clifford had the other well."

Like flashes of electricity, the energy of images crossed her mind's eye from one side to the other, leaving as abruptly as they came, and her eardrums pounded with her heartbeat: August, thinking "Where is he?" while standing by the woodpile ... Marco, shortly after Christian's disappearance, barking and whimpering, crouched as though in a cat chasing mode ... Jonathan on top of the teetering pile, David nailed to a board ... Victor and the Strate boys looking for decent boards for the tree house ... Deborah herself, numerous times, circling, selecting kindling for the shop stove, stakes for garden plants, a board for the hog fence, always looking, picking, discarding, avoiding rusty nails ... that day long ago, only months after the disappearance, when she circled and threw kerosene, pleasing Jonathan with rainbow arcs ... and then had no matches in her pocket.

"Deborah, I'm going back down."

Her head jerked up.

"I'm bringing him out of there."

"No!"

"I can't leave him there."

"No! It's dangerous. The well might cave in completely. Victor," she grabbed his shirtfront, "thank God you got out. Leave him there. It can be his grave just as well as a cemetery grave."

"Christian's my friend. I want to bring him up, and we'll give him the burial he deserves."

They argued. Finally, he no longer listened. He left her huddled on the ground and went to the barn. He came back with a gunnysack fastened to his belt.

Beyond Victor and the horse, lightning streaked across the black sky, and thunder vibrated the very air around them. Darkness was closing in, and wind stirred bits of hay and dust from the tops of dirt drifts. He came toward her, and she stopped him. With a voice strangely hoarse, she said, "So many people in my lifetime, people I have loved, people who have shared my very space, have died. I don't want to lose you too. The walls could cave while you're at the bottom." Speechless, her jaw and lips moved, and hot tears flowed into her mouth.

"You're not going to lose me." He touched her cheek briefly, and his stubbornness toppled hers.

She watched him grasp the rope, which was still tied to the saddle horn. With his back to the woodpile he squirmed beneath the boards. The last she saw of him was his face. He called to her. "I love you, Deborah."

The storm moved closer, and she lowered her head, refusing to look at the cloud-to-ground flashes, hearing their searing sounds and smelling the ozone, metallic yet spicy like cloves. She put her arm about the horse's neck, wrapping the reins about her fingers, fearful the mare might bolt in the storm. Looking back at the knot she had used to tie the lariat to the saddle horn, she saw it was secure. Time stopped, and only the storm moved about her, the lightning becoming starkly beautiful and threatening, all in one.

The rope was slack, and Deborah knew Victor was at the bottom of the well. She imagined him, groping in the darkness, filling the sack he pulled after him.

The first drops of rain were falling, heavy and cold. She shuffled her feet and tried to pray, working to focus her mind on thoughts and words. "Protect him. Bring him back safely." The wind lashed the rain at her face, and she could no longer see where the rope went below ground.

She felt the rope grow taut. "Deborah," he called, "I'm coming. Keep a hold on the horse."

She saw him pulling on the rope and coming from beneath the boards. As he crawled out over the edge of the well, a large chunk the size of two men broke off from beneath his knees, causing him to lose his leverage.

"I'll help you," she called, crouching as though to run.

"No! Stay with the mare."

She did as he said.

Then Victor was completely out of the well and held the sack with one hand, snaking the rope with the other from beneath his feet. He moved toward her. The rain was pounding, and she could see water running off the brim of his hat.

He handed her the sack, and she felt the bones in it. Again, she sank to the ground, holding the hardness against her. Victor sat on the ground with her, pulling her within the circle of his legs as he wrapped them around her. He held her, rocking, and their clothing was plastered to their bodies. Her hair had come loose, its wetness draping about their faces. When a blue-crackling bolt streaked down the sky, directing itself at the ground miles away, he lifted her from the mud. With the thunder crashing about them, he guided them to the house.

"Here." In the kitchen, he helped Deborah loosen her hold on the sack, leaving it on the kitchen table. "It's all right," he reassured her. "He's safe right there."

He pulled out a chair. "Sit here," he said gently. He started with her feet, removing her shoes and socks. Her hair straggled before her eyes, and her clothing was saturated with rain. He helped her towel dry and put on a nightgown.

She began to talk. "I was wrong, Victor. There were the times I accused him of leaving me. I was wrong."

He unbraided the rest of her hair and began drying it.

"Victor, how did it happen? What happened to him?"

"I figure it was kind of the way it happened to me—only I fell different than he did. I slid down feet first with the dirt. Maybe he tumbled, hitting head first and hard."

"So he probably went outside to see about the rain? Oh, of course he did. That was what we all figured. He loved a good storm."

"He's appreciating tonight's weather." Victor held her hands between his, warming them. "I'll bet you're right. So he was watching it come. We know for sure he put the horses and Marco in the barn. Maybe he walked out further, behind the barn where he could watch the clouds better. He just got too close, Deborah, too close. That we know for sure."

"But why couldn't we tell he had fallen there? We searched the area so many times." She pictured Maude and Martha, in their skirts, Maude with a cane, Martha with swollen, blocky feet and legs, climbing the stone wall, moving out to the edge of the farmstead. That day, men, maybe women like June Strate, carrying Jimmy and followed by little Lawrence and Harley, circled the woodpile. *John walked around the woodpile when we built the little biddy houses ... choosing old pieces to block the houses while we finished the flooring and netting.*

Victor was thinking. "It must have caved in on the edge, like it did for me—Lord, I don't know. It rained, so it probably covered up the evidence and any tracks, maybe even some of the raw earth." He gnawed at his lip. "It doesn't make sense."

She said, "The pile of wood was stacked fairly high. Maybe he was up on it—maybe the boards slid out from under him." *Lester and Paul cleaned up after building the tree house, tossed scraps of two-by-four on the pile, and made a game out of seeing who could throw the highest.* "No ... you know what? I still think he was walking next to the edge ... then maybe after he fell, some boards fell and covered up all sign."

"Could be. We'll never know."

She grabbed at her folded arms, rocking back and forth in the chair, rounding up, and corralling her thoughts. "How many times one of us went near the woodpile or right up to it to get scraps of wood! The day August died, I went there. It could have happened to any of us, just like it did with you. Oh!"

"What?"

"I was just remembering, while you were down in the well, I remembered—I suppose the summer after Christian disappeared, one of the boys, David, stepped on a nail in the pile. They had been playing there." Seeing it in her mind's eye had been bad, giving voice to it was worse. "I carried him down. Then I went after Jonathan who was balanced—

teetering, actually, at the top. I remember slipping and sliding with one or both of them as we came down."

"Try not to think on that. God watched over you, sweet girl. It wasn't meant the boys fall or find him. It was meant I do it, and I wasn't hurt."

She lowered her head to the table. "When I got the boys off the pile … I smelled something. Oh, no! There's more. Earlier, in the spring, when the weather was warming, August and I worked on the fence right there, even forked weeds from the edge of the pile, burning them, and repairing the fence. August commented … oh, Victor. He asked about the odor. I said it was probably the dead cow I drug to the gully just to the north … and there was a visiting tom cat that hid in the pile of wood … and maybe he'd died. I hadn't seen him in a while …" She shuddered. "The times I had the notion Christian had left me—and he was here all the time, close by, so close." She touched the sack.

He put kindling and coal in the range and dropped a stove lid. It clanged. "Sorry," he said. Once the fire was going well and the teakettle was on a burner, she asked him to sit with her.

He touched her hand and turned his attention back to her. "Look at you! You're shaking, you're so cold. Let's get you to bed."

He helped her into bed. He covered her up to her neck and spread Grandfather Blue Sky's blanket over her. Deborah shivered beneath the blankets, and he was concerned. "I suppose you're feeling some shock as well as cold. I'm going to make some hot tea and a little something to eat. Okay?"

She nodded. While he rattled about in the kitchen, Deborah tried to think. He brought her a steaming cup and some toast, and all she could say was, "Victor, Princess is standing out there in the storm. You've got to take care of her."

"Well. I think you're going to be okay if you're thinking about Princess. You're right. I'll go. You drink this and see if it warms you."

Deborah was drowsy when he came in later. "Is Princess okay? Did you dry her? She did a good job you know. What would Van Ricker say if he knew the horse he once owned had helped rescue you?"

"She sure did. Don't worry. She's in the barn. I milked and did what I could with the rest of the chores in this downpour. A downpour, Deborah! It's hard to believe. And you have terraces to control the run off in the field."

"You're soaked too. You need to take care of yourself." She pointed to the bottom drawer of the armoire. "There are some flannel shirts and long underwear there—if you don't mind wearing Christian's clothes. I gave his overalls to Big David just before they got married."

"I don't mind."

When Victor returned, he grinned. "My pants are drying in front of the stove." He sat in the rocking chair by her bed, balancing a mug of tea and a plate of toast. "You didn't eat much."

"I'm okay."

"You want to talk?"

"Yes." She hesitated. "I don't know what to say. I think my brain is numb."

"You rest, and I'll sit here with my supper. I just want to be close by."

"Not much of a supper."

"I guess I'm not the cook you are."

"I don't mean that. You ought to have a big meal after all the hard work in the dirt—and then doing what you did."

"I'm fine. My stomach doesn't count now. It's my thoughts that are important."

"Why? Why did Clifford Strong leave the well the way he did? Why didn't he fill it in or at least put a proper cap on it?"

"We'll never know," Victor said.

"August tried so hard to remember where the well was. Do you remember? The three of us rode the north pasture, looking for Christian. We stopped at the windmill for water, and I remember August talking about the old well, trying to remember." She felt herself growing sleepy.

Victor leaned over, kissing her cheek, his breath warm on her face. "Sleep. I'll be in Jonathan's bedroom if you need me."

*

Tonight I can only record: he is found.

Chapter 23

How Did It Happen?

By the time Deborah woke the next morning, it was daybreak. She sat up in bed, her head feeling strangely tight as though swollen. Her muscles hurt, and she knew the soreness was from all of the digging. Putting on her robe, she went into the kitchen. Victor sat at the table, drinking coffee and reading one of Jonathan's letters.

She put her hand on his shoulder and pressed her head against his. "Hi. I really slept."

"You did. Now, I want you to eat a decent breakfast." He brought her a bowl of oatmeal and went to work scrambling eggs.

"What all have you been doing?"

"Got the chores done. Kind of just waiting until the roads are good enough to travel. I figure I'd better go to Mary first and then to Moses. Who shall I call? Frank or Calvin?"

"Call Dad. He can break the news to Jonathan and the Nelsons. They won't be surprised—that he's dead, I mean. They'll be like the rest of us, I guess, dismayed as to what happened." She shook her head. "Maybe they'll be like me, finding it hard to believe we actually know. Remember all those times August and Audrey wondered what happened?"

Her dad and Calvin had recently hired a couple to take the place of the Nyfellers. She began thinking out loud. "Maybe Dad and Calvin can have the new couple take over now so Sonja and David can come home. There's certainly no rush about the funeral—perhaps in a week or two—whatever works for them."

Victor traced her jawline and then her lips. "And then," he said, "if your families would stay awhile, we could get married, I hope about a week later?"

"Yes, oh, yes!" She kissed him almost feverishly.

"If we're not careful, we'll put the cart before the horse." He thought for a moment. "Who said that?"

"Eloise said Herman and Corrine had done that, but she wasn't being critical. It didn't bother her."

Victor gave her a kiss and got the coffeepot. "A cup of coffee and then I'm off to town with Christian's bones. What do you think?"

"Yes, that's good. Go to Carl first. I suppose Carl will have to get Stoddel involved." A thought stirred her, and she laughed. "Isn't it something to think about—Stoddel will know what happened to Christian. What will he do with his time after he knows?"

"Do you suppose he'll believe it?"

Deborah jerked her head to attention, staring at Victor. "Oh, do you think—"

"Don't worry about it," Victor reassured her. "As Audrey would say, it'll all come out in the wash. But it's all the more important that I go to the neighbors first."

"I would like it if you would pick out a small casket, one just big enough for the longest bones. Christian would think it pretentious to have an adult-sized casket."

※

The Cresslers came, carrying Mary's coffeepots. She hugged Deborah. "I don't know what to say. All the way over, we've been talking, 'What are we going to say?' It seems so strange to finally know the truth after all these years."

"You've just expressed it, Mary. It is strange—and a big relief." Deborah suddenly sat down. "I'm still having to work at believing it. It has been so hard, not knowing. How many times have I said that? Now I have the answers. But I'm not feeling grief. I felt it long ago." She allowed her relief to show in her voice. "His life ended back then, and mine has gone on, almost nine years of going on."

"Well!" Mary smiled, letting her own relief show in her face.

Neighbors began to come, bringing food, staying to talk. Most of them seemed as awkward as Mary had been about what to say to Deborah. She found herself giving the same little speech to new arrivals as she had given to Mary. She could tell these folks too were relieved to see how she was handling everything.

She moved among her friends, some in the living room and the kitchen, others on the porch, even in the yard. The day was refreshingly cool after the two-and-a-half-inch rain, and everyone was enjoying a rest from hard work, a reprieve from the worries of dust and drought. Having them with her was more like a lazy Sunday afternoon gathering than for a death, which was fine with her, and she almost expected someone to break out the ice cream freezers. There was hopefulness among the group that the drought was ended.

Walking about, she heard snatches of conversation here and there, some she participated in.

"To think we looked and looked, and he was there all the time."

"Remember the search at Van Ricker's place? My!"

Deborah did remember, and now she felt bad about it.

"Deborah, I don't think you should feel bad. Tony shouldn't have made the threat against Christian if he didn't expect folks to get upset about it. All the things he's done to folks, I don't feel bad."

"We wrote letter after letter. Remember, Nila? Remember Eloise Williams and how she kind of scared you with her cane?"

"Kind of? She put ten years on me."

"All these years of wondering. Seemed like anytime some of us got together, we'd get to speculating."

"August always said Christian was good for a story. Remember how after Nelson was gone, August would tell those stories? Oh, he could tell a story, particularly if he had a good subject like Christian. He would get that grin on his face and start bouncing in his chair."

"The story about the hog almost nippin' Christian's butt."

"There was the time he was cutting the rotten tree limb."

"Set his smokehouse on fire—"

They laughed, and Deborah joined them, filled with easiness she hadn't felt for a long time.

When Victor returned and came to the house, he carried a child's casket. He held the walnut-grained box to his chest, one arm under it, the other over it, much in the way he would hold a child to him for comfort and stability.

Deborah ran her hand over the smoothness of the wood. "You chose well, Victor," her fingers tracing the brass fittings. Mary helped Deborah remove the photographs from the pedestal table, and Victor placed the casket.

"Looks like a kid's box—maybe an eight-year-old," someone said.

"Just bones. The leg would be the longest—the femur." Deborah thought the person sounded proud of his knowledge of bones.

Victor said, "Your dad said they'll plan on being here in a week. He and Calvin just need a little time getting the new hands settled in." Victor smiled at the visitors, twisting his hat brim. "You folks need to know, before this happened, Deborah and I had decided to marry as soon as the boys come home from Minnesota. We're going ahead with our plans. Deborah's dad figures there's no doubt he and the Nelsons will stay awhile after the funeral—for our wedding."

"Wedding!" O. B. Dickerson was immediately alert, and he grinned.

"Well," Gracie said, "you have just made this old man happy. He's always thinking young folks ought to marry."

"Well, sure," and O. B. tugged at her earlobe. "I want these folks to be as happy as we are."

"Hush," she smiled. "You don't have to tell the world."

Deborah went to her bedroom and rummaged through a drawer until she found Christian's college graduation picture. She stared at his face, as though trying to remember what he had looked like. Mary set the framed photo on the casket.

"Young, wasn't he?" someone asked.

"A few years older, actually," Deborah said. "This is college graduation. He died about five years later."

"Young," the voice said emphatically.

"Yes," she agreed. Christian was perpetually young, like Lendel—and the children.

Nila said, "So you're going to leave the casket sitting there until his folks come for the funeral? A week—in your living room?"

"Why not?" Mary giggled. "He's been behind the barn for nine years and didn't bother anyone."

"Oh, you!" Nila said. She flounced in her chair. "I wouldn't do it, let Reub's bones set on my best table for weeks on end."

Reub heard her and snorted. "Huh! I suppose you'd fear I'd roll over or something and scratch the varnish."

Victor stood silently in the kitchen, turning his hat around and around in his hands. Deborah joined him and could tell he had matters on his mind. "What is it, Victor?"

"Doc says not all the finger and toe bones are there."

"Oh. Well." She listened to the people in the front room. More had come in from the porch, some looking at the small casket and the picture, others sitting on the floor because the chairs were full. Someone was telling another story about Christian, one she hadn't heard. She wondered if it had been made up.

"They ought to be there, with the rest of him." Victor was still talking about the missing bones.

She shook her head. "He's not there, in the box. Those are pieces of calcium. His spirit is all around us, has been all along, Victor. Didn't you say something of the sort? That's what counts."

Reub Meyers and Herman Vinther came in from the screened porch. "Doc and Stoddel are coming," Herman said.

"I wonder why," Mary said.

Deborah was uneasy and looked at Victor. He shrugged. "Well," she said, "let's offer the sheriff some pie and coffee."

The two men came through the front room door, and the filled room grew quiet. Mary greeted them and invited them to have coffee and pie. It was evident to Deborah that Carl Hocksmith was upset. "Folks, I need your attention. This man here," he gestured toward Stoddel, "this man of authority—" Carl stopped to twist his mouth in a little sneer "wants all of you folks—women and men, out by the woodpile. He says you men need your working gloves."

"Whatever for?" Nila spouted.

Carl flushed. "He wants you as witnesses. I would think just a few of you would do, but it seems he wants everyone's attention. The sheriff's not satisfied somebody didn't do harm to Christian Nelson." He looked around the room until he saw Deborah and Victor. "Sheriff Stoddel still considers Deborah and Victor to be suspects in this case."

A commotion erupted, a mixture of indignant voices and outright mocking laughter. Herman leaped from his chair and wordlessly shook his fist in the sheriff's face.

Reub called out, "Egg, how do you know the dog didn't up and knock the man down the hole?" There was more laughter.

Herman still glared at Stoddel. Victor stepped between them. "What do you want done at the woodpile?"

Stoddel didn't answer.

Carl said, "I guess I'm still his mouthpiece. Remember, don't shoot the messenger." He went on in his clipped way, as though giving orders. "He wants every board moved off the well, one at a time. He wants to see how a man could fall beneath a pile of boards."

"It happened to Victor. He could show him," Herman said.

Carl said, "He wants a man to go down in the well. He wants these items brought up—the remainder of the toe and finger bones, Christian's clothing, his keys, and one eye-glass lens."

There were mutters. "Aw, let it go, Stoddel."

Carl held up his hand. "No. No. For many years this man has been sticking his nose where it doesn't belong. Let's do what he says—and then I, for one, do not want to hear another word about it, Sheriff Stoddel."

O. B. said, "I'd like to put a halt to this horse manure too, Doc. Come on everybody."

"Wait," Deborah said. "I saw Victor fall. The well is dangerous. You're asking that somebody else put his life in danger."

"You're right," Hocksmith said. He hesitated and then said, "Let's look matters over."

As the gathering of men and women walked out of the yard toward the corral, Deborah felt like every step she took was pounding in her head. In the kitchen, Victor had whispered to her, "Be calm." She would do her best, despite seeing Stoddel's hand on his hip, fingers tapping the gun handle. That was when her head began to throb.

It seemed so strange for the men and women to gather at the edge of the pasture and range around the old well in the sun. Deborah was thankful the weather was cooler after last night's rain. All of the men wore straw hats. Some of the women had hats, others bonnets. At first, everyone moved around the old woodpile, not getting too close but examining it closely. No one talked. Only killdeer, irate with the invasion of their nesting grounds, broke the silence.

"Well, Sheriff," Carl finally commented, "you certainly can see where Victor fell in the well yesterday evening. It rained after he got out, but there are tell-tale marks." The raw, broken edge of the well was glistening from the rain.

The man didn't respond. He turned to look at the nearby fence. "What is all this about?" He pointed at the scrape marks beneath the fence.

Patiently, although probably fuming inside, from what Deborah could tell, Victor said, "We dug out drifts of dirt before I fell in the well. We used shovels and sometimes the manure scraper." He added, "I was walking around the woodpile, throwing fuel on the boards so I could start a fire." He seemed to sense what questions Stoddel might have. "We were going to get rid of an eyesore and possible danger from nails in boards. It came to our attention because of the dirt that had blown up to it. It seemed easier to burn it and then clean up after the burning."

The men began speculating as to what Christian had been doing near the old woodpile the night he disappeared. "Well, surely you remember," John Kolter said. "We talked about it many times. Deborah there said he had a habit of going out to watch a coming storm."

"First off, we know he was in the corral," Norris Cressler said. "He had put the livestock in the barn, probably expecting rain."

"I figure," Kolter looked at the corral and barn, "he wanted to come out here at the edge of the pasture where he could see better. See how those trees on the west side of the corral would shut down at least some of his view if he stayed in the driveway or corral?"

"Sure." Ed Ratliff had been looking about too. "You're right, John. He would have come out of the north corral gate—or over the corral fence—into this pasture where he could see the cloud. I'm like you, John, I remember us all talking right after it happened. I'll bet practically all of us have the habit of going out in the night to watch a storm coming. We want to see how bad the storm is, or maybe we want to watch it and see if we can urge the rain in our direction."

The group laughed and nodded.

"In recent times," someone said, "we looked to see if the clouds were one of those black blizzards. As recent as yesterday I studied those clouds to see if they were truly rain."

Everyone turned sober, remembering.

"And don't you suppose," Levi Brownly said, "he thought he'd come sit over here on the old woodpile, just so he could watch the storm at his leisure?"

Nila sniffed. "I hope you menfolk learn from this. Stay in bed when there's a storm coming. Use your common sense."

"Well," Reub drawled, "give me a reason to stay, and I will."

There was laughter.

Moses said, "It stands to reason, he approached the west side of the woodpile so he could sit or stand and then look back to the west. The west side is where Victor fell. I suspect the pile isn't square over the well. The edge of the well on the west is close to the edge of the pile of boards."

All of the men crouched down at the edges of the cave-in, some even on their knees, and Henry Collins wormed around on his stomach, surveying the ground beneath the pile of wood. "It's hard to tell," he said. "There's quite a bit of blow dirt cutting down the view."

They decided there was nothing to do but remove the boards so they could see the well clearly. Working from every side except the west, they all pitched in and carefully lifted off each board and stick of wood, making a new pile to the side. "Be cautious," Moses warned. "Don't take a chance. We don't know if something still might cave."

Victor brought garden rakes and the men used them to pull the innermost boards to the sides. No one went near the west side. Slowly, everything was moved away. Deborah watched the sullen face of Stoddel.

Victor said to the group, "More than once August or me came out here to get an old board or maybe some kindling. Deborah remembers doing the same. But we came from the machine shop because we needed kindling for the shop stove or the forge, so we approached the pile from over here rather than the west side." He shook his head in dismay. "She even remembers the little boys getting on this pile at least once and David stepping on a nail." Deborah shivered, picturing how she had pulled David's foot off the nail.

While the rest of the wood was being moved, Victor saddled the roan and stationed the horse where Deborah had held her last night. He motioned to her to hold the reins. He had a lariat and a gunnysack.

Moses had been right. The wood hadn't been stacked evenly on all sides of the well. More had been piled to the east. Carl said, "So if he walked from the west, with intentions of sitting on the west side of the pile, his feet must have come close to the edge of the well—"

"And it caved," someone concluded.

"Then why didn't we see the caved spot?" Edmond Kolter asked. "Don't you remember August agonizing over no tracks or anything? He kept saying there was nothing to be seen, hide nor hair, he said. And that old man was alert. He said he examined every inch of this farmstead."

"It rained that night. That would cover some sign."

"Those boards—maybe they were piled higher back then, before you used pieces off the pile," Levi said. "The cave-in on the west side—it would cause some disturbance. I can imagine those boards toppling or sliding down. If that was the case, they'd fall right over the broken edge."

"It makes sense. So—let's get everything out of the well," Hocksmith said. "Let's get this done to the good sheriff's satisfaction." Carl actually removed his hat with a flourish and bowed toward Stoddel.

As Audrey would have said, Deborah was sick at heart. Everything the men were concluding made sense. She could imagine Christian, in his excitement about the approaching cloud, walking up to the well; she could see in her mind's eye, as clearly as if she had been there, what must have happened—yet Stoddel walked up, hands on his hips, holding Victor's and her lives in his hands.

Victor tied the lariat to the saddle horn. He took the end of the rope and walked to the well, approaching it from the south. "I'm going down, and Herman's offered to come after me. He'll be my witness as to what we find, and we'll put things in this sack. Unless you want to go in his place, Sheriff."

Stoddel didn't answer. His face remained expressionless.

Deborah stood with Princess, holding her reins. She trusted the rope that was attached to the saddle; she did not trust the walls of the old well.

Someone called from below, and Henry Collins stepped closer to listen. "He says to put a bucket on the rope and send it down. There's too much dirt down there from the cave-ins. We need to bring up some of the loose dirt." Norris brought a bucket from the barn and fastened it to the lariat.

Deborah bit her lip and turned to Moses. "Is there danger of more caving in?"

He tried to reassure her. "I don't think so. They went down carefully, and I don't see any cracks on the sides."

"There could be a cave-in down deeper." This time she drew blood from her lower lip and worked to control herself.

Moses put his arm about her shoulders. "Trust in the Lord," he said gently.

Henry pulled up several buckets of dirt and dumped them to the side. "The light's a little dim down there. They say to double check this dirt, look for ... anything they missed."

Hands sifted through the dirt. "Well, now," someone said, and laid two small bones out on the grass.

Finally, Herman and Victor came up the rope, and Herman had the sack tied to his belt. Deborah left the horse and moved closer to Victor. He was safe now, and she tasted the blood on her lip.

Herman slowly poured the contents of the sack onto the grass. When Victor began spreading out ragged pieces of clothing, she helped him. She couldn't prevent tears. There were the pajama top, overalls, undershorts, and carpet slippers, partly rotted away. The buckle was still on one overall strap, along with the metal buttons. The keys to the truck and car were rusted. Victor handed her the broken lens.

Sitting on the grass, she held the pieces, trying to fit them together. The lens was for Christian's right eye. It was the lens that had created a slight magnification. The small detail, one that for so many years she had forgotten until this moment, shattered what was left of the protective shell around her heart. She broke into sobs and lowered her forehead to the carpet of grass, her fingers gripping the pieces of lens until one cut her finger. Hands worked at hers, releasing the hold on the broken glass, straightening the fingers. Deborah raised her head and Victor brought her hands to his lips, kissing her fingers, and blood was smeared on his mouth. He gave her the smile she always recognized as being so full of love and caring.

Carl Hocksmith crouched down in the dirt and placed the bones in order. "This is all of them, Sheriff. The rest are in the casket." He bent to put his hands on Deborah's shoulders, lifting her. He looked at the cut on her hand and nodded. "Wash it good." Moses placed his arm around her again.

Everyone circled near the items. One by one, the men took off their hats, and their heads were bowed as they looked at the bones and clothing. "A sorry sight," someone said.

"I think it's just like Levi said, the boards sliding down and all." Henry's voice was husky and lacked its usual loudness.

"Yes," Edmond said. "That has to be it."

"Well, Sheriff," Carl said, "Mary Cressler offered us some pie and coffee. What do you say we have some?"

There was still the stubborn look on Stoddel's face, even a slight quiver to his firmly set jaw. He said, "Someone could have put the body down there after he was dead."

There was a shocked silence. Deborah wondered if she had heard the man right, and if others were thinking like him. What he had said frightened her so much that she feared she was going to vomit. She clenched her fists and held them to her mouth, whimpering. Moses tightened his hold on her.

A voice erupted in the quiet. "Now, hold on there!" It was Maude Ratliff. Just as Deborah's voice had echoed the night before when she called out to Victor, so did Maude's words now repeat themselves.

Earlier, Deborah had been surprised to see the woman carefully feeling her way through the corral, supporting herself with her teetering cane, one hand holding a floppy straw hat firmly on her head. Nila had hurried to Maude's side and guided her. Deborah looked at the woman now, seeing the same heavy brows and those eyes that seemed to burn right through a person. Maude had been aging, but she still had a strong voice.

"Maude?" Carl asked. He actually grinned.

"I think we've had enough from you, Egbert Stoddel. These are good folks here." She pointed at Deborah and Victor. "I know grief when I see it, and I've still got a good memory. Way back then I recognized grief when I saw it in a woman who had lost a husband and in a man who had lost a friend."

Other women seemed to take energy from Maude and added their voices, especially Mary. "There isn't a person here who didn't help in some way, trying to find Christian Nelson—except you. Like Maude said, we all could tell how Deborah felt, and everybody tried to help out, except you." Mary moved to stand beside Deborah. "We had no way of knowing that the instant Christian fell that there was no helping him. But we could sure tell Deborah was in need of help. I don't know if we did much good. I guess time had to do that."

Listening to the women, Deborah felt her strength return.

Maude wasn't finished. "So, Egg Stoddel. You've been offered a cup of coffee and a piece of pie and what they represent to folks around here. You turned them down—or ignored them. I think you'd better get in that old hoopy of yours and head back to town." She pushed back her hat and wiggled the end of her cane at the man. "I tell you, I'm enjoying spoutin' off to you. I'm going to keep doing it. I'm going to do it all over the county. Come November, your days as sheriff will be numbered if I have anything to do with it."

The group laughed. A number of the men began to circle the sullen man, edging him along. He moved, ever so slowly, while the men talked and joked around him as though he wasn't there. They all walked through the corral, where someone opened the gate, and he was edged a little further until he was almost up against his car.

Carl was there, opening the car door. "Sheriff," he said with a friendly tone, which wasn't usual for the doctor, "thank you for the ride from town. I'll catch a ride with someone else. Now, as I said before, I don't want to hear another word about this. I believe everything was resolved here today with plenty of witnesses in agreement." He took a paper from his breast pocket and unfolded it. His voice was growing in volume. "Death certificate, Stoddel. I showed you the vertebra this morning—it's in the casket in the house. This paper says 'accidental death—broken neck from a fall.' It's the *only proof* we have of anything, Stoddel."

Hocksmith stuck his face close to the little man. He was no longer congenial. "There is no proof of anything you've been trying to say all these years. I've got proof of this." Hocksmith waved the state paper. Perspiration saturated his shirt collar.

Deborah moved closer to the car. Stoddel's face was void of expression. Even the earlier stubborn set to his jaw was gone. She said, "Sheriff, we have coffee and pie in the house—and, as Mary said, the offer is representative of hospitality and friendliness in this community. I'm glad you took us to the well to finish getting Christian and an understanding of what happened to him. You're welcome to join us."

Stoddel, with his wide-brimmed hat pulled down low to his face, got into his car, and leaned forward against the wheel as though anticipating a starting gun. As a group, the people moved away, except someone was cranking the old car.

Hocksmith shut the door firmly. "I don't want to hold you up, so you just head on back. I'm going to have pie and coffee."

The sheriff had difficulties turning his car in the crowded driveway. He awkwardly backed and pulled forward several times while the neighborhood waited there. When he was finally gone, people milled about, talking matters over.

"Deborah, how are you doing, other than the headache I can tell you have?" Mary held her hand.

"I feel like I've been run through a wringer. But there's one more thing to do." She called out above the noise of the group. "I want someone to get a can of kerosene and matches. Let's burn the woodpile and then shovel in the well." She laughed despite her headache. "I'll do my share if you'll help me."

"It's one job I'd be glad to do," O. B. said. Everyone, including most of the women, trekked back to the old well. Shovels and a can of fuel oil were brought from Deborah's shed. Other folks brought shovels from their trucks.

When the fire was going, someone said, "One heck of a bonfire, better than the ones you build, Harold."

He grinned at the attention.

With time, they began digging at the hole, breaking down the edges, throwing the dirt into the pit. Deborah's wheelbarrow appeared, and it was loaded with drifted dirt from the fence line. Some people just filled their shovels with clumps of the wet dirt and carried them to the hole. There was laughter when a number of the men came running through the corral, pulling the wagon, not bothering with harnessing and hitching up a team. They moved it down the fence line and began loading it. The wagon was far heavier to bring back to the old well, and Deborah found Nila beside her, helping to push.

When they were done, the hole was filled level and tamped. "You'd almost think it had never been there," Deborah said. "Thank you so much."

"Now," Carl Hocksmith said, "can we have our pie and coffee?"

"You deserve it, Carl," Carlson Runnels said. "You really worked that wheelbarrow."

Deborah sat in Bethany's rocking chair, relaxed and free of the headache. The talk had turned now to Daniel Procek, and no one seemed to know what was being done with Welty.

"We won't get to go to Daniel's funeral," Carlson said. "They're sending his body to Missouri where his folks are."

There was speculation as to what Janie Procek would do with the farm. "Maybe she'll stay and work it like Deborah did," Nila said.

"She's not real well," Martha said.

"Well, this tragedy won't make it any easier on her."

After more talk, a hat was passed around the room, collecting what money they could for Daniel's family. Deborah went to her room. She took out a twenty dollar bill and folded it before putting it in the hat.

Levi said, "I understand those sacks of wheat were taken to Daniel's priest for distribution."

"That's the way it should be. There shouldn't have been any doubt about it in the first place. What a senseless tragedy."

"Deborah?" Mary stood in the kitchen doorway. "Dwight Bowers is here to talk to you."

Bowers was a little man with a big man's eyes and voice. Mary seated him at the kitchen table, pouring him a cup of coffee and cutting a piece of pie. He tackled both with enthusiasm.

"Dwight," Deborah said, "how are you?"

"Fine. More important, how are *you*?"

"I'm okay. I really am. I've had a lot of years to prepare for this."

He chewed noisily, and the fingers that held his fork were stained with ink. "I'd like to put a story about your husband in tomorrow's paper." He grinned at her, his big teeth filled with remnants of apple pie. "I would take delight in setting a few folks straight."

"I'm still miffed about the picture you printed—you know, the Welty incident. I looked awful and felt awful."

"I'm real sorry about that. I was madder than hell at the time. The bastard got by with murder."

"Well," she laughed and Mary joined her, "maybe not murder."

His voice was reluctant. "Well, folks who've been murdered probably don't put murder on an equal footing with attempted rape and a beating." He grinned at his own lack of logic. He didn't want to give up his opinion and had one last say. "Deborah Nelson, I'm never gonna sit back and ignore rape and woman beating. And I abhor anything that smells racist. If you didn't already know that, I want you to know it."

He sucked at his coffee, blowing it noisily before each slurp. "Now, I'd like to hear from you firsthand for my story." He scraped at his pie plate with his fork, and Mary slipped him a second piece.

They talked about the facts as to how Christian's body was found, not taking very long because Bowers had a deadline, but during the time, he polished off a third piece of pie and three cups of Mary's coffee.

When he was ready to leave, Dwight said, "This has been a sad day. I just came from talking to the Procek family over at Deer Run. I hope I can write an obituary that will do justice to the man."

Victor and Deborah were still at the kitchen table when Maude and Hocksmith joined them. Deborah was curious why the two of them were together and why they wanted to talk to her and Victor. Hocksmith, who could be so thoughtless, so rude, actually seated Maude at the table in a gracious fashion. Deborah had never seen him behave that way before.

Maude didn't seem at all surprised. She spoke first. "We been talking, Doc and me, about how Stoddel treated the two of you all these years. We've got some opinions about—"

"—the son of a bitch," Carl interrupted.

"Now, Doc," Maude said, "if he's a sick man, he's to be pitied, not called names."

"Sick man?" Victor was puzzled.

Carl laughed harshly. "She means sick in the head. We want your opinion. Do you think there's something wrong with his mind?"

"I sure do," said Maude. "He belongs in an institution."

"We should pity him?" Deborah asked.

"Aw, not really," said Carl. "We were just wondering what the two of you thought after all these years of abuse from the guy." He pushed back his chair and jumped up. "Come on, Maude. Your son said he'd drive me to town."

The next day, Victor stopped their work when the mail arrived, and Deborah made coffee while they read the newspaper. The story on the first page was about Daniel's death, but strangely enough, nothing was said about Welty or Henry Collins.

Victor said, "Bowers doesn't even mention Welty's name as the one with the gun."

Reading over his shoulder, Deborah was puzzled. "It's like he isn't giving Welty the time of day." Inside the newspaper was Daniel's obituary. "Bowers writes well. It hurts, though, to think that a few words about a man's conscience and kindness are all we have left of Daniel. Listen to the ending." She read aloud: "*There is justice in knowing ten sacks of beautiful golden grain are being ground, the flour added to leavening, and the aromatic loaves eaten. Such sustenance is the work of a good man no longer with us.*' I like how he says that."

She read Dwight's story about Christian. "*It was with shock we learned, officially, of a local prominent farmer's death, that of Christian D. Nelson. Mr. Nelson had been missing since October 1930. At that time extensive searches were done by his wife Deborah Nelson and members of his township. Appeals were made to surrounding communities and as far away as Nebraska, Oklahoma, Colorado, and Missouri as to his whereabouts.*

"*Although local authorities offered plenty of speculation, there was no evidence of foul play, and it was commonly believed at the time he might have left of his own accord.*

"*Two days ago a neighbor to Mrs. Nelson, Mr. Victor Whitesong, joined her in the extensive work most of us are performing at this time, digging out after the apparent cessation of blowing dust. Mr. Whitesong worked about an old woodpile that had been there when the Nelsons bought the farm from Mr. Clifford Strong's estate. It was Whitesong's plan to burn the pile and clean up any remaining debris when suddenly the ground gave way beneath his feet. He found himself at the bottom of an abandoned well.*

"'While Mrs. Nelson was acquiring a rope and saddle horse to pull the man from the dangerous depths, Whitesong found he was not the only one to have fallen in the dry well. After his rescue he bravely returned to the well, carrying a sack, and brought up the skeleton of a man. Such evidence as eye glasses and parts of clothing identify the skeleton as that of Christian Nelson, missing all these many years.

"'We join Mrs. Nelson and her family in their grief, for Christian Nelson was admired and loved by many even though he lived in this community only a year before his untimely death.

"'The finding of his body puts to rest many questions and suppositions, leaving this community with accurate facts, fodder for a new story but one far less malicious and vindictive. Christian Nelson will be remembered as a man who had nothing unkind to say about others. If only we could learn from his example.'"

"Deborah, do you detect a note of satisfaction in some of Dwight's comments?"

"Well, maybe. Perhaps it came from writing the story after consuming three pieces of pie."

Chapter 24

They Are Home

Deborah was beside Victor on the train platform, enjoying the early morning sun and a cooling breeze that was damp from the fog that lifted out of low spots. She was wearing jeans and a brightly flowered shirt and wiggled her toes in her moccasins, feeling the rough boards.

Faintly, they heard a train whistle, and she turned to Victor, doing a little dance on the platform. "For our boy David." He grinned at her. "The train is bringing so many people we love," she said. She thought she could feel the train's vibration on the platform, even from such a distance, or was it the quickening of her soul at the thought of seeing her children again?

There were old men sitting on outside benches of the station, and Deborah wondered if they were like the ones who congregated in the grain elevator and the parts shop. But some of the men she did know. Two of them sat straight and still, their thumbs hooked in their belts, and the third one leaned forward, his permanently bent back hunched over a cane held upright by his clasped hands. All stared at Deborah, their eyes squinting in the sun. A noise told her one of the old men had spit tobacco in the coffee can placed near his feet. She heard the train whistle again, the shriek much closer now.

The train pulled up to the station, its acrid, heavy smoke mingling with the lifting fog. As the train cars slid slowly past, she thought she saw a small face and hands pressed to a window—and then the image was gone. The brakes squealed harshly, but she wasn't bothered. A conductor swung down from the steps and hurried toward the rear of the train, his lips puckered in an unheard whistle in the noise. Coming down the steps were two children. Deborah was only briefly aware of adults behind the boys.

"Jonathan," she said in a hushed voice. He had grown taller, as she expected, but his features were a surprise even though she had received photographs regularly. She had been unable to put out of her mind the boyish look of the eleven-year-old he had been when he left, but gone now was the fuller little boy look, replaced with sharper cheekbones and a more angular jaw. He was fourteen, and he looked more like her than ever. For some reason, she thought of Grandfather and Fleet Foot.

He rushed to her, holding the little boy's hand, and his voice broke as he said, "Mom."

She held his tallness, and he grasped her firmly about the waist, burying his face against her neck, his hold causing her tears to begin. She felt the other, smaller body press against her side.

Deborah knelt on the platform, reaching for Baby Half Shell—oh, not a baby any longer—so tall and long limbed but still with the baby roundness she expected. Jonathan crouched down with her, and the three of them were wrapped in each other, reminding Deborah of how David, Jonathan, and she had often held Christian in a similar way.

Half Shell wiped away her tears with his fingers. His hair was shining black, his eyes so dark, and beneath the roundness of his four-year-old face she could see the bone structure of Fleet Foot. "Do you remember me, Half Shell?" she asked.

The child hesitated. He studied Deborah's face.

"Maybe not," Jonathan said. "But we've been showing him your pictures all this time and talking about you." Jonathan grinned at her, his eyes and skin dark like her own, looking so like the big brother of Half Shell.

"You're home," she cried, her quiet voice almost a groan.

"We won't ever leave again," Jonathan said.

"Ever," echoed Half Shell.

"Even if your wives and children say they want houses of their own?" Both boys laughed and hugged her again. And when she got up, Victor was there, holding Jonathan. "And this is Victor," she said to the little boy.

Half Shell reached to shake hands, but then, suddenly, he grabbed the man around the legs. Victor's jaw trembled. He picked up Half Shell and pulled Jonathan close to his side. "Hey, you fellers. Where you been for so long?"

"Minn'sota," Half Shell said.

Deborah turned to the familiar faces of Calvin and Meredith, the added gray in their hair, the lines about Meredith's mouth. "These years have seemed so long. I can tell you gave wonderful care to my boys."

Over Meredith's shoulder, she saw her dad, straight and almost like a soldier in a suit and starched collar. She released Calvin and Meredith and stood in front of Frank Jorgenson, seeing his rigid face, its skin grooved now.

"Dad." It was all she could say at first, her voice barely a whisper, and she moved into his arms, her hands on his shoulders, her face pressed against the lean hardness of his cheek, rough with a short growth of whiskers. "I have missed you so much."

Frank's arms tightened convulsively.

"I'm so glad you came," she said.

"I wanted to"—he drew back to look at her—"and I hoped you'd want me."

"Don't ever doubt how much I have needed you." So many different kinds of pain came to the surface. "Dad," she said, her voice small and weak, sounding so much like a child's.

"Daughter." He had never called her that before. It was as though August, upon his death, had passed it on to Frank, knowing she loved it. A lump filled her throat, threatening to choke her.

He looked at her face. "You've had so much sadness, Deborah dear." He had done it again. Her sorrow surfaced again, hearing Uncle Oscar's pet name.

She saw Victor pumping the hand of a redheaded man standing beside a pregnant woman—David and Sonja. "Look at you," she said to Sonja. "Look at you. You didn't tell us. A baby! How wonderful!"

"We wanted to surprise you," Sonja said.

David couldn't contain himself. "Come November!"

Deborah turned, saying, "I want you to meet some folks of the town." She led everyone to the old men. The two who were more agile stood, and one helped the bent man from the bench. She said, "This is Mr. John Warner—Mr. Homer Crawford—and Mr. Tom Deering. These are my boys, Christian's parents, the Nyfellers, and my dad."

The one man hastily shoved his coffee can out of sight under the chair with his foot. They shook hands all the way around, asking questions, talking a blue streak, remembering Christian. "Sometimes, before he drove over the tracks there, he'd stop and jaw. One time, he drove across, backed up, and came to jaw because he saw Tom there was missing. Wanted to know why. We told him Tom was under the weather, and that man went to Tom's room at the boardinghouse, just to say hello."

Reluctantly, they let everyone head for the car, their faces smiling. Deborah heard one of them say, "Seem like mighty nice folk."

Deborah and Victor had brought a truck and the car. "Sonja and David," said Victor, "we have strict instructions you're to go right to your folks. You take the truck. You might go kind of easy. Bad tires, you know. I've got a bed for you at my house." He added, "You won't believe the furniture I've got now, thanks to August and Audrey."

Victor had brought rope, and the men helped him tie luggage onto the fenders and running boards of the car. Crates were loaded in the truck. Everyone else crowded into the car, the Nelsons and Frank in the back, Half Shell on Deborah's lap. She wiped at her eyes, and Jonathan, sitting beside her, said, "It's so good to see you." She cried some more.

They drove to Deborah's farm, turning up the lane just as the late morning sun was burning off the last of the fog. There was still plenty of drifted dirt piled here and there, but whether by plan or accident, most areas showed the progress Deborah and Victor had made digging it out. Before long they would have the drifts away from the buildings; the biggest job was yet to come, finishing the fences and posts in the fields and pastures.

Probably the trees were the first things a stranger to the farmstead would notice. Frank voiced Deborah's thoughts. "Look at the homestead tree! Those cottonwoods, your shelterbelts, the orchard. A lot of planning and work has gone into this place."

Deborah was pleased by his comment. "That's right, Dad. Clifford and Bethany must have been awfully hard workers. We've seen so many instances where they thought things through carefully ... except the abandoned well." She spoke with a controlled voice. "I'll never understand it."

As soon as the car was barely stopped in the driveway, Jonathan said to Half Shell, "Come on." He held the car door for Deborah and explained. "I promised him we'd see the tree house first thing."

Half Shell looked up at her. "Okay?"

"Okay."

She watched the boys run to the tree. Jonathan was close behind Half Shell as they climbed up the ladder. She could hear their chatter, and Half Shell was excited. "Look! There's everybody. Hi, everybody!" Deborah waved at the branches where their voices floated downward like the calls of birds.

Within a few hours, everyone had settled into a routine. The men put on overalls and took over the chores. Meredith soon knew where everything was kept in the kitchen. Victor and Deborah helped the boys unpack in their bedroom and set up an iron cot for Frank.

"When you were here last," Deborah reached out to hold Half Shell, "you slept in a crib in my room. At night, I could hear you breathing, and sometimes you would thump against the rails."

Half Shell said, "Jonathan told me David was always getting turned around in his bed. He said you'd come in and tuck him back in."

She laughed. "The nice thing about you being in a crib by my bed, I could just cover you and jump right back into bed. I could also lie there and watch you sleep in the moonlight."

As she sat on the side of the bed, Half Shell rested between her knees, running his fingers from her cheekbones down her jawline. "What are you doing?"

"Trying to remember you."

"I'm trying to remember you too. You look the same, but you look different somehow. I'm sure it's because you're not a baby anymore."

He ran his finger delicately down the bridge of her nose and then outlined her lips. "When you saw me today—was it like the very first time you saw me?" he asked.

"Oh, yes! Only so much better. Today when I saw you, I said to myself, this boy, he's here to stay until he's ninety-nine and has a beard down to his knees." He giggled, and they wrestled on the bed. When she sat up, Victor was watching from the floor where he was helping Jonathan put books in the bookcase. "Your eyes are full of love," she whispered.

"Half Shell?" Jonathan turned to look at the boy. "She doesn't mean that about your beard. It'll only be down to the middle of your chest."

"You're pulling my leg," Half Shell said.

That evening, Meredith and Calvin spent time together in the bay window. They pulled chairs close to the pedestal table, sitting with their hands touching the small casket, and Deborah could hear them talking and praying.

The house and yard were full of busy noise. Voices and footsteps came and went in the house, baking pans clattered in the kitchen. In the yard, there were more voices and the whine of the separator. The horses nickered whenever the boys came near the corral. Deborah heard plans being made to fill the swimming tank behind the well house.

Chapter 25

The Letter

When Victor was gone home for the night, Deborah went to the south porch to join her dad. She carried a tray holding a teapot, cups, and lemon wafers. "Dad? Would you share some herbal tea with me before bedtime?" In the lantern light, she saw an unusual sight, the shine of tears in his eyes. Watching him warily, she listened to the sounds of the dark—an owl, the snuffling of a horse at the water tank, the distant rumble of thunder.

"I'm sorry your mother didn't visit this beautiful place. I should have seen to it."

He was gripping the arms of his chair, his knuckles white, and she was feeling too much emotion to answer him directly. "There's thunder again. I can't believe the moisture we're getting. It's like waking from a nightmare." She shook her head sadly. "A very bad memory. The feel of constant dust in your hair, in your eyes, in your lungs. It's one thing to feel dirt on your body from a normal day of working outside. It's another when it's with you day and night. Seems like we lost so many people we loved during the drought."

"I remember a similar thought because of the Great War. Like you say, a bad memory."

She was thinking about what her mother had wanted him to tell her, knowing she was avoiding the subject. "At the beginning I think August knew more than he dared to tell me. Dad, if I had let myself imagine how many years it would really be and how difficult at times—I don't think I could have faced it. Audrey knew. I realize that now. She knew, and she worked so hard to be strong for the rest of us. There were times I was frightened when I saw how hard on her the drought was."

"The memories hurt." He reached to pat her hand awkwardly. "But one part of life is remembering the pain and the people who endured it."

She smiled. "Victor and I feel the least we can do is measure up to what others have endured before us. When we were at a low point, after the boys were gone and both Audrey and August had died, he said we should pretend we were pioneers like the Goodmans were back in the eighteen hundreds. We decided modern-day pioneers have a much easier life."

She poured the tea, and Frank's hand trembled as he picked up his cup. His voice also shook. "Tea and lemon cookies. I remember your mama baking these. I've missed them."

"Lemons have been such a rarity around here. George said he hasn't been able to order them into his store for ages, not that he would have bothered. Folks didn't have the money to buy them. I guess we're more hopeful now. He said they were selling like hotcakes." She grinned. "Lemons selling like hotcakes. I think Jonathan would question that image." She felt like she was rattling on. "I baked these cookies after we got home today, and Half Shell helped me. What fun! He said Mother and he baked cookies—sometimes these lemon ones. He described biting into the pulp thinking it would be like an orange." She put one on Frank's saucer, beside the cup. "I want to eat her cookies while we remember her."

His fingers crumbled a piece of cookie into his napkin. His face was strained, and he didn't look at her.

"Daddy"—she hadn't called him Daddy since she was a little girl—"you said Mother wanted you to tell me things."

A sound he made was one of pain, and his eyes were tightly closed. "I promised her I would tell you what she wanted." His words were rushed, as though he was using the momentum to begin the conversation. "She was close to dying, and she told me things to write in a letter to you. It took her two days, and she wanted to be sure you get this letter from her."

Frank removed a thin wallet from his pocket. His hands shook and his fingers were awkward as he slowly tugged at the folded papers, not his usual onionskin paper with writing done by a heavy hand. She stared at him for a moment and then looked down at the letter, its fold lines heavily creased.

"I've been carrying it since she died. I promised Lillian I'd read it to you, that you were to hear it in my own voice. And when we're done, I've got to talk to you … things I've got to say to you, amends I've got to make."

He brushed at his hair, and a gray lock fell onto his forehead. She resisted the impulse to smooth it back. "You need to know, the boys were with me when Lillian told me what to write. We did lots of talking, lots of explaining."

He smoothed the papers on the table and fought to control his voice: "'*My dearest Deborah. I have needed to tell you this for a long time. I know you have needed to hear it just as long. All these years I have run the risk of not telling you what you should know. Just think, I could have had an accident and died a sudden death and you wouldn't know. I believe God has watched over all of us—you, me, and Frank—keeping me going until I gained the courage to tell you what is in this letter.*

"'*Deborah, Frank is not your blood father.*'"

Looking at the letter on the table, Deborah saw the handwriting was awkward, as though Frank's hands had shaken as he had written. She felt her own fingers tremble, and his face wavered because of the sudden tears in her eyes. Her throat began to ache. She rose abruptly, her chair scraping the enameled porch floor. She stared at Frank, and her breathing became irregular.

He breathed shakily and continued reading. "'*Frank has known this a long time. He found out way back when I went to Mayo Clinic. I told him then because I was afraid I would die. I showed him a picture of your blood daddy whose name is Many Stars.*'"

Words from the past rang in her ears: "You're a squaw bitch and don't belong here." Then carefully, almost gently, she sat down again, pulling the chair closer to the table.

Many Stars was her real dad. Grandfather Blue Sky's son. She was Indian … half Indian. Her hands were clammy, and her heart thumped. Many Stars … a picture … a memory tugged at her mind, but she pushed it aside to listen.

"'*Grandfather Blue Sky was your blood grandfather. He came to Minnesota with me because he knew you were coming. It was discussed with his family and me that he should be involved in teaching you—so you would know something of the Indian ways. I told Frank that Blue Sky had come to help him with the horses. That was true, but it wasn't the main reason. Grandfather loved you so very, very much, even before he knew you.*'"

An explosive build-up within Deborah erupted. "Grandfather was my *real* grandfather, and she didn't tell me before he died. I should have known." The pages fluttered in Frank's hands. Still standing, she put her hands, palm down, on the tabletop and took a deep breath. "I'm sorry. Go on."

"'I met Grandfather Blue Sky's son in New Mexico when I went there to rest. Many Stars's wife had died, and he was lonely for her. I had just married Frank, and I missed him. We turned to each other.

"'I never stopped loving Frank. I want to say your dad instead of Frank, for he's as much your dad in my mind as Many Stars is your real dad.

"'Fleet Foot is your half brother of course. He knew that when he saw you in Kansas. Half Shell is your nephew as well as your adopted son.'"

Fleet Foot ... there was the indescribable love that she had felt the moment she met him. He was her brother. Again ... she should have known. She would have insisted he stay longer so they could talk more and know one another better. There was so little time before he died.

"'Many Stars knows about you. Sometimes I've written him about you and, of course, Jonathan, David, and Half Shell. You've also told me how you have written to let him know how Half Shell is doing. I'm glad you've done that. I hope you get to meet him someday. Frank and I have talked, and he wants the same.

"'I'm sorry, Deborah, that I never told you before now. I know you've been mixed up about your looks when folks said things about your coloring and features. I remember the day you came home from first grade and looked and looked in the mirror, trying to figure things out. Jonathan has told us how some people have treated you there in Kansas and how confusing it must have been to you. He said you gave up trying to convince them you aren't Indian. He said you don't mind being considered Indian, except for the prejudice that represents.'"

Deborah began moving frantically about a small space on the porch. "I've been so naive, so stupid. I trusted you and Mother. The two of you were Mama and Daddy. I loved you and never dreamed there was something I shouldn't be trusting. It was said I looked like my great-grandmother in Sweden!"

Frank rested his forehead against his clenched hands. "You're right." His voice was tight and emotionless.

"Do you have more? Is there more to be read to me?"

He nodded and lifted the papers. "'You need to know Meredith and Calvin Nelson have known since before you were born. That's because I told Meredith why I came home from Arizona so unexpectedly. She was upset that I never told you the truth. She was upset with how Frank and I treated one another—and you. The Nelsons are proud of your Indian blood.'"

Deborah interrupted the reading. "They were so good to me when times got rough, when you and Mother …" The need to take in air struggled with the emotions that closed her throat and weighed on her chest. "Sweet Meredith, dear Calvin … *they* helped me when I needed them. They didn't tell me because Mother told them not to, but *they helped me.*"

They stared at one another. Frank's hands were clenched, his knuckles white. He whispered, "I am grateful."

A different emotion, anger, came from Deborah. "The only time they weren't there was when Kathy died. That wasn't their fault. If they had been home the night before, she wouldn't have killed herself. I know she wouldn't have."

"I know." He squinted his eyes, and his hands crumpled the edges of the letter.

Accusations were in her voice. "She shouldn't have died, you know. She was just a girl, like me, and her dad molested her. I told you Kathy's mother knew the truth, and she denied it. You, along with her parents, killed her. What did she have to live for when both her parents turned on her?" Deborah tried to control the anger. She whispered, "At the time, I knew something of that. Both of my parents had turned on me … but my tragedy was nothing like hers. I was able to face life despite my parents. She felt she had nothing to live for without the love and protection of her parents."

"I know. I let her down. I let you down. I'll never forgive myself. It was my fault." Frank's face had turned haggard, and he looked at Deborah with red, blurred eyes.

She knew his pain, but she couldn't say anything to lessen it. She could no longer look at him and turned, putting her hands on the porch railing, her body tense, much the way a vaulter might prepare to jump a hurdle. She felt the air begin to cool her face. "Finish reading," she said.

He read on, his voice hoarse and uneven. "'*Your dad, Frank, and I have got so much to make up to you. I know now I won't get to talk to you, and Frank says he'll try to do it for me. We both are so ashamed of how we acted with each other and then took it out on you. Please forgive us. We should never have done what we did to each other. We got so hurt and upset, both of us. We forgot what we were doing to you. God forgive us, and we pray you will forgive us.*

"'*Your dad just read what I have said, and I realize I almost forgot something important. I always said you had just a middle initial. Then when you asked so much I said the S was for Sarah. I lied again. It's for your Indian* name, Sky Bird. And I think it fits you perfectly. A sky bird is so free. It swoops through the sky and is so beautiful. That's the way you seem to me.

"'Love your blood dad, for he loves you even though he's never seen you. Love the daddy who has raised you, for he adores you. He's reading this to you right now. Find out from him how much he loves you.

"'Remember what Grandfather Blue Sky said about spirits. When you read this, my spirit will be with you, right beside you. I'll never leave you, and someday we'll meet again. I love you dearly. I love your boys dearly.

"'Your mother, Lillian Jorgenson.'"

The letter and Frank's hands fell to the table. The sounds of thunder were closer, and breezes stirred the trees. His breathing seemed almost ragged, reminding her of August the night he died.

Frank spoke, and what he said was jumbled together. She struggled to sort it all out. "I was a bitter, hateful man. I loved your mother. I was always picturing what it must've been like, pouring salt in a fresh wound. The thought of sharing her with someone else—and you as the result— we've had some time to think and talk. We've come a long way together, reconciled, since you moved to Kansas.

"All the regrets ... how close she came to dying from the cancer surgery, how I even wanted her to die."

"No!"

"God forgive me. I'm sorry, Deborah." He took a folded handkerchief from his pocket and blotted his eyes.

"I told you her incisions didn't look right. You didn't respond."

"Because I was ignorant and stubborn. You were a kid doing a nurse's job but you knew what you were talking about. Meredith and Calvin stepped in and insisted I hire someone.

"Your mother and I talked about how we drove you away from Minnesota and all the hard times you've had here because you felt you had to get away and stay away from us. And I wasn't any better toward Christian. If I had known he was going to up and die like he did, I would've stood in the road when he started to drive away.

"I've thought about how important you were to me when I believed you were my daughter. Then when I knew you weren't my daughter, I went crazy. It doesn't make sense, I know." He moved his hands in many directions on the table, as though illustrating his jumbled words.

"And to think, I met Many Stars when I took Grandfather Blue Sky's body to Arizona—before I knew. I liked Many Stars. He liked me. We spent time together and participated in the burial ceremony together."

Frank's eyes were painfully red from tears and wiping them. "I've wondered how I could like a man so much and then feel so bitter against him when I learned the truth.

"I never felt bitter about Blue Sky, though. He came to Minnesota because of you and gave up his family life in Arizona. He wanted to have a part in your upbringing. He was a good man and good to you. I felt like a part of me was gone when he died. I loved him, and hard as I tried—for I did try—I could never turn against his memory after I knew.

"Now, a good twenty-one years after learning the truth, twenty-one years I've hurt you, daughter, I know it doesn't matter how you came about, and I know I don't own you, like some horse in the barn to buy and sell. Even a horse has its own spirit, and if he doesn't have it, he's a sorry animal.

"You survived somehow. Your spirit is still there, or you wouldn't have endured all you have all these years. And I sometimes thought, maybe if you hadn't had your Indian blood, you wouldn't have made it through all these bad times.

"You were given to me to love and protect and teach." He repeated, "Not to own like a horse. It shouldn't have mattered how your life started. I loved you before I found out. Then you weren't any different. Believe me, I never stopped loving you. I just didn't realize it back then and couldn't let it show to you. I am very sorry for that." He sat with his clenched hands between his knees, head bowed. "You were just a kid. You didn't know and ... merciful God! How hurt you must have been." He raised his head and spoke with intensity, "I am so sorry."

She thought about touching him, needing an anchor, first his fingertips and then his entire hand. But she stood at the edge of the porch, seeing the lightning flashes grow, not the heat lightning of the drought—instead lightning cutting and fierce, yet so far away she couldn't hear or smell it. She turned to him and sat at the table, her movement rattling the cups and saucers.

"I'm trying to take in what the letter says, what you're saying to me. It's next to impossible."

"I understand."

"I tried so hard, way back then, to comprehend. I ran everything through my mind, forward and backward. Nothing made sense. I didn't know what I had done. I thought I was bad somehow." She lifted her head to look at Frank. "Like you say, I was just a kid, a twelve-year-old, a little girl with a little girl's mind. Couldn't either of you see that?

"Hannah was unpacking Mother's suitcase and took out a photo. Mother said to take the picture, to put it with my keepsakes. Nothing more. Just her cold voice—'take the picture.'

"I ran upstairs, Dad. I did as she said. No explanation from her. I stared and stared at the picture and nothing made sense, so I worked it around in my mind that the picture was of my beloved Grandfather Blue Sky when he was young. Nothing else made sense. All I knew, everything was different, that I was being treated very different."

She raised her voice, wailing, suspecting she sounded like that twelve-year-old. "I never knew why, and nobody told me." Sobs prevented her from saying anything more, and she realized how close they were to the open windows of the bedrooms where Meredith and Calvin and the boys were trying to sleep. "I'm sorry," she said, more to them than to Frank.

"The picture," Frank said, "I remember the picture. That's how I found out. Your mother had it in her suitcase and showed it to me at the hospital. Do you still have it?"

"Yes." Deborah pushed against the table top, feeling her strength begin to wobble. "I haven't looked at it since I put it in my box, for something told me it wasn't Grandfather ... yet it made no sense to think otherwise."

She turned away from him. "I need time. I'm going to look at the picture. I'm going to think about what I've heard. Then I'm not sure what I'm going to do."

"I'll be here," he said almost frantically. "I'm not going to bed yet."

In her room, Deborah struggled to light a lamp, her hands trembling, reminding her of Frank's hand on his teacup. Her legs shook also. She sat on the side of her bed and whimpered like a child, conscious that Frank was on the porch just outside her windows. The photo ... she had placed it in her treasure box, along with the headband—the headband with the Sky Bird designs. She could still see the designs as clearly as if it were yesterday when she had put the band in the box. The box was in the bottom drawer of the bureau, the same place she had put it so many years ago. The flowered satin of its cover was faded now. She placed it on the braided rug by the bed. She sat on the floor and opened the lid.

The headband, the one Meredith once made for her, heavily beaded with flying birds, was on top where she had left it. Strands of hair were still caught in the beads, hair she had pulled out of her head when she jerked off the band. The pain she had felt that long ago day as a twelve-almost-thirteen-year-old seemed as real as the pain she once felt from the beating Welty gave her. The old pain of her childhood was not physical, but its marks and scars were as vivid in her mind as the marks left on her face by Deputy Welty.

She lifted the headband, and beneath it was the photo of Many Stars. His eyes were hidden in shadow, just as she remembered, but there was a tender smile on his lips that she had forgotten. She touched his face. So long ago ... she had puzzled over who it was, concluding, yet so unsure, that it was of Grandfather when he was young. She hadn't dared to ask her mother who it was, for that was the beginning of a time when she knew she could be rejected or ignored so easily.

The photograph was grainy, yet the dark hair had picked up bits of sunlight, hair held in place with a headband, which had designs Deborah couldn't decipher. She noticed his hands, one holding the reins of the horse's bridle, the other curved around the animal's soft nose. The fingers were long and slender, and she could sense his gentleness as he touched the horse.

Deborah pressed her hand lightly on the picture and whispered, "My father. This is my father."

She caught her reflection in the mirror. She stood outside of herself, seeing for the first time what another person might—her dark eyes, high cheekbones, long, black hair—amid the darkness of her skin with an under glow so different from her mother's easily burned skin. She had noted these details probably every day of her life, but now she was experiencing a new perception. This was not the image of Deborah Jorgenson Nelson; rather she was Sky Bird, daughter of Many Stars.

Now her eyes turned inward, and she could feel her pumping heart, blood coursing through her veins, some of the same blood as Fleet Foot and Baby Half Shell ... and Grandfather Blue Sky, the old man she had loved so dearly.

She thrust the headband into her pocket and held the photo, smoothing its corner that she could imagine Frank had crumpled while Lillian told him the truth at the hospital so long ago. Blowing out the lamp flame, she went into the shadowed living room. On the little grand piano she ran her fingertips lightly over the tops of the family photos as she had done so many times when she was disturbed—they weren't normally on the piano, for Christian's small casket was on the parlor table. She placed the photograph of Many Stars beside one of herself and Grandfather, taken shortly before he died. On the other side was Fleet Foot, taken during his Kansas visit ... her family.

On the porch, Frank looked up at her, his eyes shadowed as though they had sunk more deeply into his face. She gulped her cup of cold tea thirstily. He hadn't touched his tea or cookies. She threw herself into the chair by the small table.

"You and Mama—the way you changed toward me!" She pressed her fists to her mouth and cried out, her voice muffled. "People have said things, lots of times, but all I knew was you were my daddy and she was my mama. Yet you turned on me, the way strangers have done at times when they thought I was Indian and dirt under their feet. People who didn't even know me have turned on me. One time, I saw people do that to total strangers, strangers undeserving of such ..." Her voice faded away, but the sudden memory hung there like a distant cloud in the night sky, not really visible, just a smudge that came and went in the mind's eye. She added, "That's strange, I can't remember what it was I started to say."

Frank burst forth. "Some of us human beings are worse than wild animals. What I did to you and Lillian! I thought I was justified back then. God ought to strike me dead! I was such a bully, always thinking I had to be right in everything. Thought I had to fight back if I was wronged. Over the centuries men have made prisons and tortures to hurt and control others. We sit back and say how horrible, how could they do it? Well, I did it too.

"When I had Blue Sky to talk to—now there was a man—he tempered me. He taught me so much. He taught me real gentleness with an animal—then he was dead, and after that I learned about Lillian's illness, then about Many Stars and you. I should've been kicked into kingdom come. Your uncle Oscar tried to straighten me out more than once. But all my life I fought him too. Anything he tried to get me to do or think, I did just the opposite." Frank's forehead was creased. "Speaking of Oscar, I thought maybe you did understand once, about yourself. But I guess you didn't."

"When?"

"When Oscar died. Things were said before he took sick, from what Kirsten told me, and I thought maybe you knew."

Like a door on too-rusty hinges, something tried to open in Deborah's mind, and then it was gone. "Knew what?"

"Kirsten and I had a ... talk, I guess you'd say. She said things, I said things. You were close by. Of course it was a few hours after Oscar died, as I remember, and we were all tired and emotions were running high."

She had gone with Uncle Oscar and Kirsten for a vacation to the family summer home. "I remember how Kirsten aggravated Uncle Oscar. She remarked how I looked like some young Indian girls who were selling produce near the railroad tracks. Uncle Oscar was disturbed and tried to hush her, but I wanted him to talk." Deborah grimaced. "I don't know who was more stubborn at the time, Kirsten or me."

"Well, Kirsten and I were a stubborn pair for sure. You don't remember us having a set-to?"

The tops of the trees in the orchard whipped about, and the smell of the coming rain was in the air. "I didn't ... and don't really remember anything except Uncle Oscar died that day. I know we tried to get help for him. If there was more, I guess my mind just shut things away."

"And I thought you heard what Kirsten said to me," Frank said.

"Said to you?"

"You were there, in the other room. It was that night. I had arrived after Oscar's death. She really told me what she thought of me and your mother, what we were doing to you. She and Oscar had figured out I hadn't fathered you. But you must not have heard Kirsten and me talking—or maybe you didn't understand. You must've been too young to understand."

She dwelled on that, and he waited patiently. The call of an owl and the beat of its wings as its black form went across the yard seemed to awaken her. "I remember Aunt Kirsten slapping you."

"That's right. She whacked me a good one. She was really heated up. So you must've heard the rest."

She slapped him? Again something tried to come to her memory, and she remembered, or imagined, the sound of a slap and felt her own response to something so unheard of in her family.

Frank said, "Well, I never thought of it at the time, but you probably didn't understand. I forget how young you were."

"I may have put it all out of my memory until just now. Uncle Oscar's death's has been like a black spot on the calendar for me. Could that be? Maybe that's how my mind handled things. Either that or like you said, I was just too young to understand what happened and was said that day. Looking back, I know I grew up a sheltered and naive girl. There were times you didn't let me be around the corrals. When it comes down to it, I wonder if I would have even understood the term 'fathered.'"

Aunt Kirsten and the Indians ... what Aunt Kirsten said ... and there were things I said ... someone upset Uncle Oscar, and that was when he had his heart attack. Aunt Kirsten was disturbed about me when we returned from town. Returned from town? What was there about town? Aunt Kirsten had held me, pinched me tight ... pulled? Pushed? I had wanted to do something, wanted to do it very much, and Aunt Kirsten wouldn't let me. Talk about stubborn ... like a shift in the movement of fog, something came to my mind's eye.

The stranger ... a soldier. There was blood ... and the sounds, sounds like a whip whistling through the air, birds, people shouting, was someone whimpering?

She questioned Frank. "Was there something about a soldier ... at the time Oscar died, was there a soldier ... someone who was beaten?"

"Well, yes. Don't you remember? Before Oscar took sick, you and Kirsten went to town. You were at the bus depot, is what I was told. Kirsten said some local soldiers, injured fellows, were returning from Europe. She said there was an Indian soldier, and an old man was riled up when he saw a man, a man of color, in a uniform. The Indian soldier had family there to meet him. But then there was also a Negro soldier who riled up the old man even more. All the Negro wanted was a restroom. Kirsten said the old man began beating the Negro soldier with a cane."

"Yes! I've dreamed it, monotonously, ever since. I've always been so ... horrified. I get so hot ... and desperate. I was barely thirteen when it happened ... so long ago. But the nightmare always stops just before I understand everything, leaving me upset and, like I said, desperate."

Frank nodded. "Kirsten said she had quite a time with you. Just when it looked like the whole crowd was going to attack the soldier, you decided you were going to help the Negro."

A flood of feelings came over Deborah, starting a heat and flow of perspiration about her head. "And Kirsten stopped me. How many times I've dreamed that—always someone holding me back, keeping me from doing what I felt I had to do. I felt so strongly about what I had to do. No one else was going to help the soldier. He shouldn't die.

"It was so frightening, the people—and there were birds, screaming birds—but I knew I had to help him." She rubbed her upper arms. "I remember I had bruises from Kirsten holding me back. Uncle Oscar tried to explain how dangerous a mob could have been to me ... and later I realized it was because I looked Indian."

"You figured that out?"

Deborah wasn't exactly surprised. "Well, yes, I guess I did. The first day of school first grade—I was abused for looking Indian. I never told you and Mama. Of course, Aunt Kirsten said things ... compared me to the Indian girls by the track ... and when I pressed Uncle Oscar about it, asking questions, he left, went around the corner of the house ... that's where I found him ... a heart attack."

"It would have been dangerous for you to interfere."

"That's what Aunt Kirsten said ... and Uncle Oscar. But if no one ever steps in, never helps someone ..." Deborah's thoughts were confused now.

"The dreams have been awful, the same frightening things over and over but never enough detail to tell me for sure what it was all about. Now that I understand what the dream is, I remember how shocking the beating seemed to me."

Frank sat with his elbows on his knees, his face hidden behind his hand.

"You have to be exhausted." Deborah was aware her tone sounded distant, but she couldn't seem to control it. "I guess I need time to absorb some of this. You go on to bed, and I'm going to do some thinking. Tell Victor I'm okay, I just need time. Don't look for me—expect me when you see me." Abruptly, she walked away, leaving him on the porch.

Chapter 26

Time to Think

Deborah grabbed Grandfather's blanket and flung it about her shoulders. Crossing the corral, she patted a horse here and there, choosing Christian's horse. She rode bareback and without a bridle—striking out across the pasture. A three-quarter moon was floating overhead, or appeared to, as the clouds moved across it, and in the west she could see rain clouds highlighted by intermittent lightning. She could smell rain, imagine moisture underfoot in the springiness of the buffalo grass, and touch it in the dampness of the air. She hadn't brought a jacket, but it didn't matter. After all the years of gritty dust coating her skin, working through her hair, down to her scalp, and irritating the sensitive tips of her fingers, what was the discomfort of cool dampness? The further she rode, the more her mind began to roll her thoughts like a film in a cinema, letting old images and pains replay themselves.

First and foremost was the image of being someone she hadn't known herself to be—half Indian. All her life, various people had made remarks about her skin and features, and others—such as Van Ricker and Stoddel—did more than remark. She slid off Snicker's back and led him by his nose, proceeding on foot, hoping to walk off the turmoil in her mind. She headed for the windmill where the creaking wheel turned in the slight breeze. Drinking the ebbing and flowing water from the pipe with the battered enamel cup, she watched as Snicker dropped his head, testing the water, snuffling at its coldness. He drank. Deborah leaned against his side until he was finished, and all the while her mind churned.

She thought of being introduced to a stranger on the street, learning his name and ways about him, such as his background and how it affected him. That was what she had to do with herself.

"Hello, I'm Sky Bird," she said tentatively, and Snicker lifted his head toward her voice, sparkles of water falling from his mouth. She held her arms wide and said, "Snicker, I'm Sky Bird. I'm happy to know you. Are you happy to know me? Do you know you belong to an Indian?" She ran her hand over his back. "Maybe that's why you've been ridden so often with no saddle, no bridle." The gelding swung his head back, nudging her with his damp mouth.

She laughed wryly. "Notice, Snicker, I said I'm Indian. Funny, huh? I'm half white, half Indian, but I'm called an Indian. All I can figure, it's the Indian half that disturbs most people; it's the Indian half that makes them resentful or angry. The Indian half is considered a threat somehow, no matter the qualities of the person. The Indian half is considered a contamination of the white half. The white half belongs, the Indian half doesn't." She stroked the horse.

"Just tell me to shut up, Snicker. I tend to go on and on." Deborah wrapped herself in the blanket and looked out over the grassland. The horse grazed, his teeth squeaking on the tender green grass.

Grandfather Blue Sky was her real grandfather, a man she had loved dearly and whose memory she carried in her mind and heart. He had been her friend, one she had trusted more than any other person in her life. Her teacher ... from Grandfather she learned the ways of nature and how man was a part of that nature, not a dominant figure. From Grandfather she learned Earth felt pain when man tried to change the planet's ways, change its memory of wind and water patterns, destroy its intended growth in favor of man's view of what and how something should be grown.

She learned man should not scar Earth. He should be a protector. From Grandfather, she had learned awareness of what was in nature, and, at the same time, how man was constantly trying to modify Earth's memories of mountains and prairies by moving mountains, tearing out the bowels of the land for its riches, plowing its sod, building roads and buildings, contaminating that which was original, replacing it with the unreal, the fabricated, the ugly, that which was hostile to environment.

He taught her the Hopi way of life, the nonviolent way of life, a regard for life that did not accept war. The Hopi way of life honored the spirit. "Granddaugher," he said, "Hopi means 'the peaceful people.'"

She cried, remembering him, seeing him in her memory, feeling his touch and love. And then it struck her. Grandfather Blue Sky had made the greatest of sacrifices for her. His explanation was that his wife had died, and he needed a new way of life to cope with his loss, yet he believed his wife was with him, that he carried her memory in his heart and mind.

He hadn't needed a new way of life. He loved the old way, his life in Hopi land, however controlled by white men or the Bureau of Indian Affairs. He had loved his family and home. He'd left all of it for her. Lillian had said it in her letter. He had, by choice, and with the agreement of his family, left them to go to Minnesota, solely for the purpose of being a mentor, a teacher of a half-white, half-Indian child who should know some of the ways of the Hopi.

While he was away, his family had suffered. His son Many Stars had been jailed for protesting, for standing up for his belief in the family structure of the Hopi people and in the education and values his people taught, but his children were taken away to the mission school. If Grandfather had been there when the upheaval occurred, at the very least he would have suffered too, and yet he would have been there in his family role as a sustainer, a teacher, a grandfather with all of his love and knowledge.

"The mission school," said Fleet Foot, her brother, "according to the agent, was supposed to prepare us for the white man's world. It wasn't that. It was to destroy the Indian in us."

"They weren't successful," Deborah had said to Fleet Foot. "Grandfather Blue Sky said they would never succeed in doing it."

Hearing her say that about Grandfather, Fleet Foot had said, without resentment or animosity, only with pleasant realization, "Deborah, you ended up spending a lot more time with Grandfather and knowing him better than I did." Because of her pending birth, after Fleet Foot was two, he hadn't known Grandfather.

She remembered how drawn she was to Fleet Foot, with strong and, at the same time, inexplicable love. Burned in her memory was little Half Shell's face when he sat in the mailman's car and how he had reached for her. She had thought her love for Jonathan and David was deep and strong, but a pleasant shock had come to her when her love for Half Shell was there with an intensity almost painful. He was her nephew and adopted son. He was Grandfather's flesh and blood. *She* was his flesh and blood also.

Grandfather had made the ultimate of sacrifices, not his life, his heart-beating, blood-flowing life, but the life he had known, loved, and experienced as the fiber of his being. For her, he had sacrificed—living and dying an old man in Minnesota—in order to be with her, away from his loved ones and his home … all for her.

Deborah paced about the windmill and tank, never the same pathway, not wanting to leave her footprints. The horse fed on the grass, sometimes watching her, sometimes staring into the distance, his ears pricked forward. She couldn't see what he was seeing and hear what he was hearing. She continued to pace.

If Frank had treated her as a daughter he loved and Christian as a son-law he respected, they wouldn't have left Minnesota for Kansas. Life would have been different. Christian and David wouldn't have died. She wouldn't have lost her baby and endured the blowing dirt all of these years. She would have been in Minnesota when her mother died. Deborah felt feverish and frustrated as she chalked up all of the marks against her dad.

She rode toward the pasture's biggest canyon. Upon reaching the level floor at the canyon's mouth, she urged Snicker forward, knowing it was dangerous to ride so fast into the shadows created by the high walls. At the end of the box canyon, she released the horse and clambered up the steep west side, wondering how many small animals she was disturbing as she climbed past various tunnels. Toward the top, she found a flat rock where she could sit and watch the sunrise when it was time.

As though turning a key, she opened her thoughts again. Her mother… Deborah had been adding up grievances against her dad when it was her mother who had started all of it. Was Lillian more to blame than her dad? After all, she was the one who had been attracted to Many Stars out of loneliness—and what else? Had she loved the man? Something, perhaps just sexual attraction, had caused the two of them to cross social and racial barriers, taking a chance that had the precedence of mainly bad results. The actions of others in the past had caused, at the very least, rejection and ostracism, and at the most, riot and massacre.

Her mother wrote in the letter about Deborah coming home from school and looking in the big mirror. She dwelled on the memory again. As though it were yesterday, she saw herself staring, turning, and glancing over her shoulders. She had touched her own face, feeling its contours, raising her brows, and tracing the shape of the slightly tilted eyes. She had hair her mother kinked and twisted with foul-smelling permanents and curlers. Looking back, she knew the hairdos—along with frilly, pastel-colored dresses—were an attempt to disguise her Indian looks.

That day—and other days—she had tried to see herself as others saw her. Her features with high cheekbones were regular and pretty, even beautiful, according to Christian and Victor. Her skin was dark, yet not a lot darker than "others"; her eyes certainly were dark in contrast to most people around her, pleasant lips—"always smiling," Meredith Nelson said. Always smiling—but not when Carl Jenson spit on her on the playground and another time when he attacked her in a secluded high school hallway, leaving her with breast bruises and a lump that lasted months.

Had Lillian never thought about the consequences of a relationship that might bring a half-breed into the world? Had she never thought about preparing Deborah, alerting her to the possibilities of being considered a nonwhite? The mistreatment from Carl Jenson was only the beginning. There were other happenings, such as the storeowner during her year of college who served her only when Christian interfered.

Then there were Tony Van Ricker and Sheriff Stoddel. Christian had patiently explained to the both of them she wasn't Indian, only looked Indian, but that didn't change their perceptions. Van Ricker—would it make a difference if she admitted to him she was Indian? But then, wouldn't he only feel more justified in his treatment of her? She doubted he would appreciate her honesty one bit.

Just before dawn, a heavy fog, a rarity during the years of drought, blew into the canyon, and she pulled the blanket up over her head and face. Sitting in the darkness, she smelled the dampness of the wool blanket, taking comfort in knowing it had once covered Grandfather.

Perhaps part of Tony's mistreatment of her was his indignation that she had appeared to be covering up her heritage. Did he perceive her lie as arrogance and defiance? If so, no wonder the hackles raised on his neck the moment he met her.

She had lied to everyone, not intentionally, but a lie nevertheless. She had even lied to Audrey and August—both had stood by her more than once when others had shown their intolerance. Many times she had said she didn't mind being considered Indian, but she did mind the mistreatment because of a hateful attitude called prejudice. Would it have made any difference if she had known and presented the truth to such people? She would never know about the past, yet there was still the future. Undoubtedly, she would experience many more years of racist remarks, for she had no desire or reason to hold back the truth now.

***

The sun rose, hitting the top of the canyon wall, burning off the fog, warming the rock where she sat. She bared her face, feeling the heat take away her aches and tiredness. She thought again of Tony Van Ricker, still wondering if she could bridge the chasm between them by telling the truth. The sun became too hot on her bare head, and she eased herself down the canyon wall, moving into a shadowed spot. The horse nickered and grazed closer to her.

She rode to the west, not even thinking about what she was doing until she came to the creek and the fence that bounded her land from Tony's. She stopped the gelding, feeling his hooves sink into the wet sand. The horse drank from a small pool. She got down and cupped her hands to wash her face. She smoothed her hair, loose and long, and took the headband from her pocket. Her fingertips lightly touched the blue and white beads of a sky and the black beads of a stylized but detailed bird in flight in the foreground. She placed it on her head.

The three strands of barbed wire fence, which crossed the creek, were the very ones Van Ricker had once cut into numerous pieces, for she could see the splices she and August had made to repair the wires.

With no further thought, she took the pliers out of the loop on her jeans and unwound the wires from the yellow rock post. During the ride across Van Ricker's pasture, she folded and placed the blanket in front of her. She flexed her arms and swung her legs, feeling the morning's fresh air, so unlike most days during the dirt-blowing drought. She knew Victor would be alarmed at what she was doing, especially because she was alone, but she touched the blanket again, believing Grandfather was with her.

The Van Ricker farm was silent as she approached it from the pasture. There wasn't even the barking of a dog. Fog remnants were rising from the corral, and a south breeze threw them toward the barn. She rode in through the open corral gate.

Tony was working at some machine in the yard and whirled about when he heard the gelding nicker at a bay horse near the water tank. The man watched her as she crossed the corral. He was as big and strong as ever, his sleeves rolled to where his muscles bulged on his arms. He was wearing the style of boots she remembered from his past conflict with her, heavy with metal toe covers and cleats on the heels. He was unshaven, and his oily hair stood in tufts through a battered straw hat.

There was the rank odor of charcoaled wood next to the corral. The shed where Arlene and the children had died was still not cleared; last night's shower beaded on partly burned timbers and turned ashes into a sodden mass. In the midst of the debris was the hulk of the burned-out car. One door had been opened, probably to remove the remains of the bodies, and she could see gasoline cans next to what was left of the backseat. Some of the corral posts near the shed were blackened, having come close to burning also.

Deborah rode to the corral fence, which separated her from Tony. He was holding a good-sized wrench, and his face was flushed a mottled red. "What the hell you want, squaw?"

"I lied to you and others, Tony. I didn't know that I'm half Indian, until last night. I want you to know the truth."

"You're not telling me anything new. You look Indian. You stink Indian. Now get the hell out of here." He raised the wrench.

"You have to be going through a lot of pain, living with this." She gestured at the debris. "I hold no grudges against you. I'd like to help you. Lots of people would." Did she imagine a flicker of hesitation in his expression?

"The hell," he said.

"Many of us have had our losses, certainly not as horrible as yours. But folks want to reach out to you because they know something of what you're feeling."

"I'm not feeling a thing!"

Deborah had gone too far. He came rapidly toward her, still holding the wrench. "This country, this land, was not meant for the likes of you. It's not meant that you be on the face of the earth."

She signaled with her knees, backing the horse rapidly away, afraid to turn her back on Van Ricker. He lifted the wrench, gesturing, and the fence stopped his approach. Knowing she was still close enough he could throw the wrench and hit her, she continued to back the well-trained horse to the open gate. When she was at a safe distance, she whirled Snicker about. She heard an angry call.

"I don't want anybody here." The voice was mean, yet the echo bounding back from the barn ended on a note that made her stop and turn to look back. He shook the raised wrench.

She rode to the creek where she had taken the wires down. By now, the midmorning haze could only be seen in the distance. After repairing the fence, she drank at a pool. Clouds were being reflected in the water that tasted good and cool.

Following the creek, she rode toward the tree line that spilled over the bank. The big cottonwoods that grew here and there along the edge of the creek bottom had had their roots eroded by fast-moving waters until the gnarled, powerful anchors thrust above the sandy soil in torturous shapes. She left the gelding on the bank to graze and climbed down among the roots, finding a spot where she could sit comfortably. For a while she slept, even dreamed the soldier dream again, and this time, she saw and knew Kirsten was dragging her away from the mob of people.

She woke, hot and sweaty, her heart pounding, remembering. Kirsten had driven them home in the old wagon pulled by an even older horse. At the lakeside house, Uncle Oscar had pumped water, splashing her face, cooling her hysteria.

Deborah clambered over the root in front of her, drinking at the pool's edge, cooling her face with water the way Uncle Oscar had done. The pool was wide, and opposite her were some mallard ducks and farther downstream, one wild goose floated silently, not even dipping its head or paddling like the ducks. She crept back among the roots, not wanting to disturb the birds. She watched their gliding movements among the cloud images. A deer approached from the thickets on the shore and drank. The doe jerked her head from the water, flinging droplets, and stared directly at Deborah. In a moment's breath, the animal was gone.

Talking to Tony Van Ricker had been a diversion—one she had perhaps deliberately created in order to avoid her thoughts at hand. Now she turned to her parents and the kind of life they had given her after she was thirteen. Remembering the cold, long silences, her unspoken pleas for some recognition, some appreciation she was there, she felt her face grow hot with the familiar anger. No matter the circumstances, they had no right to treat her the way they had, turning her life dangerously close to mere existence at times. If it hadn't been for the Nelsons and her books and life out-of-doors, what kind of person would she have become?

She knew she was feeling self-pity, and as she continued to stack all the blames against Frank and Lillian, she despised herself for doing so. She moved into yet another position among the roots and tried to channel her thoughts into a different direction.

A thought came to her. How had her dad's anger against her mother been any different than hers against Christian? When he disappeared, she had no idea what had happened and had thought all kinds of things against him, even that he might have left her for someone else—a thought, ironically, suggested by Frank's letter.

But the disloyalty Frank had experienced from her mother was real, not imagined. Frank had a basis, and Deborah most of all represented it. No wonder he had resented her.

Crouched among warty roots, she watched insects create ripples on the pool surface. But she didn't allow herself to be distracted, for concentration was necessary to think about the matters eating at the edges of her mind. She had to face the thoughts head-on.

Her dad was human, and human emotions could be so disillusioning, warping the sense of one reality into another, tearing at one's sanity. She of all people should know that. How could she blame Frank? Or Lillian? She couldn't. She couldn't blame her mother for loving someone enough, even fleetingly, to give herself to him. She couldn't blame Dad for loving Lillian so much that the pain of his wife's love for another man hurt him desperately. Out of the pain had come Deborah ... Sky Bird.

At that moment, the lone large bird lifted off from the shallow edge of the creek, flying above the pool of water in front of her, its wings throwing sparkles of water into the bright sunlight. She watched its silent form fade from sight.

Hours passed as she worked at sorting and rearranging her life. She placed her fingers on her wrist, sensing the pulsing blood. Was she supposed to feel different now that she knew her blood was mixed with Grandfather's bloodline? Was it like a new birth, knowing her heritage was different than she had assumed?

She climbed among the mammoth roots, and, as a relief from the heavy thoughts of what she now knew about herself, she studied the unusual tree formations much the way she might ancient dinosaur skeletons. One cottonwood's lower branches were close to the ground, and she climbed up in them, going high and still higher. The trembling, rustling leaves—the voice of the tree, Grandfather had said—soothed her raw nerves, and she settled in a branch's crotch, leaning back to rest against the trunk, losing herself among the greenness. Pulling the blanket over herself, she dozed.

Chapter 27

A Dad and a Father

Hours later, with the darkness of night, which wasn't really darkness because of the moon, she was ready to see her beloved Victor. She got on Snicker, who had hovered nearby all day as though he thought he might be needed, and searched along the creek bank until she found a shallow spot in the still water. The splashing of the horse's feet shattered the silvery surface and the moonlight made the spray sparkle. Once she was on the other side, she let the horse go and crawled through the fence.

She walked the short distance down the road and approached Victor's house. Blacky met her, as she had expected, but because he knew her, he didn't bark or growl. She knew where Sonja and David slept and passed by their window. She scratched at Victor's screen.

He came to the window immediately. "Deborah," he whispered, "sweetheart." She heard relief and happiness in his voice.

"Come out. I need you," she said and left, going around the corner of the house.

She waited at the porch door, and when he came, Deborah began hiking to the road. "I love you," he called softly, hurrying to catch up.

She whirled about, walking backward, watching his eyes shine in the light. "I love you so much. I have things to tell you."

They crawled through her pasture fence, and she chose a place to sit on the creek bank where the water had spread out to create yet another pool. They dangled their feet. In the distance, sheet lightning lit the sky, and rumbles of sound carried to them. Ducks floated with silent black forms on the far side of the pool, their slight movements putting the most minute of ripples into the moonlit surface.

"What did Dad tell you?" Deborah asked.

"Only what you told him to tell me, to expect you when I saw you."

"I have so much to say," she said, her voice choked with emotion. "I know now why my parents turned on me, why I've had the nightmares over and over all these years, why people make remarks and judge me about my looks." She was unable to speak easily with the lump in her throat. Victor moved close, putting his arm around her and pressing her cheek into his shoulder.

"My name is Sky Bird." Her voice shook, barely above a whisper.

"What? Sky Bird?"

"Dad is not my real father. My real dad is Many Stars, Fleet Foot's dad."

"Oh," he said calmly. She lifted her head, and he loosened his hold on her. "Oh, I figured that," he said.

"You did?"

"Sure. Well, first off, you sure look Indian. When Fleet Foot was here it was easy to tell you looked a lot like him, especially around the eyes. And Half Shell looks enough like Jonathan and you to be your son."

There was silence between them. Finally, Deborah asked, "Is it all right with you, Victor Whitesong?"

He laughed. "Many years ago, not long after Christian disappeared, I remember you asking if I would be ashamed of you if you were Indian. Remember what I said?"

"You said, 'Hell, no.'"

"Well, then." In their silence, he reached for her hand and caressed her fingers. "Is it all right with *you*, Sky Bird Nelson?"

"Being Indian—half Indian—is fine with me." She sighed deeply. "There are matters I'm struggling to understand. My mother—she explained to Dad she was lonely, and Many Stars was lonely, so what did they do? They turned to each other with no thought for what might be the result." In a small voice, Deborah added, "I was the result."

She pulled her hand from his as though to distance herself and went on, searching for the right words. "Victor, I have known what it is to love someone—to love you, to be so drawn to you I couldn't sleep for thinking of you, wanting to be close to you, wanting you to touch me."

Taking a deep breath, she said, "Yet we separated ourselves when those feelings became so intense we feared a sudden spark would start a fire. We talked about matters and understood one another. We waited and waited all these years because of what Stoddel might think and do and because of the boys, not wanting them to be hurt by the talk of others in the community.

"Why didn't Mother have the same strength? Why didn't she think about a possible child and what a relationship with an Indian might do to her husband and child?" Deborah was sobbing now, and her head began to hurt, so strong were her thoughts.

"So are you feeling superior to them, judging your mother—and Many Stars?" Victor asked.

A quick intake of breath hissed through her clenched teeth. "Is that how I sound?"

"Well, like you said, we could easily have given in to our feelings too. It seems to me you're resenting Lillian and Many Stars for doing what we have so often wanted to do ourselves. I guess I prefer to think the two of them had the strength to do what they did when we didn't."

"You think so?" She looked at Victor closely. "You're reprimanding me."

"I suppose I am."

After a while, she said, "I have a confession."

"Oh?"

"Once, more than once, I thought if I … had birth control, you know, like a diaphragm, a birth control device, I could give myself to you without worry. But then I knew I could only do that with Carl Hocksmith's help—and I wasn't sure I could trust him."

"Really," Victor said dryly.

"My mother didn't have an option to consider, did she? I had it but rejected it." She interlaced her fingers tightly. "But that's how close I came, Victor. That's how close I came to doing what my mother did."

"And," he said, "it seems you weren't thinking about Christian at that moment any more than Lillian did about Frank."

Deborah reacted. "But Christian hasn't been a part of my life for many years, and I've had no reason to believe he would be. She *should* have thought of Dad. Look at how angry he became. Look at what it did to their marriage and to me. The way they treated me had a lot to do with our moving to Kansas … and look at what happened, to Christian, I mean."

Full of confusion, she said, "Oh! But then I wouldn't have known you—and all the others." Her thoughts were churning. Her life was so rich; from the moment of her birth, she knew and loved Grandfather Blue Sky, and then, because she and Christian wanted to get away from her parents and experience a different life, there were all the people she came to know here in Kansas. If she hadn't come to Kansas, she would never have known August and Audrey.

If she hadn't left Minnesota, she would never have known John and the boys—and Melonie and Teddy R. She tried to imagine not having known Eloise Williams, her ways so caustic and abrasive yet so kind and giving; or Ol' Paul who feared the future and worried over the world's failure to recognize the return of renewed horrors; or Lydia, so hurt by her losses that her heart must have been shredded in pieces, yet so much wanting others to have happiness—"he loves you, you know"—oh, those words, words that seemed to cut into her own heart, bringing her right back to Victor, a man who loved her far, far more than she deserved. What would her life have been without Victor Whitesong?

She spoke the words that were in her mind. "What would my life be without you, Victor Whitesong?" She still did not let herself touch him, but their eyes bridged the distance between them.

Victor said, "I owe your mother and Many Stars so much."

She jumped to her feet and reached down to take his hands and pull him up beside her. She held him close, swinging their bodies from side to side, bringing them close to the pool's edge. She laughed, seeing her happiness, her love, and her joy reflected in Victor's eyes, his face. "Victor," Deborah said, "you know, it doesn't make sense to mourn for the life that never was when I can rejoice for the life that is."

The moon was gone. The night settled down to the intense black that comes before dawn. The sky was clouded, and the clouds thickened, covering the stars. They waited in the blackness until the horizon lightened in the east so they could see to walk to her farmstead. They talked on the way.

"Now I know why I've had the soldier dream all these years. When I was a child, somewhere around thirteen, I saw a black soldier being beaten by an old man while a crowd cheered him on, readying themselves to help the old racist. Before he focused on the Negro, he was about to attack an Indian soldier, and the crowd would have attacked that man, given the opportunity. Instead, the Indian escaped with family and friends. I wanted to help the black man, but Aunt Kirsten dragged me away. She thought the crowd would think I was an Indian trying to help another person of color."

"Your aunt was right."

She frowned. "Victor! He was already badly hurt—a soldier! A soldier who looked like he had given more than time for his country. Aunt Kirsten wouldn't let me help him."

"Deborah, you could have been hurt."

"Maybe. Maybe not. We can't go through life without ever taking a stand."

"It sounds like the crowd was out of control. Your aunt assessed the situation and feared you'd be hurt." He smiled, just a small smile. "I think you were looking for trouble."

"What did you do the day you and Fleet Foot went for tractor parts? I don't know what happened for sure, but I'll bet you didn't stand back when he was attacked."

"I thought we were safe in fighting back, Fleet Foot was such a strong looking man."

"And what did you find out?"

"That's when I realized he was also an ill man. We did okay though. It just took some doing. Deborah, we were lucky," he emphasized. "As a thirteen-year-old you might not have been so lucky."

"Someday I'm going to meet Many Stars."

"Fleet Foot knew."

"I believe he did, but what makes you think so?"

"The way he looked at you. Once he started to tell you and then stopped. He told you a lot about Many Stars. He wanted you to at least know the man that way."

She stared at him. "Do you ever miss anything, Victor Whitesong?" He grinned, and she said, "There's that big smile of yours, the one Audrey would say melts my innards. If she only knew!"

He laughed. "I love you, Sky Bird."

They walked to the corral, their shoulders and hips just touching. He held her fingers to his lips briefly. "Only a while longer, Sky Bird."

A rain shower spread its freshness over them with no threatening lightning or thunder. Victor let the stock into the barn. In the warmth of the building, Deborah wiped the dampness from the cows, and they began the milking chores. When they were finished, Frank was standing near the well house.

"Good morning, Dad." She reached up to kiss his cheek, damp from the shower—or had he been crying? He was unshaven, and the whiskers were rough to her lips.

Frank said, "You must be exhausted."

"I haven't felt this good in a long time."

His look was uncertain.

"You are my *dad*, you know. Many Stars is my *father*."

His expression wavered between happiness and disbelief. A brisk wind swirled around them, and moisture from the tree added to the rain that blew onto their bare faces and necks. Frank's eyes were almost more than she could handle, for the love in them made her realize the significance of the commitment she had just made to him. For years any problems between them had been his responsibility, or so she had thought, but now she was giving of herself in their relationship in a way she had never done before—or if she ever had, it was back when she was only a young child. She had thought she was prepared for this, but there was still more for her to think through.

Trying to voice her feelings, she said, "I've got a lot to face and absorb, Dad, so if I seem a little slow, be patient. I've learned an awfully lot in a short time. I think I've got plenty of my own past actions in our relationship to reckon with. But this I'm sure of," and she circled her hand in the air to include the three of them. "What would I be without the two most important men in my life?" Carrying the can of milk, she turned toward the well house. "Let's get out of this rain. Dad, you turn the separator."

He helped her put the separator together. They worked as though they had been sharing the tasks all of these past ten years.

"Have you been sleeping?" Deborah handed him a jar of milk from the water tank.

"I have. I guess I was worn out. I thought my mind would keep me awake, but I haven't remembered much of anything after I hit the pillow."

"Good. We've got a full day ahead of us. Let me take this jar and then would you see how Half Shell is doing? He's still a little boy, and I realize I've so much to learn about him. I've neglected him." Carrying jars of cold milk and cream, Deborah went to the house.

Calvin was stirring a fire in the stove, and Meredith was preparing to mix biscuits. She hugged Deborah and lifted her hair from her neck. "You're damp. Is it raining?"

"Just a little shower."

"Well, Calvin, get the fire going so we can warm up this girl."

He grinned at them. "Meredith just needs to mother." He worked at building a fire while Deborah removed her wet shoes and socks. He adjusted the draft on the stove. "I think I'll go see what the menfolk are doing—soon as I get these ashes swept up. I made a mess this morning."

"Deborah," Meredith said, "I'll finish breakfast if you have other things to do."

Deborah felt the headband in her pocket where she had put it when the rain started. "Sweet Meredith, Calvin, you can call me Sky Bird."

Meredith smiled, and with relief in her voice said, "You know everything now."

"Dad said you've known all my life." Keeping reproach out of her voice, she said, "I wish I had known. It might have helped me."

"I wish I had been at liberty to tell you. It hurt very much to see what you were being put through."

Calvin's expression was doubtful. "If you had known, I can't imagine Frank doing things any different than he did. He was a bitter man."

"I could have spoken up to him," Deborah said. "I could have tried to talk to him about my feelings and what he was doing to the family. I wish I had known before Grandfather and Fleet Foot died." She picked up her shoes and socks. "But at last I'm learning it does no good to live with past regrets or harbor old resentments. I've done enough of that over the years. You can't imagine how often Victor, like Christian before him, has pointed that out to me. Like the stubborn person I am, I didn't listen. Now I know. I can't blame the two of you. You made a promise to Mother, and I'm glad you were there as her friends. She needed you. As for Dad, I've reached a conclusion. I've got a dad and a father."

"That's good," Calvin said. "They're lucky men."

Chapter 28

Is War Coming?

After breakfast, Deborah spoke to Jonathan and Half Shell. "I really need to spend an hour or so with you. We should talk."

"Sure, Mom," Jonathan said.

"We need to ride out to see the arrowhead."

Half Shell was excited. "Could we?"

Jonathan said, "I've told Half Shell about the ride, enough that he feels like he remembers. And I told him about the time we sat with his dad among the big rocks and talked about lots of things."

"I remember!" Half Shell said. "It was my first ride, and I remember seeing the arrowhead."

With Victor's help, they saddled Snicker, Lady, and Dumper. Deborah stood back, watching with pride as Jonathan helped Half Shell mount Dumper.

"Are you sure you don't want to go along?" Deborah asked Victor. "We can wait until you saddle Princess."

"Another time. The three of you need to do this."

She leaned down from the saddle to kiss him. "Thank you. I love you, dear man."

Deborah searched to find the arrowhead's location, for she hadn't been there since the boys had left for Minnesota. They sat in the grass, and she held the stone first.

"See, Half Shell, the arrowhead is a part of Earth's memory."

"What's that mean?" the little boy asked.

"The arrowhead has been here a long time," Deborah said. "It's a symbol. That means, when I see it, it reminds me of things that are important. I have left it right here just as I found it, a reminder to not change Earth any more than I have to." She put the arrowhead back in its imprinted spot. "See, the arrowhead's right where it was when the three of us looked at it three years ago. I admit, there were times when I wondered if the soil around it would blow away. But it didn't, nothing's changed, and that's good. That's what Grandfather Blue Sky taught me. He felt it should be the way of all men, not just Indians. I think this means even more to me, now that I know I'm part Indian—something I'm having to get used to."

"You're half Indian just like I'm half Indian," said Half Shell. "Jonathan's quarter Indian."

The older boy grinned. "We did some talking about it. It seemed strange to us at first, I guess because I'm older than he is. We figured out we're cousins but prefer to think we're brothers."

A sudden joy filled Deborah. "Isn't that something? It makes me so happy!"

Half Shell reminded them, "What's important is Grandfather Blue Sky. He's grandfather to all of us."

"He is," Deborah said "and I'm very proud to know I have his blood in me."

"So am I," Jonathan said. "I feel bad about one thing, though."

"What, Jonathan?"

"More than once I told David I had to play Indian and he had to play cowboy—because he was too noisy to be an Indian."

Deborah and the boys laughed, and she said, "That's true, he could be noisy. But then there were times he seemed to be more Indian than the rest of us. An Indian with red hair and freckles." She looked out over the pastureland. A chorus of meadowlarks was singing, and the sound soothed her soul.

"We're going to bury your dad this afternoon, Jonathan. I don't think burying his bones changes much. We'll just be putting them in a different location. I figure his spirit's been with us all these years and will continue to be."

"It sure helps to know what happened."

"I agree. You were so young—and then I discovered you were worrying he might have left us because he no longer loved us."

Jonathan looked at the little boy earnestly. "My dad was a good man.

I've heard lots of folks say that about him. But you and me, we're going to have Victor as our dad, and he's a good man too."

"I like him a lot," Half Shell said.

"Wonderful," said Deborah. "There's nothing I need to say."

As Deborah worked that morning with Mary's help, so many thoughts ran through her mind. There was the funeral to be held at noon. What had been briefly renewed pain by the old woodpile was now just a regret she had ever doubted Christian and a sadness Jonathan and David had not known him longer. Recognizing that Grandfather Blue Sky and Fleet Foot had been more than her friends added a different dimension to the sadness she felt—if only she had known when they were still living that they shared the same blood.

She heard Jonathan calling to the house. "Idotha, Mom! It's Idotha."

The girl was riding her horse up the lane, just as she had done years ago when Jonathan started first grade. But Deborah was wondering if Jonathan was seeing the fifteen-year-old girl the way Deborah was—tall, slender, and already looking more like a woman than a girl. The two grabbed one another's hands and danced in a circle. Then Half Shell dodged in between them, and they started the dance all over again, twirling about the little boy. Idotha stopped long enough to pick up the long-legged child, and the dance continued.

"Will you look at that! She's a strong girl to lug the boy like that," Mary said. She added wistfully, "If I was younger I'd get out there too."

By noon, the yard was filled with their friends, and Victor set the small casket on the stone wall beneath the big pine trees Christian had loved.

Moses spoke to the group. "Deborah and I thought about how we could put Christian's spirit to rest today. We decided this gathering in the yard under his favorite trees is the fitting and proper way. I'm going to say a few words, and then Jonathan's going to sing with his beautiful voice.

"I've been spending some time talking with this family the past few days, and even though we now know what happened to Christian, we've still been wondering why it had to be. Then his dad, Calvin, said, 'I guess it was just his time.' What more can we say or think? It's just beyond our understanding.

"Why did it have to be? We raised the same question when the young girl, Melonie, and the young boys, Robby and David, went to heaven—and they were supposed to have had many years with us. We raised it when Eloise died—just when it seemed she was beginning a new phase of her life with Herman and Corrine. When other folks left us—Horace, August, Audrey, my Lydia"—his voice broke—"we understood a little better, for they had lived long lives.

"So we still come back to our lack of understanding when it comes to Christian, and again I hear these words: 'It was just his time.' In the Bible, in Ecclesiastes, there's a passage we've all probably heard one time or another, and here's part of it. 'For everything there is a season, and a time for every matter under heaven; a time to be born, and a time to die.' It seems that was what Calvin was saying, it was just Christian's time. The Bible says more about Christian—there's 'a time to plant, and a time to pluck up what is planted.' He was a farmer and knew how to do that for sure. Then there's the 'time to weep, and a time to laugh.' Anyone who knew the man soon learned he could laugh ... and cry while he was laughing.

"The writer of these passages sure knew what he was talking about, for he covered a lot of life when he said there's a season to do something. He also said there's 'a time for war, and a time for peace.' Any of us who follows the daily news, those words make a shiver run up our backs and into our hearts. And then he wrote, there's 'a time to mourn,' and that's what we're doing ... although I suppose you'd say we did our mourning some time ago.

"Now, if you're like me, you're saying, 'Isn't all of it so true?' All of those things are a big part of life. We don't pretend to understand. It seems all we can do is live the best we can and live on faith—for we certainly can't tell when we're going to die. We just know the time comes, sometime. Then there's faith. It's what helps us when we don't know or understand. All we know is that it's just as Calvin says, it was Christian's time.

"In this yard are Christian's friends—the ones who remain—and the family members who have loved him. We all know how he loved people and what he thought of his family—and we take a moment to say, 'Forgive us, Christian, for some of us doubted your love at times.' We also know how Christian loved the land and the skies. That's how he died, outside, checking out the land and the skies."

Jonathan sang "Amazing Grace." Deborah knew from the Minnesota letters that he was said to have a beautiful voice, but she hadn't expected this. Listening to him, she cried, as much from the sadness of Christian's death as the beauty of the singing.

They drove to the cemetery. The casket was in the back of Victor's truck, and a group of men, including Jonathan, stood on either side of it, holding on to the sideboards. Just as Victor was turning into the churchyard, his truck had a flat. Hands on his hips, he stood by the truck, looking ruefully at his tire. Other trucks and cars pulled on into the parking area, and people gathered about Victor.

"Now, I believe," Denzil Wolfe said, "if the Depression would end, a whole lot of us would buy a new tire or two."

Victor grinned. "A tire with no air is depression for sure."

The small casket was carried to the cemetery and placed next to the graves of the baby and David. Deborah could see where someone had repaired washouts or rodent holes in the surfaces of the two graves. A sunflower grew near David's stone, and she was glad it had been left there. After so many years of drought, it was good to see something growing on its own.

Moses prayed, and then everyone sang an old hymn Christian had loved. Simpson's workman was standing behind the church, leaning on a shovel. How many times had she seen the man over the years in this cemetery? He was like someone out of a Gothic novel. She turned away, seeing pile after pile of dirt against the bases of the stones. Today the blown dirt was wet because of the morning showers. By late afternoon, the wind would increase, and the drift surfaces would be moving from grave to grave, as though visiting here and there among the stones and spirits.

The line of cars and trucks drove back to the farm, and the men quickly set up sawhorses and put out planks. When the tablecloths were on, the food appeared.

Mary said, "I remember another time we sat at tables like this in your yard."

"We had been looking," Deborah said. She listened to her neighbors talk.

"Some ways it seems like yesterday, and in other ways more years than it's really been," someone said.

"All these years, I still miss Christian. One day he discovered we were picking corn and fixing it to can. He pitched right in. I never saw a man so good at cutting corn off the cob. Helped us just to be neighborly. Said it gave us opportunity to visit."

"He was a good man."

"Did you know he helped me take down an old fence and dig out those rock posts? What a job, but he just took it right in stride. I remember he grunted and said it was like those posts had sprouted roots in the ground. I've always remembered that somehow."

"When my tractor broke down in the middle of harvest, he pitched right in, like you said, and helped me overhaul it. We had it done in a day's time. I'll bet you remember that, Deborah. You helped us. I never knew a woman before or since who could work on a tractor."

"Sad, sad. So sad to lose a young man and the youngsters."

"We need more kids in this township, more young folks."

"Folks like Herman and Corrine are working on it, wouldn't you say? And look at Sonja!"

After the meal, the men, some of them smoking, gathered around Calvin and Frank.

"Maybe more young farmers will come with better times."

"Better times, shoot! It sounds like war coming."

"Someone's got to stop Hitler."

"Remember Ol' Paul Patterson's road signs? Most are gone now. He had one, 'Hitler's Germany.'"

"Why, I remember that."

"Yes," Moses said. "He was putting it up when he died, but he had worries about Hitler before then."

"Did Hitler have his fingers in the pie that early?"

"Oh, yes, and Ol' Paul seemed to know things long before the rest of us."

"That or he was just more alert to what he read and heard. The rest of us put the old gas pedal down and sometimes don't even look on down the road."

"That's the truth."

"We'd better start looking ahead. You know what's going to happen? There's going to be another war and the so-called war effort. You know what that means. It means folks will start planting fencerow to fencerow again. The badlands the government done set aside and planted back to grass? Betcha they'll get plowed again."

"I think you're right. Fencerow to fencerow."

"Deborah, Audrey told me Christian once said all he needed for sure was six foot of ground."

"But he doesn't really have six foot in his grave, his box was so little."

The women sat at a table to look at a quilt Meredith had brought for Deborah.

"We named folks who've passed on. It was nice to remember Eloise Williams."

"How could we forget her?"

"There was a good woman."

"A good woman," Corrine echoed. She was going to have a third baby and sat with her swollen feet on a footstool Mary had brought to her.

"We're sorry, Deborah and Mrs. Nelson, that Christian died, but you're sure better off knowing what's become of him."

Deborah couldn't argue with that, and Meredith nodded.

"You've had some hard times, as young as you are."

"They say war's coming for sure."

"What's that got to do with anything?"

"Folks say war brings better times. Somebody's got to make the guns and feed the soldiers. That's jobs. Gets money into the economy."

"I hate war. I've been without a dad since the Big War. Now, I've got three boys the age to go to war. And all folks think of is the jobs they'll have."

"Maybe we won't be in the war. Folks are telling Roosevelt to stay out of Europe's trouble."

"The price of wheat will go up, hogs, everything. They did during the Big War, the war to end all wars."

"Is that all you think of, wheat and hogs? What about our boys? Our children?"

"Don't blame me. I'm just stating how things were in the Big War. If we have war again, my bet is prosperity will return. Money will roll in again."

"Blood money!"

"But it's life. Deborah, this quilt is so pretty. Mrs. Nelson, you have talent at these things. I would never have thought of putting blue and green together. So Deborah, where are you and the boys going to live when you and Victor are married?"

Deborah had no chance to answer.

"Now, leave Deborah alone. This ain't the time or place to talk marriage. Christian's barely cold and you're—"

"Barely cold! Dead nine years and barely cold?"

"I mean, his body's barely been in the grave two hours and here you're—"

"Body! We didn't bury no body! Just dried-out bones—"

"Now, hush. You have no business talking that way with Deborah right here."

"Well, now—"

"Now, now. You both stop. Everyone knows there's no love lost between the two of you. We're here to help Deborah and Mrs. Nelson through this trying time."

"Well, Deborah, I'd say you did your grieving a long time ago. You were a sorry sight when Christian disappeared. We all felt so bad for you."

"Time eases the pain."

"Lord help us, if there's another war we'll have more young men dying—"

"You on to that again. Like beating a dead horse!"

"So many have lost their lives in all this dirt blowing, we don't need more dying."

"Well, it appears to be over. I'll bet you it'll rain tonight, the way my bones hurt today."

"Deborah, you never answered about Victor. You going to live here or there?"

Chapter 29

Many Stars

Deborah and Victor went to town the day after Christian's funeral and visited Bowers at the newspaper office. "I've been thinking about your picture of me," she said to the editor. "And I guess after almost nine years it's time to forgive you. Time sort of heals old grudges, don't you think?" She patted his ink-grimed hand. "And you did a reasonable story about Christian. Thank you."

"We're hoping," Victor said, "you'll write some more about Deborah here."

Deborah saw Bowers perk up, and the three of them had a good visit that afternoon. Before she left, Deborah took a strawberry sour cream pie out of a knotted tea towel. She placed it in front of Bowers.

"I hope you've got a fork or spoon hidden in your desk," Victor said.

"Don't need any." Bowers wiped his fingers on his ink-stained handkerchief and then dug into the pie.

In the weekly paper, on page two, where birth and wedding announcements usually appeared, Deborah's story was printed under a headline with the largest font Bowers owned. *Mrs. Deborah Nelson stopped by our offices earlier this week and asked that we write an announcement in her behalf to the surrounding community of Fremont. She regrets she has been party to misinformation about herself and is desirous of setting the record straight.*

"People, some in accusatory fashion, others with curiosity, and yet more with friendly interest, have assumed Mrs. Nelson to be of Indian descent. With

a few she has expressed denial and with still others, believing herself to be of full-blood Swedish descent and uncaring about what people thought, never bothered to correct their assumptions.

"With recent transpirations in her family, namely the death of her beloved mother and the more recent visit from her father, Mr. Frank Jorgenson, Mrs. Nelson has learned she is truly of Indian as well as Swedish descent. It is with pride she wishes to announce her given Indian name as Sky Bird and her Indian heritage as Hopi of the Southwest.

"We in these offices realistically know there will be those who will merely nod and say, 'So?' and go on about their business as they properly should; others will add, 'I told you so'; and still others will make comments better off not having been said and certainly not printed in this communication.

"We remind you the lovely and gracious Sky Bird gives you this information with great pride and dignity, both of which, we believe, are a natural part of her birthright."

On a later page was Christian's obituary. It concluded with "*He will be long remembered in this community as a cheerful man, full of good humor and concern for others. He knew no stranger.*" Opposite the obituaries was an announcement: "*Sky Bird, otherwise known as Deborah Nelson, will join Mr. Victor Whitesong, a local rancher, in holy wedlock on September 3, 1939. Both Mr. Whitesong and the future Mrs. Whitesong are prominent members of this community, and we wish them every happiness as they embark on their new life together.*"

The end of August was typical. Early morning blueness of the sky turned by afternoon to a heated blue that made the eyes smart. By three o'clock, the heat and monotonous drone of locusts made Deborah sluggish and irritable with worry. "It's too much like the drought days," she said.

Victor tried to reassure her. "It's okay, sweetheart. You've got to remember what's normal for western Kansas. Let's you and me take a little walk out to the African fields." He stopped at the machine shop to get a shovel. Putting it over his shoulder, he pulled her close to his side with his free arm.

They walked various sections of the south and west fields, stopping here and there to dig down into the soil. Deborah was saddened to remember a similar walk with Christian and August in the east pasture so long ago, but she didn't tell Victor about it.

"Look," he said. "Look at the moisture in that soil. It's coming back."

"You're right." Deborah hunkered down to gaze at every sample he dug. "And we've got a good crop of sudan."

After each tamping down of the soil, Victor would lean over to kiss her. They laughed with each kiss. "Do you suppose," he asked, "other critters, like badgers and coyotes, kiss with each tunnel they dig?"

Back at the farm, she looked for Frank. "Daddy, you've got to go with me to the terraced fields. You won't believe the moisture that's there." He smiled at her excitement. She said, "I haven't forgotten the five hundred dollars. We're going to repay you soon."

"No, you're not," he said.

"Well, yes, I am."

"Nope. I told you when I sent the money, consider it the college money you didn't use and an investment in my grandsons' futures."

She saluted, grinning at him. "Yes, sir."

Big David and Sonja joined Deborah and Victor each day, gathering and canning vegetables. Frank and the Nelsons worked alongside them. As they worked, they talked. Deborah felt almost like a child again, getting to know her dad.

Two days before the wedding, supper was over, and the kitchen was cleaned and cooling from a day's work. Deborah was concerned that Sonja not overdo and encouraged Big David to take her home for the evening. Earlier that afternoon, Deborah had told Sonja she should rest.

Sonja had disagreed. "Oh, I'm fine, Deborah. Don't you remember those August days a few years back? Those were hot days. This seems cool in comparison."

"I'm serious, Sonja. Think about the baby as well as yourself."

"No, really, I'm fine."

Deborah had turned to David who was filling jars with hot tomatoes. "David, put your wife in the porch swing with a tall glass of cold water and take Meredith with you."

Sonja protested. "When you were pregnant, I'll bet you didn't drop what you were doing to have a rest."

"That's just it, Sonja, I didn't. And I lost my baby girl."

There was dismay on Sonja's face. The young woman said nothing more and left the heat of the well house for the rest of the afternoon.

Now that supper was over, the Nyfellers were going to Victor's house. As he opened the truck door, David turned to call to Victor. "Don't you want to go home with us now? Lot faster in this truck than on your horse."

Victor grinned. "Thanks, but I'll come along fairly soon. My mare needs the exercise."

"Well, all right," David said. "But we just don't know what the attraction is over here."

Calvin snorted. Victor went back to reading to Half Shell. He was sitting in the porch swing, and the little boy was curled up against his side. All of them were tired, pleasantly tired. When Jonathan sat down on the steps to write, Deborah joined him with her letter writing materials.

Crows and magpies fussed in the orchard, and she lifted her head to listen. "Jonathan, one day Victor and I heard the crows carrying on when we were in the barn. We didn't pay much heed, for if we had, we would have seen they were disturbed about an approaching black blizzard." She sighed. "That was when Grandmother Audrey died. I suppose every time I hear crows screeching now I'll think about that time—and also how crows have figured in my nightmare."

Frank was reading the daily paper, and they had noticed he seemed to react to much of the news the same way August had. He erupted now. "That animal Hitler!" He rattled the newspaper and then angrily folded it. "He's attacked Poland! Why can't he be stopped? Didn't this world learn from the Great War? It was horrible! Are we going to fight the whole damned war again?"

"Dad," she said.

He angrily rubbed his chin, his day's growth of whiskers making a raspy sound. "I'm sorry, I get so worked up. There are those who think war is a great thing, a way to make the economy strong. Damn it, what a horrible sacrifice of lives!"

Deborah got up to sit in a chair beside Frank, holding his hand, hearing his breathing calm down. "Sometimes," she said, "sometimes I get so discouraged and upset with our so-called civilizations. I think mankind has too high a regard for its self-importance. History has shown us again and again how ignorant, barbaric, and idiotic we are."

Frank looked at her blankly for a moment. They both burst out laughing. "That was mighty profound, daughter."

"I thought you might think so."

Still holding his hand, Deborah idly looked out over the land in front of her, beyond the alfalfa field and on and on, over the grasslands. She noticed a trail of dust coming from the north-south road and watched it move closer.

Calvin was watching too. "There's a fellow late to supper. I reckon he's good and hungry."

"His plate will be dried out by now," Meredith said, "or it's been given to the dog."

Victor had finished the book he was reading to Half Shell, and they were pushing the porch swing back and forth. "Nice breeze when we swing," Half Shell commented.

"Deborah, that's your buddy, Corky, in his truck," Victor said.

"My buddy," she said in a drawling voice. Jonathan gave her a questioning look. "That's a long story, sweetheart. I'll tell you sometime." She continued to watch the truck as it came north.

"He's a dust raiser," Frank commented.

Victor chuckled. "Corky's a floor-boarder for sure. He's in charge of township road repairs. Likes to test the road conditions."

"He's stopping at our mailbox," Jonathan said.

"Probably coming to see your mama."

"Victor," she said, "when you sound like that you sure remind me of a certain hired hand I used to have."

A man got out of the truck and started up the lane. He was carrying a satchel and was strong looking, moving with long strides. Like Fleet Foot, she thought, and then she lifted her head, staring.

When he was closer, she noticed an oddity about his hair but couldn't tell what it was. She stood slowly, standing on the top step, watching, and then glanced at Victor. The walker was closer now, and she could see he wore his hair in braids—just like Fleet Foot had sometimes done. She turned to look at Frank.

Frank smiled nervously. "It should be him," he said, his voice husky with emotion. "It should be Many Stars. I called him about your wedding and encouraged him to come."

Deborah felt disbelief and even some alarm. Curiosity overcame her, and she whirled about. She walked down the steps with a steadiness to her legs that she found hard to believe she had. The cowbell on the east gate clunked as she went through it. The circle drive in front of the stone wall was hard packed, and she felt its surface through her moccasins. They met where the drive began and stood a few yards from one another. Behind them, the ancient and mammoth cottonwood rustled its leaves, talking to move time forward, yet bringing messages from the past.

Many Stars was an older version of Fleet Foot. He looked at her, unsmiling but with warmth to his big face, his lips twitching slightly, as though about to break into a smile. His dark hair was lightly streaked with white, and she saw Grandfather Blue Sky in the man's features. He carried under one arm a satchel and a package and under the other a small drum of Indian design.

Sudden joy rushed through her, and she said, "I'm Sky Bird, and you're my father, Many Stars."

He smiled at her, motionless.

She took the drum and put it under her own arm. She clasped his hand in hers and turned to lead him to the yard gate. "Come, meet our family."

Deborah put food on the table, and Half Shell and Jonathan sat with Many Stars while he ate. She stood back, watching and listening, learning to know Many Stars. She discovered he was doing the same, observing her, even while actively involved with the Nelsons, Frank, and Victor—and the boys in particular.

"Grandfather Many Stars." Jonathan said the name as though trying it out.

"Yes. Grandson Jonathan. Grandson Half Shell." He surveyed the two of them closely, barely looking at his plate while he ate. "What is the best and fastest way to get to know the two of you?" Many Stars smiled.

Jonathan answered without hesitation. "See what we do or what we have done."

"For example?"

"Half Shell notices things. He also can be very quiet and listen. I think he's learning to read by being quiet and listening. What do you think, Half Shell?"

"I think I can read some. I like being up in the tree house. You see trees and sky and the hills far away. I feel like I'm on top of the earth."

Jonathan told Many Stars about himself. "I like to paint and draw and write about what I see and feel."

"He sings," Half Shell said shyly.

Many Stars nodded. "So, what can you tell me about your mother?"

Jonathan said, "She is a protector of the earth and all living things."

"And Victor Whitesong?"

"He feels very deeply and then acts on what he feels."

"Your grandfather Jorgenson?"

"Grandfather Frank has learned to give love and receive it."

"Well." Many Stars was thoughtful. "Grandmother Nelson?"

"She recreates in her artwork what most people don't see." Anticipating the next question from Many Stars, Jonathan said, "Grandfather Calvin protects those who can't protect themselves—you know, like animals and children."

Half Shell nodded. "He pulled me out of the crick when I thought I could swim but couldn't."

"And Many Stars?" Jonathan asked.

"I believe in my heritage as a Hopi and that I should pass the teachings and prophecies of the Hopi to my children and their children."

Deborah woke in the night and listened to the darkness. The sounds she heard were not the usual noises of the night. Slipping out of bed, she opened her door. The voices of Frank and Many Stars and the odor of perking coffee came from the kitchen. They talked quietly, and although she couldn't hear their words, their voices sounded at ease. She smiled and went back to bed.

Chapter 30

The Indian in a White Man's World

When Deborah was saddling horses the next morning, she saw Many Stars looking at her. "So," he said. "You and I have been watching each other. Maybe we need to talk about what we see."

She said, "I see Grandfather Blue Sky. You've a bigger build but you look much like him and Fleet Foot looked much like you."

"What I see when I look at you is my mother, Gentle Dove. I don't remember much, but I've seen pictures. You look strikingly like her."

Smiling, Deborah said, "Do you suppose that means we're related somehow?" He laughed. She added, "Gentle Dove. That's a beautiful name. I love the calls of doves. Grandfather Blue Sky made me aware of them. Gentle Dove," she said again. "The name of a bird like Sky Bird."

"Exactly. That's why you have your name. Blue Sky loved my mother very much, and he wanted your name to be that of a bird too."

"Grandfather chose my name?"

"Yes."

"I'm happy to know that."

Many Stars rode over the farm with her, for he had asked to see how the land had survived the drought. "Fleet Foot told me some of what you were doing, but Frank says you've done considerably more since then."

"Fleet Foot—I loved him from the moment we met."

"So he said."

"My brother," she said.

"Your brother. He had absolutely no doubts about sending the baby to you."

A warm shiver went up her back. "That's good."

They rode to the highest point in the north pasture and looked about. Warm clouds streamed before the wind, sending fast-moving shadows across the grass and fields, much the way trout might flit through murky waters.

They sat among the tumbled rocks and talked for hours, only moving as the sun moved so they could sit in the shade, and Deborah shared water with Many Stars from her canteen. Much of what they said was about the life of the Hopi in a world claimed by white men.

"I learned many years ago," Many Stars said, "that as an Indian, I couldn't live a life of relaxation and complacency among white men. I've had to be constantly alert. You've got to learn that too. I can tell you've learned some of it already because of men like your sheriff."

She nodded. "A few days ago I was angry because I wasn't told from the beginning who I really am. All my life I've always been slightly off guard. I usually expected people to be mistaken about me, and I'd be trying to correct that—when I needed to have known I'd better be ready ... for whatever. "

"You're right, you needed to have put your energies into being on the alert. I'm sorry you didn't know. Blue Sky and I wanted you to know at birth. It was hard, and no one knew for sure what was best."

"So much wasted energy, my denying what they saw in me. Sometimes I didn't bother. Then I learned to say I would be proud to be Indian ... and for some people that seemed to work."

"Knowing and understanding who one is, that's an advantage."

She nodded. "The greatest shock I've ever experienced was having Fleet Foot tell me that he hadn't been able to buy milk for Baby Half Shell ... an innocent baby. When I fed him that first bottle of milk in my kitchen, every drop of that sustenance contained all the emotions of love, sorrow, and protectiveness that a mother can express." She lowered her head to her knees, her long hair curtaining her face. "At the time David died, Moses Bogart said we want desperately to protect a child from harm. He was so right."

Tears were on Many Stars's face, and he held her hand. "When you wrote me that Half Shell was brought to you by the mailman, I cried. You mentioned something of the pain and fear in the child's eyes, and you were working to erase his memory of that pain and fear. I still cried.

I paid money to an Indian woman I trusted—she wasn't Hopi but that doesn't matter—to take him to your doorstep." He sighed. "Another regret to follow me all the days of my life."

"Oh, I don't think Half Shell remembers."

"Maybe he should, maybe he should. It can increase his alertness."

She talked about Tony Van Ricker. "Christian and others told him he was mistaken, that I wasn't Indian. He didn't believe them, and now he knows for certain."

"And I'm afraid he believes he's even more justified, Sky Bird, to feel the way he does about you. Be alert. I suspect you haven't seen the last of his actions against you."

"I know. I worry about the children. I've got to protect the boys."

"That's good, but be certain they learn ways to protect themselves. As you know, it's the way of the Hopi to not be violent, to not fight. There are other ways, though, to protect, and being alert is one of them … seeing, anticipating—before something happens. You'll have Victor with you day and night now. I'm convinced he would give his life protecting you and the boys."

She tried to smile. "Oh, you sound so serious."

"I mean to be."

Back at the barn, they unsaddled the horses and brushed them down. Many Stars made one comment about the work Victor and she had been doing. "Jonathan's right. You're well on the way to taking care of the land."

"I haven't done it alone."

He nodded. "It can't be done alone. Everyone's needed."

The rest of the day Many Stars joined individual persons as they went about their work on the farm. He picked tomatoes with Frank, talking all the while. Deborah could hear their voices as Victor worked with her.

He said, "I can well imagine they have a lot to say to one another, and I can only try to imagine what each of them has been going through—or you, for that matter."

"I'm okay. Actually, it's like feeling whole for the first time in my life—an almost overwhelming feeling." She reached out to touch his hand. "I have you to help me."

"Day after tomorrow, Deborah. You're well worth waiting for."

"Victor Whitesong, do you know what you're getting yourself in for?"

"You bet. Of all the people in the world, you and I probably know each other better than anyone."

"And it doesn't scare you off?"

"If it was going to, I would have left long before now."

After the noon meal, Deborah worked in her bedroom, going through every drawer, the big chest, and the closet, gathering up things that had belonged to Christian; some she put in Jonathan's room and others she placed in a box in the attic for the boy. She packed what remained of Christian's clothing and went to Sonja who was working in the kitchen. "Sonja, will you take the rest of Christian's clothes to Big David? Would he mind having them?"

"Oh, I know he would appreciate them. Are you sure there's no one else?"

"No one. I could give them to Victor, but I don't want him to feel like he's getting hand-me-down clothes and wife both." She smiled. "Now, I'm going to clean my room thoroughly and if you see my dad—Frank—I mean, tell him I need a man to help me move some of my furniture."

"Shall I tell him you want him to move the huge armoire?"

Deborah laughed. "Yes. See what he says."

Frank was relieved Deborah wanted only to turn the mattress and rearrange the smaller pieces of furniture. They talked quietly as they worked, for they could hear Many Stars and Jonathan working together on the porch. "Imagine," Frank said. "Composing a wedding song. I'll be able to tell folks in Minnesota I know some composers."

He had brought Half Shell with him, and the little boy climbed on the bed and bounced to the beat of the song. "I wish I could sing like Grandfather Many Stars and Jonathan," he said wistfully.

Frank rubbed the boy's head. "What you want to bet you will? It's an Indian song, and I'll bet Many Stars could teach you a bunch of them."

Deborah said, "Grandfather Blue Sky knew lots of songs, didn't he, Dad. He taught you some."

"He sure did. On occasion, over the years, a phrase has gone through my head, at the oddest moment. Sometimes I've wondered about it and concentrated on interpreting its meaning. Made for interesting thoughts."

Deborah was thinking. "We'll visit the reservation, Half Shell. We'll meet our relatives and learn so many things. When Grandfather Blue Sky collapsed, I couldn't accept he had died. I said he couldn't be dead because I had so many things yet to learn. Now I'll have a chance to learn them with you."

"Tell me," Frank said to Deborah, "how are we going to turn the mattress on the bed with this big lump in the middle?"

"Let's just turn the lump with the mattress."

Half Shell giggled. "I think I'll go find Victor."

The little boy was in the doorway when he turned back. "Mama?" Deborah felt goose bumps on her arms. Before Half Shell had gone to Minnesota, he hadn't talked, and now, for the first time, he was calling her Mama.

"Yes?"

"Can I call Victor Dad? Do you think he'd mind?"

"Half Shell, you would make him so happy."

"Okay," and he was gone.

Frank lifted the mattress corner. "Isn't that something?"

"It is. If you only knew! Victor has so much wanted to be Dad to the boys."

"I heard Jonathan call him Dad today."

"You did? I'm not surprised. It's only right, for he's known Victor longer than Christian. Victor has always been there during some tough times."

Frank said, "He gave Jonathan the biggest grin when the boy said it. Jonathan said, 'Not everybody's lucky like my mom and me—having two dads.' That was something to hear."

"Oh, I hadn't thought of that ... I like it."

After supper, Many Stars went to the well house with Victor to remove canning jars from the cooled pressure cookers. Later, Deborah saw the two men sitting on the bench near the door of the well house, deep in their conversation. When Victor came to tell her good night, he whispered, "An amazing man—actually, both of your dads."

Early the next morning, Many Stars said to Deborah, "Could we talk in your room?"

He came with the package he had carried under his arm when he arrived. "This is for your wedding, if you like." He opened the wrapping and spread a dress on her bed. "Your sister—Miriam to some, Waving

Grass to her family—made it. She's quite an artist. She started it after Fleet Foot told her about Victor and you."

She gasped. "Oh!" The dress was made from deerskin that was almost white. Its simple bodice had flowing sleeves, and the skirt was long with a slight flare. But the bead and shell work were what made the dress so striking.

"Beautiful! My sister, Waving Grass made this! It reminds me of Grandfather's pendant." She was looking at the back of the dress with its glorious sunburst, its main color done in yellow beads, with shadings of sunlight artistically etched by numerous other colors. The sunlight seemed to spread warmly onto the sleeves and down a band the width of her hand on each hip. Another beaded band, meant to be draped around the neck of the dress and down to below the waist, portrayed graceful, soaring birds, numerous and so realistically designed that Deborah found herself holding her breath.

"My sister did this." Row upon row of thongs decorated the lower section of the skirt, each woven into the deerskin and tied, the knot in the shape of a delicate rosebud. Dangling from each thong was a tiny shell. Touching the shells, Deborah could tell they would make their own music when the wearer of the dress walked. There were moccasins and leggings also, each exquisitely decorated with more beads and shells.

"We think it will fit you," Many Stars said. "Fleet Foot described you as being similar in size to his wife, only taller and more slender. I think he was right."

Deborah held the dress to her cheek, feeling the softness and drawing in the odor of the skin. She was trying to not cry, but her voice was full of emotion. "Every year, until Grandfather died, I received my new moccasins from your family. I looked forward to those moccasins. Of any gifts I received, those were the most meaningful. And now I have this—for my wedding." She reached up to kiss the man's cheek. "Thank you so much!" She held the dress at arm's length. "My sister. Waving Grass is a very talented, artistic woman. A very giving woman."

Suddenly, Deborah realized what she had said. "I have a sister! All my life I have wished for a sister or a brother. I've been so taken with getting to know you, that I didn't think about the rest of your family."

"You have a second sister. Some call her Agnes. We call her Nodding Flower. Along with my one living sister—Morning Horizon—she helped Waving Grass do the sewing of those beads."

They decided to not tell anyone about the dress. "I particularly want to surprise Victor." Deborah laughed with delight. "All of my neighbors will definitely be surprised."

"Are they ready for this?"

"They're used to me. They had to learn a long time ago to be ready for my surprises. They've already adjusted to a woman wearing trousers and driving a tractor."

Later in the morning, Deborah heard Jonathan shout a name. "John? John and the boys are here? How wonderful!"

She hurried out the door. When he saw her coming, Jimmy shouted, "Deb'r! Deb'r!" The boy ran to her, and she hugged him, his body more long and wiry than she expected.

"Little lady." John hugged her fiercely. "You finally found Christian. I still remember the day you came looking, and June wasn't any too hospitable." His long face was sad. "I'm so sorry. When you came looking and asking, I didn't recognize how serious it all was. I've always felt bad about it."

"Oh, John." She hugged him. "It's all right."

"But now your life is moving on. You and Victor are finally getting married!"

The boys crowded around her. "You're so grown! Look at all of you! Paul, you've turned into a man."

"He's at Kansas University, you know, going to be a teacher," John said.

Paul laughed. "Dad, she knows! How many letters have you written, bragging about each and every one of us?"

Jonathan was so excited he could hardly contain himself. He tugged Half Shell about, reacquainting the boys with him and introducing the Strates to Frank and Many Stars.

"You were just a little feller when we saw you last," John said, setting Half Shell on his shoulder. "Now look at you! Taller'n anybody."

A car was coming. Mary was bringing her girls, as well as Sonja. Victor's unmarried sister Morgan was with them. Mary said, "It's sure a good thing I lost all that weight over the years. With this pregnant lady and all these girls, we couldn't have fit in my car." She went to Many Stars. "You're Deborah's father. I'm Mary Cressler. Our old neighbor used to say my Indian name was Two Pot Mary because I took these coffeepots about the neighborhood." She shook his hand and introduced the girls.

Victor's sister carried a package. "I have something for you, Deborah." Morgan ducked her head.

Deborah unwrapped the gift. It was a nightgown, simply made but ornate across the bodice with white smocking and embroidered flowers. "It's beautiful. Did you do this?"

Morgan nodded. "When I heard Victor loved you, I began working on it." She giggled. "I guess it's a good thing the two of you have taken so long, for I took a long time finishing it."

"I'll treasure this forever."

Morgan was pleased. "Marlece made remarks." Marlece was Victor's married sister.

"Oh?"

Morgan whispered, "She said it was foolish to make something so pretty for your wedding night because Victor would have it off of you in two shakes."

"Morgan! What do you know about such matters?"

The young woman smiled smugly. "I know enough—for the time being. And I intend to know a lot more someday."

All of the women worked at cleaning house and even roped the boys into washing windows. Paul grumbled. "A decade of blow dirt in the nooks and crannies of these windows and we're expected to clean it out?"

"Now," Deborah said when the windows were clean, "Jonathan, you and Paul and Lester have to do something very important for me." She went into the storage room and returned with heavily starched curtains. "One of the things Audrey and I had to do when the storms were so bad was take down all the lace curtains and pack them away. She told me I would need to hang them for my wedding—and here they are." She smoothed the lace. "All this time with no curtains—and no Audrey." She gave everyone a bright smile. "All right, you boys hang them and we ladies will supervise. They have to be done right."

When their work was done, Jonathan led her to a window. "Look, Mom." He ran his hand lightly down a curtain and then draped it back. "Have you ever seen this window so free of dirt?"

The sunlight through the lace designs put delicate patterns on his face. "Oh, clean," was all she could say.

"I can't promise you there won't be dust again, Mom. But I'll bet there won't be black blizzard dust."

Mary worked at greasing and flouring an assortment of cake pans for the wedding cake. "A tiered wedding cake," Deborah exclaimed. "Only the big folks in the cities have tiered cakes."

"Well, you're going to have one too. Meredith and I have planned it. Three tiers, two layers to each tier. How does it sound?"

"It sounds wonderful."

The girls were ready to rest by late afternoon, and they sat at the kitchen table, watching Mary and Meredith put the wedding cake together and pipe decorations on it. "An all white cake," Morgan said. "How romantic."

Mary laughed. "Deborah, isn't it a good thing you waited until the dirt stopped blowing to get married? Imagine the dust and this cake."

Shortly before bedtime, Victor and Deborah sat on the porch with Frank and Many Stars, talking about the ceremony. "I want both of you to stand with me to give me away," she said.

"Both of us?" Frank asked.

"Both of you."

Victor laughed. "This will be a wedding to cause talk for years."

"It's not as though everyone doesn't know about my dads by now. Mary says people probably cut this past week's newspaper to shreds, saving the stories."

"Now," Victor said, "are you going to have enough fried chicken and rolls for the minister and his brother-in-law?" They explained to Frank and Many Stars. "Reverend Hodgkins did a good job marrying David and Sonja, don't you think? And in all seriousness, Brown took dandy pictures of their wedding. Besides," he grinned again, "they come cheap."

Deborah laughed. "Well, sure, if you don't include the cost of the food they'll eat. I think they ate more food that night than all of John's boys when they first came to live here."

Chapter 31

September 3, 1939

Their guests began arriving by late afternoon the next day, and sawhorses were set up for tables. The men waited awhile before putting on the planks, watching Half Shell and Marlece's little girl ride the sawhorses like ponies. Robert Whitesong brought block after block of ice from his truck, and John helped him make a washtub of lemonade. Ice cream freezers appeared. "I've never seen so many freezers at one time," Frank said.

Victor caught Deborah in the pantry where she was placing a huge pile of cookies on a platter. He held her close, kissing her. "Victor! Not now."

He kissed her ear. "For years I didn't dare do this freely. I can kiss you like this now because I know we'll finish matters later." Her face turned warm. "Look at you," he said. "Look at the effect I can have on you."

Deborah was wearing her nicest dress, garter belt, stockings, uncomfortable shoes, and all. She had piled her hair on her head in an ornate style, and Many Stars winked at her when he saw her.

"Some getup," he whispered.

Deborah was determined to keep the Indian dress a surprise until the last minute and graciously thanked people for their comments as to how pretty she looked for her wedding day. When she heard the minister had arrived, she called Mary and Meredith to her, and they retreated to the bedroom. "You're my matron of honor, Mary, and you need to help me dress for my wedding. Meredith, you're my mother today, so you get to advise."

"Well," Meredith said, "I'm honored."

Deborah said, "Actually, your job is to keep an eye on Mary."

Mary giggled. "You look dressed to me. Or did you forget to put your panties on?"

"Mary!" Deborah kicked off her shoes and began removing her dress.

"What are you doing, Deborah Nelson?"

"You'll see." Deborah let her hair down and removed her slip and the garter belt and stockings. "Oh, that feels better."

When she finally stood in just her brassiere and panties, Mary said wryly, "Well, I'm sure Victor will think it's a big improvement."

Deborah laughed. "Oh, Mary, I don't know when I've been so happy. I've wanted to be married to this man for so long."

"Well, sure, girl. It's about time before the two of you dry up and blow away."

"You have such a descriptive way of talking," Meredith said. Mary's laugh was infectious.

Deborah took the deerskin dress from the closet, and the women gasped. "Oh, Deborah! Oh, my goodness," Meredith said. They continued to exclaim as they helped her dress.

"Leggings. Oh, my." Mary ran her fingers gently over the sky birds. She brushed Deborah's hair, long and straight down her back. "You should pull your hair over to your shoulder so everyone can see the beadwork."

There was a knock at the door. "Deborah?" It was Frank with Many Stars.

"Come in."

Frank was transfixed. "Many Stars told me you were going Indian today, but when I saw what you were wearing earlier—well, I wasn't sure how this was going to go with the pink dress." He was holding Grandfather Blue Sky's pendant. "Many Stars agrees it's yours now, and someday you can give it to Jonathan."

"Oh, Dad." She held the pendant, and light caught the yellow and blue stones of the sunburst. "Now I know why Waving Grass put the beaded sunburst on the back of the dress. The stones of the pendant are far more effective on a plain background. She must have planned it that way."

Many Stars said, "Knowing Waving Grass as I do, I suspect she did."

"Oh, wait." She brought the memory box from the bottom drawer and took Meredith's Sky Bird headband from it. "Look, Meredith. Those strands of hair came from a thirteen-year-old's head."

Meredith helped her place the headband. "I certainly never dreamed my simple work would be put with such a beautiful dress."

Deborah held the hands of the two men, walking between them down the porch steps and across the yard to where Victor waited with Jonathan and Mary. Victor's eyes lit up, and he gave her the delightful smile she loved. She heard the gathering of people gasp with surprise and begin to chatter, and the minister was caught off guard, as though he wasn't sure about things. Victor's eyes never left her.

Many Stars had carried his small drum as he and Frank walked her to Victor. Many Stars stepped aside, and was joined by Jonathan and Janice Cressler with her flute. The boy sang, accompanied by the flute and drum, the song rhythmic and melodious, the words full of meaning for Deborah and Victor.

Our love makes us one
With the Earth Spirit.
The song of the soaring bird
Courses through the blood of our bodies.
We are the soil, the rain.
When the moon falls in the west
The sun will rise for our new day.
We are a part of Earth's Memories.

The minister spent no more time marrying them than he had Sonja and David. When Victor placed Audrey's old wedding band on her finger, Deborah cried. He began kissing the tears from her cheeks. Seeing the kisses, the minister quickly pronounced them husband and wife.

Victor held her tightly, and she kissed him very deliberately on the corner of his mouth. "I love you, Victor Whitesong."

Deborah went through the early evening, holding Victor's hand, not wanting to let go. They talked and laughed with their friends and made sure everyone had plenty of food. Often they would catch one another's eyes, and Deborah would feel her heart quicken. O. B. Dickerson kept reminding everyone how he had encouraged Victor to get married.

"It's O. B.'s idea, you know," Victor said, "our getting married. He's a very happy man now."

Deborah said, "The sad thing of it is, our wedding isn't totally taking away his worries."

Everyone was talking about what they feared was imminent—war. O. B. was upset about Europe. "This business of Hitler attacking Poland like he's just done is the beginning, you know. Just the beginning. You know it is. He's got to be stopped!" They saw Gracie pat his arm and talk quietly to him. He began to calm down.

Victor pulled Deborah to his side. "Beside every good man is a good woman. Gracie knows how to control O. B." He looked down at her. "You look so beautiful. Being Indian compliments you. If I thought you looked Indian before, I really think so now."

"You like my wedding dress?"

"You bet! But you ought to know by now, I think you look, as John would say, 'awful purty' in just about anything."

Deborah saw Jonathan staring past the well house to the west. He was watching the sunset, the pastels interspersed with a deep orange, casting a golden glow on the faces around them. She went to stand beside him. The boy said, "Mom, remember some of the other sunsets we watched from this spot?"

"I sure do. I remember one that was very red, and you and David showed me how it made the snow red. It was an important moment for me, realizing there was more to life than feeding cattle and scooping snow. I was letting the cold and snow obliterate the love and attention you boys needed."

"I remember that time. David was sucking his thumb. I thought his hand must be cold." Jonathan was still watching the changing colors. "And some of the sunsets after dirt storms? They were so inspiring. I think sunsets like those kept us going when everything else looked so terrible."

"Jonathan, remember when we scattered June's ashes at sunset? We talked about the names of colors she taught John's boys."

"Yes! And the western sky was glorious. At the time I thought how June was a sad, sad woman when she died. Mom, maybe that sky gave her some happiness."

"Jonathan!" Deborah put her arms around him. "What a kind thought. You're a good person."

As Deborah had requested, when darkness began to fall, Harold built a bonfire on the hard ground of the yard between the stone wall and the corral, the ground that had always fascinated little David and all of the other boys with its large, drought cracks. Deborah watched the light and sparks of the fire reach out, erasing the nearby shadows.

"You have made Harold's day," Victor commented. "He'll talk about this the rest of his life, I'll bet."

Three men with a fiddle, guitar, and accordion climbed into a wagon bed and began playing for dancing. Occasionally, Many Stars would join them with Janice's flute or his drum, and when he first played, the dancers just watched. They finally seemed to realize the big Indian was just one more musician, and they returned to their dancing.

Victor and Deborah stood in the shadows for a while, watching the reverend and his brother-in-law eat. Deborah giggled. "Why are we doing this? Watching two men eat so much?"

"Because," he said very seriously, "we've got to be able to tell our grandchildren everything in detail. You know, I think the Depression has been very hard on the bellies of those men. It's an important part of our wedding day, and they are making September 3, 1939, very memorable." He put his lips to her ear. "Just think, if we remember nothing else about our wedding day, we'll remember them. And we mustn't forget our reputable newspaper editor. I've never seen a man who likes pie so much."

"Victor, you're driving me crazy, kissing my ear. Do you really think we'll remember nothing else?"

"Not if I can help it," he said.

The men played all kinds of music, but Deborah especially liked the slow numbers that allowed Victor to hold her close. He said, "I hope this makes up for the dance I tried to take you to years ago."

John interrupted and asked Deborah to dance. "Little lady, I've never seen anyone so good at stirring talk as you have today. Do you know how downright purty you look in your dress?"

"People are talking? What are they saying?" she asked.

"They think you look wonderful. They're sort of complaining, though, that Victor's keeping you to himself."

"They're right. I should be socializing better. John, do you remember what this driveway used to look like?"

"You mean all the little twigs and the roadways for the boys' cars and trains."

"Don't forget hopscotch. You were in Washington when Jimmy wanted to play hopscotch—"

"And you hopped him through the entire game and like to broke your back. Victor told me about it."

John was a good dancer, and Deborah was sorry when the number ended, but then she realized there was a conspiracy among the Strate boys. Paul asked her to dance. Lester was next in line, and she danced with each of the boys, even Jimmy. The young boy couldn't really dance, but it didn't matter. They made up their own steps.

"This kind of makes me think of hopscotch, Jimmy."

He giggled, the deep-throated laugh she loved. "Dad is always telling stories—how you let me paint Victor's house, and I ate paint and you cried, how Victor helped me swim in the tank, and how Grandpa August helped us build the tree house. I remember lots of it."

"We had good times."

"It was fun. I like our new farm, but it was fun, living with you."

Before she could catch her breath, O. B. grabbed her hand. "I sure would like to dance with a beautiful Indian woman," he said.

Deborah was surprised at how agile O. B. was. When she complimented his dancing, he said soberly, "That's why Gracie married me, you know."

"No, I didn't know."

"When we was young folks, there was a dance at the sale barn—not the one we have now, another one—oh, don't worry, they'd scraped out all the cow leavin's before the dance. I danced with her, and then we went out into the shadows and I kissed her. She said to me, 'Now you done it! You kissed me, so now we got to get married.'" He laughed. "It sure wasn't the last time I kissed her. What a woman."

At the close of the number, the three musicians sat down to rest, and Deborah saw Janice hand her flute to Jonathan. Many Stars began beating his drum, and she quickly recognized the up-and-down swaying dance rhythm Fleet Foot had taught them. Many Stars sang, as he slowly beat his drum, dancing around the fire. Jonathan picked up on the melody and played along. He also danced, sometimes whirling gracefully as he circled about.

At first, everyone, including Deborah, stood and watched. There were those who appeared uneasy, turning to look at one another. She didn't know what Many Stars was singing but recognized his voice as a good one.

She found her foot tapping to the rhythm and began to move her hand up and down with the beat. Half Shell came running to her.

"Mama? Why can't we dance?"

"We can!" She grabbed the little boy's hand and reached back for Victor. They joined Jonathan and Many Stars around the fire.

After several dances, Jonathan and Many Stars retreated, and the original musicians played a mixture of "big band" songs and schottische and polka dances. While the men rested, Many Stars and Jonathan played again, and this time the Strate boys circled the fire.

Deborah moved closer to Victor. "Look, look at John." The tall, gangly man was off to the side, swaying in rhythm to the music.

"Hey, feller," Victor called. "Come join us." That was all the encouragement the man needed to enter the dance.

O. B. was arguing with Gracie, trying to get her to join him in the Indian dance. But the woman stood in the firelight with her hands on her hips. More and more of the neighborhood children stepped into the circle, and some of the crowd began clapping in rhythm to the drum. O. B. could stand it no longer, and the man joined in with his little granddaughter. Hearing nervous laughter, Deborah turned to see Mary tugging Gladys Hocksmith through the dance.

And then, during one of the Indian dances, someone was calling above the drum. The anxiety in the sound first caught Deborah's attention. "The war! The war has started in Europe!"

One of the young men had been listening to a car radio, and his voice, shrill with tension and fear, caused everyone to be silent. "France and Britain have declared war on Germany," he said. "They fear it's another Great War."

People milled from group to group, talking, worrying out loud. "I knew it, I knew it!" O. B. kept repeating. "We're next! We'll get into it next! I just know it!" Their voices reminded Deborah of the anxious sounds of birds before a storm, and she wished for the calming song of the mourning doves.

Victor came to Deborah and put his arms around her. "We'll remember this day for more than our wedding," he said. She could hear the anguish in his voice.

"Maybe the United States won't get involved," she said.

"Maybe."

She had a sudden image of Victor in uniform, and she moved to him.

She whispered, her lips close to his ears, "All these years I've waited for you. All I ask for now is time with you. Time." He held her tighter.

Calvin encouraged the musicians to play, and the dancing slowly began again but without the same enthusiasm as before. More entered in when Many Stars played another Indian dance around the fire. Deborah thought the singing sounding less celebratory now.

When the dance number ended, in the brief silence before talking began again, Deborah detected a strange sound, repetitious and pounding. She could hear it over the voices and looking about her, saw car lights. About halfway down the lane, beyond where her neighbors had parked their cars in the ditch alongside the cottonwoods, was a line of headlights. Some of the cars were already stopped, and more were parking on the north-south road. Men walk from the cars to where the pounding was happening in the middle of the lane road.

The noise was being made by a man using a posthole digger, his up-and-down body movements catching the light. Near the digging man, others hammered nails and then raised a large wooden cross, its beams wrapped in burlap sacking. All of the men gathering about the cross wore white robes and hoods, the eyeholes black in the starlight.

"Oh, dear God above, don't let this happen." Deborah spoke loudly, unable to move, so frozen was her body with shock and fear. Her voice carried about the gathering, and immediately the people around her were silent, turning to look where she was staring. The man with the digger pounded deeper into the hard ground, slowly, gradually eating away at the soil. Each pound was like someone using his fist on her head.

The hooded figures set the cross into the hole, tamping it as carefully as any post needing a reliable, lasting base. Deborah could smell kerosene. "No," her one word verging on a shriek.

A woman wailed, "Stop them!"

Jonathan broke away from the group, walking down the lane toward the cross and the hooded men. "Victor," Deborah said in alarm, "Jonathan!" Victor seemed rooted to the spot beside her.

Jonathan's voice came floating back to them. He was singing. The cross had been lit, and black smoke boiled up into the air. Through it all, Jonathan sang as he walked down the lane. "'Mine eyes have seen the glory of the coming of the Lord—'" Deborah and Victor began to follow.

Many Stars hurried to be near the boy, and he pounded the small drum, reinforcing the cadence of Jonathan's voice and the marching rhythm of the song. Holding Deborah's hand, Victor walked beside Jonathan.

"'He is trampling out the vintage where the grapes of wrath are stored; He hath loosed the fateful lightning of his terrible swift sword—'" Many Stars sang with Jonathan, his voice deep and strong. "'His truth is marching on.'"

People marched behind Deborah and Victor in rhythm with the song, one by one joining with the singing. "'Glory! Glory! Hallelujah! Glory! Glory! Hallelujah! His truth is marching on.'"

They came to a halt a safe distance from the cross. Its flame flared up high, lighting the entire area, ferreting out the hooded faces, illuminating the neighborhood people behind Jonathan.

Then Jonathan sang alone, this time slowly, and to Deborah the drum seemed like a heartbeat. "'In the beauty of the lilies Christ was born across the sea, with a glory in his bosom that transfigures you and me; as he died to make men holy, let us die to make men free! While God is marching on.'"

The people sang the refrain again. "'Glory! Glory! Hallelujah! His truth is marching on.'" After the last phrase, the only sound was the crackle of the flames on the cross.

Deborah saw the hooded men turning their heads, looking at one another, and some shuffled their feet uneasily. They began moving away. Most of their cars had been left running, and their drivers backed down the lane; other cars had to be started. The line began to pick up speed, leaving a cloud of dust as they headed to the north.

Still no one spoke. A flash of lightning and loud rumble of thunder stirred them awake, and they turned, going up the lane to the yard. Food baskets were carried to cars, and tables were taken down. People stopped to say good-bye.

O. B. Dickerson summed up the evening for everyone. "I'll never forget this wedding, Deborah and Victor, as long as I live. Hearing the war news was tragic. Seeing The Committee was downright discouraging. But hearing the boy sing, hearing those words—that lighted cross had a whole new meaning. I'll never forget the power of this night!"

In the growing quiet after trucks and wagons had left, the family gathered about Harold's fire. Deborah hugged Jonathan and Half Shell. Victor said to Jonathan, "We're proud of you, doing what you did."

Frank and Many Stars poured buckets of water on the fire and left with the boys. They were going to Victor's house to sleep, and Deborah wondered how in the world everyone would fit into the little house with John and his boys there also.

"Don't you worry," Frank said. "We got those army cots out of the cellar, and John's boys have their blanket rolls."

Meredith gave Deborah a quick hug. "We're going to stay with Moses."

As they were driving out of the yard, David Nyfeller stuck his head out of the truck window. "Remember, Victor, you aren't to do the milking in the morning. We'll sneak over here, and you won't even know we're here." He grinned and was gone.

Deborah was skeptical. "Do you trust him, Victor Whitesong? Are you sure that's all that redhead will come here to do?"

Victor laughed. "I had a little talk with him. Reminded him what I did for him on his wedding night."

The wind came up, stirring the damp, smoky smells of the dead fire. Victor grabbed Deborah's hand. "Let's get to the house before the storm hits."

Lightning flashed, and they didn't bother to light a lamp. Victor went about closing the front door and windows. In her bedroom, she carefully removed Meredith's headband and the dress Waving Grass had created. When she put on the nightgown, Deborah smiled, remembering Morgan Whitesong's words.

"You're quite a sight with the lightning behind you," Victor said from the doorway. He had changed and wore the pajama bottoms Deborah had seen in the wash week after week. "Come," he said.

He took her hand, and they went into the living room where he turned on the radio. He tuned it to the late night station in Nebraska, and dance music came into the room, faintly and mixed with loud cracks of static. He turned to her. "I want to dance with you, Sky Bird Whitesong. I want to do the things tonight I never dared to do all these many years. Will you do them with me?"

"Oh, yes!" She moved into his arms, and they danced, barely hearing the music, but it didn't matter. He kissed her, and she responded. Then the lightning cracked, and the radio station was gone. Victor turned off the set and returned to dance with her. Big booms of thunder pounded about them, and with each startling vibration she held him closer.

"I love you, Sky Bird."

"I love you, Victor Whitesong."

They held one another the rest of the night, and many pains melted and left Deborah's heart. Sometime in the night, a name came to her for Victor to carve on the baby's headstone: Lillian Little Dove. In rhythm with Victor, Deborah thought of the future. If she and Victor should have a baby girl, she would name her Gentle Dove after Grandmother. Grandfather Blue Sky would like that, wouldn't he?

In her heart, she sang: "O Great Spirit, I honor you!"

Made in the USA
San Bernardino, CA
01 August 2013